DAIKAIJU!3

GIANT MONSTERS VS THE WORLD

Other Titles by Agog! Press:

AustrAlien Absurdities, Edited by Chuck McKenzie and Tansy Rayner Roberts, 2002/2006

Agog! Fantastic Fiction: 29 New Tales of Fantasy, Imagination and Wonder, Edited by Cat Sparks, 2002/2006

Agog! Terrific Tales: New Australian Speculative Fiction, Edited by Cat Sparks, 2003/2006

Agog! Smashing Stories: New Australian Speculative Fiction, Edited by Cat Sparks, 2004/2006

Daikaiju! Giant Monster Tales, Edited by Robert Hood and Robin Pen, 2005/2006

Agog! Ripping Reads, Edited by Cat Sparks, 2006

Daikaiju!2 Revenge of the Giant Monsters, Edited by Robert Hood and Robin Pen, 2007

DAIKAIJU!3

GIANT MONSTERS VS THE WORLD

EDITED BY ROBERT HOOD AND ROBIN PEN

Published by Agog! Press:
PO Box U302
University of Wollongong
NSW 2522
Australia
www.catsparks.net

In partnership with Prime Books:
www.prime-books.com

ISBN:
978-0-8095-7232-8 (hc)
978-0-8095-7233-5 (pbk)

Contents

for Terry Dartnall

PREFACE

This third volume of Giant Monster stories is, alas, the last for us. We've trashed buildings, flattened cities, made populations run around like panicky ants and contemplated how small we are when seen in relation to the larger inhabitants of humanity's imaginary universe. Philosophy has run riot, the weather has fumed and raged and taken monstrous form, things of unimaginable size have arisen from the sea, fallen from space, burst out of mountains and mutated in a stew of radiation, pollution, genetic engineering, digital reality manipulation and sheer incomprehensible cussedness. We've gasped in awe, stared in amazement, cried out in fear—and laughed just as much as we've shrieked in terror. Hopefully a few of you out there will have followed us through the journey and enjoyed it with us. Sometimes, maybe, it made you think.

If you've come this far, here's the final serving. For your delectation some excellent fantasy and horror writers from around the world have imagined another crop of gargantuan terrors. There are crabs as big as mountains, giant space lobsters, super-sized living action toys, planet-sized turtles, time-hopping reptiles, humungous caterpillars, an oversized mutated lizard or two, Big Birds, massive cephalopods, a titanic High Priest and a couple of vast, adjectivally extravagent Lovecraftian Old Ones.

For the story behind the genesis of *Daikaiju!3: Giant Monsters vs the World*, see the Preface to *Daikaiju!2: Revenge of the Giant Monsters*. Once they were a single oversized volume, but in the split some room was created that allowed us to solicit a story or two for this final venture. Robin even convinced Rob to include his own story—something he's a little uncomfortable with. Blame it on enthusiasm. Robin himself has provided a special treat; a detailed transcript of a little known trailer for a giant monster film that was never released. One is forced to ask: why?

Then to round off what began in the cinema, Robin and Rob have conspired to provide reviews of the seminal giant monster films of all time. Not every giant monster film is mini-critiqued, but most of them made it in. It seemed appropriate.

So as Gamera sinks slowly in the West and the *Daikaiju!* project comes to an end, we leave you with this thought: there are many daikaiju films yet to come and they may once again inspire literary writers to put finger to keyboard and create more giant monster stories. As long as cities and civilisations are still around then giant city-destroying monsters will always arise in the myths of our own making. The Monsters may die, but they never stay that way for long.

Why?

Because we love them too much, of course.

Robert Hood and Robin Pen
September 2007

Mamu, or
Reptillon vs Echidonah

Nick Stathopoulos

5.45 P.M. YESTERDAY

Sydney sweltered in a heatwave, and with the heat came the bogon moths. The unseasonal weather had provided the perfect conditions for them as they swarmed through the city on their slow migration south, to mate and die.

Swatting one away from his sweaty face, the freelance writer descended a wide concrete flight of stairs that lead to the subterranean platforms of Museum Station. The cool tiled interior was a welcome relief from the heat and hubbub of Oxford Street.

Built in the twenties, it formed part of an underground rail network known as the City Circle, linking Sydney's central business district to Central Station and the suburbs beyond.

A blast of warm air washed over him as a train rattled onto a platform below. Brakes squealed and carriages shunted to a halt.

Today the writer had been reviewing films for an online news site, and he was particularly pleased with his latest vitriolic savaging. It was directed at a big-budget Hollywood remake of a beloved old British television show, and the results armed him with plenty of opportunities to display his wit. Somehow the Yanks never got them right. He smirked with bemused satisfaction for a moment before the mood was broken.

Oh God, he could hear *her* echoing up the stairwell. That old aboriginal woman was down there again. How he detested her stupid singing. Even though she sang in her own language—Pitjantjatjara—he could still identify the tune.

"Jesus loves me, this I know ... for the Bible tells me so. Little ones to him belong ... they are weak but he is strong ..."

She was *so* annoying.

If he timed it just right she'd be looking the other way, engaging some other commuter, begging oh-so-politely.

"Scuse me Sir, could you spare some change?" or "Thank you Ma'm, God bless you." Then she'd go back to her infernal singing, but he'd be safely past.

But there was no avoiding her today. Her eyes fixed directly on him as he reached the bottom of the stairs.

"Shit."

From the pre-recorded announcement he realised the train on the platform was his, so he barreled straight past her, avoiding eye contact. He heard her pause, then sing louder. He knew it was directed at him, and didn't give a fuck.

She let him pass as she spotted a friendly young woman who was always happy to give.

"Hey lady! Don't go down there! Not today!" She held her benefactor back as she watched the critic disappear through a turnstile, and smiled knowingly.

He shimmied into the carriage just as the doors closed and the klaxon tooted. Quickly he scanned the interior, pushed past some school kids, and beat a middle-aged woman—arms full of groceries—to the only free seat. He smirked at her in triumph as he pulled out a gossip magazine from his satchel.

The woman sniffed her disgust as the train lurched forward. Madly juggling her load, she grabbed at a handrail for balance.

The writer looked up from his magazine. Something was wrong.

The train abruptly stopped, jerked forward, then stopped for good. Though the new Millennium trains were constantly breaking down, and commuters were used to the delays, a communal sigh of dismay arose from the passengers.

Strange grinding noises echoed up the tunnel, and the carriage fell silent. A bogon moth battered a light fitting.

Then, without warning, the carriage imploded.

Huge black claws tore through, then peeled back, the thin metal sheeting that formed its outer casing. A massive, fleshy appendage probed its way into the crowded compartment.

Incredulous passengers screamed as the gigantic, oversized proboscis wrenched open with a thick, liquid sound, exposing rows of needle-sharp teeth.

The woman with the groceries threw them at the maw, which, as it retracted in surprise for a moment, allowed her to dive through a gash in the floor. She crawled between the bogey and the platform to safety. But the rest of the passengers were not so lucky.

The proboscis punched deeper into the carriage, which now tilted at an impossible angle. A long sticky tongue emerged and flicked madly about, ensnaring passengers on its gooey surface, then slurped them into oblivion.

Trapped like termites, those still standing were unable to find purchase and slid toward the gnashing teeth. Others tried clambering over the backs of seats, over the passengers wedged between them, but the tongue easily located them, too.

Frozen with shock, mouth agape, the dumbfounded film critic stared in utter disbelief as the thing's tongue now flicked in his direction. His magazine flew into the air as the huge, sticky muscle coiled around him, dragging him screaming between the monster's teeth—which closed on his chubby frame with a grinding delicacy.

In the nanoseconds before he died, he should have seen his life flash before him, but no. Instead, he flashed every movie character ever caught in a death throe with some nightmare denizen—aliens, mutants, behemoths, gargantuas, leviathans— now King Kong, chewing on a stop-motion native, now Gregory Peck lashed to the side of Moby Dick, now Jon Voigt swallowed alive in *Anaconda*, and finally, the penultimate moment—Robert Shaw chomped to bits in *Jaws*—except these teeth weren't rubber. He screamed out to the only woman he'd ever loved.

"Ripleeeeeey!"

His, and the terrified screams of other passengers, echoed up into the street, where commuters tumbled from the station in panic. Someone yelled, "Echidonah! It's Echidonah!"

The aboriginal woman was swept up with the mass, and as she reached street level, spun away from the crowd, around to the back of the now deserted café, where she paused and gulped air heavily.

"Mamu,", she whispered between gulps. "Mamu."

She closed her eyes to the sounds of death, and remembered the voice of her *kami.*

OCTOBER 15, 1953

"MAMU!"

Grandmother looked up from the hole she was digging with her wira, scooping away at the dirt, and called to the tiny figure in the distance. "The mamu will get you!"

The girl didn't know whether to believe her or not, and so darted back. Like other cultures worldwide, the Anangu aborigines of central Australia used the threat of a monster to keep children in check. But that didn't mean it wasn't true.

Mamu or not, the girl preferred to follow her grandmother on her foraging expeditions than go to the missionary school. There they forced her to wear clothes that made her skin itch and to recite silly songs about Jesus. But today the girl was far from the camp, and she idly lolled behind the old woman.

Presently, they came across a sign, written in English.

"What does it say, little one? I don't understand it."

The young girl slowly made out the words, but they had little meaning to her. "I think it says to stay away," she guessed.

"Then you stay away from it! I don't trust no white fella stuff." She continued to pick her way through the spinifex, and the girl followed.

Sensing something, the old woman stiffened, sniffed the dry air, and rubbed her shoulders as the hair on her body stood on end.

The girl looked up at her grandmother quizzically.

"Kami ...? What's wrong?"

Suddenly a bright flash lit the entire sky beyond the low rocky hills. A low, distant rumble followed in its wake, and the thin clouds above them shuddered then were swept away with the shock wave. The ground trembled and an angry black cloud mushroomed over the horizon.

"A storm!" cried the girl.

But this was no ordinary storm, and the old woman instinctively knew it. "Quickly child! We must find shelter. Quickly!" She grabbed the girl by the arm and they ran for cover.

They were too far from camp to seek refuge there, so they dashed toward some caves in the rocky hills. Kami had often recounted how she and her family had hidden undiscovered there for many days when the white fellas first arrived, so the girl knew it was a place of safety. But as she looked over her shoulder, she watched in horror as the black cloud blanketed the hills and tumbled toward them.

The old woman dragged her behind some rocks as the churning pall overtook them, and shielded her with her own body as best as she could. There they huddled, until the blackness had passed.

The afternoon sun blazed a deep blood red as they staggered back to camp.

TWO WEEKS LATER

A Cinesound newsreel flickered in the darkened Victory Cinema on George Street. On the screen, a poisonous black-and-white mushroom cloud rose ominously over the barren desert. Official observers—some with berets, others with slouch hats—turned away from the blast, unprotected. Only a few scientists, in lab-coats and goggles, faced the boiling maelström.

The voice-over had a plumy British accent.

"Britain enters the Atomic Age with the successful detonation of its first atomic bomb, code-named Totem One, at Emu Junction in the remote and unpopulated central Australian desert. This and further tests help secure Australia's own atomic future, and the promise of unlimited clean, efficient energy."

MEANWHILE, BACK IN CENTRAL AUSTRALIA

There were bodies of aborigines lying everywhere, some dying, some already dead. They suffered burning red skin, vomiting, dysentery. They had thought it was measles or chicken pox—there had been outbreaks of these diseases in the past—but this was something quite different.

Only a few children and a couple of the missionaries were well enough to look after the ill. The girl brought water to her grandmother. The old woman was delirious, and kept repeating, "Irati ... irati ..."

"What is she saying?" one of the missionaries paused to ask the girl. "What does *irati* mean?"

The little girl struggled to think of a way to describe the word. "When someone gives you a bad thing to eat."

"Poison? You mean poison?

"Yes!" she nodded. "Poison. She says the black cloud was poison."

The old woman reached out to the child.

"You must get away from here." Her eyes widened. "This land is irati!"

"But where Kami? ... where can I go?" There was nowhere to run, no way to escape the irati.

"You must leave. Now. You must!

"No, Kami ... I won't leave you."

"Go!" The old woman heaved an agonised last breath, and her hand fell limp.

Sobbing, the girl ran into the night.

The missionary called after her, but the child was soon engulfed by the darkness.

And when she failed to return to camp, they thought that she too had died of the sickness. Soon there would be no one left alive who even remembered her.

THREE DAYS AGO

The two black-suited men loomed over the night-duty nurse at the Harry Seidler Retirement Village. She glanced at their IDs. They wore sunglasses in the photos. She looked back up at the men. They were still wearing them. Non-plussed, she handed the IDs back and directed them to the TV room.

"That's him."

The old man fused to the battered sofa chair was totally absorbed in "Wheel of Fortune". The ancient television screen flickered. He swore when the picture signal dropped out for a second just as the wheel slowed to a halt.

"Excuse me ... ahem ... EXCUSE ME."

The old man craned his neck at the two men and blinked twice.

"Yes?"

"Are you Cobden Parkes?" asked the first man.

The old man's eyes narrowed.

"You were the Government Architect in the fifties, during Premier Cahill's term?"

The old man nodded.

"And Government Architect for the Sydney Opera House ..." added the second.

"What's this all about?" He eyed the two men suspiciously.

"Who are you?"

The first man answered. "We're from the Australian Security Intelligence Organization. We ... think you might be able to help us."

The operative crouched down to the old man's eye level.

"Daikaiju ... what do you know about *daikaiju?*"

DECEMBER 12, 1955

"*Daikaiju*—giant monsters—it's the Japanese term for the creatures."

The Premier of New South Wales, John Joseph Cahill, was a tough, pragmatic man. Hardened by too many years of politicking, he was not exactly prone to flights of fantasy. But he could plainly see the incredulity on the faces of Cobden Parkes, the Government Architect, and Harry Ashworth, the Minister for Public Works.

"Don't look at me like I'm some kind of imbecile!" The Premier puffed on his cigarette. The other two weren't so sure.

"I know what I'm talking about. The giant octopus that attacked San Francisco three years ago ... where do you think that came from? Bloody Yanks were testing A-bombs twenty thousand fathoms beneath the ocean off the west coast. Then two years ago Japan was attacked by a prehistoric throwback that caused as much death and destruction as the two A-bombs dropped during the war."

The Premier gazed out of his office window across the city.

Parkes and Ashworth listened in silence.

"The Federal government has just granted the bloody poms full support to conduct further atomic tests in a place called Maralinga in South Australia. The Yanks are testing on Bikini Atoll. The French also have a testing program in the Pacific ... we're surrounded by bloody idiots."

He turned to face the men.

"Who knows what else they're about to unleash, or when we'll see the end of it?"

"Where do we fit into all this?" inquired Ashworth gingerly. "Why us?"

"We need to protect Sydney against the inevitability of a giant monster attack. It will come, gentlemen, I know it will come. And we all know the devastation wrought by those creatures when they intrude on a built-up area. Don't we?"

Ashworth shrugged uncertainly. Parkes stared at his own hands, clenched into fists on his knees.

The determination in Cahill's voice was intense. "Well, while I'm in power, I intend to do something to prepare for it. This will be a costly exercise, and controversial ... no doubt about it. We'll probably all cop a lot of flack before it's done, but it's one form of insurance this city can't afford not to have. Maybe not today, or even in our lifetimes, but one day ... one day ..."

He went to his desk, opened a drawer, and pulled out a roll

of blueprints, which he unfurled, balancing his cigarette on his bottom lip the whole time.

"This is what our boffins at the Commonwealth Scientific and Industrial Research Organisation have come up with to stop them." He weighed down the corners of the plans with filled ashtrays.

"This, gentlemen, is an anti-daikaiju device."

Ashworth raised his eyebrows.

Parkes scanned the blueprints and tried to take it all in. "It's huge! Where do you propose we house such a contraption?"

"Good question, Parkes. The location has to be in the city, and it can't arouse any suspicion. That's why you gentlemen are here."

Ashworth cogitated for a moment, then volunteered. "Maybe it could be disguised as grain silos?"

The Premier snorted.

"Don't be ridiculous! I don't want to make Sydney any more of a target than it is. This thing has to provide the city with its major defense against daikaiju, not ICBMs."

Ashworth was somewhat more subdued this time.

"How about a new tram terminal, then? The existing terminal on the Quay needs upgrading. How about there?"

The Premier thought about it for a moment, then scrunched up his face.

"That's no good either. Sydney may not even have trams soon, if some people have their way." He shook his head. "No, This building has to last. It has to be a landmark. Something so obvious that no one would ever suspect its true purpose."

The intercom buzzed and the Premier punched the button.

"*I'm sorry Mr Premier, it's Mr Goosens on the line.*"

"I said no calls."

"*He's most insistent.*"

"Jesus, that man refuses to give up." He tossed an exasperated glance at the two men. "Excuse me a moment, gentlemen. Yes, I'll take the call."

Ashworth recognised the name. "Isn't he the conductor of the Sydney Symphony Orchestra?" Parkes shrugged.

"Mr Goosens?" The Premier knew when to turn on the smarm. It dripped from his words, just on the verge of becoming sarcasm. "*Eugene!* It's good to hear your voice, too." There was a pause as the Premier held the receiver away from his ear. "Yes, I've read your latest letter."

He listened politely for a moment, then sighed and interjected. "I agree ... Sydney *does* need a home for your Orchestra." He'd been subjected to the same lecture so often that his eyes would normally glaze over, and they did briefly. But then the glint came back and they narrowed.

He paused for barely a second.

"Yes, Eugene, I hear you. I hear you very well."

He took a deep breath. Sighed again. This time it expressed satisfaction rather than impatience.

"Eugene, before you get too carried away," he continued, with no insincerity now, "how long have you been petitioning the government for an opera house—nine years? That long, huh?"

A twisted smile came over the Premier's face as he met the gaze of the two men in his office. They both frowned. "Well, I have some wonderful news for you. Your persistence has finally paid off. The Government Architect and the Minister of Public Works have just today come to me with a *plan* ... and I think you're going to like it ..."

MARCH 10, 1956

Over the centuries, the huge uplifted rocks at Emu Junction had been eroded by the elements into enormous round boulders piled precariously on top of each other.

Extremes of heat and cold had caused their rusty surfaces to exfoliate, not unlike the skin of an onion. But now they lay scattered, tossed like marbles by the force of the detonation.

The largest of the massive boulders began to radiate an eerie green glow. The sun had set, and it lit up the immediate area, casting long shadows around it.

Behind the surrounding boulders was an observer. Attracted by the glow, a young girl remained hidden, and watched, completely mesmerised.

JANUARY 29, 1957

The Premier rose to address the crowd. The gallery of the Sydney Town Hall was packed to the rafters with dignitaries and the press. A hush fell over the auditorium.

"And now, after much deliberation, I'd like to present the man responsible for the winning design—Danish architect, Jørn Utzon."

The lanky young Dane stepped forward, his gray suit draping loosely on his tall gangly frame, and unveiled a model of a building unlike anything seen before. There was an audible gasp from the shocked crowd as flashbulbs exploded about them. Everybody swarmed around Utzon and his model.

All except the Minister for Public Works, and the Government Architect—who managed forced nervous smiles over their concern—and the Premier, who was grinning from ear to ear. After all, a politician knows all too well how to hide his true feelings.

SEPTEMBER 18, 1959

The teenage girl approached the huge boulder with some trepidation. She had often frequented the site, and found comfort in the warm radiating glow, especially as she recovered from the sickness that had claimed her grandmother. But recently the glow had subsided. The surface of the rock had softened into a leathery shell, and was slightly translucent. It seemed to have transformed onto some kind of egg.

As she gingerly approached, something shifted inside it. Startled, the girl darted back behind the rocks, emerging only when the movement settled. As she approached the egg again, she imagined she could make out what sort of creature lay curled inside. On closer inspection she was not only certain what it was, but also knew what she must do.

She collected the largest branches she could find and slowly levered the egg away from the cluster of rocks. Whenever she felt any protesting movement from within, she stopped and gently sang to it. The song had been taught to her by the missionaries, and this seemed to appease it. With her back against it, she then continued rolling, levering when it snagged, moving it inches at a time.

Not far from where she laboured, the termites had rebuilt their mounds. They had survived the blast, but radiation had affected them, too, and now their nests towered impressively over the landscape.

Moving the egg was hard work for one so small and sickly, and it took many days before she successfully maneuvered it around each mound and into the centre of the termite field. Once there, she rested, and waited patiently.

OCTOBER 22, 1959

The phone rang downstairs in the lounge room of the Government Architect's house. The place was conservative for an architect—right down to the chintz curtains and lace antimacassars—but then Cobden Parkes was like that, and it made him the perfect government official.

The Architect answered groggily. "Hello?" Then he recognised the voice. "Oh Harry ... Jesus mate, it's 5 am ... what's up?"

"It's Cahill. He's dead."

It took a moment for his foggy brain to fully grasp the magnitude of the situation.

"Oh no ..."

"There's going to be a change in government ... and we're gonna have to go it alone."

LATER, THAT SAME DAY

The egg slowly hatched while the teenager watched with fascination. She watched as the newborn creature emerged and baked in the sun, watched as its spines hardened, as it flexed long black scimitar claws that would soon begin burrowing into the giant red termite mounds around them.

Finally, the girl approached the newborn—gingerly, so as not to alarm it. Despite being blind, it sensed her presence. It raised its proboscis in her direction, smelled her, and withdrew. She froze, and softly began singing. The creature softened its stance, then slowly began rocking to the soothing, familiar sound of her voice.

She moved closer, and, unafraid, began to gently stroke its head. It nuzzled against her as she whispered, "Mamu ... my mamu ..."

FEBRUARY 26, 1966

Cobden Parkes rolled the tile in his palm. The milky white enameled surface felt unusually warm. He passed it to Harry Ashworth.

Senior Professor Wraight of the Commonwealth Scientific and Industrial Research Organisation pushed back his glasses.

"We've just finished testing the latest batch of tiles."

Parkes and Ashworth looked hopeful. The professor smiled grimly.

"It's not good news, gentlemen."

"What? Don't the tiles work?" Parkes' face had drained white. There had been so many problems already, now was not a good time for more of them to arise.

"Oh no. The tiles work perfectly." The professor poured them coffee from a beaker, warming on a tripod over a Bunsen burner. There was an edge to his dry voice.

"What now?" muttered Ashworth, sensing a bombshell about to drop.

Wraight plunged in. "We always knew we couldn't kill the monsters—the aim was to drive them away from the city using their own ultrasonic emissions." The professor indicated a scale model of the anti-daikaiju device on the desk before him.

"These tiles were designed to coat the entire surface of the giant dome, forming a huge mirror, as it were. They would absorb the ultrasonic pulses that daikaiju emit, the same way certain moth's scales absorb the ultrasonic beeps of bats to render them invisible. The device itself would magnify the signal as we shifted the contours, create a pulse and redirect it—luring the creatures away ... packing them off to Melbourne, perhaps, or some equally deserving place ..."

His attempted levity misfired, and Ashworth remained stone-faced.

"So, if the tiles work, what's the problem?"

The professor placed on the table what looked like a large military walkie-talkie with a rotary telephone dialer.

"What's this?"

"It's a mobile telephone. It works like a small radio transmitter. The US military are currently using them in Vietnam."

"Look at the size of this thing! Doesn't look too mobile to me," blurted Parkes, failing to fully grasp the situation.

"Who's going to lug something as cumbersome as this around when there's a telephone on every street corner?"

The professor tried not to sound too patronising. "We can't underestimate the impact of this new technology in the future, Mr Parkes. There are companies already gearing up to mass-produce them. It won't be long before they're reduced to the size of a paperback."

The professor suddenly became deadly serious as he finally dropped the bomb.

"If ... no," he corrected himself, "*when* ... these telephones come into service, they could seriously compromise the device by generating hundreds, maybe thousands of signals. The interference would make it difficult—if not impossible—to focus and redirect daikaiju impulses."

The Minister for Public Works moaned as the full impact sank in. "You know what this means, Cob?"

The architect knew all right—the precious design wouldn't work. He cradled his head in his hands and rocked in his chair.

"Jesus wept ... I-am-not-hearing-this."

A defeated Ashworth threw up his hands. "How do you propose we account for future levels of interference?"

The professor's eyes widened as he rifled through the mass of plans, which spilled from the table onto the floor.

"Like this ..."

He pointed to the plans of the hydraulic systems and already enhanced framework of the building's superstructure.

"As originally designed, the anti-daikaiju device was stationary, rotating in response to the direction of the primary source signal," the professor explained. "The roofing panels open out into huge dishes already, but with a bit of modification ... OK, significant modification, I admit ... we could go even further ..."

Ashworth and Parkes listened with stupefaction as the professor's proposal assumed the implausible air of science fiction.

"Wind tunnel tests have proven that it's already aerodynamically sound, and the added offensive capability makes for a far more effective weapon."

And as he spoke, he quoted the research of Professor Hoyle from the rocket research laboratories at Woomera.

"They've just successfully tested an atomic rocket motor that could provide the initial take-off thrust. They've also secured six Rolls-Royce/Snecma Olympus 593 engines that would take over once the device is airbourne. They each give more than 38,000lbs of thrust, and were specially designed for the new supersonic Concorde aircraft. These engines can position and stabilise the device, and keep it up for maybe a whole hour."

"We couldn't possibly afford all of this!" Ashworth guffawed.

The professor was more optimistic.

"They're the prototypes—gifts from the British and French governments—reparations for all the A-bomb testing in the desert and the Pacific. I'm sure with Hoyle's cooperation, these engines could be made available to us."

The professor pushed on.

"We have the technical capacity to do this. What I need to know is whether the device can be modified this dramatically— *secretly.*"

Ashworth suddenly grabbed at the building plans—already a hodge-podge of additions and amendments—and began tracing its smallest details, running his finger along his own markings and scribbles.

The others fell silent, staring at his intensity with a mixture of expectation and giddy excitement.

Finally he looked up and met their eyes.

"Yes!" he cried, "it's a long shot, but I think it can be done." He took a deep breath. "You'd better make more coffee, professor. It's going to be a long night."

The three men poured over the plans, working out the feasibility of such an audacious proposal.

As they worked feverishly into the night, the project gradually seemed salvageable to Ashworth and they all felt a new hope. Before long, it took on the appearance of an even better plan than the one they'd had before.

"There's only one major problem, as I see it," Ashworth said.

Parkes frowned. "What? You think Hoyle might not cooperate?"

"Hoyle's fine," Wraight offered. "I know him. He'll be in it like a shot."

"What then?"

"I'm thinking of someone closer to home." Ashworth pointed to the designer's name at the bottom of the plans.

"Ohhhh nooo ..." Parkes cried. "*I* told him last time! It's *your* turn."

Ashworth's face soured.

"Bloody 'ell. These are the biggest changes yet. Utzon is gonna spew."

FEBRUARY 28, 1966

Jørn Utzon looked at the new plans with total dismay.

Behind him, huge arched concrete ribs outlined the shape of his spectacular building. Spindly cranes towered above them. The whole site buzzed with activity.

"You are not serious?"

Ashworth and Parkes steeled themselves as the Dane removed

his hard-hat and massaged his temple in frustration.

"How am I supposed to complete this project if you keep altering the brief? These changes do not even make sense."

Parkes remained silent. He was well aware what the Dane thought of him professionally as an architect, and now preferred the Minister to do all the talking.

Ashworth pleaded. "Please, Mr Utzon. It's only a minor alteration."

"Minor! All the machinery to elevate the sets into the opera theatre has been installed, and now you want to switch the opera theatre and the concert hall, and to introduce an entirely new infrastructure?"

"Mr Utzon. We are under instruction from the new Premier."

"And what does he know? Tell me! He is not an architect, he is a politician. I'm not concerned with your petty politics."

"Be reasonable—"

"Reasonable? *Reasonable!*" The usually soft-spoken Dane began to lose his temper. "I have tried to work with you ... I have made every nonsensical change you have requested, have I not?

"Yes, but—"

"But what? I design for you the most spectacular building in the world, yes?"

Ashworth grudgingly nodded.

"Then what is *this* meant to be?" Utzon slapped at the plans.

The Minister toughened. "You really don't have a choice in the matter."

"That's because you are holding me to ransom. Yes! You are deliberately withholding funds so I will be forced to comply with your ridiculous changes."

Ashworth and Parkes exchanged glances.

Utzon had had enough. "Ugghh! This is untenable! I designed for you an *opera house*. I don't know what you are trying to build, but I want no further part in it."

And with that, Jørn Utzon walked off in disgust, tossing his hard-hat into the harbour. He never set foot on the site again.

As the Minister and the Government Architect watched him wend his way through the maze of construction debris, the site around them gradually fell silent. Men downed tools, machinery ground to a halt.

Ashworth turned to Parkes and sighed, almost with relief.

"Well ... at least it's our baby now."

Slowly overtaken by a sense of foreboding, Parkes was not so sure.

"What if we can't get it to work?"

"It'll work."

Parkes sighed. "Harry ... they are gonna hang us up by the balls."

"Actually, Cob, it can't get any worse."

"How do you figure that?"

"'Cos we're already swinging in the breeze, mate, we're already swinging in the breeze."

JULY 25, 1979

At the Centre For Pacific Experiments at Mururoa Atoll, the French scientists looked on with sweaty, furrowed brows. The acrid stench of Gitanes hung heavily in the air.

The 120 kiloton weapon was meant to be lowered to a depth of 800 metres, but had become wedged halfway down the basalt shaft and could not be dislodged. After a brief consultation with their superiors in Paris, they decided to detonate it anyway.

"Cinq ... quatre ... trois ... deux .. .un ... ZÉRO!"

In a deep underwater trench not far from "Zone Centrale", over a million cubic metres of coral and rock slid away to expose what looked like a volcanic ledge, encrusted with eons of marine organisms.

As the debris settled, the ledge gently peeled apart, revealing a giant yellow pupil. The iris focused on a shoal of fish, which flashed silver with each instant change of direction.

Reptillon—the giant lizard—had been roused from its ancient slumber. Even at this impossible depth it could sense a distant calling. An old familiar opponent had been reborn, and was now burrowing towards the east coast of Australia.

The giant reptile knew it must challenge its nemesis once again. It shook itself free from the rocks and coral, raised its massive body from the ocean floor, and slowly headed westward to meet its ancient foe.

TWO NIGHTS AGO

A sledgehammer fist pounded on the apartment door.

Inside, the desperation was palpable as Kenneth Wilcox frantically stabbed at the keyboard of his PC.

An honours student completing a PHD in architectural engineering, he was tantalisingly close to an answer ... almost. Thousands of lives and the fate of the entire city depended on his results.

"Just a few more seconds."

They were now breaking down the door, and he had a pretty good idea why ...

In the course of his research to reconstruct Utzon's original opera house designs as a virtual 3D tour, he had inadvertently uncovered an incredible secret—buried within a complex jigsaw of altered plans, and tangled impossibly for decades in a labyrinthine bureaucracy.

Thanks to recent downsizing and staffing cuts, he was able to rummage through the bowels of various government departments and examine hundreds of plans and secret documents, unchecked, and without arousing any suspicion.

Or so he thought.

Just as the data he desperately sought was downloading, the door was suddenly kicked open. Two men in black, built like brick shithouses, barreled into the room. Ken leapt to his feet, and was tossed aside.

One of them pulled the plug on the PC.

"Hey! What tha ... No! Don't!" Ken pleaded.

The other rifled through files and papers, and turned to his accomplice. "It's all here."

"No! Get out of it!" blurted Ken indignantly. "I haven't done anything illegal. Everything's declassified. It's all in the public domain. What about the Freedom of Information Act? I got rights!"

"Not since nine-eleven you don't," sneered the first man in black.

Furious, the student lunged at him, but with one deft action on the part of his target, found himself pinned to the floor by the goon, who waved a badge in front of Ken's nose.

"ASIO? Awwww, fuck."

Ken was quickly bundled out of the apartment, spirited down the lifts to the basement carpark and tossed into the back seat of an unmarked car.

The first operative slammed Ken's door and jumped in the front, while the second loaded the files and PC into the boot, before climbing into the driver's seat.

A mirrored glass partition isolated Ken from the operatives. He grabbed for the door handle—missing!—and was thrown back against the seat as the car accelerated out of the carpark and into the evening city traffic.

"Who's in charge?"

The operatives listened through hidden mics.

The student pounded the partition with his fists.

"Fuckin' answer me!"

They ignored him.

Stoplights magically turned green as the car wove through the traffic.

"You don't understand. This is important. Look, I know ... I know what it is. You have to listen!"

A voice replied over a hidden speaker.

"What is it?"

"It doesn't work! I've run simulations based on calibrations made by Parkes and Ashworth in the sixties—the device doesn't work."

"Aww, shit." The driver sighed and eyed his colleague sideways. "Do you think he's for real?"

"Yeah ... I do."

The first operative contemplated the fate of the city as the car careered through Sydney's glittering concrete and glass canyons.

"That means the device is fucked ... and that means the city's fucked ... and that means we're all fucked."

"Yep. Reckon it does," agreed the driver.

The car descended into the Harbour Tunnel, heading north.

Then Ken said something that made the driver hit the brakes, hard. Cars skittled around them.

"I know how to make it work!"

The glass partition slid open, and the first operative looked over his shoulder at the student.

"Go on."

"I know how to make it work! You need to update all of Parkes' and Ashworth's original figures. Their data's now woefully out of date."

He definitely had the operative's full attention.

"Data? What data?"

Ben began spurting techno-babble. "It's the angle of incidence. The wings are all out of whack ... they've got to be recalibrated. Once the angle's been determined, the correct altitude can be calculated—"

The operative shushed him. *"Altitude?"*

The two operatives exchanged astonished glances. "You mean ... it can *fly*?"

"Uh-huh! That's the major alteration that drove Utzon to abandon the project. Parkes and Ashworth anticipated a rise in interference, though not to the extent created by mobile phones. By flying above the interference, the device can jam it, and still carry out its primary function. But it needs re-adjustment. It's just that there's no one around who remembers how to do it."

The two operatives exchanged astonished glances.

"Are you absolutely sure you can fix it?"

An exasperated Ken blurted, "Yes! In fact, I can improve it. By positioning the device above the city and angling the wings precisely, I can take advantage of all the mobile phone towers to create an umbrella shield over the entire metropolitan area. I ... I just need my PC."

"It's in the boot," the driver reminded them.

The operative's eyebrows knitted. "You'd better be right, son."

As the car spun one-eighty degrees he suddenly sounded hopeful. "I think there's someone you ought to meet."

The car shot into an emergency vehicle siding in the tunnel and gunned towards the Harry Seidler Retirement Village.

MINUTES LATER

An old and infirm Cobden Parkes sat up in his new recliner in the freshly painted TV room of the retirement village.

"Who's the kid?"

Flanked between the two huge ASIO operatives, Ken did sort of resemble a kid.

"This is Kenneth Wilcox—a PhD student in architectural engineering at Sydney University."

"Well, howdya do, Kenny."

Kenny? The student harrumphed. He detested being called that. As he opened his mouth to respond, one of the operatives placed a firm hand on his shoulder and spoke first.

"He's about to do some freelance work for us."

"With your approval of course, Mr Parkes," added the other operative.

Ken's jaw dropped. It was him! Cobden Parkes!—much older of course, but still recognisable from all the photos.

The old man looked up at Ken with disdain.

"I suppose you're another one of those arty-farty purists who thinks I'm an architectural philistine."

"N-no, Mr Parkes. Quite the opposite," Ken nervously stuttered. "I've studied all your work, read all your notes. Your theories—way ahead of their time—revolutionary!"

"Really?" Parkes brightened.

"Totally! The way you integrated the device into the infrastructure without compromising the integrity of Utzon's original design—sheer genius!"

The awe on Ken's face was gratifying to the old man.

The first operative interjected.

"Gentlemen, there's not much time. Mr Parkes. There's something important Ken has to tell you."

TODAY, NOW

Strategically located on an island in the centre of Sydney Harbour, Fort Denison was built during the Crimean War to defend the city against naval attack. Now its empty cannon pointed impotently out to sea where the water boiled and churned as the submerged Reptillon torpedoed toward it.

The behemoth surfaced east of the Fort.

"*Reptillon! Ahhhh! Reptillon!*" The Japanese tourists on the battlements had seen this reptilian horror before. Sandstone blocks were pulverised under its weight as it pulled itself out of the foam. Shaking the water off its head, it scanned the harbour, took its bearings then tilted its head back to let forth an ear-splitting roar.

In the distance, windows in city buildings shattered and glass rained down upon the pedestrians below.

The monster launched itself back into the water, sending up an enormous plume of sea-spray. What remained of the little sandstone fort crumbled into the sea after it.

☆

Tourists thought the old aboriginal woman singing near Ferry Terminal 4 at Circular Quay was just another of the many buskers that congregated there, and some even threw coins at her feet. Her quaint aboriginal Bible song bemused them.

They couldn't possibly know that the song was one of hatred, summoning the instrument of her revenge. Her voice resonated through the ages, channeling the anguished spirits of all the ancestors who had died at the hands of the white-fella.

Echidonah approached now. Through the soles of her bare feet the old woman could feel the vibration of each claw burrowing toward her. Echidonah could sense her, too, could feel her pain, and the closer it dug, the angrier it became.

She raised her arms as her chanting reached a crescendo. At that very moment, Echidonah broke the surface at Circular Quay. It crashed through the Cahill Expressway, named in honour of the once Premier of NSW. Cars and debris toppled onto the concourse, scattering tourists in terror.

The creature ignored the tasty morsels scurrying about its feet and in the tall glass mounds surrounding it—it had something bigger on its mind. Much bigger.

The aboriginal woman ran under the colonnade at the base of a building derogatively nicknamed the "Toaster". She called out to her monster from behind a column.

"Maaaaamuuuu!"

It shuffled through the wreckage and onto the wharves where ferries bashed against the piers. One capsized, hurling passengers into the glassy green water.

Unused to the sunlight, Echidonah blinked as it peered through the glare out across the harbour, where, with a mighty whoosh, Reptillon—the giant lizard—burst out of the water.

The Eyewitness News helicopter swung around for a better angle. The camera crash-zoomed tight on Reptillon's angry features.

☆

Back at the retirement village, an exhausted and sleep-deprived Kenneth Wilcox entered the room, trailed by the two ASIO operatives.

Cobden Parkes looked away from the new widescreen digital television and eyed him expectantly.

"You remembered to detach all the mooring cables?"

Ken gave a satisfied nod. "Everything's exactly as you've requested."

"Well done, Kenny my boy."

This time a proud Kenneth Wilcox didn't mind being called that.

Parkes gestured to an armchair, and resumed watching the huge plasma screen. "Take a seat, sonny. The show's about to commence."

☆

At Bennelong Point, authorities frantically evacuated the Opera House—cordoning off surrounding streets and clearing the area.

Despite the danger, hundreds of people crowded the foreshore to watch the spectacle unfold.

☆

The two ASIO operatives stood silently at attention on either side of Cobden Parkes, while Ken sat nervously on the edge of his armchair. Totally transfixed, they all stared at the huge plasma screen, where they could clearly see the two giant monsters facing off.

A bogon moth fluttered about their heads.

With rattlesnake reflexes one of the operatives snatched the moth mid-flight. His partner frowned disapproval as he went over to a window, opened it, and gently released his fingers. Unharmed, the moth bobbed away, and the operative closed the window behind it.

The blanket pulled over Parkes' lap had fallen to the ground, and the operative picked it up and smoothed it back over the old man's knees before resuming his vigil.

Parkes mumbled a vague thank you, but his eyes never left the television screen. The old man suddenly remembered his old friends, Premier Cahill and Minister Harry Ashworth, now long dead, remembered how they had all sacrificed for this one moment. Tears welled in his eyes. What political battles had they fought, and how much scathing criticism had they endured from the press and public!

The retired architect looked at the scene and whispered to himself. "Today we find out if it has all been worth it." The tears flowed freely now, and his bottom lip quivered. "Today my friends, we will be vindicated!"

☆

Back at Circular Quay, Echidonah reared onto its stocky hind legs. Its quills bristled with expectation, while mid-harbour, the giant green lizard splashed toward its opponent. Pausing between the Harbour Bridge and the Sydney Opera House, Reptillon flexed its muscles and adopted a defiant stance as its radioactive spines began to glow ominously.

Face to face at last, the two behemoths sized each other up.

☆

Before authorities could stop her, the aboriginal woman jumped a barrier and ran onto the concourse of the Opera House, where she screamed a vengeful call to attack.

"MAMU! MAMU!"

☆

Cobden Parkes leaned forward, gripped the arm of his recliner tightly, and spluttered, "Now!"

The two operatives nodded to each other, then one mouthed something into his microphone.

Grinning toothlessly, an exuberant Parkes turned to Ken, and winked.

As the giant monsters towered over the Quay, poised for battle, a loud ratcheting suddenly distracted their attention.

Together they turned in the direction of the sound, and watched tiny white tiles fly like confetti into the air, as the glittering sails of the Sydney Opera House slowly, delicately, and quite deliberately, unfurled.

☆

A huge exhaust rotated and locked into position above the aboriginal woman's head. She did a double-take as the engine core began to glow a radioactive blue.

A State Emergency Services recruit went to retrieve her, but was held back by his mate. The engine ignited, and the woman screamed at the top of her voice, before being blown back into the dreamtime.

"Kaaami!"

Her shrill scream was lost as a deep, powerful roar echoed through the Harbour foreshore and the building wrenched itself from its moorings. Wings spread, it rose into the sky like a gigantic moth.

ONE NIGHT ON TIDAL RIG #13

TESSA KUM

With the moon long gone, the night ocean was very, very dark. Against an overcast sky, empty of stars, the lights of the tower room appeared to float in the darkness. They should have been dwarfed by the beacon light fixed above them, but these nights the beacon was rarely lit. There wasn't enough oil to keep it from squeaking, and Thirteen was fond of her sleep.

Not that sleep was easy to come by on a tidal rig.

It was a great hulking mess of machinery, towering out of the water like some bad-tempered god, making toy ships out of the massive cargo freighters that passed it by. Calling it ugly didn't do it justice. Pipes thicker than subways tangled themselves chaotically and cogs with teeth a storey high spun with only metres to spare. Nestled deep amid the pistons in the heart of the rig lay an arcane generator, one of the last of its kind. Drawing on mysterious and not entirely understood energies, it drove the engines that laboured endlessly to turn the wings. A regular procession of sparks and power arcs lit up the rig's bowels in enchanted colours. Usually thirteen's iron behemoth shuddered and roared as it worked. Now the pop and sizzle echoed clearly; this close to the turning of the tide it was relatively quiet. The engines were winding down and the wings merely rolling with the powerful current they'd created.

Just as long as the number five valve didn't start venting at the wrong time, again, Thirteen paid the workings of the rig no heed.

Globes thirty through sixty-seven along the ladder were blown, shattered, or simply not there. In this unlit stretch, she paused to scrub fiercely at an itch on her nose. She shifted her tool belt, making a note to refill her oil canister. It took a moment of groping about before she found the rung again. Three supply drops ago she'd applied for a helmet light, which had failed to show up. If she hadn't climbed this ladder who knows how many times a day, half the time in starless darkness, she might have found it daunting.

"Rusty lump of crap," she muttered out of habit, and continued climbing. The dim light of the tower room glowed above her, where she would be warm, away from the wind, and with a nice big plate of sausages and mash. Only another hour, and then she could turn the tide, and go to sleep.

Thank the Ministry of Moon Loss Rehabilitation for legislating that the tide be high twice a day. She never had more than five hours of sleep in one hit, and then only if she were lucky.

Ten rungs from the top she hesitated, and then cursed, scrambling up the last part. Warm air blasted her numb face when she jerked the door open. She snatched up the ringing phone.

"Thirteen here."

White noise filled her ear.

"Can't make you out, say again?"

Garble, warble, hiss.

She hung up.

"The greatest thing about manning the oldest tidal rig on the continent is that nothing ever sodding well works."

The com speaker in the wall crackled. "What?" Fourteen, manning the next rig up the coast, had a voice full of a gravel that came from a lifetime of yelling, grumbling, swearing, and generally being a grumpy old man. She loved him dearly. Not that she'd ever say it.

"It's not even my fault," she flopped down in her frayed armchair. "No matter how many times I tighten the valve, or clean the joints, or file a report. Nothing. Ever. Works."

There was a brief pause before Fourteen answered. "What the hell are you talking about?"

She sat on her hands to warm them. "My phone, actually."

"Bloody hell, Thirt," Fourteen grumbled, "We were talking about the soccer."

"Well, no wonder I wasn't listening."

Fourteen sighed.

The tower room was dingy at best. The engineers who had designed and put it together hadn't gone to any effort to make it a nice place to live. The walls were iron sheets, the rivets holding them together bleeding rust down to the floor. The three-hundred-and-sixty degree windows were spotted and covered in salt scum and bird droppings. Cracks ran down most, and a couple were boarded up with soggy cardboard.

She pressed her nose against the closest window, seeking out the green and red flashing light on the northern horizon.

"Thirteen—"

"Yeah, I know, I'm a dork, now wave back." She wiggled her fingers at the light. The newer rigs had video and audio connections to the net, not to mention heating and carpet. There wasn't much that Thirteen could do to contact the outside world besides wave. She'd tried smoke signals once, out of boredom.

"What's all this chatter?" a third voice roared. The Coast Master. All belligerence and bile, that voice. Thirteen ducked at the whip-crack in his tone.

"Just passing time, sir," Fourteen said.

"Do it without clogging up the coastline channel. Where the devil is Sixteen?"

Although there was no one for miles who could see her, Thirteen straightened her back and sat to attention. "Sleeping, sir."

"What?" the speaker distorted. "The tide turns in less than an hour!"

"I believe she has her alarm set, sir," Fourteen said, acquiescent.

There was a distinct lack of input from any of the other riggers along the coast. *Traitors*, she thought at them. Quietly, she retrieved a bottle from the small fridge at her side.

"I need her now. Why isn't she answering her phone?"

"Begging your pardon, sir," Thirteen twisted the bottle cap in her hands, "but her phone broke ages ago."

"Why wasn't I notified?"

"I believe you were. Sir."

Static filled the channel as the Coast Master paused. "She's getting visitors in fifteen minutes. Some marine scientists making a lot of noise about this here hermit crab migration. They want to see it up close."

"What crab migration?"

"Don't any of you riggers watch the news?"—Thirteen refrained from pointing out she couldn't even if she wanted to—"Massive migration going all the way up the coast. Minister of Tourism is having a fit. All the beaches are closed."

"But if they're on the beaches, why does anyone need to come out here?" Fourteen sounded bemused.

"The Sea Walls are picking up multiple moving signals. Big ones. Not serpents. The pictures from the subs aren't clear, but they think they're old crabs joining in or some shit. They'll cruise past you guys within the hour."

A new voice piped up. "How big are we talking, sir?" Wheedling, needy, nasal: Nine. Thirteen wasn't fond of him.

"Big enough, Nine. Don't you worry, we've got the Navy on standby at Port Puck."

"The Navy? What? Do we need them? Port Puck is two hours away!"

Thirteen ignored Nine's rising panic, frowning as she stared at nothing. "Sir," she interjected, "there hasn't been a crab migration since the moon closed and the Salt Fae died."

"So? Who cares? They're on the move. Now listen up, I have four marks going by Sixteen, three coming your way Thirteen, and Ten and Eleven might get a look in as well. Smaller marks going through Six and Seven. You got everything ready, Thirteen?"

She blinked. "What?"

There was muffled mumbling, as though the Coast Master had his hand over the mic, before he spoke again. "What the hell is wrong with your phone, Thirteen?"

"Nothing," she said, not trying to hide the defensive tone in her voice. "It's old, like everything else, and doesn't work so well with the wind up and cloud cover. Sir. If I had one of those new ones—"

"You're getting a scientist, too."

"Wh—"

"Don't even start. You treat the geek with respect, make sure he has what he needs, and if I get even a whiff that you're thinking about being a prick, you won't be getting the helmet light in your next drop."

"I wasn't expecting it anyway," she grumbled.

"At this point we don't know if they're likely to pose a threat, but keep your coms on. If you need to know anything else, you'll be told. Over and out."

Silence over the channel. Thirteen stared at the scotch in her lap. There was only a couple of fingers left, so she tossed it back, screwing up her face as it burned a trail to her gut.

Then she let out a long and vicious stream of the most shocking words she knew.

"Not happy?"

"No," she said tightly to Fourteen, "Not happy."

As conversation between the other riggers slowly grew on the channel, Thirteen sagged in her chair. Her reflection glared back at her in a singularly unattractive way.

Apart from the voices of the others, she spent every day alone. Even for Fourteen, who'd been on the next rig since before she'd arrived, she couldn't put a face to his voice.

At first it was hard, but everyone adapted. She might not like it, but it was *her* solitude, and she didn't like anyone breaking it without her permission. Not to mention she hadn't had the chance to request items from the continent. Such as a new bottle of scotch.

Eight, appearing now that the Coast Master was gone, sniffed. "How much damage can a crab do?" Aristocratic accent, droll, too civilised to be a rigger.

"Thought you were jerking off, Eight," Thirteen jibed, although her heart wasn't really in it.

"*Sleeping!* For crying out loud, I was *sleeping!*"

"Uh huh," Nine snickered.

"And you're a vestal virgin. What do they think these crabs can do, in real terms? Tidal rigs aren't exactly delicate machines. The worst I can see happening is one getting caught in a wing. Hardly worth the effort."

"You have a point there," Fourteen mused. "Exactly how does anyone expect to learn anything out on our rigs? It's not like we'll be able to see anything, and with the tide turning the currents will play chaos with any fancy toys they toss in."

"Hey, guys," Thirteen fished a not-quite-finished dog end from a bristling ash tray, "my history is a bit sketchy, but it was the Salt Fae who herded the hermit crabs, right?" She discarded the butt again, and pulled out a fresh smoke.

"Yeah, I think so. Why?"

"Doesn't Fifteen have net access?" she asked, patting her pockets. Her matches were missing.

"Not anymore, her dish broke. Why, Thirt?"

"Well, given that the crabs only migrated when the Salt Fae herded them, and since the faeries closed the moon the Salt Fae are mostly dead—"

"All dead."

"—shut up! So why are the crabs migrating?"

"Thirteen, just between friends, you need to stop with the Salt Fae shit," Nine snipped.

As she struggled to think of something nasty to say, Nine added, "All that crap about you being part Salt Fae and all, getting very old I must say."

"But I am!" It sounded petulant, but she wouldn't back down. "My great-great-great-great grandmother was Salt Fae!"

"That makes you ..." Fourteen paused, "One thirty-two'th Salt Fae?"

"More like one sixty-fourth," Nine corrected.

"*Kasha ni su fakka!*"

A beat, then a bemused Fourteen. "What?"

"I said you're both arseholes! In Salt Fae-ese!"

Fourteen sighed. "C'mon, Thirt, don't shoot the messenger."

"It's not like you have gills," Nine said.

She didn't say anything.

"*Do* you have gills?"

Pouting, she shook her head. "No."

"Ha!" Nine said smugly. "See? They don't say the Salt Fae are extinct for nothing."

Thirteen bared her teeth at the speakers.

"Don't feel bad, Thirt," Fourteen said, a smile in his voice. "We love you all the same."

"Thank you. You're still arseholes." She glanced out the window, and sighed. The lights of a chopper drew near. "I'm going to go and not be a prick to the geek. So much for sausages and mash. "Ah! Matches."

"Make it quick, girl, nearly time to turn."

"Yeah, yeah. I can make it to the beacon and back before you even start, old man," she mumbled around the cigarette.

Fourteen just laughed.

The curve of her hand glowed as she lit and inhaled. Cold drafts slipped under the door, breathing through her thick trousers. She grabbed her beanie and jammed it on her head.

The wind tugged her hair as she stepped onto the catwalk. She squinted against it and hastily zipped up her coat. When she swung out onto the ladder her nose was already running. Unseen in the darkness below, the waves thundered against the rig as they had for more than a century. It was, Thirteen reflected, probably a good thing that the rig hadn't had a structural survey in more than a decade. There was probably, no, definitely all sorts of wear and tear down there that would mean the Ministry would have to spend money fixing it. Which really meant shutting Tidal Rig #13 down and loading her territory onto #12 and #14.

Hell no, this rig would be standing long after the new shiny ones had fallen to scrap.

The roosting seagulls murmured and waddled out of her way when she mounted the top platform. Her pace was slow; she could barely see, and didn't want to step on any of them. Dumb birds, she thought affectionately, and exhaled away from them.

The chopper—sleek, streamlined, top of the line—circled above, spotlight wavering about uncertainly. It caught her full in the face and she cursed, waving it away.

"Attention Tidal Rig #13. Turn on your beacon, repeat, turn on your beacon."

The birds fled screeching from the blare of the loudspeaker. Thirteen waited till the angry storm of feathers around her subsided before feeling her way towards the beacon station. Her night vision was shot. She ran her hand across a rusting surface till she found the handle. A couple of shoulder-wrenching yanks and it screamed open. Refill the oil pot, right. The light inside failed to come on.

"Tidal Rig #13, turn on your beacon, repeat—"

"I heard you the first time, sheesh."

By light of the chopper she flipped the switches, and as an afterthought slapped the com channel on. Familiar voices burbled in the wash of noise. When the tower began to hum beneath her feet, she straightened and pushed the door shut. After a last long drag on her cigarette she flicked the butt into the wind.

"Tidal Rig #13—"

"Sweet friggin'... it takes a while to warm up, alright!" Exasperation made her gestures sharp. The pilot didn't speak again.

Spider legs uncurled from the chopper's belly, the hinges snapping open with scissor-like snicks. Thirteen raised her eyebrows. Only military choppers were licensed to use spider legs, the very useful toy that they were. The mechanical arms snaked down and clamped the catwalk around the beacon, forming a temporary dome frame over Thirteen's head and anchoring the chopper safely. She held her breath, face averted, as the downdraft was full of fumes, too strong for someone used to clean sea air. The floor rattled with the equipment being unloaded. When the direction of buffeting changed, she looked up. The chopper was retreating into the darkness, spider legs curling away.

Amid the sudden mound of boxes atop her rig hunkered a figure in a much cleaner coat than hers. He scurried over, and in the growing light Thirteen made out a clean face, cheek bones to cut diamonds on, a neat hair cut, glasses, and a smile that had to be surgically perfected.

"Hello, my name is Lloyd Doyer. I'm with the Coastline Rehabilitation Organisation. They sent me out here in such a rush, I was never told your name."

His was a voice that had been raised on airconditioning and assumed it would be heard without being raised. Prior to this, she'd never found the nerdy librarian look particularly attractive, but it had been a long time since she'd seen another human being, let alone a good-looking one.

It had also been a long time since she'd talked face-to-face, and to her horror she realised he could see her quite blatantly checking him out.

"Thirteen," she said, and shook his hand quickly, too aware of the sweat and rust and grease coating her palms.

He gave her an adorable quizzical look. "I'm sorry, I thought that this was the thirteenth—"

"It is. The numbers tend to stick, Mr Doyer."

"Call me Lloyd, please. I must apologise for arriving with such short notice. Unfortunately we didn't detect these larger crabs till very late. My uncle was a tidal rigger, and he was very clear about the etiquette of visiting a rig."

"Really? What generation rig did he have?"

Doyer shrugged, "I really don't know, but it was along the north-east coast of Nova Mentus." He unslung his bag and fished around in it. "He always said to come bearing gifts. I didn't get much time to shop before they flew me out, but I did grab this."

Thirteen laughed, covering her mouth to hide her delighted grin.

"Is that scotch single malt? Yes? Okay, we like you, you can stay." He's pretty! He comes bearing presents! Oh, she liked him a lot.

"I'm glad it's appreciated," he said, seeming much more relaxed. "So, this is the antiquated tidal rig #13." He looked about the platform, taking in the rickety grid underfoot, the salt- and rust-encrusted beacon mounded high with leavings from the birds, and the single cannon mounted facing the ocean. None of it inspired awe in his expression.

"Um, where do I attach myself?"

Thirteen stared at him blankly before noticing the safety harness strapped around his waist, somewhat lost in his bulky coat.

"'Antiquated' is a fancy word for 'old', and in this particular case, 'old' means piece of junk built before the words 'safety' and 'regulations' met and shook hands." At the dismayed look on his face she chuckled. "It's not that bad. Look, the wind is coming from the west tonight. Just stay away from the east side of the platform and you'll be fine. It isn't even blowing that hard."

He gave her another doubtful look.

"Really. It took a class 3 gale to blow the last rigger off. Stop looking like that. You'll be fine. I'll be back when I'm done."

"Wait!" Doyer clutched her arm. "You're going? Where? Why?"

She gave his hand a comforting pat. "The tide doesn't turn by itself." This close he smelt of aftershave, curry, fuel and earth. Rare and exotic scents. A step back and they disappeared, clearing her mind.

"Now? Oh."

She paused with one foot on the ladder. He was afraid of heights. Typical. "Don't worry if the place starts shaking like a jackhammer. It's always quiet like this, just before a turning."

"This is quiet?"

Her top lip peeled back and she dropped out of sight swiftly. Scotch, yes, pretty, yes; however, it was one thing for her, whose life rotated around this clunky iron behemoth, to bad mouth it, and another thing entirely for him to. Geek. Nerd. Toff.

When she passed the tower room she could hear the com buzzing with talk. The ladder shook and rattled with every step. The metal coils and angles of the rig rose up around her, and even at the end of the cycle the throb and crunch of the engine drowned out the sound of the ocean. The rig never truly slept.

Far below she could make out the dim light of the switch room, a dirty yellow smear in the darkness.

This far down the ladder vibrated constantly. By the time her feet touched the bottom her palms were numb. She slapped on the com and clapped her hands to drive some feeling into them. Sixteen's voice came on loud, clear, and distinctly pissed off. The com on the beacon was still turned on, drat. Hopefully Doyer wouldn't be able to hear it over everything else he wasn't used to. Thirteen elected to remain silent until Sixteen had finished her rant, and flicked the safety systems off. Uninvited guests were not the best way to wake up.

"Buck up," Thirteen said, when Sixteen's steam seemed low, "They might be pretty." She bit down on 'too' before it left her mouth.

"Oberon's arse, they're here to look at *crabs*, Thirteen, doesn't that say something?"

There was a rare moment of silence on the channel as all contemplated the many quips that sentence prompted.

"Sod it," Sixteen spat, "I'm starting the count. All ready?"

A chorus of affirmations.

"Three ... two ... one ... Turn!"

Thirteen grunted as she put her shoulder against the lever. With a screech it clunked into place. A series of clangs and thunks followed, moving deeper into the engines. A single massive shudder shook the entire structure. Thirteen sucked her cheek in, and watched the machinery around her.

The slow roll of gears was barely perceptible at first, and she squinted until she was convinced they were turning. A sudden snake of energy discharge slithered up the pipes. The platform began to shiver with the strain of the engine turning the wings. Pushing an ocean around was not easy business.

"Hold together just a little longer." She patted the wall beside her. "Mr Doyer," she raised her voice, "can you hear me?"

"Yes, Miss, uh, Thirteen."

"What, you left your guest all alone? For shame, Thirt!"

"Shut up, Nine. Doyer, I'm on my way back up. Any idea when this crab of yours is going to appear?"

"Setting up the tracking now."

The rig groaned and pinged as she flipped the intercom off and began the long climb up the ladder.

She frowned as she ascended, staring up at the sky. The beacon wasn't turning, only pointed towards land. Bloody useless. Why on earth was it blue—oh yes. The Blue Moon Festival two weeks previous.

The wind grabbed her as she rose out of the shelter of the rig, and she halted to clutch at her beanie. Perhaps it was the remnants of chopper fuel, but something smelt off. Rank. She struggled to brush her hair out of her face, anywhere that would stop it tickling her nose. A snatch of garbled sound made her tilt her head. After a moment she resumed her climb with haste. As she drew towards the tower room, her mouth tightened. The phone, again. Some people never learned. She ground her teeth, scrambled off the ladder, wrenched the door open, and lunged for the phone.

"Thirteen here."

"Where the fucking faeries have you been?"

She flinched away from the Coast Master's bellow, half imagining spit in her ear. "Turning the tide, sir," she said, thinking that should have been obvious.

"You h...inc... —d me...oming—"

"You're breaking up, sir."

A savage burst of distortion blared in her ear, and although most of his words were eaten by interference, she knew she heard him utter 'serpent cannon'.

"Say again, or get on the coast ch—"

Without missing a beat the com speakers roared. "I said you have incoming. The biggest mark on the screen altered course to get around a rock outcrop and is now heading straight for you. The Navy have scrambled two combat moths, but they won't arrive for another half hour—"

"Half an hour?"

"Till then you're on your own. Get the cannon loaded. I don't want this thing getting tangled in the rig. The gods know how many parts we don't manufacture any more. Move it!"

"Tangled? How big is it? I mean, is it seriously going to be big enough for me even to see?"

"I said move it, rigger!"

Thirteen growled at the Coast Master. His orders unsettled her more than she liked to admit. Only twice in her time on the tidal rig had she needed to use the serpent cannon, and she considered herself lucky to have only had reason two times. It was more than a little terrifying to go up against a serpent, a creature large enough to deal some real damage to a tidal rig. In the migration years the coastline was constantly patrolled by Navy ships, for the rigs' protection. At least the newer rigs had defences more adequate than a single unautomated cannon.

She unlocked the ammunition cabinet. The shells inside were designed specifically for use against serpents. They had so many enchantments of death, bad luck, pestilence, and destruction laid on them that the cupboard itself had to be enchanted as well, to keep it from disintegrating. The amount of arcane energy saturated into it all would fetch a disgustingly high price on the black market, what with enchantments becoming increasingly rare since the moon closed. She pulled out an iron case, flipped it open to check it was full, then shouldered it. The straps dug deep.

Outside was nothing but darkness. She strained until her eyes ached as she scaled the ladder, but the night revealed nothing, least of all giant crabs.

Something squawked when she stepped onto the landing. Bloody birds. She waded around the beacon.

The gods knew what Doyer had set up. Cameras, sensors, expensive-looking machines that went 'ping!' when he touched them, and something that looked like radar.

"Can you see it?"

He whirled around, flashing a pocket torch in her eyes. "Oh! Sorry, you startled me. What did you say?"

Thirteen pointed her chin, blinking her dazzled eyes. "Tracking. Can you see it?"

Doyer shook his head. "No, something from the rig is interfering. The vibrations, maybe the arcane energy, I don't know. All I get is a big blurry blob. I thought the tidal rigs had shock absorbers built in."

"The second generation, yes."

"How do you sleep? I mean," he blushed, "What with all the noise and bouncing. Er."

Thirteen raised an amused eyebrow. "You get used to it." Carefully she sank to her knees and pulled the ammunition case from her shoulders. Everything felt a lot lighter without it. "Did you hear the Coast Master over the com?" she said, crawling over to his side.

"No, sorry. It got so loud up here, I couldn't make anything out."

The tracking was as useless as he said. Ghost images flickered around the edges. "Apparently it's coming right for us. I'm going to turn on the beacon. He didn't say if we'd be able to see it, but given he told me to load up the serpent cannon ..." She trailed off and shrugged. The Coast Master was probably over-reacting. "What are you trying to get anyway?"

"Anything. Everything! This is a phenomenon unheard of since the closing of the moon. There have been some claims of smaller migrations, but to have the elder crabs from off the continental shelf join in, why, it's just amazing. Imagine what we could discover! This is going to be one of the most exciting nights of my life."

Thirteen ducked her head and slunk over to the beacon station. His fervour was cute, but she had to wonder about anyone who thought an exciting night involved crabs. Marine type crabs, anyway. The control panel grudgingly opened.

"But this isn't just about crabs, is it?" She stabbed the rotation button. It did nothing. Cursing, she began spinning the winch furiously. "Hermit crabs don't get together of their own accord. That's why they're called 'hermit' crabs."

The beacon began to turn with a squeal. The blue light lit up the seething waters, showing up little flashes of silver as fish darted about. It turned slowly.

"Well, it is highly irregular—" Doyer, Thirteen decided, would be perfect to play poker with. He had no bluffing skills.

"I'm part Salt Fae, you know." The com chattered quietly, something about growing up in a trailer park, and she hit hard enough to make some nasty feedback. "My great-great-great-great grandmother lived in the reserves."

"One sixty-fourth?" He snorted laughter, which became a choke with the dead stare she levelled at him. "Well, I mean, you know, that's not, that's really not a lot. Um."

With pursed lips Thirteen turned back to the winch. If she ever met someone whose first reaction wasn't to laugh at her heritage, she'd marry them.

"I'm sorry, I didn't mean to offend you." His coat rustled as he moved. "It's just that I've never come across anyone who was actually proud of having faery blood."

Thirteen couldn't remember the last time anyone had apologised for getting her back up. "When you grow up in a caravan with an alcoholic mother and clinically depressed father, pretending you're a special faery princess has its appeal." Honesty made her tone curt.

"Oh," Doyer said, taken aback. He was quiet for a moment. "Do you know much of the history of the Salt Fae?"

"I know they shepherded the crab migrations, and I know that's the real reason you're here."

This time his silence was heavy with tension. "I see," he said. His voice was a closed book, and she could read nothing in it.

The beacon was nearly turned now, and her arm muscles were tiring. "Can you see anything yet?"

His coat rustled again, and there was a strangled gurgling noise.

"Doyer?"

She turned.

It was bigger than she expected.

Crabs had always been cute little scuttling things with googly eyes, irritating but harmless pinchers, and great-tasting with a bit of ginger and lemongrass.

She'd never realised how hideous they really were.

It towered above them; her thoughts stuttered at that. It dwarfed her rig, her enormous tidal rig, which she had always likened to a beast risen from the murky depths. Now she faced the real thing. The bloat of its shell was mottled brown. Barnacles and growths ruptured its surface like rancid pustules. Seaweed of all sorts hung from it in fat greasy clumps.

Something even bigger than the crab had left that shell behind.

Thirteen let out a little squeak.

The com crackled. "Thirteen, you okay?"

Like normal hermit crabs, its legs clustered to the front, bony, covered in short red bristles, and stiff and sharply segmented. It was too big for her to comprehend, she couldn't fit it all inside her head. So many legs! One rose, slow and ponderous, and reached forward. The water surged as it plunged down. Thirteen thought she felt the rig tremble, and couldn't help imagining that she could hear the terrible shell, dragging along the sea bed.

"Doyer?" she said softly, as if afraid speaking would attract the monster's attention. The scientist was frozen, a conflict of horror and delight on his face.

Beady black eyes stood high on thin stalks. It had no face to speak of. Little arms grew where the mouth might have been, and feelers flowed out among them, flicking about heavily in the open air. Her stomach lurched as though a trapdoor had opened in it, and Thirteen closed her eyes, unable to look any longer.

The sea churned as the crab took another step forward. This time she was sure the rig shivered.

It was unstoppable. The realisation hit her and the world tilted sickeningly. She steadied herself on the beacon. The sodding idiot creature was going to walk straight into her rig.

"No! You went around the rock! Go around us, too!"

"Thirteen!"

She jumped at her name over the com. "Sorry, guys." She patted around the deck until she found the ammunition pack, and dragged it over to the cannon. "I, ah, can't quite talk right now. Doyer!" The harshness in her voice snapped him out of his daze. "Whatever it is you're trying to do, do it now." Looking at the shells, covered in sigils and hexes, a twinge of doubt made her hands shake. How much effect could they have against a creature covered in its own armour?

Doyer crouched low over one of his consoles, hammering away on the keyboard. He glanced over at her, face pale and a faint sheen of sweat on his brow. "What are you doing?"

"Loading the cannon."

"What? You can't!"

"Cannon? Thirteen! What's going on?"

She turned to the huge clunky gun mounted on the platform. From the crash of the sea she knew the crab had taken another step. Its stench filled the air; rotting seaweed and mud that had never known open air. Her hands shook as she pushed the shell into the chamber and locked it in.

"You're going to shoot it?" Doyer was aghast. "But you can't! I, we, you can't do that! We have to study it, there's so much to learn, why would you do such a thing?"

He wasn't so cute now, and the look she shot him said as much. Taking hold of the trigger grips, she swivelled the gun around till the barrel pointed straight at the crab's mouth. She was unlikely to miss.

"Mr Scientist, you do what you do. I'm trying to stop it from trampling my home. Kindly shut up."

What if shooting it made it angry? Before her courage left, she pressed the triggers.

Whumpf! The concussion left her ears ringing. Doyer shrieked and flung himself flat. Leaving a curling trail of smoke and resonating with the now active enchantments, the shell spiralled through the air.

The crab lifted a leg to take another step, moving it into the path of the round. Without waiting to see the shell hit, Thirteen broke the barrel. The empty cartridge popped out and lay smoking, unheeded, as she pushed another into place. There was another crack of noise, barely heard, as the first round impacted on the crab's heavily armoured leg. Doyer yelled something incoherent at her.

She turned and realigned the crosshairs. This time she would get the timing right.

"Come on," she muttered, gnawing her lip. Her pulse throbbed in her fingertips. She could smell her own rancid sweat. A small blackened crater was the only evidence of her first shot.

And ... now.

She felt rather than heard the shot, which blew the last of her hearing away. In total silence she watched the shell curve through the previous trail of smoke. Her breath caught in her throat.

The shell hit. Bullseye.

She let out a whoop. It felt wrong not being able to hear it. The crab was so close it filled her vision. It stopped and pulled its horrible beady eyes inside its shell. The little arms around its mouth waved in panic. One of them hung limp.

Doyer grabbed her shoulders and spun her round. He shook her violently, his glasses skewed, spittle flecking his chin, mouth open and teeth flashing as he screamed soundlessly at her. Thirteen shoved him. He clung to her like a mad man.

"I can't hear you!" she cried, "I can't even hear me! Let go!" She hooked her leg around his shins and swung him down. He grappled with her coat, expression gone from fury to shock. The platform jumped with his impact. The man had clearly never been in a bar brawl in his life.

Thirteen stepped back from him as he scrambled to his feet. He slowed, the rage slipping from his movements, and stared over her shoulder.

Not again.

She half turned. One of the crab's eyes slunk out from the shell. She was positive it stared straight at them.

Then it started moving again.

Thirteen closed her eyes briefly. It had taken a shell right in the kisser. Why hadn't it stayed hidden in its shell? She would have. Despite a growing sense of helplessness she grabbed another round. The spent cartridge dropped on her foot and rolled across the platform silently. She snapped the barrel back into place without a sound, and took the triggers again.

Doyer grabbed her around the waist and flung her from the cannon. She landed hard. Something crunched beneath her. One of his gadgets. Good, she hoped it cost a lot.

She scrambled clumsily to her feet, unable to find her balance. Her shoulder throbbed. Doyer crouched suspiciously, hands in weedy little fists, and obviously had no idea what he was doing. His lips moved around clenched teeth.

Thirteen stepped up smartly, batted his punch aside, and slammed her fist into his gut. The scientist doubled over and fell to the decking, curled in a tight ball of private agony.

"Stay down." She stepped over him and took the triggers. The crab was too close and its head too high; she couldn't lever the barrel up enough to target it. Her mouth filled with bloody tang. She bit her cheeks too hard. It was too close, too late. Not caring where it hit, she fired.

The impact knocked her off her feet. Smoke drifted over her, dense, caustic, and fishy smelling. Her throat burned and her skin prickled. She covered her face, coughing.

It kept coming, it just kept coming.

Okay, plan B. Think. It was too late to abandon the rig. The life raft was at the bottom, which was a half hour climb on a good day. Death by giant crab. It didn't seem fair. Or reasonable. They weren't even supposed to be migrating; only Salt Fae directed migrations. Crabs didn't have initiative. Bloody crabs!

It took another step forward. The rig shook as gargantuan

waves crashed against it, totally unheard.

"You can't do this to me! I, *I* am Salt Fae! My great-granny was a Salt Fae! *You can't do this to me!*" What was the Salt Fae word for 'stop'? She knew it, she knew she knew it.

"*Kavara! Kavart! K'vart! Kavara ... kavarna ... KAVADA!*" She leapt up, punching her fist at the crab. "*Kavada*, you stupid animal, *kavada!*"

Doyer stepped up.

"What the ...?" Thirteen stared at him, incredulous.

For someone who couldn't throw a punch, he sure knew how to hold a gun.

Movement caught her eye, and she glanced up at the crab. Something on its head. It was dark up there, but it almost looked as though someone was moving about. On a crab? On *this* crab?

Doyer gestured with the gun and Thirteen raised her hands quickly. He breathed hard and his face was red with fury.

For a moment the world was crystal clear; the chill wind at her fingertips, the smell of stagnation in the air, the way the gun glinted in the blue light.

In surreal silence, the crab crashed into the rig.

It knocked her flat. She felt the structure scream and buckle, reverberating through her body. The platform dropped down, or she fell upwards and was thrown against the beacon station. Not being able to hear her rig tearing itself apart made it worse. The acrid smell of hot metal filled the air, sharp against the soft smell of rotting fish.

After an aeon of waiting for the whole thing to topple into the sea, she realised the tremors in the rig had subsided, were nothing more than the comforting shakes of the tide turning.

Without opening her eyes, she took inventory of herself. Bruised, battered, still largely deaf. Her knee hurt more than a little from where something, probably one of Doyer's sodding boxes, had hit her. She'd bitten her tongue. Other than that, she didn't appear to be dead, and couldn't help feeling that this was something she was going to regret.

Cautiously, she opened her eyes. The panelling of the beacon station looked battered, reassuringly so. Gingerly, she looked about.

Doyer lay propped against the station, eyes squeezed shut. Blood matted the hair at his temple. His lips moved in nervous little stutters, almost as though praying.

The gun lay between them.

Thirteen rested her head on the hard grid. Normally, scientists didn't carry guns, right? It was all wrong, but given the dive the night was taking, she shouldn't have been surprised. Just her luck that it was one of the few things that hadn't been thrown from the platform.

Slowly, she reached towards it.

Perhaps her coat rustled, maybe a button scraped against the catwalk, but Doyer heard something. He snapped out like a spring and snatched the gun up, levelling it at her head before glancing about.

It was the way he went rigid that sent shivers down her arms. She rolled over.

The crab was much, much closer than she liked. It slumped against the rig, its rigid legs resting against the platform mere metres away. At first it seemed dead it was so still, until it heaved, and the rig rocked violently. The catwalk thrummed painfully beneath her. Doyer grabbed her arm in panic, and she didn't let out the breath she held until the crab subsided. Even then, its little mouth legs and eyes whipped about manically. The crab wasn't happy about it either.

Thirteen tried to remember the structure of the west side of the rig. There wasn't much call for her to go down there. The crab was well clear of the wings, but several of the pistons were partially exposed there. She turned to Doyer.

"I think it's stuck." She almost heard her voice, a hazy mumble.

The scientist jumped. Thirteen felt a thump of air hit her face as he shot the crab in fright. She raised her hands without further prompting.

"I've already surrendered!"

Doyer scowled at her, shifting his grip on the gun. Leaning close he yelled in her ear. "On what!"

Thirteen tried to swallow. Her mouth had never felt so dry. The muzzle of the gun was inches from her face, out of focus. "Could be anything. Can hermit crabs reverse?"

The crab thrashed again. They stared at each other until it calmed. Thirteen specifically did not think of the damage being inflicted on her rig.

"It's out of the water! Not enough buoyancy! Shell too big! How did it even get this far into the shallows!"

"You're the 'marine scientist', you tell me." There were little scratches around the gun's mouth that no amount of polishing could hide. It was a gun that had been used before. Don't think about it. "We need to get off the rig."

Doyer shook his head once.

"Look, this isn't personal, I'm not trying to be a prick here, but you don't seem to be seeing the whole picture. That crab is going to tear the rig apart, and if we don't get off, we're going down with it."

He tapped her nose none too gently with the gun. "More important things here than your rig."

"Yes, our lives! Please, just listen a moment. There are a couple of combat moths en route, but I don't know how long—" The crab flailed, and the groan the rig let out echoed in her bones.

His mouth shaped the words 'combat moths' as though they left a bad taste in his mouth. "Call them off!"

"I wouldn't know how. The Coast Master called them in. Er," she licked her lips, "could you maybe not point that thing so close to my face?"

"Coast Master! You're sure?"

Thirteen nodded. Doyer relaxed visibly. He slumped against the station and adjusted his glasses with a little smile. She didn't know how he could stand waving the gun so close to his own head. He adjusted his glasses again.

Maybe, if she jumped him now. He wasn't paying attention to her, in fact he stared open-mouthed over his shoulder. Cautiously, she leaned around him.

There was someone else on the rig.

Doyer reached around until he felt Thirteen's knee, and squeezed it with excitement. Tears sprang to her eyes. That was her busted knee. With blurry vision she studied her second unexpected visitor for the night.

She lay awkwardly against the beacon station, flung there by the impact. Her skin was an unhealthy shade of grey and her round head smooth and bald. She wore a strange get-up, a dress that was almost indecent, and wet and rubbery looking. Kelp, Thirteen realised, the woman was wearing kelp.

Her mouth formed an 'O' of realisation. A *real* Salt Fae!

For a moment, she forgot the crab trashing her rig and the gun in Doyer's hand. When he turned to see if she too saw it, they shared a giddy grin. Wishes had just come true.

Doyer scuttled over to the Fae. He reached out, but stopped just short of touching her, as if afraid she would vanish.

He said something. Thirteen shook her head dumbly. The Salt Fae was *beautiful*. The scientist beckoned her over.

Roaring agony exploded in her knee when put her weight on it. Dropping instantly, she wheezed, cheek pressed against the cold metal of the catwalk until the knifing pain lessened. No left knee. Got it. She dragged herself over.

"You spoke Salt Fae!"

"Kind of. Not really."

He dismissed her uncertainty with a wave and leaned close to the Fae's face. A gleeful smile lit his expression. The Salt Fae was alive.

"Fantastic! Do you know what this means? They must have adapted. Ring in the choppers! We need to get her to a lab."

"What?"

"Need to get her to a lab!"

"She needs a hospital, not a lab. Why on earth do you want to take her to a lab?"

"She's waking up!"

Both of them sat back as the Salt Fae stirred. The clean smell of salt water drifted through the air, something Thirteen hadn't been able to smell for years. This close, she could see the gills in the Fae's ribs rippling feebly. They oozed wetly as the Fae breathed through her flattened nose.

Nine would eat his words. So would Eight. Even Fourteen. And that jerk of a bartender at the Sunflower. And her sixth grade teacher, Mr Evans. And—

It was all too much. Giant crabs, pretty scientists, her home destroyed, and her own personal fairy tale come true. She didn't know what to think anymore, so she didn't.

Doyer tugged her sleeve. She looked at him blankly.

"Speak to it!"

"No!" Not since high school had she felt this shy. For the life of her she couldn't remember how to say 'How are you?', the second piece of Salt Fae language she'd learned after 'Hello'.

"You have a satellite phone, yes? Good! Call Major Trent Necrat, of the HNS Dogmatic! Code 573-53-acrobat. Top security. Must keep this news secret. Who knows what enchantments she has access to!"

Abruptly, the world reasserted itself, and she shifted from overwhelmed Thirteen back to standard cynical Thirteen.

New enchantments. That's what this was about. Very naïve of her not to have realised. From this, it would grow into every one of the bigger crabs being hijacked, any other Salt Fae taken prisoner, and from there to military labs and questioning, and then deep sea expeditions to find the rest of them, all for a new flood of enchantments. Science, her arse. It was nothing but a cash cow.

Doyer frowned at her. There was a syringe in his hands, and as she watched he squirted the needle clear. "Get going!"

"Can't," she said, "knee is busted."

He sighed, exasperated. The Salt Fae stirred again.

"Listen, Thirteen! I need your help here. I'm sorry about the gun and all—I really didn't want to hurt you, but you didn't give me a choice. This is important. You can be a part of this." He touched her hand, his own still miraculously clean. "After this, no one will ever laugh at you again."

He looked like he cared, and he knew he was right. Damn him.

Yes, damn him.

Thirteen wouldn't have long. It surprised her to realise she'd already made her decision.

She was going to be in so much trouble.

The Salt Fae opened her eyes.

The tidal rig heaved as the crab struggled. Doyer flung himself flat. Hold together, baby, Thirteen thought at her rig, not thinking about the gun, anything except the gun. She pulled a wrench from her tool belt, and as the platform beneath her surged upwards she clonked the scientist behind the ear. A moment later she was knocked flat. The wrench skittered across the catwalk and bounced over the edge. It took a long time before the crab settled down again. The smell of cooking fish drifted up. Something was overheating below, something close to the crab. All this being tossed about was making itself known in her stomach. She concentrated on not throwing up.

When the rig was still, Thirteen checked Doyer's pulse. She'd never knocked anyone out before, well, not intentionally. There was a lot of blood. Gods, she was going to be in so much trouble. Forget the Coast Master; if this one really was a military scientist, she was screwed. "Don't die."

A hand on her arm made her jump. She looked up, into the Salt Fae's eyes.

They were dark, strange, flat, like a fish's. The hand on her arm glowed with a faint luminescence.

The woman surveyed the rig with bemusement. Thirteen had the feeling she hadn't even realised it was in their path, and now that she had crashed her crab into it, didn't care much.

She said something incomprehensible. Thirteen looked at her helplessly. The Salt Fae stood and faced the crab. She sang a piercing note that even Thirteen could hear, and wove a complex pattern with her hands. It might have been the glow of her skin, or the toll of the night, but Thirteen thought a faint trail of light followed her movements.

The crab responded to the Fae, no longer twitching, its eyes drooping slightly.

"Can you make it go backwards?" Thirteen asked, doubtful. The Salt Fae gave her a scornful look, and the rigger clamped her mouth shut. Right. Don't disturb the Salt Fae.

The Fae dropped her eyes from Thirteen to Doyer, and gave the scientist a hard nudge in the ribs. She snorted, a surprisingly inelegant gesture for such a creature, her nostrils flaring wide. Thirteen cringed away when she reached out, but the Fae only patted her head.

"You're welcome. I think."

The Salt Fae scrambled up the crab's leg, using the warty growths as handholds. At its head, she stood, and made a sweeping motion in Thirteen's direction. They were going around.

"Oh. Good. I mean—" Thirteen nodded vehemently, and then, without quite knowing why, bowed. When she straightened the Salt Fae was gone.

Ponderously slow, the crab began to move again, shuffling backwards and turning as it did. Three point turn. Perhaps it was the Salt Fae's enchantments that let it get so close to shore in the first place. Perhaps now she had placed some spell that lightened the crab's load.

It seemed a lot of effort for not much in return. In fact, she couldn't see anything the Salt Fae could hope to accomplish from this exercise at all.

Thirteen propped herself against the station. The rig shuddered as the crab backed away, but failed to collapse. She wasn't sure whether to laugh or cry.

The Salt Fae appeared again, waving for Thirteen's attention. Thirteen waved back. The Salt Fae smiled, and raised a finger to her lips. She might have winked.

Slowly, Thirteen nodded again. "Not a soul," she murmured.

Especially not after assaulting a military scientist.

Later, when the combat moths arrived, more of her hearing returned. There was a constant muffled buzzing from the com which she had turned to full volume, and when she leaned close to those birds that had returned, within pecking range, she thought she could make out their indignant caws. They hadn't appreciated their sensational eviction.

She sat with Doyer's head pillowed on her lap, partly out of guilt, but mostly so she could tell him what happened as soon as he woke. She was certain there were some details he'd need correcting on.

The moths alighted on the side of the rig, pilots peering around for somewhere to dismount. She peeked over the edge of the platform. Giant moths, she decided, were just as ugly as giant crabs. Leaning back, she finished her fourth smoke, and started her fifth.

The pilots brought more scientists with them. She was happy to play up her lack of hearing, and watched them with amusement when they attempted to mime their questions to her. She told them that Doyer had been struck by one of his boxes in one of the crab's convulsions, and that was all. They left shortly after, taking Doyer with them. Good riddance. He wasn't that cute anyway.

Later still, with the sun high in the sky and her hearing fully returned, the phone rang. She eyed it sceptically. The Coast Master never had anything nice to say, and would probably be exceedingly incensed that she'd gone and got her rig banged up.

"Thirteen here."

"Ah, so you are alive!"

She hunkered down behind the bench. "You're not supposed to use this line, Fourt. The Coa st Master will yell distortion at you."

"Eh," he said, clearly not caring, "you've been silent for ages. What happened?"

"Saw one of those crabs up close. Not cool. Blew my hearing, too."

"Mmm," Fourteen hesitated, then said, "You had your com on, remember?"

"Vaguely."

"While you and your scientist were yelling at each other, I thought I heard another voice. Some of the others did, too."

"I told you my hearing was shot. I couldn't hear shit."

"Mmm," he said again, "I think Nine is going to be nicer to you now."

"I don't know what you're talking about."

"Uh huh. You take care of yourself."

"Talk to you later."

Thirteen smiled, and hung up. With her feet on the table, she poured herself a double, no, a triple of scotch. It seemed a paltry consolation, given everything she'd gone through to get it.

She took a sip.

It was worth it.

A Madness of Ravens

Steven Savile

From the Annals of the Greyfriar's Gentleman's Club
As Transcribed by Marcus Challinor, esq.

There was nothing special about the morning the ravens left the Tower, but then the miraculous is rarely heralded.

Marcus Challinor slumped in the winged leather Chesterfield arguing with Gideon Frate about the apocryphal nature of one of his favourite nursery rhymes, Ring A Ring O'Roses. It was a familiar argument, one they had had at least three times before. Frate had petitioned for a place within the Greyfriar's Gentleman's Club, though whether he knew the true nature of the group or not remained unknown. Challinor rather liked his company, though he was a peculiar soul to say the least. But then, weren't they all?

"It's all very neat, of course, the rash around the wrist, nosegays to counter the miasmic nature of sickness and all that, but it couldn't possibly be a plague warning, Gideon. I don't care how passionate your argument, it is fundamentally flawed. Look at the actual evidence, not the fancies of so-called scholars: the Tales of Mother Goose are less than twenty years old. There is no recorded mention of the rhyme before then, thus there are no hidden truths. So what if they all fall down? It's nonsense. You might as well claim hidden meanings for Mary, Mary and Sing a Song of Sixpence. Even that fool Stoker was closer to the truth with his shambles of a novel. Forget your folly, my friend, embrace the truth."

"You take all the fun out of life, Marcus, did anyone ever tell you that?" Gideon worried at a string of boeuf from the bourgogne they had just shared. A piece of bread soaked in the wine sauce on his otherwise empty plate.

"Mother might have mentioned it once or twice," the older man agreed, drawing deeply on the briar stem of his pipe and exhaling a thin raft of smoke that rose like a veil in front of his narrow face.

They made an unlikely couple, Challinor rounded and jovial,

Frate almost rodentesque with his white-blonde hair, delicate bones and elongated features.

The verbal sparring continued long into the afternoon, between brandy snifters and thick-leafed smokes, some of it witty, some literary, and most of it utterly obscure as it shifted from the more mundane topics of fairy tales and into the nature of the monsters that peopled them.

"All I will say is this, my sceptical friend," Gideon Frate said with a wink, "don't be too quick to disregard the wisdom of those old folk tales. You'd be surprised how much of what we've forgotten as a civilisation is hidden within those simple stories."

"If you say so," Challinor said dubiously, his reason still utterly unconvinced by Frate's fancy.

The pair left the dead ends of their cigars smouldering on the silver-plate tray and took a leisurely walk along Sclater Street. The remnants of the old wooden road were being torn up and replaced with small granite stones laid in an elaborate monochromatic mosaic. Brick Lane was alive with the fancy goods market, hawkers looking to sell everything from pigs and parrots and to embroidered doilies and handmade Aunt Sallies. "Cockles and muscles. Jellied eels a penny!" a barrow-boy called, wheeling his small cart through the press of shoppers. The sporadic crack and bang of pop-guns in the shooting arcade along the left wall of the crowded alley caused Frate to flinch more than once. "Try your luck, gentlemen?" a flat-capped fellow stepped out of the press of people to wave a small brown envelope in their direction. "All of the winners from White City, right here waiting for you. Only a penny a punt, squire. Cheap at twice the price. You strike me as men of business? Threadneedle Street? Halfpenny on each dog and you'll be looking at a tidy return on your investment. Better than any bank can offer, or I'm not called Honest Hal, as everyone who lives in the shadows of the Great Eastern here can attest."

"No doubt," Challinor said, wryly. He tucked his shooting stick beneath his arm and elbow. "But I am not a gambling man."

"Name your vice, then, squire?" the patterer pressed. "A nice little hay-bag maybe?"

"The wife would not approve."

"What the old doxy don't know won't hurt her," the man winked knowingly, tapping the side of his nose.

Challinor chuckled, "Thus spake a single man if ever I heard one."

Behind them a costermonger called, "Not sixpence! Not even fivepence! Four? I'd be cutting my own throat at four, but I'm not asking for fourpence! What do I want, you ask? I must be balmy but say threepence halfpenny and this lovely cut of prime porker is all yours!" The urgent cry of another seller barked. Other voices cried on either side as the dickering for choice cuts of meat began in earnest.

Before the patterer could bother them any more, Challinor pulled away from the man with a slight nod of the head, and was off, weaving a curious path between the chaotic motion of the market-goers, down Whitechapel toward Aldgate and Crutched Friar's on Tower Hill.

There was none of the morning fog, only clear blue sky.

They turned onto Seething Lane and saw a most peculiar thing: a man in full evening dress, top hat and tails, on the steps of All Hallows, wrestling with the strings of a kite. Up above the spires of the old church a simple box kite was buffeted and bullied by the wind blowing in off the Thames.

"What the Devil?"

"The Devil indeed," Challinor spat, recognising the man: Nikoli Forte, one of the Brethren's inner ward, and most certainly not a friend of the Greyfriar's men. Forte turned, glancing back over his shoulder guiltily at the sound of their approaching footsteps on the granite cobbles. Instead of the strings, Challinor saw, he was manipulating the spars of a large brass cage, shaping and reshaping them as though they were some kind of hollow puzzle box. He had no idea what the contraption was, nor what it did. As they neared, he heard Forte's brittle voice stumbling over the words of an incantation; he recognised snatches of Arabic before they merged incoherently.

"Hold, man!" Challinor roared, waving his shooting stick at the man as he started to run, but even before he had made his fourth stride on the treacherous cobbles his legs were tying up. He dropped the metal-tipped stick. The first of the ravens surged up over The Moat in a tenacity of black feathers, and barely avoided tangling with the kite's strings as it wheeled away toward St Katharine's Docks. A moment later three more black birds took flight, cawing as they banked and swooped down toward Traitor's Gate. Five more followed them, diving from on high like cannonballs aimed at the Royal Mint, and still more ravens rose from the White Tower until the sky above the ancient building was alive with a writhing mass of wings. The sky was an utter chaos of ravens in mad flight as the birds banked and swooped and circled, breaking for the clouds only to dive low across the slates of the rooftops.

Disturbed in his mischief making, Forte reshaped the cage quickly, his piano-player's fingers dextrously reworking the metal until it resembled the skeletal frame of a bird, then let go of the kite's strings.

Up in the sky something marvellous and terrifying began to take shape as the ravens left the Tower in their droves, drawn to the box kite as it drifted higher. It took another moment for Challinor to realise that the birds were somehow restrained by the shape the Brethren's man had made, unable to fly beyond its limits so that the seething mass of feathers came together in the form of a monstrous black bird, bigger than the Tower and any individual landmark of the City it overshadowed.

Forte took off, coats trailing behind him as he ran pellmell down the length of Postern Row toward the warren of the East End and the safety of the anonymous alleys. He ran like Spring-Heeled Jack himself.

"Come on," Challinor yelled, taking off after the fugitive.

Gideon Frate was torn between the terror in the skies and the wild hunt; instead of running he merely stood, staring as the ravens flew in tighter and tighter formation. It wasn't chaos at all, far from it. Each bird still obeyed the laws of flocking, separation, alignment and cohesion. Each raven attempted to avoid collision with its enforced flock-mate whilst following the general behaviour and heading of the greater beast they had become. It was an awesome sight seen from below, a single raven with a wingspan that tip-to-tip was greater than the walk from the Tower to Fenchurch Station—more than five hundred yards as the crow flies. Somewhere lost in the middle of the polymorphous bird, the box kite and the brass frame had become its unnatural heart.

The great bird swept low, thousands upon thousands of feathers raking the parapet of the Tower and across the roofs of the neighbouring tenements of Postern Row, dislodging stone and slate as they battered the buildings. The bottom tips of the great wings toppled the nymph from her perch in the middle of the stone fountain in Trinity Square, the wretched creature shattering into a million tiny shards of stone around its steel rod frame.

"And England shall fall, monarchy, kingdom and all, on the day the ravens leave the White Tower," Frate said, the words of the nursery rhyme coming immediately to mind. The entire street was swallowed by shadow, but it was the noise that was the worst, thousands upon thousands of raucous caws melding like the feathers themselves into a single voice, shrieking out across the city as the giant bird cast a false dusk across the streets. It was deafening and horrific, a sound unlike any other.

When he finally dragged his attention back down from the impossible beast he saw Marcus Challinor walking back around the corner, breathing hard and clutching a bloody wound in his side. Each step was uncertain, Challinor swaying like a drunkard. Frate ran forward to catch him before he hit the cobbles, cradling his companion as he lowered him gently to the ground. The wound was deep; the knife had cut through his top coat, jacket, waistcoat, shirt and vest before biting flesh, but still had had enough teeth to part three inches of tissue, deep and wide. Blood bubbled up through the various torn fabrics, seeping out through the warp and weft of cotton and wool and staining everything black-red.

"He stuck you good and proper, didn't he?"

"Ruined a ... perfectly ... good ... *suit*." The last word came out through gritted teeth. All colour had drained from the wounded man's face.

Frate didn't laugh. Challinor was in a bad way. "What I would give for a cab. Just lie back and think of Victoria. If that doesn't kill you, nothing will." Working quickly, he unwound his white silk scarf and fashioned a crude tourniquet out of it, wadding a strip torn from his own shirt tail into the wound to go some way toward staunching the blood loss. "Are you with me, old man?" Challinor's eyes had glazed over from the pain, but he nodded. His skin had taken on a putty-like lustre, peppered with perspiration, his mousy brown hair plastered flat to his scalp. "Good, now do you remember what we were talking about in the restaurant?" Again Challinor nodded. "Excellent, well, I think you're about to have your eyes opened, my curmudgeonly old friend."

"I don't—"

"You don't need to, just rest. I will summon what help I can."

He reached into his heavy coats and withdrew a small tin whistle. He placed the whistle to his lips and piped three sharp blasts, summoning one of the Peelers who were no doubt policing the neighbouring streets—or at least staring helplessly at the skies above where they were powerless to intervene. He knelt beside a sewer grate in the gutter and pulled it open. The stench of corruption that was London Below reeked up through the wound in the road. Frate blew a cycle of seven notes, duplicating them seven times. It was a simple melody. Between each recitation he whispered "Come on, come on," barely vocalising the entreaty. Seven more times he repeated the pattern, the melody taking on an urgency all of its own before the first sleek-bodied rat emerged from the sewers. "Come to me, my beautiful ones," Gideon Frate crooned, spreading his arms wide. More rats emerged from the darkness, not merely through the sewer grate; they spilled out of doorways and cracks in the curbside, from rafters and up from the muddy waters of the Thames, the slick black bodies undulating as they rose like a tide of faeces from the filth of the river. They came out of the grave dirt of Trinity and All Hallows. They came out of the stocks of the bonded warehouses, fat on grain and the rich pickings of the merchant quarter. They came out from beneath the sleepers on the railway tracks as far away as Liverpool Street, as near as Aldgate East and Bishopsgate. They came from cracks and crevices of Spitalfields and Eastcheap markets. More and more rats, drawn through the streets to answer the call of one man's tin whistle, until Trinity Square was overrun by vermin.

And still Gideon Frate played his cycle of seven notes over and over, urging more of the rats up out of the bowels of the earth. He looked up at the sky where the Brethren's giant raven was banking toward the huge bell of Big Ben and the Parliament buildings further along the river, and again the prophesy of the ravens rose unbidden in his mind.

"What ... are you *doing*?" Challinor rasped as fat-bodied rats crawled all over him.

"Proving a point, my friend. Proving a point," Gideon Frate

said, grinning enigmatically.

Challinor winced as he shook his head, even the slightest movement too painful to bear. "Who are you?"

"You know me. You always have, even from your earliest days. Now make me a promise, Greyfriar. If I do this thing you need, if I save your city, you will reward me by opening the doors of your club to me. Promise."

Challinor did; how could he not?

Frate lifted the tin whistle to his lips again, only this time he conjured a different melody from it; a complex auditory spiral of diatonic scales scattered with accidentals. It was not the notes themselves that were important, it was the frequency with which they were pitched. "Rise up! Rise up!" the voice of the whistle commanded so brusquely Challinor could almost discern the words within the trill of its voice. The rats responded as a pack, climbing and crawling and clawing to be on top of one another until they were a huge writhing mass of furry bodies twice the size of the fountain that until that moment had dominated the centre of the Square.

Still taller it grew, rats seething and hissing as it grew to tower above the tallest of buildings, standing on huge legs that shifted constantly, the untold scores of bloated bodies, slick bodies, emaciated bodies and every other kind of rat imaginable fighting for its position within the great collective beast Gideon Frate had summoned.

The whistler gestured sharply with his tin whistle and the giant monstrosity lumbered forward, its body dissolving with every step as rats scrambled and fell to the road only to claw their way back into the main body of the behemoth.

"Can you control it?" Challinor wheezed, struggling to sit. Frate knelt beside him.

"Rest, my friend. You wished to see if I was fit for your little club of adventurous souls; now I prove my worth."

Challinor said nothing.

"The ravens?"

"Have left the Tower."

"Oh, gods ..."

"Not all stories are true," Gideon Frate said, smiling at the implicit irony of misquoting the wounded man's argument back at him. "The city will not fall."

"How can you be sure?"

"My rats will see to it. We must depart this place. It is imperative I maintain eye contact with the construction or it will fail. I suspect it is the same for the other, though I cannot be sure what exactly that device was he stored at the centre of his golem." He helped Challinor stand, slipping beneath the injured man's shoulder to support him as the pair of them chased the shadows deep into the heart of old London town.

The great bird pinned back its wings and dived, arrowing

for the heart of the enormous rat. But as it hit, the rat's chest parted, and the black wings and yellow eyes streamed through gaps where rats had fallen, abandoning the shape of the giant monstrosity. For a moment the two merged, then the black wings of the bird burst out of the rat's spine, exploding across the sky in a spray of blood and fur as dead vermin fell to the ground—but if there was one thing the city had it was an abundance of rats. More crawled up the legs, swarming higher and higher to fill the wounds in the body they shared. And the rat thing swiped out at the bird, scattering feathers in a chorus of shrill caws as broken-winged ravens fell from the sky. For a moment it appeared that the giant bird would be beaten with that single blow, but the laws of the flock converged to fill the ragged tears in its frame, the giant black raven cawing madly as it smashed through the body of the rat again.

The fight raged across the city, blow after blow raining down dead birds and rats as the colossi duelled from the Strand to Marble Arch, across Somerset House to the flower market of Covent Garden and the civility of the Opera House and on again to the monument of Trafalgar where the pigeons took flight in a sheet of grey, terrified by the monstrosities dominating the sky they so arrogantly believed they owned. Birds and rats hit the face of Nelson, the Lord Admiral as unflinching in stone as he ever had been in the flesh. While slates and stones fell, high walls crumbling from the battering of wings and claws, marble and granite powdered on the ground as more and more chunks of masonry came down.

The great raven banked and spiralled, swarming around the body of the monstrous rats, momentarily blocking out the lowering sun like some great and primal god.

Londoners stood in awe, the patter gone, the Cockney cockiness abandoned, faces turned to the sky where the great raven tore again and again at the ever-shifting body of the rat Frate had summoned.

Down on the street, Frate buckled, falling to his knees against the battering of the wind from so many of the raven's wings. He barely managed to get the whistle to his lips. Three more sharp blasts on his tin whistle caused the rat creature to rear up on its hind legs like a man and slash the air with fists and claws the size of a mews house. The blow cut clean into the torso of the bird as it separated and reformed around the rat, the two momentarily fused once more. But this time the rat's paw smashed against the gilded cage within the raven's breast, the thousands of tiny claws ripping the box kite from the mass of feathers. The giant bird's screams were agonising but somehow it held its shape.

"He's still controlling it!" Frate yelled over the barrage of wind and caws and ceaseless chittering. "He has to be stopped! I can't hold the rat together much longer!"

Challinor grunted through the pain and lurched away from

the man's support. He clasped the shooting stick in both hands and split it in the middle to reveal the sharp blade concealed within the seemingly harmless cane. "Do what you have to do," he said, nodding once toward the giant rat; seeing it now it was so obviously build around Frate's own elongated features, the rat man controlling the rodents, their god and maker. "I will find Nikoli and finish this."

"He has to be within eye-line of the birds," Frate said, momentarily distracted by Challinor's pain-wracked expression as he brandished the sword in one hand like some half-baked avenging hero and the hollowed out shaft of the shooting stick in the other. That distraction cost his construct heavily. The ravens split it in two from stem to stern. Thousands of rats shredded bloody fell from the sky, the great beast diminished. "Quickly!"

Challinor turned his back on the huge combatants; they could tear themselves apart without him watching them. He glanced back once, on the corner of Cockspurs and Northumberland Avenue, trying to gauge the angle of trajectory as best he could, and to extrapolate from it to the very limits of where Nikoli Forte could possibly be hiding. There was nothing to say he was even in the open street—the Brethren had resources to match the Greyfriar's, and then some. They had hideouts in every district of the city. Forte could just as easily have hidden himself away in a safe house and might be steering the bird from behind the dubious safety of glass, or from up on one of the roofs, shielded from the street by the gable.

He pushed his way through the milling people, all too intent on watching the sky to notice the young pickpockets working them over. It was the city at its finest, opportunist crime and David and Goliath scrap all at the same time. The bells of St Martins and St George Barr rang out as though calling time on a bare knuckle bout. Challinor's only thought was on finding Forte.

He had to be close, but even so, London was huge and considering the sheer mass of feathers up in the sky, "close" was not necessarily "close" as in "around the next corner". It was like looking for a needle in a proverbial haystack.

He glanced up over his shoulder again, making sure he had not broken line-of-sight with the bird monster. More bells rang out, slightly out of time with the others. The stench of the sewers was overpowering. Every cobblestone reeked.

Then, as he lurched around the corner onto Villiers, he heard a woman scream. He saw why immediately; Forte, his top hat gone, had his arm wrapped around her throat, the knife he had used to stick Challinor pressed against her throat. His eyes kept flicking up toward the great black-winged bird terrorising the city and then back to Challinor as he advanced awkwardly down the narrow street.

"Don't come any closer, Greyfriar."

Challinor dragged himself another step closer, deliberately

defying the man. "You can't win, Nikoli. It's over, let the birds go."

"The hell it is."

"There's no need for all of this destruction. This is our city, Nikoli, both of ours. I can't stand by and let you tear it down any more than you can. This city is more than us. It is London, the greatest of all the Empire's capitals. Now, let me help you," Challinor said, and anyone close enough to hear him might have believed he meant it—save for the sword in his hand which gave lie to the offer.

Above them, the ravens screamed—it was no mere caw. The scream was matched down on the street as the struggling woman sank her teeth into the meat of Nikoli Forte's palm. The knife fell through his fingers. It was all Challinor needed; ignoring the unquenchable fire in his gut, the gentleman threw himself forward, pushing the woman aside as he lunged, thrusting the long blade deep into Forte's stomach and out through the vertebrae of his back. The woman screamed yet again. Forte's own scream changed in quality from fear to unbearable pain as Challinor slid the blade free. The Brethren warrior crumpled, eyes wide with shock and horror. His lips moved, blood bubbling up out of his mouth, but no sound followed. And above them the screams of the ravens became desperate as the will binding them was undone by a single sword thrust.

"You killed me," Forte said, stupidly, his eyes glazing over as he slumped forward, pitching from his knees flat onto his face on the hard stone.

Challinor did not need to look up to know that the connection between the man and his monstrous bird was broken. He allowed the pain to wash over him, losing himself in its cleansing fire.

The woman was still screaming—at him now. He looked at her and barked: "Go!" and she ran like a frightened mare. Alone, he used the dead man's top coat to wipe the blood from the short blade then sheathed it once more in the body of the shooting stick.

By the time he returned to Trafalgar Square the birds had scattered. Gideon Frate sat astride one of the stone lions, conducting the slaughter. The rats had come down, descending upon the fallen birds, and feasted en masse, tearing wing from bone, feather from wing, and flesh from both. The Londoners walked about the square in a daze, uncomprehending at the sheer scale of death laid out before them. Frate saluted Challinor when he saw him, and raised his tin whistle to his lips, calling off the feast with a few sharp trills.

"Six birds yet live, not enough to cause any harm. No doubt they will return to their roost in the White Tower to grow old."

"Who are you?" Marcus Challinor asked again, picking his way through the blood and bile of Trafalgar Square to stand beside the man on the huge stone lion. The stories were wrong—or at least one of them was: the city would not fall despite the flight of the ravens.

"You know who I am. You've heard my story often, and now you know it is true."

"No. Who *are* you?" Challinor repeated, pressing his hand to his side. His exertion had loosened the makeshift tourniquet. Blood leaked down his side.

"No one of consequence," Gideon Frate said. "A man with a whistle, that is all."

"The rats —?"

"They obey the music of chance, the same music that binds the world together, just as we do."

Challinor shook his head in wonder. "I have seen many things but ..."

"But now you will not be so quick to dismiss the secrets hidden within the old stories, will you, my friend?" Frate said, hopping down from the lion's back.

Before Marcus Challinor could say anything, he had placed the old tin whistle to his lips and begun to play a dull threnody that settled over the swarm of rats, lulling them into lethargy. Frate walked among them, the melody changing as he past the Admiralty and left the shadow of Nelson. The rats followed him, leaving the scraps of raven to be consumed by the square's hungry pigeons. And like one of the rats, helpless to resist the lure of the man's whistle, Challinor followed Frate down to the water's edge, beneath Charing Cross Pier, and watched in silence as Gideon Frate turned his back on him and walked into the Thames. There, the man paused, the river's dark water lapping around his knees.

The rats swept past in the tens of thousands, a stream of slick bodies disappearing beneath the dirty water of the river, content to drown at their master's bidding.

"But you aren't real ... you can't be!"

"After all this time, you still think that?" Frate shook his head sadly. "After all those arguments, all those truths you tried to force upon me in the name of logic? Once upon a time I would have punished a doubter like you, Marcus. But you gave me your word. I am one of you now, yes? A Gentleman of the Greyfriar's Club? I have proved myself worthy?" Challinor nodded, speechless. "Then I am content. I shall return to smoke with you one day, my old friend, trade arguments and banter over stories and hidden truths, and I shall look forward to it. But—and mark this well for when I return—had you broken the faith, even now, one more story could quite easily have come true. You know who I am. I ask you to remember that I spared children this time 'round." Frate smiled grimly, pocketed the whistle then disappeared beneath the surface himself.

Challinor watched the rat-like man go, disappearing without so much as a ripple and leaving no air bubbles in his wake. Of course, he knew instinctively which story Frate meant. This was a day for folk tales come true, if only in part: the day the ravens left the Tower yet England did not fall.

He could not doubt the truth of one more tale.

OUT OF HIS LEAGUE

TONY FRAZIER

So just what do you plan to do about this?" Jill asked.
"I plan to have another beer," I answered.
I guess this wasn't what she wanted to hear, because all she could do for a moment was drop her jaw and make this stunned "uh" sound. Well, not really an "uh," but I can't spell the exact sound she made. Maybe I could with one of those foreign alphabets with sounds you don't find in English, but then you probably wouldn't be able to read it.

She finally found her voice and said, "But you're a superhero."

"I'm not *that* super. Look at that thing!" I waved toward the TV behind the bar. On the screen, a gigantic Thing stood amid burning wreckage downtown, somewhere near the riverfront. It looked like a cross between a beetle and a man. It was basically humanoid—two arms, two legs, one head—but it was mostly covered by chitinous armoured plates, with leathery skin visible between. As we watched, a National Guard tank fired a shell at the creature's chest. The armour plates moved suddenly, drawing together to form an almost seamless shield over its front torso. After the shell burst harmlessly on them, the plates drew back to their former positions.

The news reports put it at anywhere from 60 to 80 feet tall, they weren't sure. After all, it wasn't as if they could just ask it to stand against the Empire State Building and make a pencil mark at the top of its head. I wished they could, because that would mean it was in New York City instead of my home town, causing me problems with my favourite bartender.

"You know what would happen if I tried to fight that thing?" I continued. "You ever see *Bambi Meets Godzilla?*"

Jill shook her head at me. "Do you ever get off your couch and go outside?"

"It's a recliner. Besides, I'm kinda retired. Now how about that beer?"

"You're cut off," Jill said, taking my mug. "And if you're retired, then why do you still wear the costume?"

She had me there.

"Okay, fine, I'll see what I can do," I said, dropping off my barstool. "But it's not going to be much. I'm more a team player than a solo guy."

"We've seen how well that worked out," she said. "I'll get your tab."

"No, you'll hold it till I get back," I said. "It's the least you can do for sending me off to my death."

☆

"So you're offering to do what exactly? Hit him with your laser beams?" Colonel Fox couldn't stop looking nervously at my hands.

I couldn't blame him, really. If I was stuck next to some dude with big, metal energy blasters grafted to his hands and forearms, I wouldn't be too trusting either. They were the real reason I still wore the costume, even though I hadn't actively fought crime in years; the Driller Beam Generators don't go well with jeans. There was no way I could just blend in like some guys.

I took a deep breath. I'd spent twenty minutes talking my way into the National Guard command post, and now it looked like I'd be spending another twenty trying to convince them I could help. Hell, I hadn't even convinced *myself* of that, yet.

"I'm not really sure what I can do, Colonel," I said. "This thing's a little out of my weight class, but I'd like to help any way I can."

Major Bronson, sitting next to the colonel, asked, "How, specifically, do you think you can help, Mister, uh …"

"Digger. His name's Digger," said Captain Craun from over by the map. Craun had been introduced to me as the S-2. Bronson was the S-3. I had no idea what that meant. "You used to work with the GoDS out of LA, didn't you?"

"Used to."

"Well, where are they?" asked Colonel Fox. "Can we get the rest of them here?"

"They all died," I answered.

"But you survived," Craun said.

I shrugged and said, "I do that."

"So what exactly *do* you do?" Major Bronson asked. "Other than surviving, I mean."

"I'm pretty fast, kinda strong," I said.

"How strong?"

"I could pick up a car, but I can't throw it," I said. "Well, maybe a Mini Cooper or something, but that probably wouldn't help. I can see in the dark and climb walls like a bug. I use these to dig tunnels." I held up one hand to show off the Driller Beam Generator.

"Can you dig a pit? Trap him?" asked Captain Craun.

"Screw that," said Colonel Fox. "Can you dig *through* him?"

"If the tanks couldn't penetrate his armour, I doubt I can," I said. "And I'd be working days to dig a pit that big."

"So you can't stop it?" Major Bronson asked. I shook my head. "So why are you here exactly?"

"My bartender cut me off."

"Colonel Fox," called a radio operator in the corner. "That thing's changed direction. It's coming this way now."

"It's moving north?"

"Directly toward us, sir."

"Why would it do that?" the colonel asked.

"It's chasing me," said a voice from the doorway. We turned to see a haggard-looking man in his 30s, escorted by two MPs. He held up a stone idol of a squatting man, maybe two feet by two feet. "Actually, I think he's chasing this."

"Who are you?" asked the colonel.

"Ray Quesada," the man said. "I'm a professor of archaeology at the university. I found this on a dig on Avatu Island in the South Pacific."

"And how do you know it's after you?" asked the colonel.

"The islanders on Avatu have legends of giant beasts that guard their island," Quesada explained. "That Giant Beetle-Man is one of them."

"But how would it know where the idol is?" the colonel asked.

"It's hollow," I said, staring at the idol. Everyone turned to look at me. "There's something inside it."

"X-ray vision?" Captain Craun asked.

"More like a sonar deal," I said, shrugging. "I spend a lot of time underground. It helps to know what's in front of me."

"We're wasting time," said Major Bronson. "Who cares why it's here? The question is, how do we kill it?"

"But we don't have to kill it," I said. "Ever seen *Mothra*? We just give it what it came for, and it'll go away."

Quesada blanched and turned to shield the idol with his body. Colonel Fox just shook his head sadly. "Sorry, son. I make it a policy not to negotiate in situations like this. You give 'em what they want, it'll just encourage 'em to do it again next time."

"What next time?" I asked. "It's a giant bug ... man ... thing."

"It's the principle," he said.

"Okay, before this goes any further, we need to get you out of here, Professor," said Bronson. "You're endangering our personnel."

"Wait!" I said. "If that thing really is chasing the idol, then we can use it to lead him wherever we want him to go."

"Like where?" asked Craun.

"Like out of town, for starters." I studied the big map of the city mounted on the wall. And then I spotted something. "No, wait, I have a better idea. You guys ever see *King Kong*?"

☆

Professor Quesada told us the beast's name was Oroaku or

something like that, but to me, he was just another Thing. That's the superhero life, pretty much. You're always fighting one Thing or another.

I heard the Thing before I saw it. Hell, I *felt* it before I saw it, the vibrations from the creature's footfalls shaking the ground and making the Humvee sway and creak on its springs. The specialist driving me swore and fought with the wheel as we rounded a corner.

And then the Thing was right there, a quarter of a mile away and just *huge*! The Humvee jerked to a stop.

"This is as close as I get, sir," the specialist said.

"No problem," I said and got out. "You'd better get out of here."

"You don't have to tell me twice. Good luck, sir," he said and drove off.

I stood alone in the street for a moment, suddenly unsure of what I was doing out here. The Thing looked so much bigger in person than I'd expected.

Oh well, if I was going to die, better to do it moving than gaping. I ran toward the creature. It had eyes on stalks that protruded from the top of its head. As I ran toward it, the stalks both twisted so the eyes could look straight at me.

At that moment, a tank rumbled around the corner behind the Thing. The eyestalks twisted around to look back at the tank. I was forgotten for a moment.

As I watched, the armour plates on the Thing's front drew apart, leaving a huge expanse of skin exposed right over the centre of the chest. I could imagine the armour plates on the back drawing closed at that exact moment. The tank fired at the Thing's back, but the shot had no effect that I could see. The armour plates in front returned to their original positions.

By this time, I was so close that I was looking almost straight up at the Thing's chest as I ran. I almost tripped and fell flat on my face. Wouldn't that be a great way to die? Trip and fall, then get stepped on before I could throw a punch. What a loser! Better concentrate on my target, I figured.

The eyestalks rotated back to look at me again, but by that time, I was close enough to leap at the Thing's ankle. I flew thirty feet through the air and stuck to the creature's leg like a spitwad. Maybe I couldn't punch this Thing out, but with any luck, I could hobble it, put it on the ground with a broken ankle, and leave the Army to do the heavy lifting. I fired up the Driller Beams and took a shot at the armour plates protecting the ankle.

Nothing. I scorched the surface, but that was it. Time for Plan B.

The Thing stopped and looked down at me, perhaps debating whether I was worth the trouble of swatting. Before it could make the decision, I began to scramble up its leg, counting as I went. The creature leaned back, trying to keep an eye on me, clearly confused as I ran up the pelvis, up the torso to the centre of the chest. It finally decided to swat me off, but by the time its arms began moving, I had leapt away to stick to a nearby building.

The Thing turned toward me, raising its arm to smoosh me against the wall. I'm rather allergic to smooshing, so I jumped onto its arm before it connected, then back to the spot on the centre of its chest where I'd jumped off. I began running down, counting again. When I reached the foot, I jumped off and scrambled toward the nearest building—a luxury hotel. As I ran through the opulent lobby to exit out the far side, I could hear the building collapsing behind me.

I pressed the 'Talk' switch on the radio headset Bronson had given me. "Okay, I'm good. Get the professor moving."

☆

"Are you sure this is a good idea?" Quesada asked me as we stood side-by-side at the end of Tell Square, which was not really a square at all. It was really just a big traffic circle, hemmed in by tall buildings on three sides. And in the centre of the circle was the Progress Monument, a big, wedge-shaped obelisk, rising up to a sharp point thirty feet off the ground.

"No," I said. "But you guys turned down all the good ideas. This is what's left."

"Thanks," he said, clutching the idol to his chest. "You're very reassuring."

"It's my job," I said.

We waited there tenscly, the ground shaking with the creature's footfalls. I was so ready to head back to Jill's and get another beer.

"So what was that thing about *King Kong*?" Quesada asked. "Those Army guys rushed me out of there before I could hear the whole plan. I don't remember anything like this in *King Kong*."

"Which one did you see?" I asked. "The original or the crappy remake from the 70s?"

"Both," he said.

"Okay, well, there's this part in the crappy remake where they lure Kong into a trap," I said. "They dig a pit, just like Craun asked me to do. The pit's not deep enough to trap him, but it's not meant to. It's only meant to drop him down to where they can hit him with the real weapon."

"Gas," Quesada said.

"Right," I said. "Or, in this case ..." I looked at the spike of the Progress Monument and fingered the radio detonator hanging by a cord around my neck.

"You really think that'll kill it?" he asked.

"Doesn't have to," I said. "You ever see *The Omen*?"

And then the Thing strode into view at the far end of the square. It hesitated there, a half-mile away, its eyestalks focused on the two of us standing side-by-side. It took a step toward us, then stopped.

"What's it doing?" Quesada asked.

"It's sensing the trap," I said. "We've got to get it moving. Give me the idol."

"Oh hell no!" he said, turning away from me again. "I've worked too many years to get this."

"Okay, fine," I said and punched him in the jaw. I'm pretty strong, stronger than your average bear, so he dropped right away. I didn't have time to check to see how badly I'd hurt him; I just snatched up the idol and started running toward the creature.

"Hey you!" I shouted, holding the idol over my head. "You want this? Is this what you're after?"

The creature looked at me and leaned forward, the segmented fingers on its delicate hands flexing.

"Come and get it!" I shouted. "If you think you're big enough." I turned and ran.

The Thing thundered after me. It ran five crashing steps before it hit the wide strip of ground I'd weakened by digging tunnels underneath the surface. The ground collapsed beneath its feet. The thing tripped and fell forward.

I leapt to avoid being crushed and rolled onto my back at the base of the Progress Monument. The Thing was falling right toward me, the centre of its chest aimed directly at the point of the spike; I'd apparently measured accurately when I'd run up and down the Thing's body before. I grabbed the detonator and pushed the button, setting off the charges I had planted earlier.

The creature had been caught off-guard when it tripped, but it reacted quickly while falling. The armour plates on its chest drew together to form its impenetrable shield before it hit the spike. The Thing crashed down onto the spike and broke off the end, leaving a jagged tip. Stone rained down around me. The creature caught itself on its arms and loomed above me. The eyestalks both swiveled to focus on me and the idol. I looked into those inhuman eyes and saw my own death.

Then I heard the sound of my salvation. At first, it was a gentle pattering, like soft rain, but I knew it was stone falling onto the creature's back. The eyestalks rotated back to look up above the creature. I hoped I knew what it was seeing.

The east side of the square was flanked by the Tsuburaya Building. Its design had been "inspired" by the Empire State, down to the radio mast on top. The charges I had detonated had been planted at the base of the radio tower, to make it fall toward the spot where I lay. At this moment, the creature saw the tower plummeting toward its unprotected back, the spike pointed down like a spear, just like the lightning rod that killed the priest in *The Omen*.

The creature roared and snapped the armour on its back closed, just seconds before the radio mast struck. It was unnecessary, anyway. The tower didn't hit it point-first; instead, it struck the Thing broadside, tons of steel slamming into his back, knocking its unprotected chest right down onto the jagged, broken tip of the Progress Monument. Viscous black blood squirted out of the Thing's chest, spraying across the monument and me as I scrambled out from under it. The creature crashed to the ground and was still.

"Digger?" Colonel Fox's voice said in my ear. "You okay?"

"I'm fine, Colonel," I said. "It's dead. Got him right through the heart."

"Good job, son," he said. "I don't care what anybody else says, you're a big leaguer in my book."

"Thank you, sir," I said, not sure just how complimented I should feel.

"You want a reward, just name it," he said.

"Thanks, but right now, all I want to do is get cleaned up and go finish my beer."

And then the Thing began to move. It shook its head, then pushed itself right up off the bloody monument. It lunged to its feet, the wreckage of the radio tower crashing down behind it. Black blood pulsed from the gaping hole in its chest, and it screamed its fury at the sky.

I took off running as fast as I could, the idol tucked awkwardly under my arm, as the colonel's voice shouted in my ear, "I thought you said it was dead."

"I thought it was," I answered. "Guess he doesn't keep his heart in the same place we do. At least I made a hole. We're gonna' have to do this the messy way, I guess. You ever seen *Night Gallery?*"

"What?" the colonel asked.

"There's this episode about an earwig," I said. "Never mind. Just get me some grenades. And a beer. Digging's thirsty work."

A CALCULATED SACRIFICE

MICHAEL BOGUE

Yuriko Ishii's long raven hair bounced across her shoulders as she paced to the opposite side of the room. "Mother," she said, speaking to the wall instead of to her parent, "I thought you of all the villagers would understand."

Akiko Ishii, Yuriko's middle-aged mother, smiled but did not budge from the living room's *tokonama*, the alcove in which she'd just placed a special flower arrangement for Yuriko. Akiko's petite, kimono-clad frame trembled, just once, but Yuriko did not turn in time to see this unconscious show of sympathetic body language.

Yuriko did turn in time to make her abrupt about-face as dramatic as possible. She furrowed her lovely young brow. "I am only twenty years old, mother. Why me? Can you tell me that? Why *me?*"

Crossing the room in small, dignified steps, Akiko touched Yuriko's shoulder. "Daughter," she said, silently disapproving of her offspring's florid perfume, "you know why you. Everyone in the village from eighteen to twenty-nine drew lots. You and Kenji happened to draw the shortest lots, that's all."

"That is not all," Yuriko said, her large brown eyes flashing, their color matching the earthen tones of her simple blouse and trousers. "Midnight isn't far away. I thought I could accept being the female sacrifice to Dedorah—I know we're all lectured in the village that sooner or later, the Kaiju will make such a demand—"

"That is the way of the gods, my—"

"—but I've taught the school children of our village that such thinking is wrong, because there is no hope in it, no looking to a time when the Kaiju will no longer rule our destinies. For we must have hope. *I* must have hope. Tonight."

"But daughter," Akiko said, "just as it is on our island, so it is across all of Japan."

"Yes," Yuriko replied, her upper lip curled in contempt, "everywhere the Land of the Rising Sun is occupied by monsters in this neverending First Age of Kaiju. But it must not always be so. Don't you agree, mother? Say that you do!"

For the first time during their conversation, Akiko frowned. "We must do what is best for the village, daughter."

"Why? Dedorah doesn't care what is best for the village."

Akiko shuddered and stiffly inhaled. "Dedorah is not to be mocked."

"Then perhaps I shall curse him."

"Daughter!" Akiko covered her mouth in horror. Immediately she closed her eyes, steepled her fingers, and, shoulders atremble, began mumbling a fevered entreaty to the ever-present but rarely seen island "god" Dedorah.

Yuriko pitied her mother. But she herself refused to grovel, even for her mother's sake—she had to draw the line somewhere. Dedorah and the other Kaiju had been a scourge on the nation of Japan long enough. All her life, all the days she had spent in this simple six-room house, had frolicked in the island pond and laughed with her friends, had become the official school teacher of the village children, Yuriko had nevertheless known nothing but the First Age of Kaiju.

☆

The monsters had come in all shapes and configurations: dinosaurian, octopoid, insectile, arachnid, humanoid, sporting everything from tentacles to talons to pseudopods. They ranged in size from five to 150 meters, their origins varying from science to the supernatural to obscene combinations of the two—in these cases, the twain *did* meet. As for Dedorah, no one was certain of the creature's exact description, but the monster was apparently bipedal, amphibious, and towered more than fifty metres into the night sky.

When village elders spoke of the days before the Kaiju dominated the land, their stories sounded like so many fairy tales to Yuriko. For the monsters occupied the nation like an enemy army. Only this army was practically invulnerable; Western military forces and the UN had initially come to Japan's aid to repel the hundreds of Kaiju that infested the hapless island nation. The foreign powers' armaments—even the tactical nuclear weapons used as a last resort—did nothing to deter, much less slay, the Kaiju. In defeat, the world's armies reluctantly retreated from Japan, leaving the besieged island nation to its own devices, one of which was righteous anger.

Days before Yuriko's birth, Yuriko's father had died during the ill-fated Rising Sun Rebellion. In retribution for this would-be revolution, the Kaiju slaughtered two-thirds of Japan's population—devouring children like party favours, crushing women like grapes, torching men like shish-ka-bobs. The Night of the Great Horror was a tale that chilled the spines of toddler and widow alike; no family was immune.

One night when Yuriko was twelve, she had snuck into her mother's bedroom, and while her exhausted parent slept, she had dragged the forbidden yellowed photobook from her mother's closet. The dust that caked the book's black cover tickled Yuriko's nose, but she willed herself not to sneeze. Using the moonlight from an open window as her illumination, she opened the photobook's laminated pages; they creaked as she turned them.

Slowly, curiously, Yuriko examined the inserted photos. At first, she wasn't sure what she was seeing; indeed, it took her eyes several seconds to acknowledge that in the first photograph, she was squinting at a family—mother, father, and daughter— huddled beneath a great tree, as though in hiding. But in the second photograph, an unseen fire had roasted the family into a trio of almost-people—twisted, blackened pretzels without fingers or faces.

Yuriko was unaware of her screams until her mother scooped her up and kicked the forbidden photobook across the room. That night, her mother carried her to bed, comforting her deep into the dawn, assuring her that her father had died quickly and painlessly, and that he had been a good but foolish man.

As the years passed, Yuriko's inner screams raged. Yes, the Kaiju let the remaining Japanese keep their electricity and running water and other modern amenities—but at what cost? A life lived in constant anxiety? A world where sacrifices could be ordained by a Kaiju's whim?

After the village Kaiju priestess had interpreted the great beast Dedorah's will and told the assembled village elders that the monster demanded the sacrifice, the people trembled and swore and all but tore their clothing. All except Yuriko's husband Hiroshi.

Upon hearing of Yuriko's tragic fate of having drawn the shortest lot among the females of desirable age, Hiroshi became an active volcano. Never, he vowed, would he let Dedorah's will separate him from his beloved wife.

The next day at nightfall, Hiroshi told Yuriko that he was determined to find and kill Dedorah, and that he would set out on his journey of justice before midnight, for it was known that at that hour Dedorah made his "rounds", circling the island in the inky surf to make sure all was as it should be.

Yuriko begged Hiroshi not to go. But even after making the most passionate and soul-filling love a couple could ever know, he remained unmoved from his stated objective: Dedorah's death.

He stood at the opened door's edge, spectral moonlight accentuating his lean and handsome face as the wind whipped his hair, and he turned one last time. He kissed Yuriko, deep and full on the mouth. *I will return*, he said.

But he did not.

☆

Her prayer to Dedorah ended, Akiko turned to speak to her daughter, but Yuriko's attention had been diverted to the framed pictures of her father and late husband hanging on either side of the flower arrangement in the room's alcove. Yuriko studied them as though they could offer her solace, or worse, hope. Sadly, Akiko shook her head, and she did not hide the distress that welled up from deep inside her bosom.

Her mother's abrupt moan alarmed Yuriko. At the sight of the tears spilling down her mother's cheeks, guilt filled Yuriko's soul.

"Mother," Yuriko said in a humble, rarely used tone as she stepped near her stricken parent, "Have I upset you?"

"Do you have to ask?"

"If I have offended you," Yuriko replied, "please forgive me."

"Daughter," Akiko answered, swallowing her sobs as she wiped her cheeks with a white kimono sleeve, "I could never resent you."

"I understand," Yuriko replied, clasping her fingers together and pressing them against her knuckles. "As the hour grows closer it is just . . . difficult, that's all. Especially without Hiroshi."

Akiko lightly touched Yuriko's arm. "Daughter, I know what it is like to lose a husband."

Yuriko gently bowed her chin in recognition.

"Perhaps what we both need," her mother said, "is a breath of fresh air." Akiko opened the living room window and welcomed in the cool night breeze. The living room's white curtains rippled in the draft like languid ghosts, and though dominated by the clean scent of the woods that surrounded the village, the breeze betrayed a familiar whiff of Dedorah's unwholesome, briny stench.

"Dedorah," Yuriko said in a voice mixed with fear and hatred. "He's nearby."

"He is always nearby." Akiko's shoulders drooped, as though they bore an unseen burden.

"When will the mayor get here?"

"Soon. Honour him when he arrives."

"But mother—"

"Have I ever asked much of you before?"

"No." The small voice again.

"Then don't make me demand that you fulfill your obligation."

Yuriko wanted no such thing, for she didn't think she could withstand such a direct entreaty from her own mother. But there was a secret Yuriko had not yet revealed—not to mother, not to anyone—and it might win the sympathy of both her mother and the mayor. It had to. If not ...

The ringing of the doorbell plunged a dagger into Yuriko's heart.

In the entryway, the mayor slipped off his shoes before entering. Akiko greeted the mayor with a bow far deeper than his own; Yuriko responded in kind. After this traditional show of respect, Yuriko noted that her mother's shoulders had resumed their normal upright bearing, as though the mayor's very presence energised her.

The mayor looked upon Yuriko with eyes both severe and

considerate. His magnificent mane of silver hair was brushed straight back, as was his custom at formal ceremonies, and his black silk gown was adorned only by a small, circular family crest in white. Towering over both Yuriko and her mother, the mayor uttered three words: "It is time."

But Yuriko had her own three words to offer in return: "I am pregnant," she said. "I carry the child Hiroshi will never see."

Her mother's brows lifted. The mayor frowned. Then his tense face relaxed, and the sun broke out across his creased features. "Yuriko," he said, "that is wonderful!" His radiant smile showed off his famed polished teeth which, to Yuriko, resembled neon gravestones.

"Yes," Akiko said, obviously following the mayor's lead. "Happy news indeed, my daughter."

Yuriko couldn't believe her ears—they were *happy* she was with child, knowing that she was the female sacrifice?

"Are, are you saying," Yuriko said, "that even though you know I am pregnant, you still insist on going along with—?"

"Dedorah's will is the will of the gods," the mayor intoned simply. "And seriously, I don't know why your pregnancy upsets you so. It is the best possible thing that could happen, given your fated path."

Dizzy with shock and disbelief, a sick feeling in the pit of her stomach, Yuriko turned to the mayor with one last plea. "Surely you are not as superstitious as the others. Surely you know that letting Dedorah have his way with the village is wrong." Yuriko's resolve toughened. "We must fight. We must! And we can start tonight. The whole village can revolt against—"

"Daughter!" Akiko thundered. *"You go too far!"* Only once before had Yuriko heard her mother use such a tone of voice.

Yuriko groped for the momentum to keep her protest rolling. "But, but mother, how—?"

"Do you believe," Akiko stated, her voice hard and resonant, "in respecting your own kin, your own flesh and blood, the very mother who gave you entry into this miserable world?"

For a moment, Yuriko's resolve wavered atop a steep precipice. Her mother had raised her on her own, without the help of a husband, and she had unfailingly loved Yuriko and sacrificed for her. Could Yuriko truly be a good daughter and do any less? Her resolve in shambles, she mentally flung her independence into the bottomless abyss of surrender. "I respect you, mother."

"Then," Akiko asked, her voice less harsh but no less determined, "will you honour me?"

Yuriko studied the floor. "Yes, mother. I will honour you."

With a show of mixed relief and sorrow, Yuriko's mother embraced her and let an abundance of tears wet the front of Yuriko's blouse. But she said nothing. Neither did Yuriko.

At the mayor's behest, Yuriko left the home of her birth, slipped into her sandals, and resisted the temptation to take one last look over her shoulder.

Walking past the familiar wood-framed, tile-roofed houses that lined the town's main street, an avenue whose cracked asphalt was gouged with potholes that would never be filled, Yuriko felt as though she was a prisoner trapped in someone else's dream. Surely she would awaken soon.

But she did not.

Whistling a familiar island dirge, the mayor strolled beside her, his hands clasped behind his back; undoubtedly, he wanted to make sure that Dedorah's instructions communicated through the village priestess were obeyed to the letter—no one was to speak to Yuriko, or gesture goodbye, or come out of their houses at all. Yet the warm, buttery light that glowed from the village windows made Yuriko ache for home—for her friends, her students, her mother. But she kept the tears inside.

It was a short trip to the edge of the village. There, awaiting her, was twenty-one year old Kenji, the village's male sacrifice. He carried his wiry frame ramrod straight and held his chin high, but the sweat that slicked his face and shimmered in the full moon's radiance betrayed his unease.

The mayor donned his grim duty face. "This is as far as I go. You must climb the lookout tower on your own." He bowed quickly to Yuriko and Kenji, who returned his bow with interest, then pivoted on his heel and hiked back into the village.

Yuriko swallowed and smiled at Kenji. Weakly, he returned her amenity. Then they walked through the island foliage towards the lookout tower that the common good demanded they ascend, a site some three hundred metres from the village.

Oblivious to the drama going on around them, island insects chirped and whirred and buzzed. The dark undergrowth that flattened beneath Yuriko's footfalls was more moist than usual, the forest's exotic smells more pointed. A warm breeze rustled through the palm fronds of the surrounding trees, causing them to clack together like dinner plates. *Or dangling bones*, Yuriko thought.

Upon reaching the wooden lookout tower, Yuriko and Kenji climbed the full twenty metres to the top without incident. The most serious mishaps on the way up were the splinters that Yuriko's palms acquired from grasping each successive ladder rung. But the stinging pain seemed irrelevant, even absurd, given the magnitude of what was to come.

From the top of the lookout tower, Yuriko and Kenji gripped the landing's railing and gazed out over the night-blanketed island. A thick canopy of trees—ficus, fir palm, camphor, and others—covered the land's northern sector. The island's central volcano appeared as ominous as ever, rising high above the earth like a dark, conical temple. The village to the west, looking from this height like a quaint collection of storybook houses, appeared peaceful and serene beneath the star-strewn sky.

Then it started.

At first, Yuriko thought the thrashing in the forest to the far west was caused by a gust of wind. But next came the wet snappings of tree trunks and the spectacle of dozens of trees collapsing around a central location the size of a baseball stadium. A cold finger grazed Yuriko's heart. Whatever was active under those trees was big, and it wasn't the wind or any other natural phenomenon.

A dark shape half the size of the island's volcano rose from the funereal woods like a great black wraith, and when it did, Kenji gripped Yuriko's arm so fiercely that his nails dug into her flesh.

Slowly, regally, Dedorah attained its full height of fifty metres, towering above the surrounding woods like an upright crocodile lording over a thatch of weeds. Darker than the night and blotting out the stars caught behind its stygian silhouette, the Kaiju favoured the vague outlines of an immense allosaurus. But its rounded, Tyrannosaurus-like head was much too large for its body. Like a bulbous watermelon fitted with shark's teeth, the massive head wobbled atop the beast's thick torso as though it might slide off.

Instead, it swiveled in the direction of the lookout tower—and grinned.

Kenji gasped and stumbled backwards. Winter flooded Yuriko's hands, but she refused to budge from her vantage point.

Dedorah's head then pivoted towards the village. From the firetower in front of the village hall, the tower's bell began to ring out the time, each clang rippling through the night air like a summons. The last chime would signal the advent of midnight.

The Kaiju moved to the edge of the village, yet it didn't so much stalk there as it seemed to half-glide across the earth, its means of motivation hidden by the thick woods that came up to the creature's knees. And it wasn't so much as though the ground shook—it was more as though it wobbled, Dedorah's curious tremors radiating all the way to the top of the lookout tower and vibrating through Yuriko's legs and arms and face, making her teeth rattle.

The last chime sounded.

Midnight.

Without preamble, Dedorah opened its massive jaws. Its tongue—a pulpy, gray, worm-like thing—slithered aimlessly over its bottom row of teeth. Its jaw hinges snapping and creaking, the Kaiju's mouth gaped so wide that it appeared as though its head might split in two, and the slick, pinkish-green roof of its mouth was seen to be pocked with red and white lesions. As the mouth widened even more, the lesions popped open, revealing yellow, mucous-filled eyes that, in unison, turned their diseased gaze upon the village.

"It's time," Yuriko said, more to herself than her lookout tower companion Kenji.

A single green burst erupted from Dedorah's jaws and struck the village.

Blinding light burst upon the night like a sun exploding beneath the sea. Yuriko shielded her eyes, yet the heat seared her protective arms. The explosion was soundless save for a pronounced popping in her ears, yet its concussion wave shook the tower as surely as though Dedorah was shaking it himself.

It was over almost as quickly as it had begun.

Hesitantly, fearing yet knowing what she would see, Yuriko took her arms from her eyes.

The entire area that the village had occupied less than sixty seconds earlier had become a barren swath of blasted gray earth. Nothing remained—not even the firetower. Streams of pinkish-gray vapour carried on the wind, the stench funneling into Yuriko's nostrils like smoke from a freshly used crematorium.

Dedorah, apparently pleased, gazed upon the destruction it had wrought; the flat, moon-like tableau that had once been the village was now an ugly gray scar on the face of the island's otherwise lush green expanse. The creature's head swiveled in Yuriko and Kenji's direction; for several seconds, it stared at the sacrificial couple with a curious intensity. Then, a look of feral satisfaction distorting its demonic visage, it glided away, disturbing the island foliage as it departed.

The Kaiju had vowed never to let the Japanese become so numerous that they posed even the hint of a threat ever again. So periodically, human populations were cleansed and allowed to begin anew. Randomly chosen sacrifices were chosen to be the progenitors.

Yuriko and Kenji were their village's sacrifices. They had been ordained to live, though the rest of their village had now perished, and the memory of their murdered loved ones would sear their sleep for the rest of their lives. Such was the sacrifice the Kaiju demanded.

The Kaiju also demanded that Yuriko and Kenji now be fruitful and multiply. Since Yuriko was pregnant with a child who wasn't Kenji's, that was a distinct possibility.

Of course, Yuriko pondered, so was death.

BEACHED

LEE BATTERSBY

By the time I arrived, over two hundred people were on the beach, trying to push the monster back into the water. From my vantage point on the bluff, overlooking the strip of sand where it lay, I could see how hopeless the task was: the beast, positively identified as Irukaguma, was too vast to be shifted by such insignificant creatures as humans, and as I'd learned from the car radio, the military would arrive long before it could be returned to the waves. Nevertheless, here I was, and there it lay, and all I had to do was climb a few dozen steps down the side of the bluff and I'd be touching the same sand as my nightmares. My shoes and socks were in the car; I'd rolled my trousers up past my knees. There was nothing to stop me from stepping down and crossing the beach, laying my hands upon its skin, feeling the salt and the sweat and the essence of its flesh.

Even so, I might have sat upon my perch forever were it not for the hand on my shoulder, and the girl, meeting my jump of surprise with a smile and "Are you here to help?" in her soft voice. I must have stammered like a fool, but eventually my mouth worked as it should.

"Yes," I lied. "Here to help."

"Fantastic." She held out her hand, and I shook it gingerly. "Susan Monroe."

"Tom Burns."

"A Burns on Burns beach? Do you charge rent?" She laughed, as if the coincidence of my name delighted her.

"Not quite. It's anglicised."

"Well, it's close enough." She scrambled ahead of me, dropping the last couple of feet to land with a soft thump. "Come on down."

What could I do? I followed, closing my eyes as I took the last step. The sand was warm and gritty, and blew back and forth with the furnace-blast of the beast's breath, siroccos beating against me with every exhalation. Susan coughed. I opened my eyes, and gasped.

"It looks much bigger from this angle, doesn't it?" she said, and I nodded in agreement rather than speak.

He'd been larger before; at least, he had seemed so. Now, devoid of strength and rage, it was as if the sunlight leached him of his mass and majesty so that he was just another dumb animal washed up to die, a mountainous expanse of flesh certainly, but just that. Flesh and breath, and the stink that all dying creatures carry.

"Come on," Susan said. "There's plenty of space."

She stepped past me and I followed her up the beach to where a small tent stood behind a circle of camp chairs. A group of volunteers gathered around a portable barbecue, ladling soup out of a pot. Susan made introductions, grabbed two cups, and handed me one.

"Truth be told," she said. "The job's impossible. It doesn't matter how many people join us, he's just too big."

Some of the others nodded. I sipped from my cup, and stayed quiet. Pushing wouldn't work. They were right about that much. Irukaguma was almost one hundred metres long. His dorsal fin alone weighed several tonnes. I glanced at it as it pointed towards God like the outline of a mountain. If I squinted, perhaps I would see a scar at the front, towards the tip, a sign of impact ...

"What do you think, Tom?" Susan's words brought me back to myself. I blinked.

"Sorry, what?"

"Grant says he knows a guy who used a kind of collar to drag sperm whales back into the water." She nodded to a thin, bearded man leaning forward to refill his cup. "He thinks we could contact him, maybe get him to jury rig a couple together, get them here by morning."

"Uh huh."

"We can't work against the bulk," Grant said. "We have to find a way to redistribute the force, pull it down the slope of the beach—"

"Then we're underneath the damn thing when it hits the water," another person interrupted. "Do *you* want to be there?"

The argument broke out again, but to my ears it sounded well-worn, as if the participants were fulfilling a duty rather than making a case. I turned away from them and gazed again at the behemoth. I felt a presence at my shoulder and wasn't surprised to find Susan there again.

"It's almost hypnotic, isn't it?" she said. "It draws you in. Have you ever seen anything so huge, so ..." she shuddered. "It's incredible."

"No," I said, and it was only partially a lie. "I've never seen anything so huge."

Ankylobuta is not so big, nor Urufuki, and a semi-submerged fin is not so massive as the entire beast.

"Well," she said, and clapped me on the back like we were hunting buddies, "it's about to get a lot bigger. Let's get down there and see if we can tip the balance, hey?" She set off down the beach. "Come on." I stared at her happiness, failing to recognise it for a moment, then drank the last of my soup and followed in her wake.

Up close, Irukaguma resembled nothing so much as a building that flexed with the wind, each breath shifting the wall of its flesh more than a foot either way. Those volunteers who still persisted in trying to push the beast slid back and forth with the movement, their feet digging tracks in the moist sand. The noise of the creature's breathing destroyed all other sound, so that we shouted at each other as if in the midst of a gale.

"Just pick a spot," Susan yelled, gesturing to metres of free flesh between each labouring human. "Damned if it'll make any difference, but what else can we do, eh?"

She strode over to a nearby spot and planted her hands against Irukaguma, leaned into the task, and pushed. What could they do? Hire two front-end loaders to dig a series of progressively lower trenches between the beast and the sea—the way the Japanese have rescued large whales for years? Call any one of several friends I had made in the aviation industry, hire as many skycranes as it would take to harness and drag the monster's extremities towards the ocean, hoping the bulk would follow? Give up and count shipping lanes as safer places? Susan looked at me again, and I flexed my fingers, curled my hands into fists. My legs would not take me forward. She frowned and came back to me.

"What's the matter?"

"I ..."

"Are you okay? You look pale."

"I ... I'm sorry." I broke away, turned from her worry and stumbled up the beach. I was almost to the grass and the press of the gawking crowds when she caught up to me.

"Hey. Hey!" She grabbed my shoulder and swung me round to face her. "What's the matter?"

"I'm sorry. Really I am. I can't ... I just can't, okay?"

"Can't? You mean ... hey, hey, it's okay," she said as my tears began. I clenched my fists tighter, squeezed my eyelids together until I saw green and purple lines in the dark. "Listen, listen." She grabbed my hand, rubbed it in both of hers. "It's okay, really. Some of the others had a similar reaction, at first. It's elemental, a creature like this, something overpowering and emotional. It's okay. I understand. Just ..." she pulled gently, led me a step or two back towards the monster. "Come back, as close as you want. Take your time. When you're ready—"

"No!" I pulled my hand out of her grip, so savagely that she stumbled from the sudden release. "You don't understand, okay? You don't understand a fucking thing about it."

"What?"

"Elemental, emotional." I heard the sneer in my voice, saw it slap her. "What do you think it is, a fucking stuffed toy?"

"No, of course not."

"Let me tell you what it is, okay? It's a monster." My hands were waving; my body pushed forward like a drunk about to take his first swing. She stepped backwards, out of my reach. "A fucking indiscriminate killer. You want to save it? For what, so you can pat yourself on the back and feel all warm and conservationy every time you see it sink a ship on the news?"

"What? No!" She looked around her for support, but the watching crowd stood silent. If the beast were one type of spectacle, we were another. "It's in pain, Tom. It needs our help. It doesn't attack ships. We've done the research. It lives in the deep—"

"It hunts, you fucking moron!" Several of the crowd laughed at my scream, and behind Susan, a number of the volunteers looked up, noticing our confrontation at last. Susan blinked. I stopped, stunned by the force of my outburst. "Oh, oh hell. I'm—"

"I beg your pardon?" Now Susan stepped forward. The heel of her hand hit me in the chest, hard. "What did you call me?"

"I'm sorry." My anger had deserted me. I retreated like an empty man. "That was wrong."

"Yes, it was." She pushed again and I stumbled against the grassy lip of the beach's edge. "Exactly who do you think you are to talk to me like that, huh? At least I'm out here doing something. At least I'm *saving* something."

I sat down, as much to avoid the scorn in her voice as the thought of another thump to my chest.

"If you don't like it, Burns, then fuck off."

I stared at the hurt and fury in her face for a second, then lowered my eyes in defeat.

"I can't," I mumbled.

"What?"

"I can't."

"What do you mean, you can't?" She stood above me, hand on her hip like an angry lover. I sniffed, closed my eyes for a moment. When I opened them again it was to look past her, over the concerned gazes of the soup-drinking volunteers, to the wall of flesh at the water's edge.

"I have to be here," I said. "I have to know."

"Know what?"

"Why." I barely heard my own whisper.

"Why it beached? Is that all?" She snorted in disbelief. "God's sake, is that what all the histrionics are for?"

I shook my head. "I can guess why it beached. Cold water climate change, sonar haemorrhage. Christ, it could even have dilated cardiomyopathy for all I know." I shrugged. "It's a type of whale, we've always known that. Whatever they have, it stands to reason—"

"Then what?" She kneeled down in front of me, put her hands on my knees. "Come on, Tom. What's the matter?"

"You don't understand what you're doing. You don't understand."

"Understand what, Tom?"

"It kills people, Susan."

"It doesn't. We've—"

"It does!"

"When? Where?" She shook my legs, gently. "Tom, I've been working with this group for two years. Everything we rescue, we're organised. We do the research. There are no recorded instances of Irukaguma attacking shipping or causing destruction of human property."

I raised my head, looked straight into her eyes. "You're wrong."

"And how do you know that?"

"I've seen it."

"You what?"

"It comes out of the dark," I said, pinning her gaze with my own. "It feeds on colossus squid like we do on whiting. It moves all the time, it doesn't care about humans, and if it hits a refugee boat you'll float for days before the helicopter spots you and you'll never, *ever* find a trace of your parents again." I blinked, and she shook her head, released.

"And is that it?" she asked. "Is that what you came down her for? Revenge, or something?"

"No." We helped each other to stand.

"Then what?"

"I need to understand." She let go my hand, and I felt a moment of regret. "I need ... it can't be just an animal. It can't just ... I don't know."

She stood with head bowed for several seconds and I looked anywhere but at her, or the monster, or the few members of the crowd who still gawped at us now that we had exhausted our sideshow value. Finally she shrugged.

"I don't know what to tell you, Tom."

"I ..."

"I'm sorry, I really am. I'm going back down there and I'm going to keep trying to save him. If you can't help, well, that's okay. But I've got to go."

She moved away, turned her back on me and made her way to the staring soup drinkers. They gathered about her, asking questions, making sure she was okay. She brushed through them and kept walking down to the monster. Several of the volunteers glared at me, before they all returned to their task, leaving me alone with only the catcalls of the crowd for company.

I watched them for twenty minutes, pushing against the oblivious bulk. Susan tilted her head from time to time, peeking at me over her shoulder before returning to her labours. I don't know who they were trying to persuade: me, the sightseers, maybe each other. But more and more of them stopped hurling themselves against the unfeeling flesh as I watched, and joined those who ran buckets of water up from the surf to throw over its skin. Little by little, the act of rescue was becoming that of giving comfort. Whatever I wanted, whether I understood just what that was or not, was being taken away from me. Even Susan, eventually, leaned back from her task. I watched as she moved forward, running one hand across Irukaguma's skin, moving along its flank and down its jaw until she stood below the ranks of massive teeth. She pressed her head against the jaw, and I saw defeat in the lines of her body. As volunteers ran past her with buckets she began to pat the beast. I stumbled forward, rushing past bucket bearers until I stood no more than three or four feet away from Susan and the monster's maw.

"What the hell are you doing?"

She turned her head to look at me, her hand still patting away at the monster's skin.

"Nothing."

"Are you out of your mind? Get away from there!" One twitch, that's all it would take. One twitch of those misshapen jaws. I doubt it would even notice Susan as it crushed her between its teeth, wouldn't even taste her as her body bounced across the ragged ground of its tongue and into its throat. I lurched forward, to within an arm's reach of her, before my legs froze and refused to carry me the rest of the way. "You'll get killed."

"No, I won't." Susan let her hand drop, and faced me. "How can this animal kill me, Tom? Look at it. It's helpless."

"*You* look at it!" I swung my arm at Irukaguma's mouth, hanging above us like the entrance to a timeless cave. "Look at what you're doing."

"I am looking. I see an animal dying, a unique life form that needs us, and I can't help it." I saw the tears on her cheeks. "What am I supposed to do?"

I held out my hand. "Come away from there. Please."

"No." She sniffed, and ran the back of her hand across her face, obliterating all proof of her tears. "You come here."

"I ..." I looked above her, felt the blast of meat breath across me. I took one step, then another, stiff-legged, my feet dragging through the sand. Susan reached out and took my hand. I squeezed her fingers, and in the next instant she pulled. I tripped forward, and righted myself by wrapping my free arm around her, drawing us into a hug I didn't have the strength to release. Her hand was around my wrist now. She braced her arm, hauling my hand towards the jaw. I could reach out, extend my fingers and brush against wet skin. I strained against Susan's grip. My fingers tensed, then curled in upon each other until I was twisting my fist out of her hold, raising my arm away from the monster, unbalancing myself, and Susan, so that we collapsed against each other, sprawling full length on the sand.

Susan regained her feet in an instant, splashing sand across the side of my head as she rose. I lay still, my face pressed into the sand, eyes closed. I could breathe, I thought, draw in a deep lungful of earth, scour my throat and lungs clean, drown in earth like I couldn't do in the water. I'd been too young, then, to understand. I fought against drowning. Now ...

Susan's hands dug into my t-shirt and pulled. I raised my head, reluctantly, missing the grip of the beach the moment my face emerged. She let go and sat backwards.

"Jesus. What the hell is wrong with you?"

Up on the bluff, moving along the road towards the public side of the beach, khaki-coloured vehicles. I blinked sand out of my eyes and stood.

"It doesn't matter now," I said, brushing myself down.

"What do you mean it doesn't matter? All you've done since you stepped foot onto this beach—"

"Look." I pointed, and she saw the convoy.

"Oh, crap." She began to retreat up the beach towards the camp. "What the hell are the military doing here?"

"What do you think?" I followed her. "There's a giant monster here. Of course they're coming."

"It's a beached animal, for Christ's sake." We reached the tent, and she began scooping papers from the tables and stuffing them into cardboard document holders. "They've no right to be here. Marcus, ring Admin. Get hold of Irene. Tell her the shooters are coming down. See what she knows and what we can do."

A gaunt young man sitting nearby nodded and raised a cell phone to his ear. Horns blared outside. I ducked back onto the beach. The trucks had arrived, and already the crowd was being dispersed by friendly and uncompromising troops. An officer was climbing down from the lead vehicle, all gold braid and shoulders. He hit the ground and looked around him at the soldiers herding bystanders away then strode over to where Susan had joined me in front of the tent, a staff sergeant at his heels.

"This site is under military jurisdiction, ladies and gentlemen," he announced, with far too much satisfaction for a man just doing his job. "Under section 64 of the Natural Attack Act of 2010 I order you to leave this area and come no closer than three hundred metres from a perimeter as set up by the men under my command. You have fifteen minutes to comply. Do you understand?"

Susan stepped towards him, and I recognised the desire to fight in her stance.

"Listen, bucko. We're here under the jurisdiction of Greenpeace, the WWF, and at the request of no less than a dozen local residents, to help a beached animal back into its natural habitat. So you can get off your Natural Attack high horse and piss off, unless you want to provide a court with evidence of what attack you're supposed to be talking about."

She may as well have been shouting at a cliff face for all the reaction she received. The Major, according to his insignia, looked straight over her head at me. I lowered my eyes and turned my head away, but not soon enough. He stepped down onto the beach and brushed past Susan.

"Mister Burns?"

I kept my stare fixed upon the distant hills. The Major stopped well within my comfort zone. I smelled his aftershave and his sweat, nearly strong enough to drown out the stench of salt and dying beast.

"I am talking to you, Mister Burns."

I sighed and turned my eyes to him.

"What is it, Major?"

"Exactly what is it you are doing with these people?"

"Wait a minute. Wait a *minute*." Susan pushed between us and faced me with her hands on her hips. "They know you?"

"You don't?" The Major might have smiled, had he not been the career type. As it was, his voice gave away his amusement. "You haven't even told them who you are?"

"It's not relevant."

"Not relevant?" Susan's voice, on the other hand, barely kept a lid on her anger. "Who the fuck are you, Tom? What have you been doing here?"

I reached into my pocket and withdrew my wallet, folding it out so that my identification card peered at the Major through its plastic window. "These people are with me, Major. They're doing important work."

Susan stared at the card.

"Leave them be. Please."

This time the Major did smile, a small puff of scorn escaping his lips.

"I don't think so."

"What the hell is this?" Susan snatched my wallet away, read the card more closely. "Department of Natural Response? Assistant Director?" She let the wallet drop to the sand, and looked at me. "Who the fuck are you?"

"Mister Burns is the Government's acknowledged expert on Giant Animal behaviour, Miss," the Major said with no little satisfaction. "He wrote our book, didn't you, Mister Burns?"

I tried to look Susan in the face, and failed. I settled instead for her feet. "It's easy to study the ones you don't know," I said. "Easy to advise on how to capture them, how to neutralise them."

"Kill them."

"Not always." I thought of Urufuki and how we'd neutered it, lobotomised it, sent it back to its island where it could wither away and die in peace. "Sometimes." I felt the bulk of the beast at my side, almost as if it recognised me now and listened like the others, deciding whether to hate or understand me. "All these years I've been studying maps and charts and footage, finding patterns, finding behaviours, telling the hunters: they're animals, yes, misshapen and irradiated, angry, destructive." I caught my breath, managed to raise my eyes to Susan's. "It's easy to tell them when you don't know where it comes from. But this one..." I raised a hand towards Irukaguma, lowered it, let it twitch by my side. "I had to know. I had to know."

"Know what? That it was dying? That you could see it go?"

"Whether it knew!" I smelled the stink of the raft, heard the screams and the snapping of wood, saw the top of the fin like a building, sliding back underneath the waves. "Whether it meant to do it!"

There was a moment of silence. I bit my lip, scared now that I had no more truth left to hide. Susan nodded once, twice, her face reflective. Then she balled up her fist and hit me square along the jaw. I slumped to the ground, blinking stupidly at her back as she stalked away to rejoin her comrades. The Major retrieved my wallet and tossed it into my lap.

"I want you off my beach, Mister Burns," he said. "You can study the animal after we've finished with it, but you will not return here until you have my express authorisation. Your consorting with these people will be in my report." He turned away. "Sergeant, escort this man from this area."

He strode back up the beach to supervise the ejection of the volunteers. I could hear Susan, still protesting, her voice moving further away from me with every moment. The Sergeant bent down and extended a hand.

"I have to say, sir," he said as he helped me to my feet. "You know how to pick them." He pointed me away from the soldiers and the volunteers, back along the path I had first taken. "This way might be best, sir."

I sat on the bluff and watched as the soldiers cordoned off the beach with their usual courteous efficiency, sweeping the sand clean of volunteers with too much speed and politeness for any real resistance to organise itself. The evicted saviours trudged past me on their way back to the carpark, their stares angry and accusing, but otherwise leaving me alone. Now that I was outed, I was too protected to harm, and beneath their contempt. I ignored them all, my gaze fixed upon the spectacle below. I heard the crash of something heavy breaking a windscreen. By the time I got back to my car, the tyres would be slashed and my petrol tank full of sand. Below me, surveyors pinned Irukaguma to their notebooks with laser sights and measuring ropes, pencils and equations. Photographers clambered this way and that over the giant body, impaling small white flags into the flesh and taking shots.

"Happy with yourself?" I didn't need to turn to know the look on Susan's face. Still, I did. "Is this what you hoped for ... why are you crying?"

I returned my eyes to the beach.

"Oh, God." She sat down beside me. "You're going to be complicated, aren't you?"

Across the sand, humans measured and quantified, oblivious

to our observations. As they worked, I began to talk, explaining their thoughts and strategies to Susan. My notebook sat beneath my leg, a lifetime of observation inside. I gave it to her, told her what it was. She tucked it inside her jacket.

When it fell dark, the soldiers set up floodlights and kept working. I don't know whether it was the change of light, or just some animal instinct, but not long after, the beast, silent all this time, gathered its breath and began to call. At the first sonorous thunderclap of sound, the guards clamoured for their weapons, while the civilians ran for whatever high ground they could reach. Susan gripped my arm.

"What's it doing?"

I closed my eyes and listened to the fear and despair in that giant voice. Irukaguma breathed in again, and nobody present could have missed the gap in its inhalation, the catch that spoke of something broken deep inside the monster's gut.

"It's really dying, isn't it?" Susan asked, and I didn't need to answer.

The beast called again and a hundred times more over the next few hours, each time a little more weakly, each time betraying more pain and alarm as gravity, and its own immense bulk, worked to crush it beyond life. No answering voice came from beyond the black waves. No mate or monster responded to ease Irukaguma's terror. The creature on the beach was unique, and in dying, alone. At some point I noticed that Susan and I were holding hands and I could not bring myself to mention it in case she realised and pulled away.

Irukaguma called, and we listened, and some time after midnight the calling stopped. After that there were only the waves, and the sound of my own breath inside my skull.

☆

The sand under my feet was cold as we made our way to the cordon of guards, staring at the corpse as if they half-expected some obscure monster trickery. I had no need of Majors; I approached the man nearest the radio array, his Sergeant's stripes visible in the glare of the spotlight. Men raised their rifles at our approach. He glanced at me then ordered the men to lower their arms.

"Mr Burns."

"Sergeant."

"The Major ordered you from his beach."

"Yes, he did."

He nodded, glanced past me at Susan then let his eyes meet mine.

"If the Major discovers you here when he returns no earlier than nine o'clock tomorrow morning you will be in serious trouble."

"Thank you."

He stood aside, and we walked to the low side of Irukaguma's body, away from the light and the curious stares of the soldiers.

We rounded the great bluff of its nose and the half-open mouth, yellowed teeth the size of a full-grown man displayed like so many ancient stalagmites, walked down the elongated and misshapen jaw until the body hid the spotlights from us, and I stood in the cold sand with only the ocean behind me and the insurmountable wall of Irukaguma in front.

I let go of Susan's hand and stepped forward until no more than an arm's length separated me from the creature's flesh. At this distance, the smell was overpowering: meat and death, overwhelming my senses. No memory of the world remained. All was Irukaguma, and Irukaguma was dead.

I raised a hand, held my breath, and reached out to touch the monster.

Terrapin Suite

Mikal Trimm

She swam through galactic eddies, driven by instinct and necessity. Worlds shuddered in her wake, their paths disrupted, their orbits undone. No matter to her—they were cold, empty, lifeless things that no longer registered in the slow pattern of her migration.

Suns reflected dully on her carapace, passing as streaks of warmth across her scutes as she navigated the endless night of the Universe.

☆

"So, what do you really think of all this?"

"All what?" Deej wheezed the words as the last hint of smoke left his lungs. *God, I hate guys who try to make conversation when they're stoned.* Radiohead blared from the boombox, and the night sky wavered in front of his eyes, an ocean of stars rippling through the marijuana haze.

"*You* know," and Randy paused to take another hit, "*all zis!*" Teeth clenched, voice tight, and he waved his free hand in the vague direction of *up.*

"What, like the stars and crap?" Man, he was missing his favourite song! No, wait, that was the next one. Still ...

"Life, dude! Eternity! Like, where did this all come from? God? The Big Bang?" Randy paused, craning his neck back so far to see the extent of the night sky that he fell over in his beach chair. He didn't seem to notice. "Du-u-de ..."

Deej cranked up the boombox. His favourite song (yeah, *this* one) was on.

Randy stirred. "Killer song, man. We got any more beer?"

☆

She could not feel fear, but there was a sense of unease as she traversed the sea of stars. *Cold,* not just the suns themselves, but the barren rocks in thrall to them. *Not mine, not mine.*

Her eyes weren't meant for small things—they took in solar systems at a glance—and it was hard to bring the microcosms of the tiny suns into focus. She shook herself, throwing off a billennium of cosmic dust, and submitted to instinct alone, eyes closed, forelimbs driving her through the endless night.

☆

"Black holes, dude."

Deej reached over to turn the boombox louder, realised the music was done. "Wait, wait ..." He shuffled through the rest of his CDs, trying to read the covers, failing. *I am so stoned.*

Randy pulled another joint out of his fanny-pack from a seemingly endless supply, sparked up. "Black holes, dude. Sucking in light. Big ol' holes in the universe." Sparked the lighter, burnt half the joint down in a gargantuan breath. "What's *that* about?" He passed the soggy remains of the joint to Deej.

Do I need more of this? Deej watched the surf pound the beach, noticed the glimmer of the stars dancing across the waves, saw tiny fairies leaping from crest to crest to keep their feet dry. *Yep. I need a lot more.*

"Dude. The music's over." Randy stood, a stop-motion leviathan, and Deej had to laugh as he watched Randy try to navigate the short distance from his collapsed chair to the stack of CDs between them. Randy shuffled the jewel cases like cards, finally spilling them out across the sand in a drunken flourish. "Hey, dude, which one has that song I really like?"

Deej took another toke, realised that he wasn't sure if he was looking at the stars or the ocean, and giggled.

☆

She feels the pull. There is a heartbeat there, faint, but enough to give her a direction, enough to carry her through the boundless ocean of the Universe. *Soon*, she knows.

And the milky miasma of the Universe knows, as well.

☆

The surf stroked the Florida coast, teasing it with licks and caresses, promising a long, sweet path to oblivion.

Dude, I'm really stoned. Deej tried to focus on one point, *any* point, failed miserably. The only constant in his sinsemilla-scented world was Randy's voice, still rambling on about ... whatever.

"So what I'm saying is—" Randy paused to take another swig of beer and chase it with a heady hit, "—like, why are we here, y'know? Is it a Supreme Being, or an old explosion of nothing, or some hoobledy-doobledy that we just don't understand?"

"Hoobledy-doobledy?" The only thing that stood out from Randy's ravings. Deej heard it in his head, over and over, *hoobledy-doobledy, hoobly-doobly, hooby-dooby.* He had to giggle again. *Doobie. He said doobie.* That was pretty damned funny.

Randy stared at him for a long time. A looong time. Deej tried to stare back, lock eyes, play the game ... failed. "Dude. What the hell are you *smoking*?"

"What made the world, man? Why do we exist?" Randy craned his neck enough to take in the entire star-laden sky. "Why ...?" Randy sat up, dug in the cooler, found another beer, and pressed it against his forehead, then dropped it, still staring into the endless sea of stars above him.

"Oh, man. Black hole, dude."

☆

The Universe spins around her, the focal point, the Creator. She swims the black sea of vacuum and ice and finds warmth. *There you are*, and the cosmos begins to revolve around her, as it did before, as it always will.

☆

Deej giggled again, couldn't help himself. The stars were disappearing as he watched, blanked out by a shadow that grew larger with each blink of his eyes. *Dude, don't blink!* Too late, though, too late to shut Randy up as he went on and on about black holes and Armageddon. Deej could only see one image, the kind of shape you'd imagine when you were staring at clouds as a child. He watched the shape swim closer, took a last, nostalgic hit off the joint in his hand.

Something cracked with a noise loud enough to wake the braindead, and he and Randy watched as the ocean disappeared, ebb and flow invalidated in one mad rush.

In the moment before the killing steam burst from the jagged hole that was the Atlantic Ocean, Deej grabbed Randy's arm, exhaled his last breath, and said, "Black hole, my ass. That's a *turtle*."

☆

She felt the clutter of parasites, as she always did. They appeared when circumstances were right, when the pattern of her laying met with the perfect conditions for incubation. Billions of eggs, strewn across the endless wastes of the cruel Universe. Sometimes, circumstances conspired in her favour.

The egg wobbled in its orbit, great cracks appearing in its surface. The tiny mites covering the egg died in the first moments of birth, superfluous. The Universe shuddered, fell apart like the forgotten fragments of the shell.

There was a moment of nothingness.

Time to lay, she thought, and she shepherded her child through the endless Void, teaching as she went.

THE RETURN OF ZOTH-OMMOG

LEIGH BLACKMORE

(Found Among the Papers of the Late Jack Leyton, of Sydney)

*I*t was a star-spawned abomination, a monumental cosmic horror *from a universe beyond imagining. The thing lumbered towards me, its great faceted eyes protruding, its membranous and semi-transparent squamous flesh quivering, slime dripping from its ravening maw. It was a god awakened from slumber, a being of hideously appalling size and terrifying vastness. It crashed across the temple's rock platforms, its cone-shaped body dwarfing the gigantic eel whose size had shocked me before this even more massive creature had appeared.*

"Zatomaga! Zatomaga!" chanted the Pohnpeians, massed to witness the spectacle in their ritual temple.

The abominable creature slowed in its lumbering tracks and extended hideous appendages that sucked and chewed at the air, writhing blindly as they sought prey. The thing was a behemoth, positively Brobdingnagian. Extending one of its appendages to the nearest chained Pohnpeian, it ripped the head cleanly off the screaming man. Blood spurted ten feet through the air, splashing me on the chest. The remains of the man's body slumped to the ground. The gargantuan thing had four broad, flat, starfish-like arms with suckers, but it seemed to prefer to use its head-tentacles to clutch and grapple. It was a god, an incredible mutation, sheer muscle and killing power.

Zatomaga! Yes, and Zoth-Ommog—for despite the native name for the creature, I knew this was the Dweller in the Depths, the One referred to in the Ponape *Scriptures. Dozens of feet above us, Zoth-Ommog brandished the man's head in its tentacle—a revolting trophy, dripping blood.*

I backed against the temple's cold stone wall. The natives brandished their weapons, giving full vent to their fury. In hellish ecstasies of adoration they howled their god's name. "Zatomaga! Zatomaga! Zatomaga!" Their god, the one they had worshipped for generations, was making a rare, if shocking visitation. It was the time of the Red Haze, and Zoth-Ommog had come again!

☆

My name is Jack Leyton. It is ten years since the events of which I shall write. I am not overly imaginative. At least I was not until unexpected adventure befell me. Now, my dreams are shockingly haunted, and I intend to seek in death a peace I can find no other way.

I am without heirs or relations. I leave this diary account of my Ponape adventure for whomever may find it, for I am almost maddened by glimpses of forbidden aeons, of shattering truths that flashed out at me in that fated year of 1863.

"*Pwoahng Mwahu*" said my companion, Sturges. "Good night". He lay down with his back to me.

Since escaping our captors, we had eaten our fill of bananas and breadfruit, and then later cooked yams on our campfire. We saw a large monitor lizard in the distance. Sturges told me they will eat chickens and occasionally a small piglet. I wondered if we might catch meat tomorrow if that monitor didn't sample us for breakfast. I don't remember falling asleep; I was so exhausted from our escape.

We had awoken to the sound of heavy bodies smashing through the jungle's perpetual green daylight. To our night-camp came the crunching of splintering branches, feet splashing through shallow water. Startled birds screeched as they wheeled up and away from the column of men bearing down upon us.

I rolled over on my grassy bed, my eyes crusty with sleep. I scrabbled for my knife and the few remaining possessions I had with me. Folding stiffly into a half-crouch, I turned my head, listening. I heard the *thwack* and stomp of men chopping their way through tangled knots of jungle growth. The ship's masters might send men from the *Lady Armitage,* moored in the lagoon separating Pohnpei from its surrounding reefs. It may have been natives. In either case, we didn't want to be caught.

I gestured to Sturges, pointing forward through the rain-drenched forest canopy. We plunged into the bougainvillea, thick stands of pandanus. Moments later, we climbed a monkey-pod tree to elude our pursuers. Rain came again and the splashing muffled any noises we were making. Our pursuers lost us, passing on the muddy overgrown trail beneath. We waited a long time in that tree, listening past the rain for any sound of danger.

Only three months before, I'd been enjoying old Sydney town. But in 1863 the colonies' publican houses were the stalking ground of press-gangs. I was a naïve landlubber, and I didn't expect to be whacked on the head, certainly not by naval troops.

I had finished work, and passed along the Rocks' cobbled twilight streets. Everywhere muffinmen rang their bells, pigs'-trotter men plied their trade, piemen cried out for people to buy their wares. I arrived at the Hero mighty thirsty after my day's work.

The Lord Nelson was a sandstone pub, as was the Beehive,

both built with stone from the Argyle Cut where I'd been working. I didn't want to drink at places reminiscent of my workplace, so I usually drank at the Whalers Arms or the Hero of Waterloo. Tonight it was the Hero. The place was favoured by Garrison Troops, but its open log fires and well-stocked bar provided welcome relief from the ramshackle, rat-infested dwellings of the Rocks' mean streets.

I often drank there, and had never run into any trouble before. I generally avoided Cockroach Lane or Frog Hollow, more dangerous slums of the colony, which were filled with unsavoury grog shops and shanties.

On this particular night, however, a sinister atmosphere filled the air as I downed my pint at the bar. Rum smugglers were said to use the place, but I had no idea that tunnels ran from the hotel's cellar down to the Harbour.

This week had been hard. After a couple of hours I was full as a boot. Just as I thought of heading home, two men clad in rough blue naval dress accosted me, suddenly gripping my arms from both sides. A stunning blow to the side of my head sent my vision black as I slumped to my knees.

Before I could recover, I was dropped through the trapdoor into the cellar. Kegs of beer rolled away from me as wrought-iron gates opened on rusting hinges. I was half-dragged, half-carried through a maze of stone cellars, smelling the sweat of my captors and the dankness of the underground tunnel that led from under the hotel to a house nearby.

I had no time to regain my senses or look about me, before the same two men took me from the house. They manhandled me down to the wharves, where many whaling ships were berthed, and unceremoniously bundled me aboard an even more foul-smelling clipper. They thrust me into the hold, rough quarters for a motley crew of other gang victims—some (I soon learned) as shocked as I was to find themselves there, aboard the *Lady Armitage*.

"Slogger Ball got ya did he?" one of the sailors jeered.

"Who's he?" I asked groggily, fingering the tender spot on my head, where I could feel a patch of bloody, matted hair.

"Press ganger. Does the Darling Harbour beat. Hard to miss—wears a stovepipe hat and frock coat. The back rooms of his house have hidden trapdoors. Poor bastards like you get shoved into the dungeons there before they turf you out to crew this sorry ship."

I tried to think. "No, I was drinking at the Hero of Waterloo, down Lower Fort Street".

"Ah, matey, that place is just as notorious. Could have been the naval press gangs, then. They're licensed to roam the streets and seize any able-bodied man. Or maybe it was the larrikins from the Rocks Push got ya. Well, make the best of it—you're bound on a voyage for Micronesia!"

And you, too, I thought, but said no more, for shock overcame me at this moment. Upon my recovery, it wasn't long before I concluded the crew of this ship constituted ruffians of every description. Many had been pressed into service from the gaols. Others had been taken from their places of employment, or (like me) simply kidnapped off the streets.

Once at sea, I realised that conditions on board the full-rigged ship promised to be little worse than those I had endured in servitude. The masters reminded me of the brutal guards at the Argyle Cut, where I had been doing hard labour cutting sandstone with hammers and chisels, and witnessed the first horrific experiments with explosives. The place was becoming the underground home of thugs, petty gangsters and rats, and cases of plague were cleaning out the convict labourers.

Most of the crew endured rough treatment at the hands of the master, Henrik Janssen. Under Janssen, there was Karl Jacobs, the bo'sun; and Dan Metcalfe, the second mate. The men all slept in bunks in the ill-fitted berth below decks.

I wondered at my change of fortune. One place was as good as another if I was a free man. Maybe I'd even be better off sailing all the way to Micronesia. The warm dark nights refreshed me, as did the ringing of bells at the various watches, the sky's blue during the day, the rolling of the waves. The masters still treated us brutally, but at least I began to make acquaintances amongst the crew.

"We're bound for the Carolines," snapped one of the men when I asked our destination, but he didn't seem to know exactly why. The master played his cards close to his chest.

Over the course of a month, the ship sailed north, up Australia's East Coast, past New Guinea and on through the vast landless reaches of the Coral Sea. Heading further northwards, it reached the Solomon Sea. I thought we might make landfall in the Bougainvilles, but instead the ship pressed on, sailing past New Ireland and further north. After another month we crossed the Equator, past tiny Kapingamarangi Atoll, and kept going. In my dreams I imagined escaping when we made landfall, but each time we weighed anchor for supplies we were beaten below decks and hardly saw the earth let alone the green forests of those islands in all that time.

Eventually, three months out of Sydney, we came into the region of the Eastern Carolines.

One night after second dog-watch I was scrubbing the deck around the after-deckhouse—one of my allotted tasks to earn my meagre provisions—and overhearing snatches of conversation between Jacobs and Metcalf, who leant over the rail smoking.

I learned one of the reasons for them heading for Micronesia. The sea around Truk and other islands in the region was full of sunken wrecks, they said. Some contained treasure. Some, the men claimed, were in lagoons, under only a few feet of water, shallow enough that it would be simple to salvage whatever treasures were still aboard.

"Those wrecks are going to make us rich," whispered one man to the other. "Just think of all that gold!" At one point they discussed heading for the mysterious and darkly rumoured Sequeiras Isles in the West Carolines, but after arguing they decided to head for Ponape.

There was a place on the island called Nan Madol. Some legends, according to the men, said that Nan Madol's canals had been formed by a giant dragon or lizard. Jacobs ventured this may have derived from the New Guinean crocodile, a large species that often swam in the open sea, but Metcalf held the legend true, superstitiously believing the giant lizard or eel still dwelled in a secret chamber in Nan Madol's largest temple.

I contrived to win the confidence of one of the crew. Ship's provisions were meagre; we lived on ship's biscuit, tins of corned beef, salt butter and tea. By saving some of my corned beef, I managed to get Eli Sturges to engage in conversation with me. Initially surly, he warmed to me after I offered him my extra corned beef, and I found he was simply being guarded.

Sturges was a tall, lean man who had worked up north with the Kanakas in the Queensland cane fields. He had been a blackbirder—one who specialised in stealing young Melanesians to put them to work in Australia's cane fields. He confessed as much.

"We used to lure 'em on board with promises of treasure— muskets, mattocks and axes, pipes and tobacco were treasure to them. Naïve, they were. Then we'd take 'em back to Australia and put 'em to work for our wealthy colonial betters. The owners found us white scum died if forced to labour in Queensland's tropical heat." A bitter laugh escaped him. "I earned good money to stand over the kanakas on horseback, with a stockwhip."

I shuddered. Sturges seemed proud of his former job, which amounted to no more than slavery. In fact, he was morally little different from the pressgangers. How galling he found his enslavement now! Despite my repugnance, I kept up our conversation, for I hoped the stories he offered might provide something useful towards my escape.

As we stood together up near the forepeak one evening, he began to reflect upon some peculiar lore which preoccupied his thoughts.

"Ever heard of the *Ponape Scriptures*? It's a manuscript found in the Carolines by Captain Abner Ezekiel Hoag sometime around 1734. It was old even then." He eyed me, gauging my receptiveness to his statement. As I didn't react, he went on.

"The book's pages were made of palm leaves; it was bound in a now-extinct cycadean wood and lettered throughout in Naacal— the language of Mu."

"Mu?" The name sounded strangely on my ears.

Sturges looked around furtively. "Mu—Lemuria—can't tell

you everything at once. I knew an army man from Ceylon. Churchward was his name. He got in with those priesthood cults—studied various megalithic civilisations, especially in the South Pacific—was entrusted with the secrets from certain stone tablets. He was full of tales of a great early civilisation, known as Mu or Lemuria. It vanished beneath the sea 25,000 years ago. Imagine that! Mu was an immense continent covering nearly half of the Pacific." He waved vaguely to the southwest. "Mu sank under a great volcanic eruption. Now fifty million square miles of water cover it over. Churchward said Mu's history dated back 200,000 years."

These were numbers and measures of time for which I had no reference. I couldn't help but shake my head. Sturges scowled.

"Well, Hoag wasn't making it all up. That's all I'm saying. He managed to translate the manuscript. But when he tried to have it published, religious leaders strongly objected to the book's references to Dagon and the publishers turned him down. I know some copies survived amongst secretive cults such as the Esoteric Order of Dagon."

I didn't know what he was talking about. "Esoteric Order of—Dagon?"

Sturges reached into his inside coat pocket. He drew out a volume bound in dark cloth, stained with salt and water-marked on its covers. "Here. You'll need it where we're going."

I couldn't imagine how he had kept the thing secret, but followed his practice of keeping it hidden at all times. In my bunk below decks, and by the feeble light of a stolen stump of candle, I read it through; it was the testimony of a crazy man. It claimed the original *Ponape Scriptures* was authored by Imash-Mo, high priest of a race of beings known as the "Old Ones". The book claimed these Old Ones ruled the Earth before humans existed. They were gone now, inside the earth, and under the sea, but their dead bodies had told their secrets in dreams to the first humans, who formed a cult which had had endured throughout the ages. The author raved that the *Ponape Scriptures* detailed the story of the legendary lost continent of Mu.

Paging further through the volume's tattered pages, I read penciled annotations which Sturges must have scribbled in the margins: "*Churchward says temple built over network of cellars and crypts connected to a canal. Centre—room shaped like pyramid. Similar ruins (to Ponape) at Kosae, near village of Lele. Huge enclosures—cone-shaped hill surrounded by high walls. Natives say people here very powerful—travelled east and west in great vessels. Some believe legendary lost continent of Mu, or Lemuria, may lie off its waters. Nan Madol, ritual centre, built as mirror image of sunken city that, at time of construction, could still be seen lying beneath water's surface?*"

I hid the volume away and fell into a restless sleep haunted by visions of distant wastes and dark places. Hoag's words seemed to appear before me in letters of black flame: "*Some day the Old Ones will call, when the stars are right, and the secret cult is always waiting to liberate him.*"

My reading of Hoag's book, and Sturges' recent bizarre rantings, confused and bewildered me. But there was a weird credulity to the tales that almost convinced me despite myself.

"*What has risen may sink, and what has sunk may rise!*" said Sturges. "We have to try and stop what's happening on Ponape."

I fell to studying the volume's contents with ever-increasing fascination, keeping an eye on the captain's cabin to ensure my secret studies were not observed. I would be soundly flogged if the senior crew discovered me slacking off my on-deck duties.

Starboard lay Kosrae Island. The sailors whispered anxiously of its ill-rumoured ruins, which stood on the smaller island of Lelu. Off to port we glimpsed the atoll Ngatik; but we would make landfall at Ponape.

Despite fair weather for most of our voyage, we weathered a small typhoon once we reached the Carolines. Fortunately the ship was undamaged.

Gradually we approached the islands, coming in through the coral atolls, with their sprinklings of coconut palms. Sturges pointed out the peak of Mount Totolom, easily seen from out at sea. Occasionally a cortège of sea turtles would cross the clipper's wake. Gorgonian fans of bright coral loomed up beneath us.

Another night, Metcalf and Jacobs talked of the strangeness of Ponape.

"Did you ever hear tell of old Captain Obed Marsh?" asked Jacobs. "He learned of strange creatures he called the Deep Ones. Alien, half-fish and half-frog things, he said they were."

Metcalf responded with rumours of bountiful gold offered to people in certain South Seas areas, given in exchange for human sacrifices. Sometimes, he whispered, the Deep Ones even mated with the humans, producing hideous hybrid entities. Their vast cities lay beneath the sea, and the alien creatures lived in them for millennia. Other whispers centred on brooding reefs and black abysses, and an underwater city, Cyclopean and many-columned Y'ha-nthlei, which some thought lay beneath the harbour at Ponape's mysterious Nan Madol complex. Some said this was identical to a legend of a sunken city the Pohnpeians called Kahnihniweiso.

☆

Zoth-Ommog had returned! As I backed against the temple wall, I thought how foolish I was to have ventured here. Zoth-Ommog's cult had consumed the people on Ponape, and I had been captured through my careless enthusiasm for adventure and the lure of the mystery of Nan Madol's bizarre architecture.

Zoth-Ommog thrashed colossally before my eyes. Its head was tremendous, razor-fanged and reptilian, but covered in tentacles. Bending forward, it extended another prodigious tentacle writhing with mouths, each lined with viciously sharp fangs. The tentacle snaked towards the next man in line—it was Janssen, master of the Lady Armitage. Though he had done me no kindnesses, I didn't wish to see him die. But I could do nothing to prevent it. Janssen pulled out a flintlock musket he must have hidden on his person. Before he could fire, the tentacle lashed around, smashing him across the face. Half the skin was flayed off at the first blow. The musket clattered to the floor.

The tentacle returned, whipping gigantically around and opening fully in front of the terrified man's head. The teeth gleamed an instant in the red maw, then the mouth snapped shut, splitting Janssen's skullcase with an awful crunch. Zoth-Ommog, stupendous in his alien ghastliness, undulated, shook Janssen's limp body furiously, then tossed it aside. The natives shouted, in a hoarse chorus of approval: "Zatomaga! Zatomaga!"

Zoth-Ommog roared its mountainous satisfaction. I now knew this to be Great Cthulhu's third son, imprisoned by the Elder Gods beneath the seabed near Pohnpei. I had read neither The R'lyeh Texts *nor the fabled* Zanthu Tablets, *but enough had been whispered to me by my compatriot Sturges for me to know Zoth-Ommog was perhaps the most dreaded of the Great Old Ones.*

The creature known as Zoth-Ommog slobbered and groped, a gelatinous immensity that promised nothing but fear and death. It roared again, and the temple walls shook. I knew I was about to die.

A beautiful young Pohnpeian woman with eyes like the dark moon was suddenly beside me. It was the girl I had seen earlier on the island, and who had not given away my presence. She was offering to help me escape! As she cut my bonds with a stone adze, she said one word: "Pwoakapwoak". As I looked into her dark eyes, I didn't have to speak the language to know that meant "love".

She gestured to a dark recess, an exit, in the temple wall nearby, and pulled at my wrist. I needed no urging to run with her, desperately seeking refuge from the monstrous horrors I had witnessed. A shout from manifold throats rose behind us as we made our escape.

This was not my first escape in recent times. As I ran hand in hand with the girl, my mind swam back to Sturges. Had he known what fate awaited him the night we escaped from the Lady Armitage?

☆

Sturges and I had decided to escape as soon as the *Lady Armitage* entered Nan Madol's lagoon. The night before, I grabbed a canvas bag and stowed in it what supplies I could. At dead of night, we climbed overboard and took the dinghy towards the shore. Someone on board raised the alarm. They fired on us, shots ringing out over the open waters. We were sitting ducks in the dinghy.

"Dive!" I called out to Sturges. We were a long way from shore, but we leapt into sea, and struck out hard. The water was not cold, but the distance was long. Nearing shore, I could tell Sturges was as exhausted as I was. I scrambled out of the water, onto an exposed rockshelf, shivering on the edge, then reached down to help the dripping Sturges from the pounding surf. The wind's stinging fingers struck ice into my veins. I remember little else. Memories of wide, cold ocean splashing up against the shores— pools of water topped with slippery algae scum—wind buffeting— then merciful unconsciousness as we dragged ourselves to the treeline and collapsed.

When we awoke, we found ourselves on mountainous Ponape. From our position on the coast, we could see numerous volcanic peaks dominating the island.

"The name Pohnpei translates as *upon a stone altar*," said Sturges. "I don't understand what it means, but that's how it translates."

We looked around. Dense forests surrounded the lagoon, within which the *Lady Armitage* lay at anchor. The coastline consisted of unending reefs and inlets. One spectacular outcropping was a place Sturges pointed out to me as Sokehs Rock. It was a sheer basalt cliff face—the boldest natural landmark, rising 500 feet.

"You get tidal flats and mangrove swamps on the coast," said Sturges. "The interior is more treacherous—it's filled with hidden brooks, snaking rivers, and secret valleys."

I agreed with him that we didn't want to venture into the interior rainforest. The moss-covered trees and abundant rainfall there would make it difficult to reach and harder to get out of.

One morning we stole an outrigger canoe from the beach, and hid it in the forest on the point at Metalanim Harbour. To my puzzled queries, Sturges replied: "Insurance."

"We have to watch out," he added. "They don't like Westerners here. If the ship's crew doesn't get us, the locals will. In 1854 the whaler *Delta* brought smallpox. An outbreak of sores followed the fever. I saw the aftermath—hundreds of natives groaning and dying through the breadfruit groves. People, some alive, were buried in shallow graves. Sometimes those buried alive returned to their families clad in their burial clothes. Over half the island's population died, including many chiefs. The epidemic abated, but they blame the Westerners—if they catch us, we're dead meat."

"That was only nine years ago!" I exclaimed.

Seeing the look on my face, he added, with his bitter laugh: "Oh, it's quite safe now."

We climbed a rise, where from a bare stone ledge we could see down to a local village: huts made of mangrove wood, thatch, rope and bamboo, all painted in contrasting colours. Most backed onto pens of squealing pigs. Baskets spilling bananas and yams sat outside some of the thatched huts.

A dark-skinned fellow worked on an outrigger canoe model. I could see on the ground next to him models of manta rays that he'd carved from ivory-palm nut.

"Clever people. They use hand-twisted coconut sennit rope to tie the beams. See how the wood pillars are set on stones up off the ground."

"They seem really peaceful," I said. Boys in loincloths played with dogs that ran about the paths, which were lined with moss-covered stone walls. "But you don't trust them?" I asked him, as dark-furred fruit bats circled overhead, and screeched towards the treetops.

"Keep your head down," he flinched. "Not at all. They have their sinister and fanatical side. Let's hope we don't find out about it." He looked away into the distance. His eyes saw unbidden memories and his jaw set tight.

Bare-breasted women wearing hibiscus skirts did laundry in the streams. Young children ran laughing and naked in the heat. Men walked about, occasionally spitting a squirt of chewed betel-nut. Some were adorned with brightly coloured trochus-shell necklaces and beads. Many seemed heavily tattooed, on the arms and legs, with complex cross-hatched patterns. Some of the women were tattooing their men as we watched. The design that recurred most often depicted a writhing creature with a tentacled head.

"And what about the tattoos?" I asked.

Sturges shrugged. "The *pelipel*? These people wear history on their bodies. Clan histories and great island events show up in them. They see the ability to endure pain as honourable. They take 'em to an isolated hut. For up to a month, the person being tattooed withstands the ordeal of having elaborate patterns etched into their skin with an ink-dipped thorn. Colourful, aren't they?"

The women were also tattooed, largely around the thighs and buttocks, though Sturges told me they were often also tattooed around their genital regions. I grimaced.

"You think that's bad," he said. "Another male rite of passage is the *lekilek*—the castration of the left testicle." He laughed at my obvious discomfort.

Sturges pointed back to the forest, and we returned to our camp-cum-hiding place. Just as were making our way into the trees, I turned around, and spied a Pohnpeian woman, one of the most beautiful island girls I'd seen, staring after me with eyes like the dark moon.

A red orchid was in her hair, and her brown skin glistened. For a moment I stood stock still, terrified to have been spotted. But she smiled shyly, inclining her head in a way that signaled me to keep going. Perhaps she had seen something about me she liked. I continued under cover of the trees, and saw her return to work, weaving her net, saying nothing to those around her.

Sturges and I hid in the forests for two weeks. Bored with eating breadfruit and fresh mangoes, we made our way to the beach, and caught fresh fish in the lagoon's shallow waters.

Back at our camp, Sturges told me another Pohnpei story he considered important.

"Eight years ago," he said, "in July 1855, a dense, smoky haze surrounded the island, and the sun and moon glowed red. The *sanworos* (priests) got upset. They thought it the work of Isohkelekel, displeased over the people's failure to perform *karismei*, the breadfruit season offering. They immediately made feasts to his principal priestess. Soon afterward, the Red Haze disappeared. It was around that time I was taken captive. I nearly lost my life then. Something's brewing again now." He looked worried, and wouldn't say more. But that night the dark sky was tinged with red.

We were, I learned, in the Madolenihmw district near Nan Madol. I enjoyed watching the people from afar. One day I could smell the Pohnpeians preparing *sakau*, a potent narcotic brew like kava. They had taken pepper plant roots and were pounding them upon huge basaltic stones made from rounded river rocks. The men would then squeeze the *sakau* through some inner bark of the tropical hibiscus, which contributed a viscous sap to the *sakau*.

An atmosphere of anticipation began to build amongst the people. Sturges recognised it as ominous preparations for a major ritual. The people held a canoe-building competition, feasting, singing, dancing and *sakau* drinking over a number of days. Gradually they worked themselves into a state of frenzy. We saw them drink the *sakau* from coconut shells, passing it around communally.

Meanwhile, I felt my obsession to see Nan Madol growing.

Eventually, we crossed from the jungle to the tidal flats of hilly Temwen Island, where we beheld Nan Madol. Mysterious megalithic ruins of ancient walls ... dykes ... columns ... Cyclopean stoneworks ... all built of black basalt rock. The Venice of the Pacific!

☆

The island girl and I fled that poison temple of madness through a secret exit known to her, running for our lives across the outer precincts. Why did it seem that the stones were oddly angled beneath our feet, the endless vistas of rock seeming phantasmally variable and prismatically distorted?

The girl took me to the islet's edge. Behind us were a thousand angry Pohnpeians and a raging Old One, an aeons-old immensity that lumbered and floundered after us.

We had one advantage as it would take Zoth-Ommog some time to find a way out of the temple. The black-haired girl guided me skilfully through the twisting waterway; without her I wouldn't have had a chance. I rowed the canoe back through the canals.

She pressed into my hand a flintlock musket; it must have been the one Janssen had dropped. It would be no use against Zoth-Ommog's might, but perhaps it would help me somehow.

The moon shone fitfully down over the scene. Behind us, a thunderous crashing told us Zoth-Ommog had broken out through the temple wall. I felt a pulsing of alien thought pressing on my mind, threatening to overtake it. The star-spawn was using its telepathic powers to try and sway me, but it was not close enough. It wouldn't take long to catch us, though.

Leaping off the canoe and back onto the fringing beach, we ran for the shelter of the coconut palms. The ground trembled beneath our feet. Looking back over one shoulder I saw It through the haze—a cloudy impression of great wings, of writhing head tentacles, and a face only an Old One's mother could love.

The grotesque monstrosity came on after us, its outspread starfish arms clawing at the midnight sky. With a few strides it crossed from Ihded islet to the very shore where we had stood scant moments before. We scrambled forward through the jungle, over rocks and fallen trees. Our one hope lay in the dark, and in the Red Haze, which now lay low above the ground. From Zoth-Ommog's height, we puny humans would seem the merest insects.

Zoth-Ommog's misshapen head turned to sight us. Its stupendous legs crashed on the ground. Trees splintered and fell before It as It entered the forest in search of us. The girl cast terrified glances behind, but I tried to urge her forward.

Thank God Sturges and I had stowed that spare outrigger canoe around on the point of Metalanim Harbour. If we could just reach it and get off the island!

I didn't think Zoth-Ommog could stray far from his lair, for I had seen the graven seals on the rocks around Nan Madol, and now I knew what they were. They were the ancient seals and signs of the Elder Ones, the immemorial gods who had imprisoned Zoth-Ommog here in the South Pacific. The return of the Red Haze had allowed the Old One to rise, but we still had a chance. We must get out to sea!

As we continued to stumble through the jungle, my thoughts returned again to Nan Douwas, to all that had led us here.

☆

Sturges and I descended from Temwen island. There they were—ninety-two islets made by human hands, across eighteen square kilometres, covered with liana and mangrove. I could see that in places the fast-growing tropical trees, underbrush and vines were starting to destroy the ancient stonework.

We descended the rock footpath through scattered ruins to the reef. Nearest us was Nan Douwas, Nan Madol's largest structure. Some of the corner stones here might weigh fifty tons, I thought. The islets were connected by a network of waterways.

Sturges continued to lecture me. "At its height, Nan Madol was a vast capital. It supported more than a thousand people—Ponape's ancient elite chiefs (the *Saus*) and their servants—on the islets alone," he said, gesturing around us.

I was stunned. This was a city built by people as sophisticated as the ancient Egyptians.

He shrugged. "Let's get cracking. We can approach by canoe and move along the central lagoon that leads through Madol Pah."

Numerous outrigger canoes were pulled up along the stony beach near the entrance to the canals. We commandeered one. The high tide enabled our small transport to navigate the grid of twisting mangrove-choked waterways that wound through the complex. The place must have been vast in its day. Some of the stone walls towered as high as fifty feet above our heads.

Looking over the canoe's side, I glimpsed variegated coral beneath crystal clear waters. Passing jungle-covered islets on both sides, we caught glimpses of Nan Douwas' southwest corner through the lianas and trees.

With Sturges steering the canoe, we maneuvered and slowed, sliding up beside the west front's main entry landing. I gazed in wonder at the magnificence of Nan Douwas' west facade—the stately podium, the noble entryway, and the steps ascending to interior courts, enclosures and tombs. Enclosing walls surrounded the huge crypts.

"How did they do it?" I sat in the canoe, staring awestruck.

"One legend claims the brothers had magical powers, and the basalt blocks were brought from nearby Sokehs and made to fly through the air, settling down in the right positions to form Nan Madol."

The prevailing northeasterly ocean breezes ruffled our hair as we continued gazing up at Nan Douwas.

"How do *you* think they did it?" I asked. "Did this black magic have anything to do with it?"

Sturges shook his head. "I don't believe so. There's yet another—more credible—theory, that the prisms were dislodged by large fires built at their bases. The stones were rapidly cooled and fractured by the seawater, then placed on rafts and floated within the fringing coral reefs to the building site.

"Not all the stones reached their intended destinations," he added. He gestured to the coastal lagoon's bottom, where I could see long blocks lying on coral and sand. Some appeared to have mysterious carvings, like signs or seals engraved on them. The sunken blocks suggested coral-encrusted formations in the deep, and I thought again of the book, with its suggestion that a vast sunken city underlay Nan Madol.

Sturges shrugged again. "They may also have used levers, maybe inclined coconut-palm planes. They would have made strong hibiscus fibre ropes. Moving megaliths was definitely within their capabilities. They're a smart people, even if I don't trust 'em."

"What's the area to the northeast?"

"That's Madol Powe. It's the upper town, the ritual and mortuary sector. They built major tombs there—the biggest is a central stepped tomb. It's where the *Saus* lived. Nan Madol is divided into two main areas. To the southwest is the lower town, known as Madol Pah. It used to be the administrative sector—the royal dwellings and ceremonial areas."

A cycle of whispered legends clustered around the practices of the ancient peoples who had built and worshipped here, averred Sturges. Some of the legends centred on Zoth-Ommog, a being of the Old Ones, who had been spawned near the double star Xoth. He was the eldritch progeny of Great Cthulhu and the female being known as Idh-yaa.

"So why is it called Nan Madol?"

Sturges needed no encouragement to display his knowledge. "'Nan' meant place, and 'Madol' was Ponapean for 'between places', so Nan Madol meant 'space between' or 'the place between places'."

I could see that 'space between' could be a reference to the canals that intersected the islets. But it didn't seem to be a full explanation. What could that phrase possibly mean?

"Is that all?" I pressed him.

"Well, the Sadeleurs originally called it *Soun Nanleng*, which means 'Reef of Heaven'. But they renamed it when the Old Ones trickled down from the stars. I think it's a reference to the Old Ones' rulership of the city. I once saw a copy of Abdul Alhazred's *Necronomicon*. There's a passage I know by heart."

His gaze became distant as he recited. *"The Old Ones were, the Old Ones are, and the Old Ones shall be. Not in the spaces we know, but between them, They walk serene and primal, undimensioned and to us unseen ... They walk unseen and foul in lonely places where the Words have been spoken and the Rites howled through at their Seasons. The wind gibbers with their voices, and the earth mutters with their consciousness ... The ice desert of the South and the sunken isles of Ocean hold stones whereon their seal is engraven, but who hath seen the deep frozen city or the sealed tower long garlanded with seaweed and barnacles? ... They wait patient and potent, for here shall They reign again ..."* Sturges stared at me, challenging me to call him crazy.

"Not in the spaces we know, but between them!" I thought of the seals on the sunken rocks—*"... the sunken Isles of Ocean hold stones whereon their seal is engraven."* Despite my reluctance to believe Sturges' more outlandish ramblings about the Old Ones, the evidence seemed to be piling up in their favour. We clambered out of the canoe and onto the islet.

We hadn't gone more than a few steps onto the rocky platform when out of the shadows came a party of Pohnpeians, armed with slings and stone adzes. We were captured!

They took us, struggling and cursing, to the main Pah Kadira islet. The whole temple complex seemed ominously desolate under the moon's dim glow. We were thrust into a bamboo cage, and locked in. It was an uncomfortable night, and I dreaded what was to come.

Next day, the tribe assembled. From our bamboo prison we saw them bring forth a great turtle, which they anointed with coconut oil and hung with ornaments. The chief priest killed the turtle with a blow from a club, breaking its shell. The men cut it up, cooked it, and served it to the priests, with muttered prayers and ritual.

"It's a *kamatihp,* a feasting ceremony," said Sturges. The men seemed to forget about us. For the feast, they killed and ate a dog, and served giant quarter-ton yams. Native women arrived in canoes, and the Pohnpeians worked themselves into an orgiastic frenzy. They fell to having sex, openly fornicating and continuing the feasting.

The natives' wild ceremonies were now building to a crescendo. Next, the priests made an offering of cooked turtle innards to Nan Sanwohl. During this bizarre ancient ritual, the natives loudly chanted "Zatomaga! Zatomaga!" and "Nan Sanwhol!" The latter was the name of the Sacred Eel, also known as 'the Thing That Lies in Wait'.

"The *Saus* take this very seriously," said Sturges.

After a fortnight of near starvation, we were taken into the vast main temple, its stacked prismatic walls glittering darkly. A low monotonous chanting greeted us—voices raised in dark praise. Two tattooed Pohnpeian acolytes dragged us forward and bound us to a stump of upright rock with hibiscus-fibre ropes that chafed our wrists. I knew this must be the place Churchward wrote of as being mined by cellars and crypts, for the temple's inside was shaped like a vast pyramid.

In the temple's central precinct was a huge dark pool, surrounded on all sides by tattooed Pohnpeians wearing beads and other ornaments. It seemed human sacrifice was to be the culmination of the ceremonies.

The Sau chief picked up a large, bound volume, and began to intone some incantation from its pages. I recognised it from its palm-leaf pages as a copy of the fabled *Ponape Scriptures.*

There now lay revealed a horror that threatened to overwhelm us. What Stygian depths yawned beyond the frightful pool we shall never know, though I suspect some accursed infinity of lightless pits led down towards the ocean's nethermost reaches. God knows what unhallowed elder worlds exist in those ghastly caverns of inner earth.

Next to the pool, on the square basalt cobble paving, tottered aeon-old mounds of broken turtle shells, where the Pohnpeians had cast the remains of the food they fed to the Thing That Lies in Wait. The shells seemed mixed with more sinister remains. From where I stood they appeared to be human bones.

Beside us were chained several of the local women, like us, potential sacrifices. Beside them were chained the captain, the first mate and the bosun of the *Lady Armitage.* Evidently they had been careless enough to be caught while trying to track us and take us back to the ship.

Now they were in deep trouble. They cast around in panic, struggling against their bonds, or stared at their feet, awaiting their desperate fate.

The Pohnpeians tethered Sturges at one end of the line of native prisoners, and me at the other. I looked helplessly at the faces of Janssen, Jacobs and Metcalf. They seemed to sense death was near, but they could hardly have anticipated its nature.

One of the Pohnpeians brought forth, with great ceremony, a turtle-shell bowl containing a pale blue transparent sea creature. I could see it had tens of long straggling tentacles and guessed it was a deadly sea wasp or box jellyfish, its tentacles armed with thousands of stinging cells. The man picked it up with an instrument resembling wooden tongs.

The chanting from the assembled Pohnpeians grew louder and more intense as the native took the jellyfish, its long tentacles dripping with brine, and walked the length of the line, stopping finally before Jacobs. Jacobs screamed as the man thrust the jellyfish at his face. The thing wrapped itself around his head.

I knew as the venom went into his face that the attack on his nerves and heart was immediate. Someone called his name but I doubt he heard it; the pain must have been excruciating. I could see the thing's tentacles were becoming sticky and adhering to his flesh. He clawed at his face, trying to pull the creature off, but the tentacles started to rip away portions of flesh, leaving his face bloody. In a few moments he went into toxic shock and, no longer able to breathe, contorted, fell to the ground, writhed for a few moments, and then lay still.

The natives picked up his body and threw it onto a raised basalt platform at the edge of the pool. I recognised this with a shudder as a *pei*, a stone altar of incredible antiquity—*perhaps the very stone altar that gave this island its name.*

There came a stirring in the black water at the pool's centre. A ripple of dirty foam signaled something alive in the pool.

The eel was not simply gigantic. It was stupendous, titan, horrifyingly enormous. Most of its gargantuan bulk lay submerged in the pool's brackish water, but its vast head and upper body gave a clue to the ghastly enormity of the whole. We stood horror-struck. It was a gigantic Viper Moray, its immensely strong curving jaw and rows of needle-sharp, pointed teeth on view as its maw gaped ravenously.

I threw a glance back at the line of native women prisoners. The *Sau*'s men were bringing forth more turtle-shell bowls, each containing a deadly box jellyfish, which they started placing over the faces of the helpless women. Each in turn writhed, screaming in agony as the poison took effect, and then fell in death throes.

I knew it was only moments until I met the same fate. I looked back at the pool, with its hideous oceanic denizen. The creature's disgusting body smelled half-rotten—with leathery skin covered in hideous purple-brown blotches. It was a creature that ought not to exist in this world. Had it come from the incredible deeps of the Mariana Trench? It could have lain here in the dark for thousands of years, being worshipped and fed by the Pohnpeians.

Suddenly, it reared up, snapping its massive head in our direction. The few prisoners still alive reared back in panic as it slithered mountainously out of the pond toward where we were tethered. If the smaller eels could take off fingers or toes, this massive creature could undoubtedly bite our heads clean through, or chew us in half.

The thing came onward, its slavering jaws exuding the foulest stench imaginable. The Pohnpeians waved their spears and chanted. The beast's thick, leathery skin was proof against any weapon. Of course, we had no defence. The high priest intoned a passage from the *Ponape Scriptures*, as the assembled Pohnpeians bowed in supplication before the creature.

Sturges was unable to dodge the thing, which lowered its great ugly head toward him. He screamed. Razor-sharp teeth sank deep into his flesh. The rope binding him broke, but he was now lodged in the filthy thing's massive jaws. It tossed its head this way and that as it savaged him. Blood spurted from Sturges' neck and chest. His arms still flailed, but his chest had been pierced by the needle-like teeth, and the Thing Which Lies in Wait smashed Sturges' body upon the stone altar of the podium.

His skull cracked loudly as the body slammed into the rock. His attacker started rending him limb from limb, chewing the human flesh bones and all, and within a few minutes what remained of Sturges had been chewed and gouged into an unrecognisable state.

I closed my eyes. Through gaps in the temple walls, I could hear and see great crested terns and frigate birds wheeling overhead, crying like banshee children. More than that—I could see the sky had become a Red Haze. It was the time of Zoth-Ommog!

☆

Zoth-Ommog was catching us up. The closer It came to us, crashing through the trees behind us, the more strongly I could feel the intensity of Its alien thought-forms. My head swam with visions of strange geometric cities. As we came out on the sand and continued our desperate rush for the canoe, our last hope of safety, the girl fell beside me, clutching her head.

Surely she saw the same things I saw—incredible inclined planes and walkways, vast alien cities of abnormal and un-imaginably non-anthropomorphic construction, beneath iridescent skies filled with triple crimson suns, and far-flung gaseous nebulae of unguessed-at cosmic alienage.

I pull her to her feet. "We have to keep going!" I shouted at her. She couldn't speak my language, but maybe the sound of my voice would get through to her. "Snap out of it!"

She shook her head, trying to free herself of Zoth-Ommog's intrusions.

We stumbled across the moon-litten beach, wisps of the Red Haze drifting around our heads. Just the other side of this distinctively shaped rock was where Sturges and I had hidden the canoe. I scrambled to a halt, clutching my companion in shock. The canoe was gone!

Zoth-Ommog appeared hugely above the trees. His enormous wings flapped thunderously against the still-present Red Haze. The Haze was blocking his senses somewhat, but his head-tentacles wavered in search of us.

I cast around for the canoe, hoping against hope. There it was! The very tip of a prow was jutting out from beneath a pile of fronds Sturges had used as camouflage. He must have covered it up with palm-fronds while I searched for fresh water.

The girl pulled me forward, for she too had spotted the canoe. We threw off the palm fronds and pushed the vessel the short distance down the beach to the water's edge, where we forced it through the shallows. Leaping in, we began to paddle it into deeper water.

Zoth-Ommog, silhouetted gigantically against the moon, advanced implacably onward. Trees fractured like matchwood as It stomped onto the beach, sending up an earsplitting howl that echoed out for miles over the darkened waters.

We looked back as we continued to paddle our hardest. The outgoing tide was with us, and the outrigger, built by the natives for fast travel, cut swiftly through the waves, making good time. But would it be fast enough?

Zoth-Ommog was now at the water's edge. It waded in, sending up great plumes of spray, displacing tons of water as it ponderously crashed forward into the ocean. It continued striding colossally after us. I could not believe we would escape it. My heartbeat thumped in my ears. The distance between the creature and us began to diminish by the moment. The girl screamed, her dark eyes flashing.

"Keep paddling!" I yelled.

Zoth-Ommog let out a howl of triumph as It lashed one of Its starfish arms into the ocean beside us, causing our tiny craft to rock uncontrollably.

We were prepared to be crushed, dismembered by the almighty Old One, when its roar changed timbre. A plaintive note of anger had crept in—then one of terror, as it lashed its head tentacles in frustration.

A stone column, barnacled and dripping with weed, was rising slowly from the ocean surface. As the girl righted our canoe, I peered down through the waves and from the seabed came another, then another, rising like dripping sentinels, forming a ring barrier between the gigantic monstrosity and our vessel. They were *the seal-engraven columns of the underwater city, long set in place by the Elder Gods to protect humankind, setting a boundary that Zoth-Ommog could not cross.*

The monster flailed helplessly as our canoe continued out to sea. Later we would head for Yap or another island whence we could return to civilisation. For now it was enough that we had escaped.

The last we saw of Zoth-Ommog was Its mountainous form surrounded by the fading Red Haze, covering its hideous head with its tentacles as it averted its face from the aeons-old seals of the Elder Gods—and retreating back to land.

☆

My companion's name was Lipahnmei. She remained my devoted friend through all that followed, travelling with me, working for our passage back to Sydney, sharing in adventures comparatively mundane. Lipahnmei learned to speak English quickly but sadly no children came to bless our marriage bed. Perhaps the trauma of that night had taken something of the life from both of us, for I always dreaded Zoth-Ommog's return.

We both remained troubled by the memories of the Old One. One day I found her tattooing herself on the thigh with the seal of the Elder Gods, a final, desperate attempt to stave off the madness that seemed destined to overtake us. She died last year, of natural causes. Now I lie alone at night without her strong arms to hold me in the dark.

Of late, a strange red haze has been reported drifting about some of the South Pacific islands. I do not care to live on a planet where alien monsters may yet be liberated, and rule again over a puny and defenceless humankind.

Here, on my desk, is the flintlock musket given to me by my wife, and with its aid I shall, tonight, bring an end to the horrors I have known and can no longer stand.

PATIENT X

KIEL STUART

Kouichi Minnamino bit his lip, gazing anxiously at the unconscious girl. Patient X. Her chest heaved, and her skin glittered with perspiration.

The terrible noises outside raged on, but he could not tear his gaze from her. *How could she?* he wondered. *How?* Delicate, upslanting features, blue-green hair waving back from her face like wings.

It wasn't the hair colour; kids parading the Ginza strip wore far more outlandish hues, though they did not dye their brows and lashes to match as this one had. No, it was the state in which she'd been found that was beyond Kouichi's understanding.

Dr Nakajima tapped Kouichi's shoulder, jolting the young man from his reverie.

"Kouichi-kun, why don't you have her ready?"

"Sensei, notice her skin—" Seeing the doctor's scowl, Kouichi stopped short. Her skin seemed opalescent, beyond the sheen of sweat, but now was not the time or place for flights of fancy. "Is the chopper on the way?"

"Don't know." Dr Nakajima raised his voice to compete with the roar of distant aircraft. Thick and muscular like a bulldog, stubborn, demanding, Sensei was one big scowl today. "Couldn't raise it."

The girl whimpered. Did she realise the horrors unfolding around her? "If the chopper's not coming—"

The doctor snorted. "I called ahead to the hospital. Hate to take her out by car, but it can't wait. Not with all this."

Kouichi nodded. The hospital lay upland, close to where his mother lived. It made sense to travel away from the harbour. "But, Sensei, her skin—"

"I'll bring the Jeep," interrupted Nakajima. "Can you manage to strap her to a gurney without breaking either one?"

Kouichi snapped to attention. "Y-yes, Sensei."

The doctor left him alone with the girl. In his mind, he had named her Hikaru, *the shining one.*

As he wheeled the gurney near, Kouichi realised that if he

dwelt on what was taking place down below, in the Seto-Nakai, he would be overwhelmed.

On a late-summer eve such as this, the inland sea should be alive with commerce—fishing boats, an oil refinery, tourists. Not alive with fighter jets defending against an attack.

The trick was to keep his thoughts at an angle. He was good at it by now.

Carefully, he reached for water to dab the girl's brow. There was a glass on her bedside table, a spoon beside it. As he shook open a sterile cloth, the glass trembled. Kouichi stopped in mid-action. Not an earthquake, not now!

Perhaps it was just a sonic boom.

Quickly, or Sensei would be furious. Kouichi slid one arm under the girl's narrow shoulders, another under her knees. They had determined there were no broken bones; they simply could not discover nor treat the cause of her raging fever.

Fukai Mori was a small clinic, no more than a way-station tucked into the tree-shagged hills around the Inland Sea. The gum-cracking chopper pilot (who insisted on being called Buckaroo Kansai) was a friend of Kouichi's. Buckaroo ferried the more serious cases to the hospital, and they were far more likely to be presented with some careless hiker who'd gotten a twisted ankle than a strange girl with a mysterious fever. Sensei had consulted specialists about the girl. They all said the same thing: bring her in.

Kouichi slid the girl, hot and rag-limp, onto the gurney. She mewed. "Shh," he crooned. He must not think of the curve of her neck, of her soft little hands.

Then a flash of light at the bedside claimed his attention. Kouichi watched, astounded, as something quite impossible took place.

Outside, jets zoomed past on their way to do battle. Sirens wailed. He scarcely heard, rapt with what he was seeing. A strange almost-music pierced the air. It did not take much time. One second, two, three. Then it was over, and his hand darted out to seize the impossible.

Dr Nakajima burst in. "Aren't you done with her yet?"

"Sorry, Sensei. I was—" Seeing the thundercloud look on Nakajima's face, Kouichi quickly secured the girl.

"The Jeep's running," said Nakajima. "Don't drop her."

"No, Sensei." Kouichi helped steer the gurney to the car.

This was a big American model, with left-hand drive, and Sensei was as proud of it as Buckaroo Kansai was of his daredevil piloting. Kouichi settled into the back of the Jeep, wondering again how this frail creature could have allowed herself to reach such a shocking state.

Nakajima gunned the motor. "We'll be safe once we reach the hospital." The Jeep's headlights stabbed a path along the narrow road as they climbed toward the hospital.

"I saw something," began Kouichi. "Back in the room—" A sonic boom killed his words, and he steadied the girl. *How can she burn so and still live?* None of the usual methods of reducing fevers had worked. They had dosed her with aspirin, splashed her with alcohol and ice, but the fever raged.

Dr Nakajima turned on the radio. A shriek of static, then it cleared: "—sending blasts of flame throughout the harbour—" Static rose again, almost drowning the scream of jets. "— battling the monster, but Mahou Aku appears unaffected—"

Nakajima turned off the radio.

"He is beautiful," said Kouichi.

"Eh?"

"Mahou Aku. When I saw him on television."

"What a crazy thing to say!"

Kouichi did not respond. All glitter and dash was the monster, the shape of his flames like a calligraphy of music. For as long as he could remember, Kouichi had been in love with music. As a little boy, he'd hummed the mournful strains of traditional Enka. Sang on street corners with friends at school. Even now wrote snatches of music whenever possible.

But real musicians played full-time. They did not work for irascible doctors.

The girl mewled again. A blushing young couple had brought her to Fukai Mori, wrapped in a rain poncho. They were hiking, they said, and found her on a rock, unconscious, without a stitch of clothing.

"Hold on!" bellowed Nakajima. Kouichi flung himself over the girl. A tremendous crash rocked the car; brakes squealed.

"All right back there?" asked the doctor.

"*Daijoubu.*" Kouichi glanced out. Inches away from the car, a boulder blocked the road.

"It fell," said the doctor, shaken. "Barely missed us."

The boulder was glimmering, but the gleam faded even as Kouichi stared. Nakajima put the car back into gear.

It was slow work, inching up the steep, tree-furred shoulder to get around the boulder. Kouichi's shoulders cramped with the need to hurry. "Almost there," he whispered to the girl, reaching to check her forehead.

Then, she simply sat up.

But I did strap her to the gurney!

The gown slipped from her shoulders. She was like a pearl all over. Blushing, Kouichi pulled the gown up to cover her.

The girl gazed into his eyes. Hers were a deep garnet. Then she opened her little mouth and began to flute.

"Sensei!" he cried.

Dr Nakajima braked, hard. "What?"

"Listen." The girl fluted once more, shrill and urgent.

The doctor scowled. "What language is that?"

Kouichi shook his head. It wasn't English, nor Chinese, nor

Korean. "French?" he suggested.

"French! You're crazy. She's got a high fever, she's gibbering. Why have you got her sitting up in the first place?"

The girl's mouth moved, silently. Then, slowly, in heavily accented Japanese, she said, "Take me back!"

Kouichi and the doctor exchanged startled glances.

"Take me back!" she repeated.

"She's too ill," said Nakajima, as if the girl wasn't there, then added, "You just lie down and we'll soon be safe."

"From what?" she asked.

Nakajima hesitated. "From the monster in the harbour. But don't you be afraid. We'll soon get you out of here."

The girl did not seem frightened. "Monster?"

"Mahou Aku," said Kouichi. "It's burning up the harbour front."

She stared out the window, twisting her head to follow the dim glow of the treetops. With a piercing cry she fell back.

"It's okay," soothed Kouichi. "We're almost there."

"Pyroglyphics," she whispered. "Calling me."

But as Kouichi settled her back down, the straps slid away and the girl struggled upright.

Kouichi thought of the thing he had seen in the clinic. Of the boulder crashing down. Now the straps.

"Sensei," he cried. "Please! Stop the car!"

"What is it now?" Nakajima again stamped on the brake.

"The boulder. What I saw in the room."

"Now you're the one babbling. Of course, you seldom make sense in the best of times."

"Sensei, something occurred when the girl was crying in her sleep. The spoon—" Kouichi gulped down his nerves. "I think we have a case of psychokinesis."

"Kouichi-kun, what is this nonsense?"

"Within hours of the girl's arrival, the monster attacked."

Dr Nakajima's eyes narrowed. "And you accuse this sick child of having something to do with it?"

"Back at the way-station, a spoon, an ordinary spoon, under my very eyes, emitted a faint glow. And then it began to bend."

"You were distraught—"

"I saw what I saw." Kouichi reached into his pocket and withdrew the bent spoon; it looked like a large silvered hairpin. "I brought it with me."

Dr N stared at the inert spoon. "It got bent in your pocket. You know how careless you can be."

Kouichi lowered his head. His cheeks burned.

"No," said the girl, "Only watch." She mewled again. A faint hum, just below conscious hearing, filled the car. The music pierced Kouichi like a lost dream.

The spoon began to glow, as if tickled by moonlight. Then all the hum and quiver in the air flew to the spoon, making it tremble.

For a moment the spoon was in agony, and Kouichi burned along with it, but then the struggle passed. The spoon flowed, smooth as liquid, and slowly straightened out.

Nakajima glared as if the spoon had personally offended him.

"You see for yourself. And now you must take me back."

"Young lady," said Nakajima. "I cannot. I will not. Our only hope is to flee."

"The planes will have no effect. These fires in the sky—I know their meaning."

Kouichi burst out, "Their shape reminds me of musical notation. The monster communicates with fire, doesn't it?"

Nakajima waved an impatient hand. "More nonsense on your part."

But the girl held Kouichi's gaze steady. "He is calling me."

Nakajima said, "No more of this pointless bickering. You really must get to the hospital."

She lowered her head. "Then you condemn me to death."

Kouichi cast a helpless glance at the doctor.

"And why is that, child?" sighed Nakajima.

"Your planet is poisoning me."

"Our *planet*?"

"The one destroying your world is my partner. If you want to save your city, take me back."

"Back where?"

She slanted an odd look at Kouichi. "I am not from Earth."

Nakajima took an audible breath.

It made a crazy sort of sense. Kouichi whispered, "So that's your real hair colour. No wonder the brows and lashes match."

"Something in your atmosphere sickens me," she continued. "I made a hard landing. Mahou— that is, my partner—looks for me, and will not stop, under any circumstances."

Nakajima peppered her with questions, but she shook her head. "I have said too much already. But something is wrong. I should have been able to call Mahou from here. I can't. I will have to get closer. There is no choice."

"Sensei," pleaded Kouichi. "*I* believe her."

"Planes ..." rasped the girl. "Call them off!"

Grumbling, Nakajima put the car in reverse. "This is crazy. Running *toward* a monster."

By the time they reached the way station, the alien girl was so weak they had to carry her. Kouichi sat at her bedside, and the doctor went to try the land lines, leaving them alone.

I don't want her to go, Kouichi thought, *but she must.*

She gripped his hand. "Help me up," she said. Kouichi gulped down his nerves. For modesty's sake, he slipped off his jacket and buttoned it round her shoulders.

She gave him a tiny curl of a smile, making him wonder what her lips would taste like. Quickly averting his gaze, he said, "You learned our language from listening to me and Sensei exchange a few sentences?"

"I'm a quick study." She gave him another little smile. Then the lights flickered, and went out. She pressed close to him. She smelled of vanilla.

Kouichi's pulse raced. *She'll feel my heart.*

The girl's voice was muffled against his chest. "They won't be able to stop him," she said. "And he will not stop until he finds me. Dead or alive."

He wanted to tighten his arms around her. "Then I will see that he finds you alive."

Dr Nakajima stormed into the room. The private moment shattered, Kouichi eased the girl into a chair.

"I think I might have gotten through to someone in charge," said Nakajima. "But the static—"

"Sensei, the Army won't believe me," said Kouichi. "But they'll believe *you.* You can keep trying to get through. This one will die unless she reaches the monster. Let me take the Jeep and drive her down."

The doctor shook his head.

"Sensei, you'll be safe enough here for the moment."

"It's not my own safety that concerns me."

"If we don't succeed in uniting the girl with Mahou Aku, nowhere will be safe—for anyone."

Dr Nakajima glared. Sweat beaded Kouichi's lip. At last Nakajima growled, and thrust his keys at Kouichi. "I am warning you, boy," he said, "don't even scratch the paint."

They helped the girl into the car, and Kouichi focused all his attention on driving. The faint tremble of the wheel under his hands, the spear of headlights marking the way, the thrum of tyres on the road, smells of gasoline and motor oil.

Gasoline. Motor oil. With a painful jolt, he remembered. *The oil refinery!* Kurashiki's oil refinery at Mizushima. If the monster's flames should hit there, or a plane should crash—

He jerked the wheel hard, and hurtled offroad down a narrow path, meant only for foot traffic.

There was a cliff overlooking the harbour, more than big enough for a car. He streaked over the path. Trees flew past, scraping the doors. Pebbles flew up. The car bucked. Kouichi fought like an angel, the Jeep fishtailing, trees leaping in front of them. He wrestled the car to a smoking halt, heart loud in his throat. "Are you hurt?"

She shook her head.

He got out and surveyed the damage. Bad enough.

Yet they had stopped just past the trees, in plain sight of the harbour. "Will the monster be able to find you from here?"

"I don't know." He helped her from the car and they picked their way to the cliff's edge. She leaned out, crying into the air.

Below was the monster. The one the media had dubbed Evil

Magic—Mahou Aku. It hung in the sky, weightless for all its bulk. Its head ranged back and forth, spouting flames.

The fighter jets seemed like flies against it. Long segmented body, pale glittery blue, a dragonfly delicacy darting on translucent double wings. Its head was a dinosaur's with a glowing mane, and two useless little T-Rex hands dangling down.

But then it turned, and there was the startlement of enormous, jewel-faceted eyes. That was when Kouichi could no longer think of the monster as "it."

Even from such a distance, even through the gathering dusk, Kouichi was stricken with the force of Mahou Aku's intelligence. There was more: a sense of duty, of concern for the girl. All in a moment, Kouichi and the monster had a commonality.

Fanged jaws opened. A curling blossom of white fire rose. The jets peeled away, then came together to attack once more.

Kouichi's heartbeat slowed. He felt himself diving towards a dream, drowsy, heavy-eyed, hypnotised by the monster's beauty.

Mahou Aku was moving up the coastline. The oil refinery—

The alien girl cupped her hands to her mouth and cried out. The effort cost her, and she crumpled against him, a burning feather in his arms.

From her pearly skin rose gemdrops of vanilla-smelling sweat. *I am here, I am here*, insisted a small girlish voice. Kouichi could not know if the voice was real or imagined. But his chest flattened; he could not take a breath, and then both voice and pressure vanished and he gasped in relief.

"You see?" she whispered. "No use. Whatever mind-connection we have, your planet's atmosphere is interfering."

"If we could only get closer. Close enough for him to see you."

With the car useless now, there was no way down. He could perhaps carry her, but by then she might die. And the monster would turn his rage on the city, and then—

Kouichi willed himself to focus, to calm. The sky was blue in his mind. Clouds parted. As in a daydream, he saw the image of the monster, peaceful, reunited with the girl on his back.

But one would have to fly through the air.

He turned to the girl. "There is a way. If I can get through." He loosed one hand and got out his phone.

Connection. He spoke a few tense words, heard a reply, pocketed the phone.

She was a candleflame, weightless, trembling. Hold on, he willed.

To distract her, he spoke. "I went to work for Sensei last year. I like him, I like the work. My mother is happy I have a good job. However ..." He shrugged. "And you?"

"We are explorers," she replied. "The big ship waits unseen while Mahou explores the space around a world. A crew member takes a scout ship to the planet. We try not to be seen. What is this 'however' you leave hanging?"

"I know a boy who sings. He has a good voice, and if he had some original music ... we talk of it now and then, but I'm too scared to begin."

"You, scared? But you are brave, taking me down here."

He shook his head. "I hold myself at an angle always."

From the hills behind them came a roar of wind, a stab of light, as if the monster himself were descending.

Kouichi spun round as the alien girl hid her eyes. "What is this?" she wailed.

He gave a huge grin she could not see. "That's our ride—Buckaroo Kansai!"

The chopper set down, and Kouichi led the girl forward. The gum-cracking Buckaroo tipped his shaggy head at them. "Hey, pardner. I'm heading back from the hospital and I get this call on my cell. Any chance you need a lift? And who's the gal?"

"Long story," said Kouichi. "Are you game for tricky manoevres?" He helped the girl into the chopper.

"When am I not?"

"Did you happen to notice the monster?"

"I might have at that."

"You'd have to get right alongside it."

Buckaroo popped his gum, shrugging. "No problem."

"And I'm not sure Sensei can call off the planes."

"Well, who wants to live forever?" Laughing, Kansai lifted them off. They hung in the air a moment, the rotors beating back the treetops. Then the chopper threaded its way toward the monster, its pilot humming an American cowboy tune.

There was the girl, crowded into his lap. Her pearly little body was radiator-hot.

Kouichi had never loved anyone before. He knew he loved this one, wanted to wrap her in his arms, keep and protect her forever.

But that would mean her death.

Mahou Aku hovered in midair beneath a futility of fighter jets. Up close, his skin flashed fire, as if each individual segment had been breathed to life by a master glazier.

"Hold on!" Buckaroo hammered right at the monster's head.

The girl gasped. A jet cut from formation, came screaming down on them. A second jet broke off, roared in diagonally. The monster's head snapped up, forming the apex of a triangle, trapping the chopper in the middle.

The monster's glittering eyes zoomed in on Kouichi's. *I am about to be destroyed by beauty.*

The girl's hand crept over his. He could do anything now. "Steady," he urged Buckaroo. "You can manoevre better than the jets."

The creature's mouth opened. The white heat of a firebloom raced toward them.

Buckaroo yanked the controls, slamming the chopper

vertical.

The fireblast roared by, just skimming their landing gear. Kouichi barely had time to let out a breath of relief when, inexplicably, both jets veered off.

Buckaroo dragged a hand across his forehead. "That Sensei of yours must've got through to the army."

The girl gave Kouichi's hand another squeeze.

"Bring us close," he said. The monster hovered quietly now, his eyes like big calm gems.

The *thok* of rotors was the only sound until the craft nudged right up to Mahou Aku. "Whoa, he's a biggun," mused Buckaroo.

"Closer still," Kouichi encouraged. "That's it." He shifted the girl from his knees. "I don't want you to go," he said.

She held onto Kouichi's hand. "Neither do I."

Kouichi smiled. "I won't let you fall."

She gave an odd little sound, perhaps a laugh. "Fall?" she said. "Only watch." She worked her way to the door and balanced on the rim. Hand in his, she leaned out like a beautiful ship's figurehead.

The monster waited.

Eyes shut, head thrown back, the girl began to hum.

The glitter of her skin increased, as if an inner light was working its way to the surface, beading up in sugar-dusted clumps until pearls stood out on her arms, her face, her legs, and finally detached and pattered from her body.

Seaweed mane thrashing in the wind from the rotors, the monster stretched his neck.

Already regaining strength, the girl let go Kouichi's hand. In a glowing escort of pearls, defying gravity, she floated onto the monster's back.

A blaze of light engulfed them, blinding Kouichi for a moment. Then it faded to a sunset glimmer, and he could see.

With the girl safely on his back, Mahou Aku voiced for the first time, a low hollow sound filled with anxiety and relief. The girl fluted in answer, and then they sang as one—up and down the scale. Kouichi shivered. The alien and eerie melody filled him with a beautiful loneliness.

The girl rode Mahou's neck slightly behind the head, as though she were born to it. The little beauty on her beast was leaving him forever.

United, they backed slowly from the chopper, one, two, three lengths away. Then the monster darted skyward, departing in a glimmer of icy blue.

Below, the earthly wail of sirens rose as help rushed to the scene. People were already going about the business of restoring normalcy.

Through streaming eyes Kouichi watched the effort, able to pick out firetrucks battling the flames. Water met fire. Steam billowed, scenting the night.

Good-bye, Patient X.

"Hey, pal," said Buckaroo. "Look up!"

Kouichi looked. A faraway speck resolved itself into the monster, which spun in mid-air, and came floating back. Closer, closer, until the girl was eye-level with them.

Plumes of smoke drifted past, now veiling her, now revealing. She gave him that tiny curl of a smile.

Kouichi's phone trilled. Without taking his eyes from Patient X, he clicked it open. Nakajima's voice—thin and masked with static: "Well?"

Kouichi nodded, knowing the doctor could not see him. "Your Jeep," he began, "I'm afraid—"

"What happened?"

"Stuck near the cliff. Scratches. Flat tire. Bent wheel." The seconds stretched out, but he drank in the sight of the girl and waited for the doctor's tirade.

"Ah well," Nakajima said at last. "A good assistant is more valuable than a car. See you back at the way-station."

Kouichi pocketed the phone. "Hikaru," he began, "not Patient X."

Her garnet eyes were swimming. "You forgot this." Shrugging her shoulders, she slid out of his jacket and held it out to him.

Kouichi swallowed the lump in his throat. "Keep it."

"But I have nothing to give you."

"Oh, you're wrong about that. Keep the jacket—look at it now and then."

"I will never forget." Hikaru gathered the jacket to her chest. Kouichi felt the hug, as if her arms were around him and not the cloth.

Then she and the monster darted up and away, driving toward their unseen ship. In a last spangle of light, they vanished.

Furiously wiping his own eyes, Buckaroo Kansai held the chopper steady.

The air was thick with smoke. Below, people were still struggling to extinguish the fires. A first alien invasion, successfully repelled. That is what the papers would say.

Kouichi let out a long sigh. Maybe he had been wrong. Maybe a musician could still work for a doctor. He would take Buckaroo for a drink and they would talk about it tomorrow. Today had supplied him with enough experience to write a lifetime of songs. He laid a hand on his friend's arm. "Great job. Now let's go home."

Kouichi shut his eyes. Hikaru, riding the dragon, her sea-coloured hair waving. He took a deep breath. The scent of vanilla. The hum of alien music. The warmth of her pearly body.

CREAM OF THE COP

STEVEN CAVANAGH

I apologise for not telling you in person, but it's a lot easier for me to write this down than talk about it. I hope you understand. You can't read the statement I made at the time; it hasn't been released to the general public. Even if you could, there were one or two things that were either too personal or too embarrassing to put on an official document.

Yes, I was in Sydney when it happened, but being there was pretty much all I did. I actually *worked* with Sam Jackson, though. She was just a senior constable then, and I was a rookie barely three months out of Goulburn when that bloody great thing heaved out of the harbour and started smashing everything in sight.

When you graduate you're a bit of an idealist, keen to get out there and change the world. I was at the stage just after that, when you discover the heady delights the uniform can bring. Some call it the 'discount uniform', and there's a certain breed of woman that finds it an aphrodisiac. I was still new enough to the Police Service to pronounce the 'o' though, and keen to get whatever field experience I could.

That was why I was glad to be working with Sam. She was rough as guts and cute as a button, a combination that got my attention. There were girls that looked as good as her back at college, but I thought delicate beauty was *delicate*, that when they got out into the world of domestic violence and suicides they would crack like china dolls.

Sam showed me different. She didn't take crap from anyone. One guy saw how good she looked in the uniform and thought she was a stripper. Two minutes turned him into a little boy in a principal's office. If some neckless bikie tried to push her around, a squirrel grip would soon get him to Assist the Police in Their Inquiries.

I knew where the hole was in her armour, though. I learned pretty quickly that police don't get much thanks from civilians, no matter how much they put their lives on the line. Most of the guys at the station couldn't see past that figure of hers either, and she was too much of a workaholic to find a husband. So who was there to tell her it was all worthwhile? An awestruck rookie, that's who. We needed each other.

The day before they started putting biologists in the army, Sam and I were going pee pee on Circular Quay. That's what she called Police Presence, where you stroll along and be seen so all the suits with coffee nerves feel safe. We were checking buskers licenses when Incremental Sergeant MacPherson's voice came over the four-channel on my belt. He was usually a stickler for procedure and 'professionalism in the service', but that day he sounded like he was calling a horse race with his crotch on fire.

We'd seen him earlier that morning on George Street, but didn't know where he'd gone. I'd asked him to repeat when there was a thud and the ground shook. I mean *bam*, like someone banged on a table and we were all pepper shakers.

My first thought was that something happened at the train station just behind us, but then I saw Sam's eyes bug out. I followed her gaze and saw a head poking over the top of the opera house.

You've seen it a million times on the news by now and everybody's so familiar with it that it's hard to imagine what it was like to *see* something like that for the first time. We could only see the head and neck; the caterpillar bit in the middle was behind the building, and its tail was probably still in the water. The bloody thing looked like an emu with those round, mad eyes. A scaly emu that was vomit-chunk orange and breaking off slabs of the Opera House like pavlova.

What was just as weird to me was that so many people didn't see it at first. Sure there were some that began to run and scream like movie extras, but a good half of the people just looked around a little as if construction work was going on.

I don't remember what my first words were, but I doubt you'd hear them on TV until late. I picked my jaw up and said to Sam: "Is this a joke?" But it wasn't one of those inflatable monsters they put on buildings to promote movies, or some animatronic tourist thing. It was *alive*, as big as an ocean liner and growling like a tassie devil.

I thought I stood there for only a second, but it must have been longer because Sam grabbed my arm and said "Move!"

I only ran toward the creature because she did. By the time we'd passed the ferry terminals and a few shops, the Opera House was smoking and people were starting to run back toward us. One of them was the Sarge.

He had his Glock out of its holster and was shouting at us to get the people back. He'd called it in with base, and we had to hold the thing off until the State Protection Group could get there. I don't know how he convinced the operators at base that it was real. I know *I* wouldn't have believed it.

I'd had a steady hand on the range, but when I pulled out

my nine mill it was shaking like I had Parkinson's. The thing was down on the Opera House steps by then and we could see all of its legs rippling under that striped body, as if it was a caveman-powered bus.

It wasn't easy to miss. That was the first time I'd discharged my weapon without ear protection, and I thought I was deaf after putting a few shots into it. It wasn't worth it either; it didn't even notice. It just pointed that big flat beak at the Toaster building—you know, the square one that was next to the Opera House—and let fly.

The papers said it breathed fire, but I've seen more flame on farts. It breathed *heat*, and the air in front of its gob shimmered like the road to Roma. As the building hit flashpoint I saw a light post wilt, and half a dozen *al fresco* chairs ran like silver yolk. When I saw that, I was bloody glad it ignored us.

By then there was bedlam. The Manly Ferry had been coming in; it did a rocking waltz and churned water to get out of the Quay. The Opera House was burning, and the Toaster turned out to be pretty well named. The crowd that ran screaming only made it a hundred metres before running into the crowd that had come to look.

All we could do was stay ahead of the beast and try to keep everyone out of its way. That wasn't hard—it didn't move all that fast, and still wasn't paying much attention to people. Maybe we were too small for it. The thing seemed to be annoyed with *buildings*. It went to town on any structure it could see, breathing heat and smashing with that club of a tail.

Sam, always proactive, prompted the Sarge that we needed a plan. I guess she could tell that even when the SPG guys showed up they wouldn't be able to do much more than we could.

You have to remember that this was the first time anyone had seen one of these. The Navy probably had something we could have used at their Garden Island base (it was less than a click away), but it was like when the War on Terror first started. There was no communication between services. The Macrofauna Division didn't even *exist* back then, and the largest net you could find at that time was strung on a soccer goal. There was just us, and a lot of milling people.

MacPherson shouted that he'd take any ideas we had. I couldn't see any way of stopping it that didn't involve one hell of a lot of explosives, not that we had any. Besides, the risk to civilians was too high for something like that. Sam looked dubious, but said she thought she could buy us some time. She winked at me and ran into a convenience store.

In the madness of the moment I almost laughed. Maybe she thought the creature would stop for chips and a drink. But that was when it got stuck under the train overpass, so I forgot all about Sam in a hurry.

The footage of that bit did the rounds of the Internet, so

you've probably seen how the creature thrashed like a Rottweiler with its head through a cat door. It buckled the train line and the expressway above it—you wouldn't believe the noise! Later I saw the cars, a spilled box of dominoes. It was a good thing the peak hour trains were so late, or there would have been even more of a mess.

A couple of idiots with cameras approached it from the front, before we could work our way around there to stop them. I guess they wanted good shots of its squealing and squawking. When they were crisped, the whole place began to smell like burnt pork. We had no trouble in keeping civilians away from its gob after that, and I wasn't so keen to get more field experience.

The Fire Brigade turned up then, and our guys were right behind them—the SPG had sent the Tactical Operations Unit. They spilled out into the street and went to work without even consulting the Sarge. I thought that was a bit arrogant, but I guess if you're used to waiting for hours at a house siege, one-hundred-and-fifty metres of many-legged urban renewal comes with a pretty clear-cut objective.

If I'd only known how much the creature was into 'urban renewal', I would have gone home then and there and saved myself a lot of counseling.

In our Code of Conduct and Ethics, one of the core values we're told to strive for is 'Citizen and Police Personal Satisfaction'. There was a lot of striving. All a clip from an mp5 did was embed some lead in its hide. They tried hosing down its beak, but that just made it madder. It pushed itself free in a cloud of steam and snapped up the fire truck, shook it like a chew toy and tossed it to the road half melted.

It sure noticed people now, and didn't like us one bit. It breathed all around, microwaving a few cars and people. I kept my distance but the guys at the station still called me lobster face for days.

After that it started up the old AMP Building—that tall striped one behind the train station. It gave some steam whistle hoots as it climbed, those chorus-line legs punching into the concrete and glass.

The Sarge came up to me with his radio in his hand. "When a courier turns up from forensics," he said, "take his package to Sam."

I told him Fokay, but I was busy just then. The workers in the building were following their fire evacuation drill, filing calmly down the stairs and right out under where the creature was dropping big chunks of masonry. I'd grabbed a megaphone from one of the firies and I directed the workers to stay inside, until the creature moved around to the side of the building.

Then I spotted the bike courier; he was balancing a big drum on his knee, labeled by our forensics lab. I grabbed it from him and radioed Sam. She told me to take it to the top of the building.

She was already on the way, 'cause the Sarge had somehow got her a chopper. I think it was one of those radio station traffic ones that had come to look.

I had to run in the main entrance. The building was apparently the biggest in Sydney once, but it was only 20 stories or so. Still, I didn't want to go up that many stairs, and the drum was heavy.

The doors had barely closed in the elevator when it (or the whole building, I couldn't tell) began to shake, *bambambam.*

There was nothing I could do about it, so I popped the lid of the drum to have a look. A wisp of winter breath wafted out. It was used for freezing perishable evidence, like DNA or sperm, but there was nothing in it except dry ice.

The *bambambam* didn't stop. I was sure it was the whole building by then, and was starting to wish I'd taken the stairs.

The radio gave a crackle. The Sarge felt a need to tell me his theory why the creature had attacked the other buildings but not this one. It must have been discouraging the competition, because it had started to mate.

Now I've never felt any great empathy with the building I was in, whether it was my office, home or pub, but that day the beast was a dog and the office block was my leg.

Even if you *could* imagine the sick combination of terror and revulsion that idea puts into a man, you can't begin to understand what happened next. See, that building is one where you have to change elevators to get to the top, and Murphy's Law being what it is I got off where ... well, where *it* did.

That's all I'll say about that part, except that I still have nightmares and I haven't gone through a car wash since.

The top floor was all boardrooms and those stupid success posters on the walls. I had to find some cowering dweeb in a suit to tell me how to get to the roof. The newer buildings are covered with aerials and receiver dishes, but this one had enough room for Sam to be set down.

She had a shopping bag in her hand and was looking over the edge at the thing, and didn't notice me until I was right next to her. She spilled some cans from the bag and grabbed the drum from me. "Quick!" she said. "It's seen me. Dip these in and flake off the metal."

You've probably heard from the papers how the police had special foam that we used on the monster. Truth is, Sam remembered a high school prank. You take a can of shaving cream and dip it into dry ice. It freezes the stuff, gas and all, and the can turns brittle. Pop the unwrapped creamsickle into someone's car, and it begins to thaw. When the poor sucker finds their car, it's as full as a cappuccino. I could imagine Sam doing that as a kid.

When it went into the creature's beak, that shopping bag had six frozen cans of General Gallagher's Rapid Shave.

Sam figured it'd gum up its gob a bit to at least stop it burning things, but in the heat of that maw it took only a few seconds for its lungs to be full, frothy and scented like a Real Man. It snorted foam clear over my head and then fell ... Well, you *know* where it fell, don't you? There's that shiny memorial there now.

I joined the service to catch criminals, not gargantuan horny fiends from the depths. I quit as soon as I could. It put Sam's career through the glass ceiling, though, and she got enough recognition for anyone's lifetime. All I got out of it was a drinking problem and a whole new appreciation of architecture.

I still see her from time to time. I asked her once how she thought of throwing that stuff in its mouth, and she said that she got the idea from one of the bystanders that we pushed out of harm's way.

See, she reckons that when the creature first crawled down from the Opera House a little Asian man pointed at it and shouted: "Gob filler! Gob filler!" If that's what she says, that's good enough for me.

ACTION JOE™ TO THE RESCUE

NICK FOX AND JOHN HEEDER

A t a time before time was measured, a time at which no history was kept, great alien forces fought a vicious battle to determine possession of a newly discovered blue-green world.

Of all these forces, and of all the horrors unleashed on the fragile young planet, none was as terrible or as awesome as the Terror. Towering over the combatants that raged across the continent, the Terror wreaked total destruction with every attack. At 300-feet tall, its shadow was as great as a mountain. Each step the Terror took shook the earth, its trailing tail gouged massive ruts into the ground.

Despite being outnumbered a hundred to one, the Terror was not afraid. The Terror wielded six terrible weapons of destruction, one for each of its six hands: the mighty Sword Piercer, which disrupted the air itself as it hummed towards its targets and sliced through them with great ease; the Mace Devastation, which could penetrate even the armour of a Rolling Dreadnaught; the Spear Butchery, which could fly at a speed greater than any sensor could track and always returned automatically to the Terror's hand; the Sceptre Domination, which used a yellow beam for scanning enemy locations, a red beam for warning of enemy targets, and a blue beam for sending distress calls; the Scythe Annihilation, which could hollow out mountains in seconds with its curved blade; and the Axe Destruction, which could smash through Oblitercannons as easily as splitting logs.

No, the Terror was not afraid as it cut down two Tainted Obliterators, the last of its enemy's forces. But then the Sceptre Domination glowed red.

The Terror smashed the Mace Devastation into the ground, again and again. It used its Scythe Annihilation to clear away the debris, creating mountains around the hole it dug—a hole that could have swallowed a lake. At last, after displacing enough dirt to create an entire mountain range, the Terror discovered what had set off the sceptre's warning: a Planet Smasher bomb.

The Terror's enemy had been cunning in their attack, the campaign on this remote world a clever feint. A whole planet, green with life, teaming with large lumbering reptiles, and lush with exploitable resources ... *sacrificed* just to destroy the Terror.

The bomb's visible timer neared the end of its countdown. Not knowing what else to do, the Terror swung its Sword Piercer down on it.

The explosion shook the planet. It was as though a massive comet had punctured the atmosphere and struck the surface. The results of the explosion were catastrophic.

☆

"Give that back!" Steve Fellowes cried. The slim black teen lunged unsuccessfully for his backpack, and the cuffs of his crisply pressed khaki pants slipped up over his calves, exposing his white dress socks.

"Whatcha gonna do about it, nerd-boy?" someone from the ring of tormenters taunted. He tossed the backpack over Steve's outstretched arms to a boy in a letter jacket.

"Maybe he'll cry to his mommy," another boy said.

"Come on, you guys! My portable hard drive is in there." Steve stood inactive, unsure of which direction to go as the backpack quickly passed through several hands.

The crowd parted to let a tall boy with red hair through. His letter jacket had three stripes on the left arm. He shoved Steve, hard, causing him to bang his eye on a locker before crashing to the floor.

Dick Hairyson leaned down and pointed his finger in Steve's face. "Are you in my hallway again?"

"No, I ..." Steve looked around frantically, seeing nothing but a wall of leering faces.

"I told you to stay out of my hallway." Dick grabbed Steve by his cotton button-down shirt and lifted him to his feet. He pulled back his fist. "Good night, nerd-boy."

Someone grabbed Dick's fist. "What the hell's wrong with you?"

Dick spun on the voice, his face red with anger. When he saw who it was, he stepped back, dropping his arms to his sides. A shaky smile crossed his face. "Just having a little fun, Kurt."

"If you ever want to catch another pass and impress the college scouts, Dick, you'd better lay off my friends." Kurt Aikmen turned his back on Dick and yanked Steve's backpack from the kid holding it. A can of cola fell out, but Kurt didn't notice it. He returned the backpack to Steve. "Here you go. Don't let this jerk get you down."

While Kurt's back was turned, Dick snatched up the can of cola. He jabbed his finger at Steve and mouthed, "Kick your ass," then joined the departing crowd.

Steve couldn't look Kurt in the face because his own face burned with humiliation. "Thanks," he said to the ground. "See you after school."

"Hey man, it's all right," Kurt said.

Steve shot him a lacklustre thumbs-up as he walked toward the computer lab.

☆

In the eastern Canadian Artic Islands a new iceberg was born. The glacier that gave it birth seemed reluctant to let its child go free, but at last the iceberg floated off into the waters of the northern Atlantic. At about thirteen miles long and ten miles wide, it was one of the largest icebergs of the season.

Deep within the white ice laid a dark object. While dwarfed by the iceberg, the object was so big as to defy human comprehension. The shape was basically humanoid, but had a number of extra limbs.

Moving at about a half of a mile every hour, the iceberg made its way south. As it moved into warmer waters, the combination of the temperature change and the incessant slapping of the waves against its edges caused the iceberg to break apart.

The form inside the ice moved.

Smaller icebergs broke off as the warmer water and the waves took their toll. Large cracks appeared along the middle of the iceberg.

The figure in the ice moved again.

This time, the figure strained, pitting its strength against the tomb of ice. The iceberg put up a valiant fight, but lost. With an explosion of crystal ice-shards, the fault line gave way.

The Terror tumbled free from the icy prison that had held it for thousands of years. All those millennia ago, it had destroyed the Planet Smasher bomb just in time. Rather than planetary destruction, only localised devastation and rapid climate changes had resulted. The Terror had been thrown unconscious into a newly forming lake that eventually became a glacier.

Now, the icy cold water fully revived the Terror. It came to its feet, still wielding five of its six weapons. With a mission of destruction and revenge on its mind, the Terror trudged along the bottom of the Atlantic Ocean.

☆

Steve and Kurt sat in folding chairs at a haphazard arrangement of four tables in the Fellowes' basement. Each table held a variety of computers and other electronic devices, in various states of assembly. Empty cola cans competed with lamps, piles of magazines, stereo speakers and other miscellaneous items for what little tabletop real estate the electronics weren't using.

Their friend, Duck, a teen of large girth, sat on a ratty old couch against the wall. A lamp that shone behind him made his pasty white face look almost like a full moon. He smirked at Steve. "Why are you wearing those shades in here?"

Steve pushed the Ray-Bans up his nose. "Because they're cool."

Duck snorted. "Everyone knows that Dick gave you a black eye today. It's all over school."

Kurt looked up from his computer. "Dick's ass is as good as kicked. Just as soon as Friday's game is over, that is. Can't mess him up before then because Coach seems to think we need him and if we don't win that game, Coach'll kill me."

"Guys," Steve said. "I don't want any—"

"Dude," Duck said to Kurt, "you oughta kick Dick's ass now."

"Do you not listen? I just said—"

"Guys," Steve said, his voice raised a notch. "I'm sitting right here!"

Duck smirked at Steve. "Kurt's lame," he said. "But it's okay, the word around school is that you already took care of Dick."

"He *did?*" Kurt looked at Steve quizzically. "Did you brain him with your laptop or something?"

Steve took off the Ray-Bans, revealing that his left eye was nearly swollen shut. He looked confused. "I have no idea what Duck's talking about."

Duck put on a sly grin. "Come on, you know what I'm talking about—you obviously caught on to the prank I pulled with your soda, right? And so you let that jerk Dick take it."

Steve shook his head. "What *are* you talking about?"

"This." Duck pulled a weird, shoebox-sized, wire-covered device out of his backpack. "Your *osmosis* thingymabob. You told me that it could make the cola go out and something else go in right through the aluminium without the can being opened. I thought it'd be funny to give you a little taste of cafeteria grease."

"You didn't!" Steve exclaimed, eyes big. "They use peanut oil in the caf, and—"

"And Mr Tough Guy Dick Hairyson is allergic to peanuts. Yeah, I know. I don't know how you knew what I did, but passing it on to Dick was a real stroke of genius, even for you. From what I heard, the chunky grease splashed all over his face when he tried to chug the soda. His face looks like he sprouted a gazillion big zits!"

"I didn't know!" Steve said. "He *stole* my soda, and—"

Kurt burst out laughing and Steve couldn't help but join in. They held their sides and howled. Steve laughed so hard that he fell off of his chair.

Duck waited for his friends to regain some semblance of calm, then said, "I just happened to mention your cleverness to a few people. There's a new laughingstock in school. It'll be hard for anyone to take Dick—or should I say, *Crater-face*—seriously for a while, methinks."

"I don't believe it!" Steve said, wiping a tear from his eye. "He's such a psycho, he'll probably claw his face off."

Once the teens finally stopped laughing, Steve went back to helping Duck with his homework. "Here's your problem," he said, staring at a computer screen.

"What is it?" Duck didn't bother looking up from his copy of *Sports Illustrated's* latest Swimsuit Edition.

Steve frowned at him. "You didn't close a for–next loop. Honestly, Duck, that's about the simplest error you can make."

"Look at the maracas on this brown beauty." Duck held the magazine sideways for Steve's inspection.

"She could use 'em to slap your face," Kurt said. "But then again, she probably wouldn't want your oily face-sweat all over her—"

"—maracas," Duck said enthusiastically.

"Do you know it's now three-thousand times this week you've mentioned brown maracas?" Steve asked. "Wait, what's that about?"

Steve turned up the volume on his media player's news broadcast.

Seismic listeners all over the globe were detecting powerful seismic shocks erupting from the Atlantic. The shocks were regular, and they were moving. Scientists were baffled by the phenomenon.

"Ah, it's probably just some *hump*back whales doing what they were named after," Duck said. He quickly lost interest and glanced over at Steve's collection of Action Joe™ action figures and accessories. "What are you doing with this stuff?"

Approaching the table with the toys, Steve carefully removed a mint condition Action Joe™ from its box. The six–inch-tall poseable figure dressed in combat fatigues clutched an M-16 in his Action Grip™. "I'm scanning the box art into protected subdirectories on my web server."

"Oh. Why?"

"Why not?"

Steve went back to the computer screen that displayed Duck's program. "Close that for–next loop. Count the open and close brackets and compare them, doofus."

Kurt scrutinised some perplexing items on another of Steve's tables. "What is this stuff, Steve?"

"My latest invention. I finished that prototype last night."

"Another invention. Great. You're not going to turn the town's drinking water purple again, are you?"

Steve affected a look of pained dignity. "If you want to make a science omelette, you have to break a few public-nuisance-citation eggs."

"Omelettes ain't purple," Duck said. "Hey, I'm hungry. Anyone want a taco?"

Kurt opened his wallet and retrieved a fiver that he wadded and hurled at Duck. "I'm in. If you eat one of mine before you get back ..."

Duck snapped the fiver out of the air, then heaved himself to his feet and started up the stairs. "Then it'll taste good. Hey, that was an excellent if–then statement!"

"No, it wasn't," Steve called after his departing friend.

"So, Steve, what does this gizmo do?" Kurt asked.

The device consisted of two five-gallon hermetically sealed jars, one with a red lid, the other with a blue lid. Each jar rested on a clear polyethylene box, displaying several circuit boards and wires. Cables ran from each jar to a computer.

"This is the Fellowesmodeller," Steve said proudly. "The blue jar is the scanning stage. It's a vacuum environment to keep out dust and any foreign debris. A laser reads every dimension, every line, every curve, and even the texture of any object in the blue jar. This information is fed into the computer. Next, Fellowesvapour is pumped into the red jar."

"Fellowesvapour?" Kurt chuckled. "Another invention named after yourself, I see."

Steve reddened. "Why not? Anyway, the Fellowesvapour is key to the process. It's actually a super-heated version of this weird goo I found out back when I buried the remains of my failed rid-the-world-of-PMS experiment."

"What do you mean, weird goo?" Kurt asked, a grin crossing his face. "It's not Fellowesgoo?"

"The *weird* goo's carbon dating came up so old that I think the stuff broke the carbon dating machine. Anyway, when the Felloweslaser focuses on the absorbent Fellowesvapour—"

"Felloweslaser?" Kurt laughed. "What next? A Fellowesinflate-a-girl?"

"As I was saying," Steve said, avoiding Kurt's eyes, "the Felloweslaser carries information from the computer and uses it to solidify and shape the Fellowesvapour. The Fellowesvapour is used to create a new version of the scanned item."

"So it's sort of a copy machine?" Kurt asked.

Steve shrugged. "Close enough. But the original parameters of the scanned object can be adjusted in the computer before you send the information to the Felloweslaser."

"Steve, are you telling me you can turn lead into gold?"

A wide grin was the only answer Steve gave.

☆

Duck descended into Steve's basement, clutching two bags labelled 'Taco Time'. Kurt and Steve were gone. "Huh, guess he doesn't want these," Duck said, reaching into Kurt's bag.

While he munched on a super-taco, his eyes fell on Steve's Action Joe™ collection. He picked up Action Joe™ with his free hand. "Look, up in the sky, it's flying soldier-man." Duck made an air-rushing sound and flew Action Joe™ around a computer monitor.

"Flying soldier-man senses a nude and oiled exotic dancer in distress! Her dancing studio is in flames! I'll save you, nude and oiled exotic dancer!"

Duck flew Action Joe™ in a sudden dive toward the monitor. Action Joe™ hit the edge of the monitor case, jerked out of Duck's hand, and landed in the blue jar. The sudden jolt of the action figure's landing caused the jar's hinged lid to swing into place and snap shut. The jar automatically began pumping air out to create a vacuum field.

Duck looked over at the jar. "Poor flying soldier-man, trapped in a bottle like a bug. Farewell, flying soldier-man. Your valiant yet painful end will earn you a posthumous medal of honour."

Unnoticed, Duck's super-taco crumbled and pieces of it fell onto the computer keyboard. As Duck picked up the taco bags and went upstairs in search of Steve and Kurt, the values on the screen changed. A ball of ground beef, balanced precariously on the backspace key, wobbled, then finally rolled away, pressing down the Enter key.

A green light came on in the blue jar. A laser in the base of the jar scanned Action Joe™. Fellowesvapour pumped into the red jar from a tank in the corner.

☆

On a Saturday that was the worst day for South Carolina since the Civil War, the Terror came ashore at Myrtle Beach. Teams of scientists, tracking the seismic shocks of its footfalls, were the first humans to witness the horrendous warrior from outer space take its first step on land in modern times.

It was the last thing they ever saw.

The Terror arose from the Atlantic and waded through the twenty-foot deep shallows, breaking upon the shore like a tidal wave. It smashed a dock to slivers, then stomped the scientists' van with its forty-foot long foot, flattening it as thin as aluminium foil.

The Terror's every stride covered 100 feet, and each step it took sent shockwaves that flattened local buildings. As the shockwaves spread, windows shattered on every building within a twenty-mile radius.

Throughout the city, people streamed out into the streets. "Are they shooting a movie?" someone asked.

The police didn't have time to organise as the Terror smashed through Myrtle Beach. Its long strides quickly carried it through the heart of downtown. The damage was massive. What the Terror's footfalls knocked down, its swinging tail reduced to rubble. Those locals and visitors who had not had the time or sense of mind to flee were left dead or dying in its wake. Geysers of water shot up as waterlines ruptured. Fireballs blossomed in the wake of the giant as transformers overloaded and natural gas lines burst.

The Terror did not register any threats to its existence, so it strode on unconcerned, following a beacon only it could sense. Lost in the colossal explosion all those thousands of years ago, the Sceptre Domination now called to the Terror. The Terror anticipated with great anger the moment it would use the sceptre to contact its masters. Then it would finish the job it had come to this planet to achieve: it would conquer this world, subdue it. Great worldships would follow. All the water, all the ores, all the atmospheric gasses would be stripped away. All organic matter would be broken down into chemical solutions that could easily be warehoused. The hot lava that was the planet's lifeblood would be siphoned and stored.

The planet Earth would be left as lifeless and as pitted as its moon.

☆

"What have you done?" Duck hissed. "This is even worse than the time your Fellowesfogger buried the whole town in sticky, caramel-flavoured mist."

"I didn't do *this*," Steve said. "I'm lucky to be alive!"

The rumble of a motorcycle engine came from behind them. Kurt cruised up on his 1985 Hog and came to a stop next to Steve. He pulled his helmet off, his eyes reflecting the awe and astonishment in Duck's eyes.

"What have you done?" he asked Steve.

"I didn't do this!"

The phenomenon in question was as amazing as it was alarming.

A huge man lay prone in a crater in the empty field behind Steve's house. The giant's skin was a dull pink. He clutched a massive M-16 in his Action Grip™. He wore green battle fatigues, black combat boots and a Kevlar battle helmet. His Action Accessory Belt™ was loaded with massive grenades, ammo, and other weapons of war.

"It's almost like the Fellowesmodeller made a duplicate of Action Joe™," Steve said. He studied the motionless action figure. "But I didn't do it. I didn't even go back into the basement last night."

"It must be 500 feet tall," Kurt said. He swung the hog onto its kickstand and hopped off.

"288 feet tall," Steve said. "You take the length of the shadow, the time of day, and plug them into the formula x equals—"

"Fine," Kurt said, "288 feet tall."

"What's this about the basement?" Duck asked.

"That's where the Fellowesmodeller is," Steve said, as they walked toward Action Joe™. "But I didn't use it last night."

Duck avoided Steve's questioning gaze, so Steve stopped at the edge of the crater and examined the gigantic soldier. "It's Action Joe™, there's no doubt about that. What's going on?"

Steve felt a small tremor in the ground beneath his feet. Kurt grabbed him and pulled him back.

Even as the teens retreated, the tremors increased. Suddenly, the earth shook so violently that they were thrown off their feet. Steve tumbled to the ground; Kurt rolled into his fallen Hog and knocked his head against the front suspension fork.

"Whoa!" Duck exclaimed as he landed on his backside.

"Owww!" Kurt cried, rubbing his head.

"What the heck!" Steve exclaimed.

"Sir, reporting for duty, sir!" a giant voice called out.

The voice was so loud that the vibrations bounced Steve and his friends around like ants on a trampoline. Hands over his ears, Steve looked toward where the voice had come from.

Action Joe™ had risen to his feet. He towered over the teens, his face so far above them that Steve could hardly see it.

"Reporting for duty, sir," Action Joe™ bellowed.

Steve had to steady himself as the ground shook. "Can you whisper or something?" he screamed.

"Oh, sorry, sir," Action Joe™ responded in a tone that was enough to rattle teeth, but much more tolerable nonetheless.

"It must think you're the Commanding Officer," Kurt said.

"Where did you come from?" Steve asked.

Action Joe™ saluted. "Hostile Alien Eradication Squad. I am deployed under your command, sir."

☆

Myrtle Beach International Airport had the misfortune of being right in the Terror's path. A 727 jockeying for a landing found itself on a collision course with the Terror. The aircraft was clumsy and slow compared to the alien warrior; with the Sword Piercer the Terror sliced it first down the long fuselage, then in fourths just behind the wings. The jet and its passengers went in four directions to their deaths.

The Myrtle Beach Police Department finally responded. Five squad cars with sirens screaming barrelled onto the tarmac and came to a screeching stop behind the Terror. Ten cops exited the cars and quickly formed a half-circle. They raised their handguns and shotguns and fired.

The Terror barely felt the rain of bullets and pellets along its calves and the back of its knees. It quickly dismissed the attack as having a zero threat rating, and stomped on. It smashed through Terminal C, reducing the building to splinters. Electric transformers exploded. People ran screaming, some jumped from windows as high as thirty feet above the ground just to get away.

Having at first taken news reports of the Terror as some kind of joke, the local National Guard division lurched into action. Twenty M1A1 Abrams Main Battle Tanks rushed along a plotted intercept course with the Terror.

☆

Steve couldn't believe it; he was actually in the shirt pocket of Action Joe™. The view was incredible. With his head and shoulders poking out of the pocket, he felt like an Olympian god striding across ancient Greece, master of all he surveyed.

Action Joe™ set a crisp military stride, the M-16 slung over his back. Steve directed the giant soldier along country roads and the sparsely inhabited areas around his hometown of Bucksville. Kurt and Duck followed along behind on the Hog.

Steve had no idea what to do with Action Joe™, but for now he was having the time of his life. "Yee-haw!" he screamed.

His cellphone rang. He fumbled in his shirt pocket for it, then answered, "Top of the world!"

"Steve," Duck said, "you won't believe what's on the news!"

"Right now, I'd believe anything. Did the Martians invade?"

"Well, yeah, that's probably it."

"Duck, did you eat ten Big Macs at one sitting again? You know all that rheumy-eyed cow meat gives you hallucinations."

"Check your phone's web browser."

"Whatever," Steve said. He ended the call just as Action Joe™ halted. The sudden stop nearly sent Steve flying out of the giant pocket.

"Sir, enemy sighted," Action Joe™ said. "Due east fifty miles."

"Enemy? What do you mean *enemy*?" Steve worried about what in the world a gigantic action figure would consider an enemy.

"Sir, alien invader has commenced operations."

"Put me down!" Steve shouted.

Action Joe™ proffered a palm. Steve hopped onto the *handy* platform, and the giant soldier lowered him to the ground.

"Ready for orders, sir!" Action Joe™ said with a salute.

"Now hold on," Steve said. "I know you're big and everything, but I don't want you to attack anything."

"Sir, enemy campaign has destroyed property and lives. Recommend immediate response."

The hog pulled up next to Steve and Duck hopped off. "Did you check your phone's browser?" he asked.

"Duck, Action Joe™ has gone insane here, all right? I don't have time for your jokes."

Duck pulled up a web browser on his own phone. "Quit with your little fit and check this out."

Steve grabbed Duck's phone and scanned the headlines. His eyebrows shot up and his mouth gaped open. "This can't be—"

"Sir, recommend immediate response to hostile," Action Joe™ said.

The teens exchanged glances. "What do I do?" Steve asked.

Duck shrugged his shoulders.

"Look, Steve," Kurt said. "You're the quarterback now. You have to check out the defence, call a play, and fearlessly execute that play."

"Screw the sports analogies! A huge monster is stomping the hell out of Myrtle Beach, and my Action Joe™ is seeing imaginary enemies."

"Maybe the monster *is* your toy soldier's hostile."

"How can Action Joe™ know about a monster fifty miles away?"

"Maybe he has a wireless internet connection?"

Steve turned and looked up at Action Joe™. He hadn't planned to create the giant, yet he felt responsible for this seemingly sentient creature's well-being. "What if the alien is ... well, *hostile?*"

Action Joe™ squatted down on giant haunches, and said, "I've been trained and equipped by the Hostile Alien Eradication Squad for this moment, sir. It's my duty."

Steve balled his fists in frustration. A thousand thoughts rushed through his mind, least of which being, *What the hell is this Hostile Alien Eradication Squad, anyway?* Finally, he said, "Action Joe™, bring me aboard. Let's go kick some monster ass!"

A smile somehow crossed Action Joe™'s moulded face. "Sir. Yes, sir!"

"Double time to the enemy!" Steve shouted.

Action Joe™ ran across the South Carolina countryside, thunder followed in his wake.

☆

The battle wasn't going too well for the South Carolina National Guard tank squad. The forty-miles-per-hour top speed of the seventy-ton behemoths was much too slow to deal with a being that took 100-foot strides. Two tanks had been crushed, their four-man crews along with them, when the Terror stepped on them.

The explosive bursts of the tanks' 100-pound shells didn't do much more than disturb the monster. The Terror's armour shed the blows as though they were raindrops against a windshield.

The tanks settled into a run-and-gun attack. Several fired while retreating, while others scrambled and took new positions. Each time the monster lashed one of its weapons at a tank, the other tanks fired.

The Terror had never seen tactics like these. It was confused. Finally, after taking a pounding from several direct hits, it decided to focus on one tank at a time. The Terror swung the Mace Devastation down against the nearest tank, ignoring the direct hit the tank made on its chest. The force of the blow caused the fuel and ordinance aboard the tank to erupt into a massive fireball.

The Air Guard arrived with a splashy entrance. Like a swarm of wasps erupting from a disturbed nest, AH-1S Cobra Gunships converged on the Terror. Anti-tank TOW missiles flashed from the Cobras. The anti-tank missiles crashed against the Terror's armour with ear-piercing explosions.

The Terror flung the Spear Butchery. Before returning to its master's hand, the deadly missile smashed through two Cobras as though they were made of plastic.

The attack was a complete failure, leaving several guardsmen dead and millions of dollars of war machines destroyed. A retreat was called, and the Cobras hung back to cover the Abrams tanks' retreat.

When the Terror realised that the attackers were retreating, it felt a surge of lust for destruction; it wanted to demolish every enemy that had dared challenge it. But its mission to retrieve the Sceptre Domination took precedence. The Terror resumed its original course.

One last tank stood in its way. The Terror lunged for the unlucky tank. More missiles from the Cobras smashed into the monster, but it ignored them. It picked the Abrams up, reared back, and flung it. The seventy-ton war machine spiralled across the sky like a football from the hand of a star NFL quarterback.

"Got ya!" Action Joe™ exclaimed, reaching for the tank with both hands. He caught it and carefully lowered it treads-down to the ground. "Good job, soldiers. Now you pull back and leave that big ugly thing to me."

For only the second time in its existence, the Terror was caught off guard. All of its senses focused on the strange warrior it now faced. At last, a truly worthy foe to battle and to destroy.

"Sir, you evacuate the area with these soldiers," Action Joe™ said, gently placing Steve on the tank. "I'll report for a briefing after I've kicked this monster's ass from here to the Moon."

"Wait!" Steve said as the Abrams tank drove away. He braced himself to jump off the moving vehicle, but a guardsman grabbed him and held him down. As the tank fled to safety, Steve felt like he was leaving a friend behind to die.

Action Joe™ trained his M-16 on the Terror. "All right, you ugly slab of anus butter, drop your weapons and prepare to be taken prisoner."

The Terror didn't understand the words, but it recognised the tone. Such a challenge would be answered in like fashion. The Terror flung the Spear Butchery at Action Joe™.

"Sweet maple syrup!" Action Joe™ exclaimed as the Spear Butchery came rushing for his heart. Action Joe™ sidestepped as quickly as he could, but the Spear Butchery still managed to score a wound along the left side of his ribcage.

"That's gonna leave a mark," Action Joe™ said. As the Terror caught the returning Spear Butchery, the giant soldier levelled his M-16 at the alien. "First blood to you. It's gonna be last blood to me."

Action Joe™ fired a burst at the Terror. A dozen bullets, each one nearly five feet long and weighing 500-pounds smashed into the Terror at supersonic speeds.

The Terror's armour dented slightly as it was driven back under the onslaught. With a bellow that was heard clear in Washington DC, the Terror moved its five weapons into attack position and charged Action Joe™. The charge was terrifying; the ground shook as it rushed its opponent.

Action Joe™ tossed the M-16 aside. "Bring it on, you clot of lung-spew."

☆

The camera crews were arriving from all of the major networks. The cable news outlets were already there, as were crews from local TV stations. Even from this position, five miles away from the battle of the titans, the ground shook as the combatants struggled.

It was impossible to mount cameras on tripods; the tripods kept falling to the ground. The news vans shook intermittently as the thunder of the distant battle rolled over the hill country of South Carolina.

A tent city had sprung up. People swarmed around the area, but were kept at bay by a barricade of soldiers and traffic pylons. Steve Fellowes found himself hustled along by a ring of soldiers.

In the command tent, they plunked Steve down into a chair surrounded by several tables set up with communications equipment. Steve sat upright, keeping his spine stiff. Angry men and women in the uniforms of at least three branches of the armed services, as well as state, city, and county cops, and those in the uniforms of various emergency services, converged on him and peppered him with questions.

"How many times do I have to say it?" Steve said, his voice riddled with irritation and anxiety. "I *don't know* where that big monster came from."

A red-faced, four-star general jabbed a fat finger into Steve's chest and shouted, "Who are you working for? The commies?"

"Did you construct that giant toy soldier out of environmentally safe chemicals?" screamed a woman in a lab coat.

"This is a scheme by the vast right-wing conspiracy to steal the election: tell the truth!" the bulbous senator from South Carolina shrieked, the whiskey on his breath evident even at a distance.

Steve valiantly protested his innocence, but his efforts were in vain. After what seemed like an eternity of harassment, he was dragged away by a soldier and locked into an armoured personnel carrier.

Steve rattled the locked doors. "I thought these things were supposed to carry soldiers, not innocent high school students," he yelled as the soldiers left.

"You're not innocent," a voice snarled from behind him.

Steve turned around in shock.

Dick Hairyson peered back at him through the main window from the carrier's cab. Ugly red and purple splotches covered Dick's face and neck. They looked like a male baboon's swollen mating marks.

"You're going to pay for what you did to me," Dick said. He pushed the ignition button and the engine roared into life.

"What are you doing, crater-face?" Steve shouted. "You can't drive this thing."

"Shut up, nerd-boy!" Hatred made any remaining pink skin on Dick's face flare red. "You're gonna need your breath to cry after I give you the ass-kicking of your life!" Dick fumbled with the controls, switches, and pedals. Suddenly, the carrier lurched.

Dick stomped on the gas pedal, and the vehicle shot through the barricades.

☆

Action Joe™ threw himself to the left as the Terror slashed at him with the Sword Piercer, the Axe Destruction, and the Mace Devastation. The trio of weapons scarcely missed the giant soldier, cutting through the air where he'd stood a split second earlier. Action Joe™ smashed through an abandoned farmhouse as he dodged the attack.

The Terror swung the Scythe Annihilation, the cutting edge of the curved blade aimed at Action Joe™'s exposed throat. At the last second, Action Joe™ stepped back from the attack—a feint designed to get the Terror to commit to an unbalanced strike.

"You fell for the oldest trick in the book, you wad of bloody snot," Action Joe™ said, as he grabbed the scythe's handle. With the alien off-balance from the attack, it was easy to give the handle a good twist.

Action Joe™'s move knocked The Terror off its feet and sent it flying. Its passage toppled trees and dug a massive trench. It bellowed in rage as it clambered clumsily to its feet.

Action Joe™ lined up a huge cast-iron water tower just like a football ready for the kickoff, then booted the cistern, sending it smashing into the Terror's face.

"That's right between the uprights for three!" Action Joe™ said as the Terror stumbled backward. "This kid is having a great season!"

Taking advantage of the Terror's confusion, Action Joe™ ran at the alien and tackled it. The two huge combatants flattened hundreds of acres of wooded hills as they rolled and grappled. The Terror howled in frustration as Action Joe™ caught it in a bear hug, effectively neutralising its ability to bring its weapons to bear at such close proximity.

"Say 'uncle,' you hairy armpit on a reeking hippie!" Action Joe™ screamed.

☆

"Get out here," Dick said, pulling Steve from the personnel carrier.

Dick had stopped the vehicle in the shadow of the fighting giants, but he was so focused on his hatred for Steve that he didn't pay any heed to the ongoing struggle.

"Are you crazy?" Steve shouted, backing nervously away from Dick. "We're gonna be stomped into little blobs of jelly out here."

Dick picked up a tyre-iron from the carrier's tool chest. He whacked the business end of the heavy metal tool into his palm.

"You did this to my face, nerd-boy," Dick said. *Whack*, he smacked the tyre-iron in his palm again. "Because of you I had this allergic reaction." *Whack*. "Because of you, everyone at school calls me crater-face." *Whack*. "Because of you, everyone is laughing at me."

Steve backed away with a cautious eye on the tyre-iron. "It's kinda ironic, you know," he said, "how you hassled me without mercy for three years of high school, and it took this for you to get how it feels."

Dick advanced on Steve, still smacking the tyre-iron against his palm. "I'm going to kill you, do you know that? They're going to find you out here so smashed up that they won't know your ass from your head until the autopsy."

☆

The Terror dropped its weapons and grabbed Action Joe™ with all of its hands. Then, with enormous strength, it hurled its enemy away.

"Whoaaa!" Action Joe™ cried as he flew though the air, ploughing into the ground like a vast humanoid meteor. By the time he'd extricated himself from the gash in the earth, the Terror was on its feet, reclaimed weapons in its hands.

"Oh, there you are," Action Joe™ said. "I was hoping you hadn't chickened out. I'm not through kicking your ass yet."

☆

"Don't do something you'll regret later," Steve said. He backed away as Dick advanced brandishing the tyre-iron.

"Oh, I won't regret it," Dick said. "You will, but then, hey, you won't be around anymore, so maybe regrets aren't high on your list of things to worry about."

Steve turned and ran, a blind panic spurring him on. Unfortunately, he ran in the wrong direction. Looking back over his shoulder, Steve didn't notice he was headed right for one of the huge gashes dug deep into the earth by the fighting giants. Screaming "Aaah!" Steve fell into a vast chasm. Fortunately, he didn't fall far; after about five feet, he hit the sloped sides of the pit and rolled down the recently churned up soil.

Dick hopped in after him, easily sliding down the slope on his feet. He came to a rest a few feet away from Steve. "I was really hoping you'd run faster than that. I don't want this to be over too quickly."

"Look, Dick," Steve said, "I'm sorry about your face, really, I am." He frantically searched the pit for anything that might be used as a weapon. "If you do this, Kurt and Duck will know you were behind it."

Dick kicked a cloud of dirt at Steve. "I don't care. I don't care if the whole town knows what happened. All that matters is that you'll be dead."

"Have you lost your mind?" Steve shouted, and was horrified to see the answer displayed in Dick's psychotic grin. He turned and tried to run, but the soft dirt of the trench was treacherous and he stumbled to his knees.

Steve felt Dick's hand on the back of his shirt just before Dick spun him around and thrust his face down into the dirt.

"This is it, nerd-boy," Dick said. He brought the tyre-iron up. "This is where you feel ... *the pain*."

☆

The Terror stomped towards its foe. The whole planet would suffer for the disrespect of this insolent warrior. When the processing ships were through, the dust ball that remained would serve as a warning to anyone who ever dared challenge the Terror again.

"Whenever you can spare the time," Action Joe™ said as the Terror continued its deliberate march.

The Terror wheeled back the Spear Butchery and hurled it. Action Joe™ saw nothing more than a blur as the missile screamed through the air at him. He looked down in surprise to see the Spear Butchery in his guts, hanging there from his innards.

Action Joe™ staggered back, his legs not seeming to want to support him. "That ... hurts," he said. He looked up at the Terror. "But if you think this soldier is down for the count, you'd better think again." He wrapped his hands around the shaft of the spear. Biting his lip to fight back screams of pain, Action Joe™ pulled at the Spear Butchery.

The Terror stopped to watch his enemy attempt to remove the weapon. For a brief moment, the Terror knew respect for this warrior. In the entire universe, such a feat had never been attempted. Indeed, no warrior had ever been left alive after being struck a direct blow from the Spear Butchery. Respect turned into admiration as Action Joe™ succeeded in pulling the Spear Butchery free.

The Terror continued its advance as Action Joe™ fell limply to the earth. It planned to grant this valiant warrior a quick and merciful end. The Terror reached Action Joe™ and lifted the Sword Piercer to the sky. The Sword Piercer flashed in the sun as the blade that could not be turned slashed towards Action Joe™'s neck.

The Terror failed to notice that Action Joe™ had not released his hold on the Spear Butchery. At the last possible second, Action Joe™ held the Spear Butchery up in both hands, taking the brunt of the Sword Piercer's slash on the shaft of the spear that could not fail. A massive explosion rocked the area.

☆

"Don't do this, Dick," Steve said as he struggled to push Dick away. "This'll screw up the rest of your life. Do you want to end up in gaol?"

Dick smashed the tyre-iron into the ground inches away from Steve's face.

Steve screamed.

Dick grinned, and lifted the iron up for another strike. "So what? This world sucks with a nerd like you in it anyway. You think you're so smart, so smug with your perfect grades and teachers sucking up to you. You need to be brought down—you deserve it for thinking you're so smart. I woulda done this a long time ago if Kurt hadn't been there, babysitting you. I don't know why he's your friend."

"I don't know either. How about we go ask him?"

"Shut up! After you're gone, Kurt will hang out with his own kind, instead of losers like you and Duck. I'm doing him a favour."

Steve saw on Dick's face that he'd worked up the hatred and anger necessary to smash down with the tyre-iron.

Steve made a final plea for his life. "Please! Dick, please?"

"Die, nerd-boy, die!"

The tyre-iron came down in a brutal blow.

☆

To Action Joe™'s pleasant surprise, the Terror was knocked back from the force of the explosion. The alien's flight tore up more hillside, digging a gash big enough to bury the fifth fleet. Leaning on the Terror's spear, Action Joe™ climbed painfully to his feet.

The Fellowesvapour that gave Action Joe™ life leaked away through the wound inflicted by the Spear Butchery. It wouldn't be long before he was non-operational. He was the Hostile Alien Eradication Squad's best hope, and now he faced imminent failure. Oddly, he felt an irrational desire to save a nude dancer from flames.

The Terror regained its feet, still clutching the Sword Piercer, which sparked and smoked.

Action Joe™ ignored the tempting thoughts of brown maracas and fixed a hard look at the Terror. "You'd better know that this nephew of Uncle Sam never gives up." He held the Spear Butchery out, tauntingly. Then, in one swift action, he brought the spear down and shattered it across his thigh.

The Terror roared in fierce rage. The Spear Butchery, like all of its weapons, had been forged in the heart of a star and was supposed to be unbreakable. Now the spear was in three pieces, one in each of Action Joe™'s hands and a third piece on the ground.

The Terror charged. It would brutalise the enemy for this destruction of the Spear Butchery. It would rip the warrior into pieces. And then it would call for the mother ship, and strip this planet clean.

Action Joe™ slumped to the ground, holding his hands over the hole in his gut. Fellowesvapour continued to ooze from the wound.

☆

An explosion went off as Dick brought down his blow, a blow with which he'd meant to crush Steve Fellowes' head. The ground shook so hard that Dick completely missed his target.

Deep in Steve's gut a new feeling took root. Deep in his magnificent brain, a new thought struck. It came to him in fiery letters, in clarity such as he'd never experienced in a life of bringing scientific clarity to everything he did: *he did not have to take this. He did not have to be a victim.*

He did not have to allow others to bully or unduly influence him. He would not allow Dick Hairyson to take his life.

Steve lashed out, planting his fist squarely in Dick's crotch. The madness faded from Dick's eyes as pain engulfed him. Steve struck his target again, compounding his foe's pain. Dick fell to the ground wrapped around himself in the foetal position, clutching his throbbing genitals.

"That's right," Steve said, pulling himself up. He jabbed his finger down at Dick. "You can't bully me anymore—I'm *not afraid* of you! And if you ever mess with me again, there's more of the same in it for you." He kicked the tyre-iron out of Dick's limp hand for added emphasis.

"Steve," someone called, "can you hear me?"

Steve recognised Kurt's voice. "Down here!" he yelled back, looking up the slope to where his friend approached. His gaze continued on around the massive devastation that covered the countryside as far as the eye could see.

"The whole thing was on the news," Kurt said, sliding down to Steve. He looked over at Dick, then turned to Steve. "Are you all right? It looked close there for a minute. The news helicopters were shooting the whole thing. They even picked it up on audio."

"Helicopters?" Steve asked, looking up and seeing the helicopters flying overhead; until that moment they had been nothing more than background noise in the fight for his life.

"They've been broadcasting everything—the monster smackdown *and* your fight with Dick." Kurt clapped his friend on the shoulder. "You're a hero, dude."

☆

Action Joe™ watched the frenzied approach of the Terror. The alien monster was so enraged that it charged without its weapons held up.

Action Joe™ had one move left. As the alien drew closer, the giant soldier reached his left hand behind his back and struggled to his feet.

The Terror lunged, howling.

Action Joe™ smiled as he popped a pin from a grenade. "This is courtesy of Uncle Sam." He threw himself at the Terror and thrust the grenade deep into the alien's throat. He wrapped his fingers around the monster's snout and held its mouth shut. The Terror stumbled back, frantically trying to throw Action Joe™ off.

The massive explosion left a crater two miles wide.

The Terror's head blew off, never to be found.

Action Joe™ disintegrated in the blast, his mission completed at the cost of his own existence.

☆

Steve Fellowes wandered the crater and all the devastated areas with Duck and Kurt trailing along, looking for any sign of Action Joe™. Hours later, with tears pooling in his eyes, Steve gave up the search.

His cellphone rang. In shock from all of the day's events, Steve ignored it at first. Eventually, he numbly answered the incessant ringing. "What?"

"My name is Mr E," an obviously scrambled voice said. "I'm the commander of the Hostile Alien Eradication Squad."

"Action Joe™ kept mentioning—"

Mr E cut him off. "You've done your country a great service today, Steve. Our Action Joe™ intelligence software combined with your Fellowesmodeller saved the country and the whole world."

"Your software?" Steve asked. "But how did you get it into Action Joe™?"

"There's a tiny chip in all of 'em toys. Some of 'em damn aliens can read our minds, but they can't tap into the plastic brains. It's a failsafe ... Look, I've said too much—sorry, Steve, if I told you more, I'd have to kill you. We'll visit again when you finish college. HAES can use bright lights like you."

The line went dead. Steve stared at the phone.

"Action Joe™ was a hero, just like you," Kurt said, leading Steve back to the camp.

"He was my kind of guy," Duck said. "Loud and huge."

☆

Steve Fellowes made history that day. On top of being responsible for the soldier that saved the world, his Fellowessniffer, which tracked alien radiation, was invaluable in finding the Sceptre Domination where it lay buried. Government agents promptly hid it, along with all of the Terror's remaining weapons, and teams of researchers with millions in budgets began the work of deciphering the technology behind them.

The autopsy on the Terror was never started. Minutes after its head exploded, the Terror's body melted into pools of chemicals.

With Dick Hairyson locked away for psychiatric evaluation, the Fellowesmodeller carefully disassembled, and the Fellowesmodeller's gooey fuel carted off by government spooks, life returned to normal for Steve and his friends.

But many a late night Steve Fellowes sat in his bed and imagined himself perched in the shirt pocket of Action Joe™, stomping across the countryside like an Olympian god. And on those quiet nights, Steve felt the presence of Action Joe™ and he knew that Action Joe™ was far more than software and plastic and Fellowesvapour.

Action Joe™ was the spirit of freedom, the force that made men rise to the challenge when their homes were in danger. Steve knew that if ever he were needed again, Action Joe™ would return.

THE STRANGE CASE OF STARBASE 6

TERRY DARTNALL

Monsters," said Sherlock Holmes, tapping out his briar pipe against the heel of his boot, "are products of the imagination. They only exist in the mind."

Everyone knows that I have the highest regard for Holmes's acumen, but I wasn't sure about this one.

"What do you mean?" I said.

"Monsters are the product of fear, Watson." He looked at me with those sharp eyes of his. "What do you fear the most?"

"Well, Holmes, I ..."

"Forgive me. That was impertinent. What do most people fear, do you think? Come now, you're a doctor."

"Blood?" I suggested.

"Blood," he said. "Yes, people are afraid of blood."

He stood up and straightened his waistcoat.

"I shall tell you a story about blood. And fear and monsters. A terrible monster, Watson."

"Good show," I said, and settled back in my leather arm-chair.

☆

"My story begins with William FitzGibbons—William the Doctor. I shall refer to him as William. William had a morbid fear of blood, so it might surprise you, Watson, to discover that he was a medical fellow, like yourself. He became faint at the sight of blood—sometimes at the mere thought of it. But he came from a family of doctors and nurses and so he followed the family tradition."

"Sounds like a brave chap, Holmes. Didn't like blood but became a doctor anyway, eh?"

"Quite so, Watson. Medical School was an ordeal for him, but he got his medical degree from Edinburgh University and with his family's help acquired a practice in Sussex. It was shortly after this that he met Gladys Goring. Gladys was a fine young woman from an aristocratic family. She had been widowed at an early age. It is not clear what happened to her first husband. Some say that he died on an expedition to Africa whilst others say that he took his own life."

Holmes paused and sucked on his pipe.

"The incident that I am about to relate happened shortly after William and Gladys were married. They were staying with her family at the family estate in Falmer, near Brighton. It was here that William met Gladys's uncle, Sir Henry Throgmorton. Sir Henry had made a fortune out of fences."

"Fences?" I said.

"Haven't you noticed that iron and steel fences have sprung up all over the country, Watson? You see, but you do not observe."

"Made by this Henry chap, were they?"

"Throgmorton Industries. Sir Henry was obsessed by metal fences. They were all he talked about, as William found out."

☆

"Uncle Henry, I would like you to meet my husband, William."

"Good to meet you, William. So you're a doctor, eh? Good show! We need a doctor around here, that's what I say. Got any views on fences, then, eh? What do you fancy? Wrought iron? Steel? Decorative? Antique?"

"Well, I—"

"Fence Posts? The FC005's six feet of solid iron. All sorts of finishes: Scottish, Home Counties, Urban, Rustic." He put his big face close to William's and breathed brandy on him. "Southwestern? Asian? Chap like you would appreciate something like that."

Lady Agatha intervened. "I don't think William wants to hear about your ghastly fence posts, Henry. Do you, William? Now, I was going to ask you, would you like to address our society?"

"What society would that be, Lady Agatha?"

"The Society for the Preservation of Culture, William."

"Which culture would that be, Lady Agatha?"

"You young people, you're so blasé! Henry was like you before the war. After the war he only wanted to kill things. And talk about fences, of course. English culture, William—Agincourt, Trafalgar, Waterloo! How about Thursday?"

"It would be a pleasure, Lady Agatha."

"So proud of you, darling."

"What'y riding, William?"

"Riding?" said William.

"Didn't tell you, eh? Going huntin'. A few of the fellas and Gladys. Got a damned fine seat on her, that one. Good to have a doctor along, that's what I say. We were out huntin' last week and a fellow fell orf. Onto a fence post. An E29A, five foot with a decorated Rustic Finish in deep green. Quite nice. Mind you, I prefer the FC005. Went straight through 'im, spleen, liver, guts all over the place. Said to m'self we need a doctor along. Eh, Agatha?"

☆

"As you may have surmised, Watson, William was a studious fellow and he couldn't ride. But he didn't want to be shown up in front of Gladys's family, so he did something very stupid."

"You're not going to tell me that he went on the hunt?" I said.

"Indeed I am, Watson, and with tragic consequences. The weather was fine the next day, so any hopes that he might have had about the hunt being called off evaporated in the early morning sunlight. Gladys's family turned out in their hunting regalia, the dogs milled around, and suddenly they were off! William hung on bravely for a while, but when they were galloping downhill he slipped forward and hit the horse's neck with his riding crop. She was a skittish filly. She bolted downhill and headed for a fence."

"One of Sir Henry's—"

"—six-foot constructions. The horse pulled up before the fence —"

"Thank goodness!"

"And threw William into the air—"

"No!"

"Onto the fence. It impaled him before it snapped off."

☆

"Two in a fortnight," said Sir Henry. "Damned shame."

William lay on the bracken with the paling through his chest. His back was broken. Sir Henry's brandy-bloated face loomed over him. He planted a boot on William's chest and heaved out the bar. There was a fountain of blood.

"Urrrgh," said William.

"S'pose not, old chap," said Sir Henry. "I'll put it back."

He replaced the railing, presumably to staunch the flow of blood. It was too much for William's delicate constitution.

"Good Heavens!" said Sir Henry. "He's dead!"

☆

"He's a bounder!" I shouted.

"Just a victim of his genetic inheritance, Watson."

"Is he our monster, Holmes?"

Holmes smiled. "No, he isn't our monster."

He continued.

"Sir Henry looked puzzled. His dull brain heard strains of music, mysterious and wonderful. For the second time he withdrew the spiked railing from William's body. He examined it closely. How beautiful it was! What power and passion it possessed! With a sense of destiny he hurled it upwards, laughing. The music cascaded over him—Strauss! *The Blue Danube*! Up and up went the railing, twisting and shimmering in the sun. It grew bigger and brighter and acquired a light of its own. It grew beams and girders that curved and folded in upon themselves, with little twiddly bits stuck on it like holly. It became an oblate spheroid and a curved hexagonal lattice. And far, far below, Sir Henry Throgmorton dwindled into history."

☆

Towards the end of his story Holmes had taken his bottle from the corner of the mantelpiece and his hypodermic from its neat morocco case. He inserted it into the brown fluid and drew it into the shaft. He rolled back his left shirt-cuff with his long, nervous fingers and inspected his sinewy forearm, dotted and scarred with puncture marks.

"What I have told you so far is mundane," he said.

"Mundane?" I said.

"Dull, sublunary. It does not engage the imagination or tax the spirit."

He inserted the needle into his arm. I had seen him do this many times and it always filled me with apprehension.

"What is it today?" I said. "Cocaine? Morphine?"

"Cocaine," he said, "a seven-percent solution. Would you care to try some?"

I did not reply.

"From the sublunary to the sublime, Watson. From a yarn, a dull documentary, a tale you might tell your family around the evening fire—"

"Hardly!" I cried.

"To a vision, a revelation of the future."

Holmes sank back into his velvet-lined armchair and sighed. His features slackened. The corners of his mouth curved upwards in a smile. For a long time he did not utter a word or move a muscle. When he spoke again, he related the strangest story I have ever heard.

☆

"William FitzGibbons stood on the bridge of the Starship Victory and witnessed the docking at Starbase 6."

"I thought he was dead!" I shouted.

Holmes became silent again. Then he said, "Dear friend, let me continue. Suspend that quick mind of yours and all will be revealed." Then he added, as if he was talking to a child, "This is another William FitzGibbons, Watson. A descendent of William the Doctor. Gladys gave birth to a son six months after her husband's death. She named him William, after his father, and it became a tradition.

"Two hundred years have passed since Sir Henry's vision and how the world has changed! Gone are poverty, chaos and disorder. The Society for the Preservation of Culture has seen to that."

I sat bolt upright in my chair at this, but Holmes held up a laconic hand.

"In the last twenty years, Watson, we have seen the typewriter, the telephone, the gramophone, the telegraph, the electric light bulb, the internal combustion engine and the transatlantic cable. In two hundred years we shall have mastered the nuclear furnace, colonised the oceans and gone forth into the stars. But these are technological achievements. The real challenge will be social. The

British Empire will continue to expand and will soon control the planet. Then we will spread out into the universe. That is our inevitable destiny. To fulfil it we will have to impose order on the world."

"Kill everyone who's not British?" I said.

"Sir Henry had political influence and there was some bloodshed," he said. "Considerable bloodshed, in fact, for there is nothing as effective as six feet of iron railings in the hands of aristocratic bigots, backed by the British army. But the situation isn't as bad as it seems, Watson. You told me about Dr Mendel's work on the units of heredity."

"That's right, Holmes. He says there are hereditary units that remain unchanged from one generation to another."

"And that," said Holmes, "explains the supremacy of the British upper classes. We have superior hereditary units. We must ensure that they retain their dominant position in the world. There will be some initial culling, of course, but after that all that we have to do is to make sure that our units aren't polluted. And that the other chaps don't breed too much, of course."

"Good show, Holmes!" I said. "Carry on!"

"But suppose it is not so simple," said Sherlock Holmes. "Suppose that we *need* a large pool of units."

"What's that, Holmes?"

"Have you not noticed that pedigree animals are often sick and frail, whereas animals that breed indiscriminately are healthier and fitter? I shall assume that we need a large pool of units, Watson, and that without them our genetic flaws will multiply and be passed on to our children. So we have a problem. On the one hand we need to nurture our hereditary units, because they make us what we are—superior. But if we guard them too zealously we will become inbred and we will regress. This will be the real problem that we shall have to face as the Empire spreads out into the stars. So in this future, Watson, Captain William has inherited his ancestor's fear—"

"Of blood!" I shouted.

"Quite so, Watson, but in this future he is not alone, for everyone has phobias."

He was silent for a long time after this. I could see that my interruptions had disturbed him more than he was prepared to admit and that he was finding it difficult to return to his story.

Then he said, "Morphine."

"I'm sorry," I said. "I shouldn't have interrupted you."

"Not at all," said Sherlock Holmes. "The vision is subtle and it fades." He looked absently at the Persian slipper in which he kept his tobacco, then opened a drawer and took out a bottle of morphine, repeating the operation he had performed a few moments before. I had been concerned for a long time about this morbid and pathological process and had reminded him of the black reaction that comes upon him afterwards, but on this occasion I felt that my admonitions would be futile.

For the second time he sighed deeply and sank back into his chair.

☆

William FitzGibbons stood on the bridge of the Starship Victory and witnessed the docking at Starbase 6.

"*It's an oblate spheroid,*" *said William.*

"*It's a curved hexagonal lattice,*" *said Henry.*

"*Hello Station 6. Come in Station 6.*"

"*Station 6 receiving you. Come in Victory.*"

"*What shape are you?*"

"*OK, thank you. Rather bored.*"

"*Not you. The station. Put us on Mainframe.*"

"*Why?*"

"*To see what shape you are.*"

"*Who are you?*"

"*Captain William FitzGibbons. I've got four stripes. What've you got?*"

"*Oh, all right. Mainframe on.*"

"*Mainframe, relay configuration of Station 6.*"

"*CONFIGURATION OF STATION 6, READING: HORIZONTAL PROJECTION, RHOMBOIDAL POLYHEXADRON. 5 DEGREES FROM NORMAL—*"

☆

"Holmes!" I said, interrupting his story. "Why are you shouting?"

"That is the voice of the Universal Engine," said Holmes. "Remember our friend Charles Babbage?"

"He's working on a Universal Engine," I said.

"In two hundred years they will have perfected it," said Holmes. "It is massive, and it shouts."

"Why does it shout?" I said.

"Because it's massive," said Holmes. "Do I have to explain everything? The bigger something is, the more noise it makes."

☆

"*CONFIGURATION OF STATION 6, READING: HORIZONTAL PROJECTION, RHOMBOIDAL POLYHEXADRON. 5 DEGREES FROM NORMAL—*"

"*You're making it up!' said William. 'Look in your database!*"

"*IT'S ROUND. WELL, NOT REALLY ROUND. SORT OF SQUASHED ROUND. LIKE A TRAIN TRACK. NOT A REAL TRAIN TRACK OF COURSE. A TOY TRAIN TRACK, HORNBY OO SORT OF THING. NOT—*"

"*Forget about it! We're coming aboard.*"

William and Henry were soon having tea and crumpets with the crew.

"*Nothing happens here. It's boring.*"

"*No aliens?*"

"*No aliens.*"

"No meteorite showers?"

"No meteorite showers. Milk? Sugar?"

"MAINFRAME ALERT. CONDITION YELLOW."

☆

Holmes was becoming agitated. "Are you all right, Holmes?" I said.

"Your continual interruptions are affecting my train of thought, Watson."

"I'm sorry, Holmes."

☆

"MAINFRAME ALERT. CONDITION YELLOW "

"Well, as I was saying, I hate creepy-crawlies. Nice thing about spaceships, that is, I always say."

"My friend Cedric, he's on Station 8, and he's an agoraphobe. I think that's wonderful really, up here in space and being an agoraphobe."

"MAINFRAME ALERT. CONDITION ORANGE."

"Well, I don't know. It's all in the mind really. I mean if you don't think about it it's the same as being anywhere else really."

"That's what he says. I never look out, Eric, *he says.* All that space, ooh, I couldn't bear it."

"CONDITION RED ALERT. REPEAT RED ALERT. ALIEN CONTACT TWENTY-FIVE SECONDS. CONFIGURATION: MANTIS WITH BLOOD SAC. LENGTH 3.08736 MILES. HEIGHT—"

"That's attention seeking, Mainframe. Just because we have visitors."

"NO, HONESTLY. I SAID I WAS SORRY ABOUT THE LIFE SUPPORT SYSTEMS. I WAS BORED BUT THAT'S ALL OVER NOW. FORGIVE AND FORGET, I SAY—"

Click.

"That's shut him up. I don't like things on the left. It's the side sinister, you know. All those medieval etchings of demons carrying women off to the left. Ooh, it's creepy."

"Woodcuts, not etchings."

"I'm in charge and I say they're etchings."

There was a jarring thud as the station collided with the mantis.

"Christalmighty, what's going on? Activate Mainframe! Mainframe? Mainframe?! He's moping. If you don't answer I'll pull out your circuits."

"YOU WOULDN'T DARE."

"Like in the film, y'know, not Star Wars *... the other one."*

"CASABLANCA? NO, IT WAS ..."

☆

"I've been there!" I blurted. "It's in North Africa!"

"Watson!" said Holmes. "Shut up!" He enunciated the words very slowly, one at a time. "I have taken a grasshopper by the wing. Its chirping will drive me mad."

I know that I can be irritating at times, but I was so captivated by Holmes's story that I had entirely forgotten myself. And I was agitated, too. Why was the Universal Engine, located on something called a *starship*, talking about a place in North Africa?

Holmes took a small key from his waistcoat pocket and held it out to me. "This opens the small drawer in my bureau," he said. "What you will find there is for your eyes only."

I turned the key in the lock and the drawer opened easily. Inside were three coloured bottles.

"Pour the morphine into the cocaine, Watson, and shake the bottle."

"Holmes, I—"

"Just do it! Now add the contents of the coloured bottles."

I put the green one to my nose. "Chloroform!" I said. "It's illegal, Holmes!"

"So are the other drugs, Watson—opium and curare." I was about to remonstrate, but I saw there was little point. If I had refused to help him Holmes would have done it himself. I realised that he was in the grip of an obsession and I thought it best to stay there as a helper, rather than be turned away.

For the third time that night Holmes rolled up his shirtsleeve and thrust home the needle. This time the drugs took him differently. Rather than sinking into his armchair with a sigh of satisfaction he gasped and clutched at his collar.

"Holmes!" I stood up, but he waved me down.

"I see it!" he cried. "The great screen is filled with horror. Eyes ... Dear God, they're bigger than the station! Horns! Mandibles! They are in its claws!"

☆

"ALIEN RESEMBLES TERRAN MANTIS."

"A praying mantis?"

"AFFIRMATIVE. SPECTOGRAPHIC ANALYSIS CONFIRMS PRINCIPAL CONTENTS OF SAC TO BE HAEMOGLOBIN, NOT INDIGENOUS TO ALIEN. SAC CAPACITY ROUND FIGURE 118 BILLION GALLONS REDUCING."

"Of blood?"

"Not only that—it's drinking it."

"Urrrgh," said William.

"ORIGIN UNKNOWN."

"It resembles a mantis?"

"WITH BLOOD SAC."

"Give us a rundown on the species Mantodea."

"THE MOST INTERESTING THING ABOUT THE MANTIS, I THINK, IS ITS SEX LIFE. THE MALE SNEAKS UP ON THE FEMALE AND POUNCES ON HER. THEN HE STICKS IT IN AND SHE BITES HIS HEAD OFF BECAUSE SHE GETS BETTER SEX THAT WAY BECAUSE THE CORTEX INHIBITS—"

"The body keeps going without the head?"

"AFFIRMATIVE. THEN SHE EATS HIM UP. YUM YUM."

William was on the floor, clutching his collar. "Cut! Cut!" he gabbled.

"Christalmighty, it's going to mate with us. I don't want to be fucked by a mantis. I'm scared of sex."

"Of sex?"

"Why d'you think I'm fifty light years from the nearest woman?"

"Are you afraid of sex or women? We should get to the bottom of this. Could you relate to a woman if you didn't have sex with her? Would you enjoy sex with something that's not a woman?"

"Not a praying mantis."

"Starship Fucked By Praying Mantis. They won't believe it."

"Cut! Cut!"

"Poor fellow's upset. Chin up, William. Brave face in front of the natives."

"It's not a native. It's a three-mile vampire."

"Come on, William, sit up and talk to us."

"Neural impulses," gasped William. "Check its reaction time."

"Of course! Neural impulses are slow and this thing's monstrous. We might be able to cut our way out before it can respond. We can't sever the claws from this angle, so we'll have to go for the top of the forelegs. Mainframe, how long would it take a neural impulse to travel from the top of the forelegs to the brain and for the response to get back to the claws?"

"WELL, I WOULD SAY, PERSONALLY SPEAKING—"

"Compute it! Compute it!"

"NEURAL IMPULSE TIME: 48.536 seconds."

"It wouldn't respond for 48 seconds?"

"AFFIRMATIVE."

"You're a genius, William. It won't respond for 48 seconds. That'll give us time to sever the legs from the body. Then we decapitate it and cut the sac of, ah, red fluid from the abdomen."

"How do we cut it?"

"Our ship's a cutter. Does that mean it cuts?"

"We use lasers. Anyone afraid of lasers?"

"Only red ones."

"Green lasers then. We sever the legs from the body ... here and here ... then sever the neck and the collar between sac and abdomen. I can't help because I'm a Quaker. To your stations ... Fire One! ... FIRE ONE! ... FIRE FUCKING ONE!"

"It's the button. It's a funny shape."

"Change over. Edward on the funny button. William, you aim. Henry on second laser ... Fire one! ... Now what's wrong?"

"Can't look at it. Large, uh ..."

"Insect."

"With ..."

"Billions of gallons of blood."

"Aargh!"

"Henry, are you OK with insects?"

"Not furry ones."

"No fur. It's a praying mantis."

"Aargh!"

"Henry aiming. William on button, eyes closed. Edward on second laser. FIRE!"

Pencils of lights stabbed at the mantis, at legs, at neck, at the collar between sac and abdomen. For a long time it did not move. It had the raptured look of the very old imparting wisdom to the very young, ruining their lives forever. Then it came apart. Slowly. Very slowly. The head and legs drifted from the body. The great sac burst.

"You were right, William. There's no response. Look, it's breaking up."

William peeped between fingers and saw the sad eyes of the mantis, as huge as moons. Did they see him? What if they did? He'd conquered his fear! He'd conquered his stupid fear! Look at the blood! BLOOD! Streaming in the firmament!

☆

At this point Holmes tugged at his collar and shouted, "SEE WHERE CHRIST'S BLOOD STREAMS IN THE FIRMAMENT! ONE DROP WOULD SAVE MY SOUL!"

"Is that the Universal Engine?" I said.

"That was me," said Holmes. "You're a moron, Watson."

He sat up in his chair and focused on something I could not see, his voice hoarse with strain and apprehension, his eyes bulging in his head.

☆

Forty-eight seconds have passed since they fired the first lasers. The mantis's response has gone out, through the thorax and down the long length of the severed legs.

Forty-eight seconds have passed and the response has reached the claws, which clamp onto the starbase and move it towards the monster's cavernous mouth. William realises that they had much less than 48 seconds to sever the legs from the body. That was the time it took for the response to reach the claws, not the barbed femurs at the top of the legs. They had severed the legs within 48 seconds, but by then the signals were travelling down the long forelegs to the claws.

The jaws loom over them. Oceans of drool stream from the salivary glands and bubble into space. William wonders if it was sentient. Did it see them? Did it know they were there? He realises that the protruding eyes are a curved hexagonal lattice.

For a moment he thinks they will escape. The severed legs are drifting away from the body but they are clamped onto the starbase and are moving it into the mouth. The smooth surface of the ship slips out of the inner, auxiliary jaws. But the main mandibles get them.

The starship is stationary for a moment. Then the spiked roof of the mouth pierces the thin layer of metal and plastic that stands between life and nothingness.

And it is over.

☆

We sat in silence for a long time after that. Night had fallen and the gaslights in the streets were flickering on, casting pale shadows across the room. I had heard Holmes tell many tales over the years, but none as strange and terrible as this, and my mind reeled with the wonder of what I had heard. But I was worried about my friend, because I had no doubt that he had drunk too deeply at the well of knowledge and travelled too far into the forbidden realms it had opened before him. I resolved to wean him from the drugs that put his soul in peril and threatened to deprive him of the great powers with which he was endowed.[1]

"I see what you mean now, Holmes. Monsters are in the mind all right, even though this one was three miles long and ate—what was it?—the starship. You mean it was their fear that made it seem like a monster to them. Otherwise it would have ignored them and not eaten them at all, what?"

Sherlock Holmes sat in his velvet-covered armchair and did not answer. He seemed to be studying the flickering shadows on the walls. Then he said, in a voice that was barely audible, as if he was talking to himself, "Perhaps I was mistaken. Perhaps they are real after all."

I struck a lucifer and lit the gaslight on the mantelshelf.

"Our landlady will be waiting for us," I said, consulting my pocket watch. I held out my hand to Holmes and helped him to his feet.

"Dear, dependable Watson," he said. "You're right, of course. It's time for crumpets and tea."

---

1   In *The Adventure of the Missing Three-Quarter* (published in 1904 and dated December 1896 in Holmes's time), Watson tells how he gradually weaned Holmes from his drug dependence.

THE RETURN OF CTHADRON

RICHARD A. BECKER

His eyes were the eyes of frogs, cold and impersonal with lemniscate pupils; his scales were great green-black shields no missile could penetrate—five hundred feet tall, hundreds of thousands of tons, a walking, breathing denial of the laws of science and squared cubes. He was an eighth wonder of the world, a king of the monsters, rising from twenty thousand fathoms' depth, the mighty CTHADRON!

The year was 1954—

With each mighty step he destroyed a vast swath of our human civilisation, so vital and alive; with each step he destroyed jukeboxes spud guns drive-ins hot rods with rumble seats tins of Folger's Coffee sock puppets vaporisers skylights Lugers cans of Vienna Sausages telescopes penny arcades toy xylophones player pianos chemistry sets strung popcorn and cranberries linked-construction paper loop garlands Lincoln Logs model railroads circus sideshows and midways penny-molding keepsake machines fold-out turkey centrepieces EC comic books decoder rings music boxes three-D glasses boxes of cumin leather jackets Davy Crockett hats Mausers stained glass hedge mazes Korla Pandit shows model airplanes made with tissue paper and balsawood dime museums pianos burlesque houses soda fountains pogo sticks milkmen Queen Anne furniture and necklines kinescopes of Vampira and Zacherley orchestrions music halls and vaudeville houses and movie palaces and nickelodeons sidecars martini glasses motels shaped like teepees and spaceships wax-cylinder recordings airstream trailers roadside zoos carhops wood-paneled rec rooms bomb shelters brick barbecues Mediterranean hanging lamps swimming pools tromp l'oeil paintings Bettie Page loops rope ladders Roman candles woodburning sets spookshows old-time radio shows stereopticons Saturday matinees and serials bringing death and destruction to us all.

Who named him? The newspapers blamed the scientists, the scientists blamed folklorists, folklorists blamed rumour-mongers in the street, and no one knew who the rumour-mongers blamed. In the end, the creature was Cthadron, and no human on Earth didn't know what the word meant. Death is an impersonal force in the universe, sweeping away the good with the bad, but most of all, kicking apart the embers and dust of the old in favour of the new. Death does not care what form the new may take, but clears a path for it—a herald of newness.

So Cthadron heralded the new world, from out of the old, with roars that thundered past outrageous, impractical teeth; teeth that looked like knives but were too huge to do anything but crush and rend any living thing on Earth besides their owner.

I tell you this now, because I was there, and because it's been so many years since we've lived in terror of his thundering roar. That roar was enough in itself to turn skyscraper windows to a fine powder that would rain down, shredding your lungs and eyes if you were unlucky enough to stand too close, did you know that? Of course you do; we've all seen the photographs, but I remember seeing and hearing the horror with my own eyes and ears. When I could keep them open, that is.

I was a reporter for the Patterson-Gilman Company, and not a very good one, having been part of the forgotten coverage of the forgotten Korean War. It wasn't a war, as you know, being only a police action, and so it was poetically just that I should cover it. I'd wanted to be like the great reporters of World War Two, riding in a Jeep with the troops as we paraded in triumph down the streets of Pyongyang. But the communists were under the cloak of our larger enemies, whose nuclear weapons were brandished at our own home cities, and we would never dare to push them so far in their own backyard. And as for me, well, they said my prose was too florid and that I rambled on and on, and that they had no use for me on the frontlines.

They were right, and I know it, as I knew it then. I worked every angle they gave me and then they felt sorry for me when the war ended. Sent me to the Philippines, with the cheap booze and the little hookers of Subic Bay. Nine years since the war in the Pacific, I was sitting in bars drinking with ageing Marines and sailors, talking about victories that gathered dust, and knew I would die in Subic listening to tinkly xylophonic jazz on cheap radios in tropical bars with rats on the roof.

They were talking about television, the new medium I was too un-photogenic for, in the bar—the Marines were playing "smiles" in the corner with a group of underage b-girls—when the city began to shake around me.

The Phillipines were the first landfall of Cthadron.

At first I thought it was an earthquake, and I staggered outside with my drink in my hand to wait it out. But then I noticed that the rhythm was wrong; it was a rhythm of slow and inexorable footfalls instead of a deep bass drumroll. And I saw the faces of everyone in the streets. They were staring, shocked, into the sky: drunks, whores, thieves, servicemen, food merchants, garbagemen, knife-wielding toughs, and soon enough, failed reporters.

Words cannot describe the first vision of the monster, Cthadron. It was taller than any building, it filled our eyes like an eighteen-wheel truck fills the eyes of a cockroach on an interstate highway. Its weight was so massive that concrete pulverised into billowing, choking clouds of white dust under its footfalls. It had claws. Claws whose sharpness was meaningless—in cross-section, their finest point or edge would be broader than a plow—broader than a hundred plows! Claws that could not have been meant for anything smaller than a blue whale, claws that would've left little edible meat on an African bull elephant. It was terrifying, obscene, insane, absurd, impossible. It made your mind and body scream YOU CANNOT EXIST!

It stood in the sunset of the world, the sky a blazing crimson behind it, and Cthadron roared. It was the trump of Gabriel, the voice of Shiva become the destroyer of worlds, and it knew no bounds.

They think today that atomic testing may have awakened it. Others say it was a strange configuration of the stars, possibly counterfeited by the passing of a secret early satellite of which we were never told. I have clung desperately to each of these theories, and many others, in turn, and found no solace. Cthadron existed, and that was all that mattered. The mighty dragon, enemy of God, gave voice to its rage and everyone ran.

"Everyone, please remain calm. Cthadron is approaching the city. Please evacuate in an orderly fashion ..."

That is what the docudramas say policemen repeated, over and over again, in the first of his reigns of terror. The docudramas are full of shit, I tell you. The policemen used their guns and billy clubs to clear paths through screaming mobs driven insane with fear, seasoned troops broke like Boy Scouts and fled for their lives when he was within half a mile of their lines. For all that his movements wavered between rubbery flexibility and jittery stop-and-go strangeness, Cthadron could move impossibly swiftly when he wanted. Half a mile, twenty miles, depths of the ocean: nothing seemed a long enough distance for him. The world was not enough.

I gazed up at him. Today you know that I was the only journalist on the scene. It was my lucky break. After his roar, the stench of his breath flowed over the city like a wave of smog. An aroma of fire, brimstone, rotting things, and the unmistakable reptile odor of a fat snake in a cage at the zoo. His body, as everyone knows, was like a heavyset Tyrannosaur, one with a bizarre bone disease that made warped spikes and ridges like vast Pacific coral reefs grow forth from his flesh. Even at the great distance between us, I could see small lakes of seawater rain from his shoulders, dying fish wriggling in sudden rainbows.

I would be a terrible Zen philosopher. Although it's true that impartial death is the harbinger of the new, I can hardly think of that when it's my old ass that's about to be swept away in favour of a fresh pile of rubble, a younger generation of carrion-eating rats, and a brand-new layer of ash. I survived the crushing mobs trapped in narrow passageways of the city only because I was frozen with heart-hammering shock for long minutes, and when I found my will to live, I ran after all the rest of them. But I couldn't get very far; the bottlenecks were bloodbaths, and I took refuge (ha!) in the minaret of a cheap fake pagoda restaurant called Chinese Dream Number Eight.

That's where I was when I phoned in the world's first report of Cthadron, and where I began my new life.

He walked past me. That's as close as I ever was to Cthadron, at least three blocks away no matter what my official biography says, and it was near enough to see the filmy nictitating membranes that oozed across the huge, gleaming black eyes; it was near enough to see the vast swathes of tarmac rip and slip under its tread and its long dragging tail like loose patches of glued-down paper. It was near enough to feel the heat of Cthadron's Death Pulse.

Science fiction writers lost to cheap drugs would have been the only earlier witnesses to the Death Pulse. It was madness incarnate. Cthadron reared back, concentrating in some reptilian fashion, and suddenly an eerie green glow welled up inside his head. The bones of his spine, his skull, and his surprisingly delicate-looking fanged jaw all transformed into a glowing inferno of green-white light that shone through his tonnes of flesh like a nightmare moon. And then he unleashed the fury of the green-white nuclear fire through unscathed eyes, mouth, nostrils— really his entire face became a conduit between mankind and thermonuclear devastation. The electromagnetic pulse killed my telephone, all the lights, all the policemen's Jeeps, every electrical device in the city; the sound shattered windows for miles, the heat crisped my eyebrows before I could jump for cover in the room. And where the Death Pulse struck, ashes and slag were the remains of the fortunate ones.

For the unfortunate, blindness, deafness, crippling injuries, disfigurement, slow death by burns, hideous bleedouts from radiation, and worse.

It was the Death of Manila that came that night, but I survived it, cowering in the abandoned restaurant until the United States Marines came and took me under their wing. My report had made me a hero. I had lived while many thousands had died, and Cthadron had returned to the Pacific in a wake that seethed like a boiling cauldron. My survival was my curse.

I was to be Cthadron's albatross. Where he struck, there I would be also, telling the story of his horror and the fight for mankind's survival. "This is Guy Gene Marten, reporting from Singapore ... Saigon ... Tokyo ... Honolulu ..." The Far East became the Far West as I rode on his tails to success amid death and doom. Manila was terrible, but Singapore was worse (Jesus, the orphans!), Saigon beyond belief (the bravest troops who ever faced the thing!), an SOS from Tokyo (Christ, I hope I can forget the faces!): the worst of all.

He marched like Sherman, not to the sea but from it, and every time the military's efforts turned out to be worse than useless. The Eisenhower administration debated using the Bomb on Cthadron, wondering if such a physical impossibility might be stopped by the splitting of the atom. But then, it seems, a quiet transformation occurred—someone told someone else that it was "time for the truth."

You would never know it today, but there was a time when Government Tech was a closely guarded secret. The disparity between public access to high technology and the products of black laboratories across the American Southwest was not always apparent. We honestly didn't realise that, just as there are starships based on Greytech nowadays, Washington had access to jet planes when the Wright Brothers were gliding at Kitty Hawk. The men in black suits and mirrored sunglasses loved their secret handshakes and nods as much as their vaults of wonder crafted by carefully silenced engineers and scientists. Only genuine shrieking fear could have made those Illuminati release their stranglehold on the truth. Only Cthadron could force cards onto the table.

It was Honolulu that decided matters. I was heavily tranquilised on the back of a truck, ready to report for the Dumont Network on the approach of the demon-thing that had incinerated and crushed over a million human souls and left millions more wounded, shattered and broken in its path. My suit was impeccable, my wallet was full, and every single split second was meaningless in the face of ultimate death. The Navy had listened with undersea microphones to the hellish approach of Cthadron, ripping up forests of kelp and smashing reefs full of life between his splayed toes, and the charts didn't lie. Honolulu would be next.

An hour before noon, Cthadron rushed up from Mamala Bay into Honolulu, his body swamping forward in the midst of a gigantic Hokusai tidal wave. Sailboats caught unawares surfed the peak of the tsunami for short screaming seconds before pouring down into the city. Thousands were crushed and drowned on his arrival, and Navy sea mines fell from Cthadron's arms and legs to explode in our midst. The same mesmerising cycle as always had begun: Cthadron waded up onto land, began to kill and destroy, and the military rushed to attack. And as always, missiles were useless, five-ton shells launched from battleships erupted in fire and shrapnel on his hulking abdomen, high-tension lines and fuel depots were irritants to his prehistoric hide.

But then the strange airplane came. It was like a flying wing out of the late years of the Big One, or a silver pterodactyl out of a dream; it burst through the sound barrier with a chain of boom-boom-booms across the sky and it cut across our retinas with a searing white light as it burned at Cthadron with a continuous stream of charged leptons and baryons and muons, oh my.

We watched, more incredulous than ever, as a machine no human being had ever known could be built did battle with a living monster that every human knew could not possibly exist. Our huge, clunky, black-and-white, live-television cameras and sixteen-millimetre news colour-film cameras darted this way and that, an ocular ballet to follow the struggle in the sky. Minutes passed as Cthadron's march into Honolulu came to a standstill. He stayed his ground and screamed out his awful warcry, unleashing his Death Pulse at the hypersonic jet again and again, bellowing with pain when its radioactive, ionised stream of power actually burned his outer scales. We were too stunned to cheer, and too surprised to realise what was happening.

Cthadron had been releasing his Death Pulse into the sky, missing the jet again and again. And it took longer and longer for the Pulse to happen each time. After the longest five minutes in human history ... there was no more Death Pulse. Only the crackling boom of the particle beam, burning Cthadron over and over, until the jet had also lost its charge.

At the time, we didn't know what was happening. The military pressed their advantage, but it didn't mean anything. Artillery of all sizes meant nothing to Cthadron, who was too heavy and dense to be budged by shells that destroyed city blocks. But the temporary extinguishment of his Death Pulse seemed to dishearten him. And something else. He stood in the hail of artillery and took a colossal step forward.

And vanished.

With the flooded city crowned in dirty flames, an Armageddon, a kali yuga, a Mrs O'Leary's cow armed with fuel-air explosives, one could not help but think—if one had the right perspective—how the world appeared to be one thing but was truly another. While the camera crew and the other reporters cheered, thinking Cthadron had been finally blown to atoms by shells and missiles, and the professional worriers argued that the creature had burrowed under the salty soup of blood and rubble it had made, all I could think was that there was more to all of this than we knew. A giant magician's trick, making the elephant disappear, Cthadron had vanished and no one knew how or to where. Mankind makes death disappear every day, by pretending it doesn't exist. So that was what we did.

But ...

I was the Man Who Had Survived Cthadron, a Pulitzer-prize-winner, graduated from cheap booze to expensive prescription pills, braver than The Shadow or Tom Mix in the eyes of the public, the gravelly voice of American courage facing the living incarnation of Armageddon, and I had Huntley, Brinkley, Cronkite and Murrow looking to me as a peer. How lucky could a man be, when all it cost was a sea of human ashes and concrete dust?

We forgot death. It was with us every day, so we forgot it, and went on. That's what people do, of course. I did it, too. Married the blonde cheerleader in the cocktail dress and listened to my jazz and ate my steaks and smoked my pipe and lived in the house in Levittown and clucked my tongue at the Army Hearings and never quite got off the tranks. My kids were born at the tail end of the 1950s, spoiled little Baby Boom brats but I loved 'em. Our world wasn't the same as it had been pre-Cthadron, but it never is the same, is it? The incredible punctuates our lives like a heartbeat. It punctuates the lies we tell ourselves to get through the days before our deaths. The years passed in a dream-nightmare of Cold War and repressed peace.

And then the year was 1964—and the thing returned, to take his unbelievable revenge, as Cthadron raided again!

The year was 1964—

With each mighty step he destroyed a vast swath of our human civilisation, so vital and alive; with each step he destroyed Russian nesting dolls lavalites The Green Ghost water rockets go-karts Don Post Calendar Masks neon signs skybucket rides Creepy Crawlers Spirographs hanging paint-by-numbers kits wood-paneled wagons with running boards wicker chairs Frisbees air hockey Uncle Miltie's Ant Farms A&W root beer stands Harley-Davidson bikes 8mm monster reels shooting galleries Major Matt Mason Moon Crawlers Ca Bala minibikes toy pianos Fizzies Colossus Rex injected-plastic memento machines cigar boxes fondue sets Sheriff John tiny hand-moulded plaster bricks red plaid Betty Crocker cookbooks carved-soap sculptures Ripley's Believe It Or Not Museums boxes of Captain Crunch and Quisp foozball glow-in-the-dark posters Barbie dolls animated billboards Sears wishbooks Lum's restaurant nightclubs spotlights casks of aged rum pick-up sticks filmstrips spouse-swapping parties Castle of Frankenstein magazines Viewmasters diners Hobo Kelly convertibles Barnabas canes and posters and rings and boardgames and paperbacks G.I. Joe X-ray specs communes monster hot rod models Chinese puzzle boxes Mars Attacks cards Water Wiggles Nehru jackets yo-yos Bogart posters layered drinks stilts skeeball Rockem Sockem Robots waddle books tiffany lamps Big Little Books hula hoops Slip 'n' Slides Chris-Craft companies ornate room dividers Easy Bake ovens electric organs with pulsating colored lights wax candy lips grabbing-hand banks Hot Wheels and Hot Wheels track King Kong Posters Smokey Joe's Cabin Winky Dink ghost on a wire tricks nudist colonies Famous Monsters of Filmland and Famous Monsters Speak CARtoons soapbox racers Microbots touch plants air-puff guns denim jackets bringing horror and sudden death to us all.

If you trace a path across the seas, you find that Cthadron must have originally arisen from the icy waters near Antarctica, inhaling pods of whales and frantic polar bears as it walked and swam (it can do both, and burrow as well, and maybe other things it never showed us) toward Manila, Singapore, Saigon, Tokyo, Honolulu. It marched from the East to the West, which are human points of reference on a vast geoid ball that doesn't care what you name it, and when it evaporated in a microsecond before our eyes in Honolulu, it faced the east and our nation's West Coast.

Why were we so surprised when a vast whirlpool swallowed up an ocean liner between Hawaii and California? Why did we never anticipate that the thunderstorm that hammered Los Angeles that night was the black banner of Cthadron? Why doesn't a cancer victim think their tumors can ever return, after the doctors pronounce it a five-year cure?

Cthadron's crushing footfalls ignited the Firestone rubber tyre plant in Southgate; the Death Pulse brought equality to the white palaces of Bel Aire and the black hovels of Watts; orange groves, freeways, corrupt building inspectors, concrete-lined rivers and Mexican-American family households were annihilated in a vast stew of carnage. Cthadron's shock-surprise reappearance had caught a fat and lazy America off-guard; even I couldn't arrive in LA until hours after the hellfire had been laid down. There barely was a Los Angeles by the time I set foot on the tarmac at March Air Force Base—it was a fiery ruin dotted with hills of radioactive dung dropped and smeared by Cthadron as he strode with a milestone figuratively around his neck. The monster himself had already returned to the sea. Strangely, his particle-beam wounds from a decade earlier were still fresh, though he ignored all the barrages aimed at him by mere artillery.

An evil old man once lied that two is a suspicious number, because two is everywhere around us—look at yourself in the mirror, if you will—but twice in a lifetime was too much for most of us. It shook our faith in a just God; it was one thing for throngs of Asians to meet screaming death under the toes of a prehistoric reptile, but honest-to-Christ Americans vaporised by the Death Pulse? Unthinkable. Unspeakable. There had still been some innocence left in America a half-year after Kennedy's brains were the reddest pennant in the Dallas motorcade, but a second Cthadron on American soil was enough to kill our souls. There'd never been such devastation among Americans on American soil in all of history (apart from the War of 1812, the Civil War, the Little Big Horn, the Labor Union battles). The religious called it the curse of God, or turned from God altogether. The politicians used fear as leverage, as they always do. Military men saw their roles expand, and did not resist the heady wine of power. America was on the move, but so was Cthadron. And so was I.

They gave me a ranch house safely inland in Denver, and a new Corvette Stingray, and my wife and two kids loved my big new salary. My doctor didn't even raise an eyebrow when I tripled my prescriptions. I was back in the saddle again. All I had to do was watch the slaughter from the front-row seat and tell everyone the horrible details to their sick little hearts' content. So I did.

Cthadron and I roved up the Pacific Coast together. We were like two drunken Marines in Subic, too long in-country, drinking blood and spiking our veins with fiery destruction. Cthadron was the Toho Chi Minh of our Second Vietnam, proof that the wonders of the world need not be benevolent. He tore down the Golden Gate Bridge and swatted streetcars into the far horizon; turned the Willamette River red with death; snapped the new Seattle Space Needle in two and actually devoured Pikes Place Market; set fire to Vancouver Island and then set his sights on the Alaskan oilfields.

They kept the nuclear option out of the question, despite the screaming battles of Teller and McNamara. ("Aren't things radioactive enough?!") But they used napalm, reptile-specific viruses of the deadliest sorts, enormous clouds of oxygen-free gases that proved for all time that Cthadron did not need to breathe. They used electricity, lasers, liquid hydrogen, armour-piercing ammunition and explosives in a bewildering variety. Soldiers drugged into fearless berserk hyperactivity were parachuted onto his mountainous bulk in hundreds, using climbing rigs and powerful satchel explosives to try and crawl under his scales like fleas and detonate their bombs against softer flesh beneath. But Cthadron was no wyrm of legend, and unlike Fafnir or Smaug he had no weak spot. Men were crushed, shrieking like trapped animals, under his scales; smeared redly across him by outsized claws, plucked and dropped into his awful mouth to become a soft paste on contact with superheated live steam.

Without oil there is no industry, without industry there is no wealth, without wealth there is no power. Millions had died already, but as Cthadron steamed north toward Anchorage, and I popped valiums with my black coffee and powdered-sugar donuts, a gleaming geodesic Plexiglas dome rose from the sea in the monster's path. The youngsters were more surprised than I was; after the silvery V-shaped aircraft in the '50s, I was frankly more surprised that something like this hadn't happened when it could've saved more lives. But then again, a carefully orchestrated victory can be worth a lot to the right people.

In any case, Cthadron climbed up the sloping undersea shelf toward Alaska, a thousand waterfalls shimmering down his body and face in the cold morning light. He was huge and darkly emerald against the white sky, and he saw his reflection a hundred times over in the panes of the geodesic dome.

The State Department never had admitted to being the source of the Delta Plane in 1954, but they'd hinted about it. Now they kept their mouths shut again about the gleaming dome gently rocking in the waves as Cthadron cautiously approached it.

I don't know what I was expecting from it. I suppose I'd thought all along that there were people inside the dome, watching and preparing some sort of weapon. I didn't think the dome was the weapon itself. But when it erupted like some strange bursting Amazonian flower, gushing a weird plastic web hundreds of feet into the air, I was as surprised as Cthadron.

Cthadron cried out with his Ragnarok voice, but choked midway through the roar. The plastic stuff was all over him, leaving only his tail untouched, a thin glistening shroud that knit together furiously with a powerful chemical reaction. He fought and struggled, casting up vast waves onto the evacuated shoreline, and the military had some sort of secret orders because this time there was no artillery barrage. They merely watched and waited as the eerie drama played itself out. Cthadron staggered this way and that, unable to roar, until it finally used its Death Pulse—but that freed only the monster's gigantic mouth. The plastic clung too snugly for Cthadron to chew or claw it; it was between his scales and deep in his pores. His vision must have been distorted, his hearing muffled, his sense of smell nonexistent. Cthadron smashed the remnants of the dome with his tail, then stumbled forward and crashed into the surf.

It wasn't deep enough to fully submerge the monster, but it did. We wondered if Cthadron had smashed upon some subaquatic cavern, or yanked his claws free to burrow deep into Earth's bowels, but we later discovered that neither was the case. He'd simply disappeared under the swirling waters, dropped below the concealing murk and no one knew where he'd gone. He was the Amelia Earhart of natural disasters, the Judge Crater of sudden death; we fretted and speculated about possibilities for two whole years before we forgot him again.

Hard to believe, isn't it? We forgot a five-hundred-foot juggernaut of agonising death after just a few years. What can I say? I had bills to pay. The wife grew up and the kids got older, I got fatter and everybody was so proud of me for sitting in a military helicopter half a mile away from Cthadron watching the whole thing through a pair of $200 binoculars.

Around the world, kids watched cartoons about thinly-disguised Cthadrons who were "good friends to man", protectors of the world, friends of children. I really didn't mind that part. We all deal with death our own way.

☆

"Cthadron has appeared twice in human history," said the narrator of the educational film over the perky, tinkly background music, an animated green line cutting up from Antarctica along the Pacific Ocean and toward the Arctic Circle. "Although legends of mighty beasts of centuries ago, like the Tarrasque (CUE MEDIEVAL WOODCUT), have alleged things not unlike Cthadron, we know now that Cthadron is clearly some sort of mutant dinosaur (CUE STOP-MOTION DINOSAUR FOOTAGE) or possibly a very dangerous form of extraterrestrial life (CUE CAMERA TILT-UP INTO MYSTERIOUS, BEAUTIFUL STARSCAPE) ..."

Clearly. Clearly we knew nothing then, or now, about what Cthadron actually was. Taxonomically, a reptile or amphibian. Two forelimbs, two legs, bipedal, long dragging tail, thickset body, short thick neck with large wedge-shaped head and snout, four claws per extremity, short thick forked tongue. Swam and burrowed (but it burrowed only rarely) with all four limbs and tail in motion, walked upright on land using its tail as a counterbalance, stereoscopic vision in its lidded eyes, no apparent ability to see in non-visible spectra, human-like range of hearing in its pit-like ears, not a particularly good sense of smell, breathing only to emit its roar. Gender unknown, but we assumed it was male. Somehow, I always felt like Cthadron was male, but God only knows. At least the damn thing never laid any eggs. We hope.

The beatniks got too old to be cool and the boys and girls of the Boom took their place, growing hair and talking about free love and free drugs and free everything. I was too old to understand what the hell they were talking about, a well-sedated and substantial journalist at the overripe point of my late 30s, but my kids were just close enough to teen age to make my wife uncomfortable with what they understood. People still blew the hell out of each other with bombs, especially in Indochina. Vietnam, whatever they want to call it. I still refuse to say "Kampuchea".

The age of Aquarius was the age of Satanicus for a lot us; a little Charlie Manson and Sirhan Sirhan went a long way to cooling off the Summer of Love. The seventies came around, and as I hit my forties I decided I was tired of being old and—yes, I went in for the love beads and the Nehru jacket and all of that. You would have, too, if you'd been me. The one thing I've wanted above everything else is to stop being myself, so if you're in the market, let me know. You can be me for a song.

In any case, I'd talked the missus into experimenting along with me. The kids would be in high school soon, and hell, we didn't want to be uptight. We made sure the kids were all right (we thought) and we did a lot of crazy stuff. Key parties, drugs other than the booze and pills—especially psilocybin, the fungus of terror, and LSD, the bodysnatcher from Hell. It was a party for three whole years, especially once the kids went to college, and it was me versus my own death all the while. Young again, so I wouldn't have to grow old, or face the end as suddenly as all those people in those burning cities.

And time passed. And suddenly, shortly after the dinner hour, at a lonely Canadian Arctic research station, an unknown object of gigantic size crashed into the tundra. Geophysicists inside one of the aging quonset huts thought at first it was an earthquake, until they heard the hissing rush of superheated air, the thundercrack of giant bones flexing, and a familiar and terrifying roar that smashed the lenses of men's glasses and the glass surfaces of their delicate scientific instruments. A few survived there, but their warning to Northern Canada came in vain—for Cthadron had reappeared!

The year was 1974—

With each mighty step he destroyed a vast swath of our human civilisation, so vital and alive; with each step he destroyed CB radios 8-track tapes of Mahalia Jackson and Chicago and The Best of Carson and Harry Belafonte Zap-Action model kits Hilly Rose Wizzers kids' toy soda fountains waterbeds Trackballs planterns Mego Star Trek dolls mood rings Bill Ballance Cinemagic magazine Chicken Delight Kathryn Kuhlman bubble-windowed Vans with shag carpet interiors and Vans shoes Jack LaLanne Nieman-style posters of King Kong and Star Wars Koogle Shrunken Head Apple Sculpture Kits Maskatron Dave Hull the Hullabalooer Icebird Lone Ranger burger stands plants hanging in macramé nets Stan Chambers Pizza Man life-size posters of Kirk, Spock and Jack Davis' Frankenstein Monster Dynamite magazine Carol Hemingway the D. Jack Frost military surplus store People's Almanacs and Books of Lists monster trading cards Ben Hunter Howard the Duck For President buttons waterbeds Saturn Five moon rover and LMD models plastic Star Trek models of ships and equipment Skydiver rides Radio Shack stores Ken and Bob carnivals Gypsy Boots Spider-Man rock albums and coins Happiness Is A Warm Puppy mood fish self-adhesive mirror tiles Micronauts novelty erasers and pencil cases Herb Jetko old-fashioned iron parks Weebles coffee shops Papa Bach's and A Change Of Hobbit Big Wheels Ray Briem Seymour and his Slimy Wall Yummy Mummy Fruit Brute and Booberry Charlie Tuna radios Aurora monster models with glowing heads and hands pinball machines FOOM posters superballs executive toys with click-clacking steel balls Swanson's frozen fried chicken Karkoff Is Coming billboards British books of Naked Yoga and The Illustrated History of Horror Movies Prehistoric Scenes toothpick sculptures Nixon masks copies of The Glass Tower, The Fan Club, Allan Eyles' Marx Brothers Books, The Fan Club, Comics and Comix, the Star Trek Concordance and Star Trek Blueprints Pong

The human loss was less than before, but the numbers increased with time. The environmental damage was staggering, but human beings are rarely as concerned about animals and plants as themselves. We'd be happy with just ourselves, the things we made, the animals and plants we domesticated, and lots of concrete. A tiny minority disagree, but who cares about those treehuggers?

In any event, Cthadron raged unchecked along the Arctic coastline of Canada. From Victoria Island to Baffin Island, from Devon Island to Ellesmere Island, to Greenland (where the Danish military demonstrated why they're a noted force to reckon with in the modern world), to Iceland (where Cthadron paused at the volcanoes, but no one knows why), and then—into the Atlantic.

They called it malaise, they called it post-Nixon incompetence, but nobody apart from the Canadians was all that worried about Cthadron. Maybe he'd be satisfied with using the Death Pulse on moose and pine trees. Maybe he'd wear himself out. Maybe Vietnam and Watergate and Munich and JFK and RFK and MLK had worn us out—I should say, US out. Humans are communal animals—though we scorn sheep for the same behaviours. When some of us are weary, all of us are weary, and I certainly didn't mind the fact that they weren't sending me out there to watch Cthadron at work. Yet. Regardless, it wasn't until Cthadron had rounded the Earth and was bearing down on Western Europe that we took him completely seriously again. He surfaced off the Shetland Islands, bound for the North Sea and its oilfields. What a surprise to us all, then, that suddenly action was underway.

Satellite systems existed that none of us had heard about. The governments of the world had been pressured since '64 to explain more about these sudden appearances of technology, but partisan politics stalled every effort since the Kennedys had been murdered. Johnson didn't plan to tell anyone what he knew (and said he knew nothing, anyway); Nixon certainly wasn't going to talk, and we all believed that Ford didn't have a clue. But there was a lot of anger in the air that The Powers That Be hadn't taken a hand in things until their own interests were threatened.

We never worried about the fact that there were Powers That Be at all; only that they weren't watching over us with the proper diligence of a shepherd. O Lord, save thy flock!

When the monster's course was clearly set for the North Sea, and possibly Scotland, Northern Ireland, or anywhere along there, the network brought me back from reading the news about federal-level corruption and plopped me back into the field with a mighty "Hi-yo Silver, away." I packed as many drugs as I thought I would need to get through this one, and then a little bit more. That's the funny thing about covering the end of the world live via satellite, you never know when you're going to lose your mind with yammering idiot fear and begin to scream for your mommy on global television. Which is good for ratings—once. Having a great desire to continue life and my current lifestyle, I made damn good and sure I would remain calm as Cthadron approached. Tousle my thinning hair just a little to look sexy and harassed by the terror that was claiming the lives of everyone else in its path. Good stuff for the camera.

Another funny thing is that there comes a point when the tranks just aren't working as well as they ought to. We were out over a misty, miserable North Sea and the pilot, who was just a kid, pointed out the front of the bird. He was jumping up and down like a tot with their ass on fire, telling me to look, look, there it is. Hell yes, there it was. Cthadron, swimming like an oil tanker through grey twenty-foot waves, headed straight for a big oil rig. The guys aboard it had already evacuated, so the only thing at risk was a CEO's ransom in crude, and it was going to be my first reunion in a decade with my old "buddy". I could see the fresh-looking particle-beam marks on his leviathan body, even with such lousy visibility, and he trailed quarter-mile streamers of plastic crud that looked brand-new.

We were due to go live when everything went black.

They told me later at the hospital that I'd had a panic attack, maybe too many of my pills, all sorts of possibilities, but thank God we weren't live on the air. My blood pressure had spiked and my heart had gone arhythmic, and I just blacked out. They did their best to keep me alive while we headed for a hospital, and somebody else got the first look at Cthadron in the North Sea. They also were the only ones there to see the latest secret weapon against the walking death, namely some kind of freeflowing silvery metallic substance that adhered to him and then glowed orange as it negated gravity. The video footage was spectacular; it was like watching a Macy's Thanksgiving Day parade balloon float up and up and up into the sky. Before I came out of it, cosmonauts reported seeing the monster from space, and even some backyard astronomers told of watching Cthadron's voyage into the void. The world rejoiced. Apart from Canada, Greenland, and Iceland, of course. This time, no major cities had been destroyed. This time, it was Earth one, monster zero.

The public was told I'd had a heart attack, and I guess I had, in a way. The truth was that I was so damn afraid of Cthadron I overdosed and almost died. The wife was glad I was alive, and so were the kids, but I wasn't quite as enthusiastic. We could hope for an end of Cthadron, but I was never so sure as other people were. Three times was enough to make me doubt. I didn't know if I agreed with Jeanne Leek or the other so-called psychics that Cthadron was a primal human death-urge that couldn't be stopped until we conquered ourselves, or that he was a scourge across the universe that would destroy all planets until he returned, but I did know he'd come back before. He could do it again.

The brush with death? All it was, was blackness. The same darkness you see in Cthadron's eye. No tunnel of light, no angels. That's all I knew. But I wanted to live, so after they checked me out of one hospital I went to another one, on sabbatical, and got myself cleaned up. "Got myself cleaned up" being four short words to describe a quarter-year of shrieking, delirious, filth-drenched horror and insanity as they took me off half the legal and illegal drugs known to mankind. But finally it was over, and I no longer even drank Bloody Marys. I took up golf. And crossword puzzles.

And I waited, hoping it wouldn't happen again, as my kids left school and met their spouses and my wife had her back broken in a car accident that left her in a wheelchair and me as her part-time nurse for the rest of our lives. I liked the stripper at my 50th birthday dinner a little too much for the wife's comfort; stopped caring which party I voted for; had to put the dog to sleep. And Jimmy Carter came and went, and Ronnie Reagan got elected, and my father died from his lifelong cigarette smoking, and my mother moved into a trailer park, and I got traded over to the fledgling CNN for beaucoup bucks.

And I waited.

People were afraid of mass famine in Africa, the new threat of AIDS, and the old threat of the hydrogen bomb. Cthadron was still a favourite of the kids (well, any kids who had never really had to face him), and he was still the giant footnote to my career. But although the Freedom of Information Act had forced the government to admit that there had been a secret Lincoln Advanced Research Program (Project LARP) since the 1870s, precious little had been revealed and Ronnie Reagan clamped the lid back down. The main thing was, it had always come through when we needed it, right? Right. It was morning in America, and that was enough. Wake up, it's time to go do a hostile takeover and some lines of cocaine.

This time I wasn't at all surprised when the warning from space came. Something large was approaching the Earth at high but not planet-threatening velocities. The intruder's trajectory had been tracked for a couple of years and was highly erratic— apparently they'd lost track of it once in a while (which was itself nearly impossible) and then found it again someplace completely different. But now it was headed for Earth, and it was probably going to burn up in the outer atmosphere.

I wasn't quite so sure. The object was about 500 feet long, very oddly shaped, covered in cosmic dust and meteoritic bits which were concentrated much more heavily on one end. I was very certain that smarter men than myself were thinking the same thing I was thinking. And I had my credibility to consider. What if it wasn't ...? What if it was another Kahoutek? What if it was just a myth, like a UFO? What if I went out and played another round of golf with my hands shaking like I had Parkinson's? And listened to Mantovani on my headphones for hours, damn whatever the kids laughed at?

Cthadron didn't burn up on reentry. He glowed white-hot when he climbed up out of the crater that had been the port authority at Marseilles, leaned down and screamed out his roar so close to a crowd of people that many of them literally burst in a spray of blood and intestines from the overpressure shockwave.

The year was 1984—

With each mighty step he destroyed a vast swath of our human civilisation, so vital and alive; with each step he destroyed ice cream sandwiches packets of Kool-Aid ham radios Pez dispensers 7-11 convenience stores Otter Pops life-size standees D&D books by the truckload toy robot arms wax museums Bomb Pops orange-crate art soldered-together tinscrap folk art fold-up shopping carts Flexipop wrist rockets two-liter bottles of Doctor Pepper tiny wax bottles of sweet liquid games with little aircraft supported on tiny jets of air the Z Channel thrift stores pop-culture conventions dark rides Winchell's Donuts ship models Ouija boards Gyruss magnetic sculptures Flintstones Chewable Vitamins collage art model rockets plastic model kits coin collections fireworks assortments meerschaum pipes McDonaldland playgrounds ham radios Budweiser Clydesdales bowling alleys Cracked Magazine toy jack-in-the-boxes Swanson's frozen dinners silent movies on flammable silver nitrate film Dover Books catalogs fern bars Galaga the Illuminatus Trilogy racks full of plastic-and-metal pins which formed impressions of faces and hands CO2-powered pellet guns aircheck tapes of Doctor Demento videocassettes of Elvira disks of Styx and Triumph and Queensrÿche and Dokken Zombie the boardgame drawings by William Rotsler Cragmont Cola wave machines grapnel hooks the collected wisdom of ODF Pillsbury Doughboys ice cream men Harem Games paperbacks vinyl LPs and 45s and 78s Betamax machines hot tubs volumes of Vonnegut and Robbins screamers sparklers snakes color-changing mood shirts gooey rubber erasers

and he put the last nail in that Age of Aquarius that had spawned the yuppies, because the fire monster that had arisen from the pit to destroy all mankind was no mere product of the human subconscious.

It was the best-covered of all Cthadron's rampages, this time, as he blitzkrieged along the Mediterranean. France, Italy, Sicily, Greece, Albania: it was all live on television each time the monster from the surf thundered ashore. The Death Pulse was feared again, although secretly little kids and their Boomer parents thought that it looked "cool", and Americans forgot all about Lafayette and smirked at the deaths of Frenchmen by the city-full.

The network remembered what had happened to me at the North Sea. Viewers of Cthadron Watch: Mediterranean would have been surprised to discover that I was never any closer to the front line than Majorca, but with clever camera setups and good editing, you can convince people of anything. They put young guys out there in the field, just as they had all along, but the "dean of Cthadron reporting" was strictly an anchor on this one.

I felt much better for it. Please don't assume that this meant that I was any less afraid of the damn monster, but when he was that far away even I could relax. I still stuck to decaf, though.

Government Tech was the answer we all expected, but things went a little differently this time. Apparently the people at CalTech had been doing a little Cthadron-watching of their own, and they'd noticed a pattern with him. The monster always seemed to be continuing his previous rampage with direct continuity, but with "hiccups" in time and space between them. They were roughly 10 years apart, true, but data seemed to indicate that the time between his appearances increased in small increments each time he came back. Similar figures existed for his physical location. Each of his disappearances seemed to correspond with a low point in his own energy levels. They weren't sure what it all meant, or how it all came to be, but ... they thought Cthadron might go away without anyone doing anything.

Since Cowboy Ronnie was in serious discussions with European heads about exercising "the nuclear option", despite millions protesting in the streets, this theory was loudly proclaimed by Sagan and the Concerned Scientists and all that crowd. Personally, I expected some new miracle from the Shadow Government as soon as Cthadron kept going east and threatened to become the terror of Mecca.

But instead, ground forces from NATO did their best to slow the creature down—nation by nation—and he seemed to get tired, eventually, after enough billions of dollars in damages and enough teeming throngs of dead children, women and men. Before Cthadron could proceed eastward, he stalked back into the Med and we waited in vain. He didn't resurface. They searched with nuclear subs and found nothing. Tad Schumann, the best-looking young guy in a suit we had on camera, became "Tad the Cthad Stud" for his earnest coverage of the apocalypse in the Med. We were all covered in glory and great ratings at the network. Inland real-estate values, and coastal insurance premiums, continued to rise.

Months became years. My grandchildren starting popping up, the little brats. I golfed with ex-presidents and went to a millionaire's retreat every year up in Mendocino, went yachting in Martha's Vineyard, and kept the wife happy in her little world. I was a spry, potbellied, balding sixty-something and I'd cheated the odds since 1954. I'd looked Cthadron in the eye four times, which might be something of an exaggeration but you get the point, and I'd lived to tell it to the whole world. I wasn't that poor kid reporting from Venice who'd just kept talking a mile a minute while a skyscraper of reptilian doom loomed over him, raining dead fish and blackened metal, and then mockingly crushed his prettiness to death underfoot. I was alive, and I was like Cronkite, a symbol of the world's ongoing tradition and continuity. "Humanity is indomitable," my jowly countenance seemed to say on TV. "We have always been here and we'll always be here. Not even a cyclopean, impossible angel of death can bring us to our knees. The human spirit can never fail."

A notion I didn't believe one bit, and never will. The human spirit fails all the time. Just look at me.

By now we were all aware that Cthadron would almost certainly be back. There was always a slim hope that he would never be seen again, and scientists argued the point interminably, but no one under the age of 10 really believed that he was permanently gone. The only question now was what to do about it. The gap between what the government admitted to having and what they really had, technologically speaking, was still a Grand Canyon of silence and disinformation, but every year we learned more. It was a tiny trickle of information that began to add up, at least for scientists and engineers. Of course, they were as careful of their reputations as I was of mine, so things changed far from swiftly.

We rang in the new year, 1990; we rang in the new year, 1991; we rang in the new year, 1992; we rang in the new year, 1993. We bought emergency supply kits, special Cthadron Detectors (cheap electronic seismographs that went off when your dog scratched at the front door), gas masks to filter out smoke and dust, anti-Death Pulse suits for only $79.95 plus tax, shipping and handling—

We watched as Cthadron waded ashore in the Persian Gulf we'd bombed the living hell out of only two years earlier, humans blasting other humans to oblivion or a crippled eternity of existence, and cried our eyes out as he did to us what we did to each other.

The year was 1994—

With each mighty step he destroyed a vast swath of our human civilisation, so vital and alive; with each step he destroyed resin-cast models Slim Jims ironing boards boxes of Lego crazy straws Hostess fruit pies Johnson-Smith catalogs nunchakus wooden blocks Renaissance Faires beanbag chairs Swiss Colony gift sets Wonder Bras sealing wax and seals bulletin boards Mister Bubble used bookstores potbellied pigs cans of Spam and Play-Doh bead curtains feathered Mardi Gras masks Thrifty Ice Cream African fainting goats craps felts art cars skateboards Mexican Flag suckers rollercoasters high boots Pre-Raphaelites Silly Putty Art Deco Art Nouveau Magic Rocks Soviet Realists postage stamps hedgehogs swordcanes bagged comic books cinderblock shelving tinkertoys Masonic pins grindhouse theatres seesaws ferrets supplements for the Paranoia roleplaying game Mexican Christmas star ornaments made with sticks and colourful yarn Loompanics Books catalogs belt-buckle punch knives autographed pictures of Alan Rickman and Gary Sinise Slinkies hacky sacks glowsticks peepshows Erector Sets magic trick kits seashell collections Grateful Dead rocket-shaped playground slides waterpipes bubble-lights accordions dragsters slide whistles monster trucks

and I could not have been less distant from my fellow men and women than if they had been aliens from space. I suppose the bell had tolled for me. One day we hosed each other's guts off bombed-out streets and the next we stood together in solidarity against the Great Outsider who didn't have the right to kill as we killed, or displace us so obviously in the food chain. One night we watched green nightvision scopes showing Scud missiles burning, mashing and eviscerating living flesh and blood and waited for a commercial; the next we shuddered because something inhuman and abominable was stalking the planet and might come for us next. Just because Cthadron had always manifested in or near the oceans didn't mean that he couldn't appear in or near your home town—not unless you lived alone in a remote desert, more inhospitable than the Arctic or the Antarctic. He was a random H-bomb coming down on a town that didn't look that different from yours on TV; he was the enemy that didn't need any propaganda to make you dread him. Cthadron was a doomsday machine running loose, and we feared that more than we feared what we did ourselves.

I felt the fear melting away. That's probably the result of getting old, and closer to death, but I had never felt this way about Cthadron before. Whatever he was, he was inevitable and apparently unstoppable. All the miracle cures were pointless. He'd only vanish anyway. The government's secrets didn't really mean anything. What good were particle beams and plastic gloop when death could just appear out of nowhere and destroy anything in its path? We'd never saved one person from Cthadron yet, wonder weapons or not. What he wished to crush, he would crush.

I actually requested the field assignment and was turned down. "Too valuable a resource to risk," they told me. An aging coward who never did a meaningful thing in his life but be a figurehead. And a figurehead for what? Hope. The hope of human beings who lacked the simple courage to love each other instead of killing each other. We didn't deserve hope.

I frankly did not and do not understand how Government Tech saved the day in '94. It was some sort of arrangement of four-dimensional mirrors and a neutron warhead shunted sideways in time, according to the best theories anyone could come up with, and if it did the trick I'm damned if I know. Cthadron vanished, and they took the credit for it—whoever they were. But as I say, he would've vanished anyway.

In 2000, there was a global summit to discuss a final option for the Cthadron problem, which no single nation and no coalition of nations had ever solved yet. The public wasn't told what they decided, apart from some simple platitudes about global cooperation and aid from the World Bank after the next Cthadron rampage, possible proactive solutions, various projections of his exact next appearance in terms of location and time, and so forth. We had George W. Bush in the White House, and his people didn't like to share information, and the attitude was catching.

As for me, I coasted into my seventies as the wife passed on from kidney failure (only God knows why that woman ever loved me, and I kid myself that she did), one of the daughters-in-law miscarried, and my prostate turned to a rock. It was almost comforting—like listening to your heartbeat in the night after you've contemplated your own death for much too long and actually grown bored at the prospect—when Cthadron reemerged into the world.

I was listening to another hour of angry, backbiting talk radio, with people babbling on about the conspiracy to make Cthadron come to life and all the genetic engineering that went into building an ambulatory thermonuclear device, when the emergency people broke in and told us the monster was bound for Bombay. I pictured the lights of Bollywood's movie studios glinting in the creature's eyes as he crumbled mighty buildings and rained death from above onto that oh-so-Western city. I put on my sweater and drove to the studio, imagining a city built by British Imperialists on hills in a bay, returned once more to its primal state by the death I no longer needed to deny.

The year was 2004—

With each mighty step he destroyed a vast swath of our human civilisation, so vital and alive; with each step he destroyed lace bodystockings cases of Guinness Stout boxes of Count Chocula and Frankenberry BDSM gear pop-tarts shinai cans of Dinty Moore beef stew Sea Monkeys candles theme parks Figi's for the holidays boomerangs old matchbooks Tri-Ess Scientific catalogs single-malt scotch kukri knives yellowing issues of TV Guide CDs of The Floating House plastic army men electroluminescent wires themed restaurants swagged cords Old Spice Fruit Rolls shurikens cider World Press Review magazine children's swimming pools Depression glass fezzes model Cars and motorcycles peel-and-press writing pads IKEA stores Pixy Stix fencing masks and foils Joshua plants wind-up toys trampolines Risk and Monopoly and Operation and Candyland old lobby cards ionizers kazoos wooden Indians pooltables posable artist mannequins pre-fab Christmas trees coffin-shaped furniture overhead projectors fibre-optic sculptures diamondvision screens Sideshow Toys action figures self-contained ecosystem spheres bottles of Goldschlager

and so much more, so many precious lives lost. I think they were precious, at least to God and their owners, even if I no longer held much faith in them.

I was "colour commentary" for this rampage. They gave me five minutes on the hour, talking to other old reporters, retired generals, professors emeriti, and the other detritus that a younger generation had never learned about. There were shiny computer-generated logos and three-dimensional cutaways of the latest theories of what it looked like inside Cthadron, sophisticated scientific speculations reduced to USA Today charts and Fox News soundbites. Cthadron destroyed Bombay, and was about to turn Sri Lanka into an abbatoir, when the most incomprehensible of all his defeats occurred.

They showed the video again and again, around the clock,

for the next two days. All it showed was a blurry light that lasted 1.21 seconds (according to the timecode on the tape) and seemed to visibly go through a Doppler blue-red shift as it came from one horizon, rounded Cthadron, and streaked off over the other. Less than 0.8 seconds later, Cthadron vanished again.

Less attention was paid when Russian and French scientists published a paper that explained that Cthadron was somehow transcending time and space by his very nature. They explained in some impenetrable scientific gibberish how he existed differently than we do, in eleven-dimensional spacetime, and that Cthadron's rampages were really all continuous with one another from his perspective. That we grew old while he was the same creature we'd always met in battle, and that for him this entire struggle had only lasted a couple of months.

It was a fascinating revelation, but it meant nothing, really. Purely academic. If anyone in the world knew where the monster came from, they weren't talking, and if anyone knew where the Government Tech came from, they didn't talk, either. Most of all, if there was a way to permanently stop Cthadron, no one had known it. Or if they knew they didn't want to use it.

My kids were getting older, their kids were growing up, and I was headed for my 80s. I thanked God I didn't need Social Security as the network expressed their deep gratitude for my lifelong achievements with the customary rubber steak dinner (I deserved better than the rubber chicken dinner) and the 21st century equivalent of a gold watch. I had finally retired, a legend in a journalistic field that no longer merited being called journalism. I was as good as they deserved, really. A field that no longer had any Murrows or Woodwards or even Rathers, but instead had pretty boys and me. Après moi, le deluge, boys and girls.

The Dubya Years were even worse the second time around, and the War On Terror kept everybody feeling productive. Even a change of administration didn't prevent the economic disaster that came along next, but it was good to be a fat old bald failed fake of a reporter with millions of dollars. I didn't suffer, my kids didn't suffer, my grandkids didn't suffer. But I think we needed to.

Instead, we outsourced our suffering and I watched on TV as the young boys from 1974 took my place as Stuffy Old Cthadron Expert. They waded through the blathering theorists and the hideous footage of victims and their suffering. I sat in my easy chair and listened to the maid cleaning and the images flowed over me. Cthadron lived, still the same as always, bearing the scars of every encounter with our species and carrying on.

The year was 2014—

With each mighty step he destroyed a vast swath of our human civilisation, so vital and alive; with each step he destroyed guppies and hermit crabs crystal prisms Obon festivals tiramisu snow

*globes glycerin soap with toys inside Brut aftershave plastic
dinosaurs Hallmark greeting cards fuzzy dice lifemasks Edmund
Scientific catalogs bottles of absinthe bound editions of Sluggy
Freelance geodes paintball guns and masks scrimshaw carbide
cannons paintings on black velvet of card-playing dogs and
Elvis and a laughing Satan Travelodges dirigibles hearses estate
auctions and garage sales tons of cheap champagne harps PVC
corsets Apple computers Bailey's Irish Cream DVDs with extras
moonbounces smoking jackets romance novels Etch-a-sketch jet
packs antiques model submarines and blimps quarterstaves bows
and arrows and crossbows jumping beans cellphones with special
ringtones Persian carpets*

and I fell asleep, now and then.

Where was Cthadron? Did it matter? Wasn't he really
everywhere, throughout our time and space, haunting us with
the spectre of our own mortality? I recalled them talking about
Djakarta, Haiphong Harbor. There was talk of robotic cybertanks,
of Thor's hammer falling from the sky to poetically smash the
Midgard Serpent and the death he foretold, talk of time and space
and death so near at hand.

They said that it was possible, just possible, that if Cthadron
crossed his own earlier path through the world, he might somehow
close his circuit in time and space. There was talk of it, while we
waited for secret men with secret weapons to descend from God
knew where to end our pain. They were like the masked surgeons
who treated me for my stroke; faceless experts with cool voices
and cool hands, saying nothing that we could understand and
administering what they felt was necessary. Left in their hands,
left in their hands, what could we do but hope?

I have little control left over my body now, sleeping most of the
time, diapered like a baby. The children never have time for me,
the grandchildren say I whisper so low they can no longer hear
me. They said on the TV that the monster was bodily driven by
some sort of gravity wave away from Tokyo, out to sea, and onto
the path he'd taken across the Pacific on his first journey from
East to West. I vaguely recall that Cthadron wavered visibly, like
an old celluloid film rippled before an overhead light, the nearer
he came to his own path. A serpent swallowing his own tail, he fell
into himself and vanished one more time.

Was it the end of Cthadron? Was it the end of his long, short
walk through our world?

It is for me.

Cephalogon

Alys Sterling

W hat is this?" Will poked his chopsticks at a tentacle slowly writhing its way out of the mound of rice-shaped algal starch in front of him.

"Think of it as a Martian delicacy." Maura grimaced at her own plate.

"Just so long as I don't have to think of it as dinner." Will waved his arm, indicating the dining hall around them, its three long, yellow-topped tables occupied by scientists of various persuasions. "My kingdom for a steak."

"It's supposed to be a horse," Maura said.

"I'd rather eat a horse than this." Will teased the tentacle out a little further. The suckers showed bright red against the orange flesh.

"If this is anyone's kingdom, it's mine." Pete picked up a slimy lump of his own dinner and shoved it into his mouth without looking at it.

"My coring rig then."

"No way," Pete said, still chewing. "That's company property."

"A whole horse would feed all of—"

A series of loud thuds rattled the plates on the tables and drowned out Will's last words.

"Do they have to do that while we're eating?" Maura shouted, as the noise of the bombing run died away.

"Of course. You know there just aren't enough hours in the day to test weapons." Will held up the tentacle, now captured between his chopsticks. "Personally, I'm more worried about things like this. I don't mind eating seafood, but this isn't even a real squid. Vern is serving up mutants again."

"It's all the bombs." Pete nodded. "There's radiation or something else they're not telling us about. That's why we're getting so many mutations."

Maura shook her head. "Nah. It's all that crap the last team kept putting on the fields to try to get crops to grow. Those chemicals just went straight into the lake."

"And they still never got anything to grow," Will said. "Some of the stuff they used, I'm surprised the rocks aren't sprouting tentacles."

"We need to get the proper bacteria in situ." Maura gestured with her chopsticks, as though jabbing bacteria into the Martian soil with them. She never seemed to lose enthusiasm, no matter how many of her experiments failed. Even her hair bristled with it, short blonde curls shooting out energetically from her head. She looked like an avenging angel in a white lab coat.

"Chemicals aren't the answer."

"I don't notice anything growing in your plots yet," Pete said.

"The soil is toxic. I just need to breed a strain that can—"

Another round of bombing cut off Maura's reply. The mess hall windows shook in their insulated frames.

"That was a little close," said Pete.

Before anyone had time to answer, another run commenced. The floor rippled. Will's chair rocked, then tipped backwards as the lights flickered and went out. His shoulders hit the metal ridge of the chair-back, and then his head hit the floor.

He woke in darkness, feeling something sticky on his cheek. A cold, writhing worm was forcing its way into his nose. He tried to breathe, and choked on rising nausea.

Beams of light cut the blackness; someone had found the emergency torches.

"Helb!" Will shouted. "I'b udder addag."

"Silly." Maura knelt over him.

Will felt her fingers on his cheek. Her nails scraped his skin as she pried at the thing stuck there. It came away in increments, trying to hang on.

"It was only your dinner." Maura dangled the red-suckered tentacle in front of him.

"No way am I eating that now," Will said. "You can have it for a specimen if you want."

Maura sighed. "If I analysed all the mutants Vern catches, we'd get nothing to eat. Besides, my field is microbiology. Compared to what I normally look at, this thing came from a giant."

"Hey, when you two are finished discussing the food, there's something you might want to come see." Pete beckoned from the door.

Will let Maura help him up. He walked over to the door, gingerly running his fingertips over the back of his head. By the feel of it, he had quite a lump. Then he reached the open door and stood shivering in the chill night air, lump forgotten.

Between the mess hall and the lab huts, a thirty centimetre high escarpment now broke the once-flat ground. Looking from side to side, as Pete swung the beam of his torch, Will saw the irregularity continuing into the distance towards the lake, and on in the other direction through the rest of the Lewin Agri-Industries compound.

"That last one was no bomb test," Pete said softly.

"Bloody hell," Maura whispered. "Marsquake."

"Idiots!" Will shouted, as though he could make the managers of Conglomerated Armouries hear him across the lake. "Fools. Military-minded assholes. I told them months ago there was a fault zone here, and what do they do? Bomb the shit out of it, that's what."

☆

The damage looked worse in the morning. Cracks ran across the dining hall windows. One of the oldest buildings on Mars, constructed eighty years ago by a team of terraformers, had collapsed. The Quonset hut, which housed Will's equipment, was still in one piece, but a quick look inside before breakfast revealed the equipment itself had not fared so well. Toppled shelves and broken core samples littered the floor. Everything would be cross-contaminated now. Will groaned. Weeks of drilling wasted.

He stomped off to the mess hall hoping to find Maura, but she wasn't there. He spooned up algal porridge at several times his usual speed, his mind filled with visions of twisted metal. He had to get out and inspect his drilling rig. It would take months to get a replacement up here. Not to mention an extension on his grant. As he gulped down the last slimy mouthful, Pete came in followed by a man with a Conglomerated Armouries badge on his jacket.

"Will, a word with you." Pete beckoned him out of the mess hall, leading the way across the broken ground outside to his office. "This is Andrew Short, from Conglomerated Armouries. Will is our geologist." He waved Short through the door ahead of him. "He may be able to explain what's happened."

"What's happened," Will said to Short, "is that your bloody bombs have gone and caused a Marsquake, that's what. Don't say I didn't warn you."

Short looked taken aback. "We have yet to determine the cause of the quake. The planet may still exhibit some post-terraforming instability. Besides, it's by no means certain that our test site was the epicentre."

"Very good, Short." Will applauded soundlessly. "Look out there." He pointed back out the door, at the miniature escarpment bisecting the compound. "That says we're awfully close right here."

"In any case," Short continued after a moment, "we have a more serious problem. The lake is disappearing."

"What? You—"

"I'd like you to go have a look," Pete interrupted, before Will could decide what to call Short.

Personally, Will wouldn't mind if Lake Edgar disappeared off the face of Mars. At least then Vern would have to stop serving mutant squid. But Pete hadn't exactly given him any choice about going.

Short drove Will out to the lake in his Mars buggy, an ATV equipped with huge, cleated tyres and a state-of-the-art locator system. If not for the satellite location, Will might have believed they had reached the shore of the wrong lake. Slimy patches of algae, now dying in the chill sunlight, marked the old waterline. The ancient lakebed, refilled fifty years ago by the terraformers, lay once again bare and exposed for a good kilometre before water came into view.

Short manoeuvred the buggy forward. Will felt the wheels slip, breaking through the dried crust of the algae patches and sliding on the slime beneath. He put a hand out to brace himself as they rolled down a steep incline. The vehicle bounced down a final step in the ground, and Will hit his head on the roof. It was the last straw.

"Why do you have to drop so many bombs on Mars, anyway?" Will burst out, no longer able to contain his frustration. "Isn't it enough you made the moon so radioactive no one can land on it? We've barely made Mars habitable, and now you're destroying it, too."

"Habitable? You know better than I do how many scientists have tried and failed to make crops grow here. Without a source of food, Mars can't support large settlements. We might as well get some use out of the planet. After all, we can't test these things on Earth."

"Why not? Where do you intend to use them, if not Earth?"

"Think of the damage to the environment." Short seemed honestly horrified. "We can't just go blowing big holes in our own ecosystems. These are deterrents. The government would never actually use them."

"Then why test them at all?"

Short paused for so long Will thought he finally had him stumped for an answer. "For the joy of it." Short held up a hand, forestalling Will's reply. "Because having dreamed the things up, figured them out, made the prototypes—how can I not want to see if they *work*?"

Will turned in his seat to look at Short, reassessing his opinion of the man. "You actually design them? I thought you were military."

Short grimaced. "It's an honorary rank. Couldn't have a civilian in command, even up here."

When they reached the edge of the water, Will could practically see it ebbing away in front of him.

"Shit," he said. "Must be some kind of underground fissure." He opened his door, letting in the stench of dying algae. When he stepped out, something squelched underfoot. He looked down. Dead and dying squid littered the slime-covered rock of the exposed lakebed.

Will tasted porridge at the back of his throat. He tried to hold his breath as he stacked pebbles to mark the current waterline. It didn't work. He leaned forward, spewing the contents of his stomach into the water. Behind him, he heard Short losing his own breakfast. Will spat to clear his mouth, and walked back to the buggy.

"Shouldn't have had seconds on the eggs this morning." Short slid behind the wheel.

"You get eggs? Where from?"

"Earth. Send them up dried. Army supplies." Short swallowed between words, looking like he might spew again at any moment.

"I think I should drive," Will said.

"You know why the water's gone already?"

"See there, where the fault line goes into the water?" Will pointed at the uneven seam the buggy had bounced over. "I think it opens up again under the lake. I'd have to dive to know for sure. You wouldn't have deep-water equipment on hand, would you?"

Short shook his head.

"Damn. Of all the things not to bring—" Will thought longingly of his own hardsuit, gathering dust in his lab back on Earth. There was something else he had seen gathering dust lately... "Wait a minute. I know where I can get an old outdoor suit that might work, but I'd need some kind of propulsion unit."

"Suit jets?"

"Yeah, if I had any."

"I might be able to help you out with that."

They detoured through Conglomerated Armouries' facility on the far side of the lake to pick up the jets, a slim, white-enamelled backpack unit with bars reaching out at hip level for control. While they were there, Will had as much of a look around as he could. He was surprised to see a number of soldiers marching in drill, on a rectangle of ground so packed down their stamping boots raised no dust.

"What's all that about?" he asked Short. "Do you really believe you'll be attacked up here?"

"No." Short glanced over as the drill sergeant shouted something. "But it keeps them busy."

Reddish dust coated what looked like a pile of junk in an old crate in the corner of Will's Quonset hut. Some of the core samples had fallen into it, but the suit's hard shell had taken no apparent damage. Will lifted out the top half of the suit and put it on the work table.

"You sure about this?" Short wiped a finger across the suit's shoulder, leaving a clean, bronze-finished trail behind.

"Looks all right to me. Soon find out if it's not watertight." Will grunted as he lifted the bottom half of the suit out of the crate.

"What about air?"

"Suit has an integral supply. About enough for four hours' dive, I reckon. And it's insulated, so the cold won't be a problem." The hard outer shell, meant to protect the wearer from windblown debris, ought to protect Will from the pressure of the depths. At least, so he hoped. He didn't voice his doubts as Short helped him attach the manoeuvring system to the suit with heavy webbing straps. As a final touch, Will glued a self-rewinding reel of nylon cord to the front, just under where the straps crossed.

"What's that for?" Short asked.

"Guide-line. If there is a fissure under the lake, I'll have to go in and see how deep it goes."

"You're enjoying this. You want there to be a fissure." Short pointed a finger at him.

Will grinned. "Hell, yes. Think about it. The only unexplored territory on Mars, and I get to see it first. Imagine what it must have been like for the teams who came in before the terraformers. Every day, you'd get to see something no one had ever seen before. Now it's all mapped and gridded, and every day we change it more."

They took Vern's runabout back to the lake, towing the fishing boat. The algae along the exposed lakebed crunched under the runabout's wheels, already freeze-drying in the Martian wind. The new waterline lay a metre or so back from Will's marker.

"Looks like it's slowing down. It may reach equilibrium soon." Will hefted his helmet up. Just in case he was wrong, he wanted to dive while there was still some water left.

Short finished winching the boat out from the trailer and cast off. The water parted viscously around it as they headed for the middle of the lake.

☆

Beneath the water the light quickly faded, obscured by floating particles of algae, so that Will swam through a tea-coloured murk. He switched on his helmet light, thankful the terraformers had seen a need for night-time navigation. The light made a tunnel through which bits of detritus spun aimlessly. A squid jetted through the cone of light, emitting an ink cloud behind it. Its tentacles alone stretched a metre long.

"Hey!" Will said, startled.

"What is it?" The suit radio made Short sound a thousand miles away.

"A squid nearly as big as me. I didn't know they grew that size."

"Oh, sure. They come much bigger than that on Earth. Don't worry, they didn't seed any giant ones up here."

"You don't call a two-metre squid a giant?"

Will let the weight of the suit pull him down to the lakebed, searching for the fault line. He grew used to seeing squid flit past, rippling bright red and white stripes at him, or shooting out ink.

The terraformers had covered the lakebed with a layer of finely ground Martian rock, mixed with chemicals and bacteria, which was supposed to simulate natural soil. It seemed to work better for growing seaweed than for growing wheat. Slimy green growths up to half a metre tall covered the bottom of the lake. Will poked a finger at a particularly bulbous one, meeting a jelly-like resistance. When he pulled his hand back, a small plume of green motes spun out into the water.

It took him a while to locate the fault line, due to the limited range of his light. At last, his beam illuminated a ribbon of bare red rock slashed like a wound across the lakebed. Will followed it, feeling the tug of a current speeding him along.

Suddenly, the ground beneath him opened up into a dark slit, the gap widening to ten or fifteen metres across in the centre. Will fought the current pulling him down towards it.

"Shit." He hovered above the fissure, his light failing to penetrate its depths.

"What now?" Short asked.

"I've found where all the water's gone. There's a bloody great hole in the rock here. I'm going down to take a look, see how deep it goes. Don't worry if you lose radio contact with me for a while."

Will unreeled the end of his safety line from the chest of his suit, tying the thin white cord around a projection at the lip of the fissure. He double-checked the fastening before swimming downward, into the darkness.

The fissure opened out into a cavern so huge his light couldn't reach the other side. He struck out from the fissure, using a slight push from the suit jets to move himself along until he came to a wall. Then he let himself sink down again, following the curve of the wall, noting red and yellow banding in the rock. A few minutes later, he found a hole. The opening, and the tunnel beyond, had five sides, smooth and suspiciously regular.

Will swam through the tunnel, his light glancing off rock close around him. It came as a relief when he finally emerged into another huge cavern.

"Short? Can you hear me?" As Will expected, Short didn't answer. The tunnel had sloped downward; the rock above him must now be thick enough to interfere with radio reception. Nonetheless, it made him uneasy to be cut off from all communication. One mistake down here, and no one would ever see him again. Will checked his guideline, took a deep breath, and went on. He had enough air for an hour's exploration before turning back, and the feeling that an hour was not going to be enough.

Will's light reached further in the algae-free water of the new cavern. He saw more openings, low in the cavern walls. He checked the suit's wrist-compass, and chose one to the northeast. He swam through several more linked caverns, one with a frozen waterfall of yellow flowstone ten metres high. From there, he entered a long tunnel. When the tunnel widened, he found himself floating in an almost spherical chamber, with tunnels leading out in all directions. Directly below him a huge tube plunged straight down. Will's light caught odd shadows on the black rock of its sides. Peering closer, he saw ridges set in semicircles covering the rock. There seemed no purpose or pattern; perhaps they were the work of some rock-adhering creature like a Martian barnacle, eons ago when these caves had formed.

Will swam down until he reached the largest cavern yet. A forest of thirty-centimetre-thick columns filled the chamber. Their surfaces exhibited the same sort of ridges as the tube above. Will jetted slowly forward, weaving his way in between them. Some distance in, he found a broken column. He searched the cavern floor for a small enough piece to take back as a sample, stirring up black sediment that glittered in his helmet light. At last, he found a fist-sized bit, one side showing the strange markings. Perhaps Maura could make some sense of them. The hardsuit had no pockets, but Will managed to wedge the rock between the crossed harness straps of his propulsion rig. The broken edges sawed at the straps as he pushed the rock under them. Odd. Will took a closer look at the stump sticking up from the floor. Conchoidal fractures. This rock looked glassy, like obsidian. What were pillars of volcanic rock doing in a clearly water-formed cave?

He looked back through the forest of columns. Their consistent size tempted him to believe they must be artificial, but their layout followed no pattern he could discern. Surely only natural formations would exhibit such a random placement. And besides—who could have built them? No evidence of ancient Martian life larger than nano-organisms had ever been found. His barnacle ridges could make Maura famous. Will grinned. If he could get her to analyse something so large.

He checked his guideline, making sure it had not fouled on any columns. He would need it to find his way out of this cavern, for sure. He gave it a sharp tug. The line went slack in his grip.

Will's stomach congealed into an icy lump. He knew he had tied the line securely, but what if it had caught on some sharp projection, and been cut? He forced himself to remain still; not to yank on the line again. He might still be able to follow it back to the exit from this cavern, at least. Will began backtracking along the line, swimming slowly so as not to disturb it more than necessary. He was directly underneath the hole in the ceiling when the line suddenly went taut.

The pull strengthened, yanking him through the hole. He let out a yell as he rushed upwards, unable to figure out what the hell was happening. At the top of the tube, the line jerked him sideways, through a tunnel, out into a cavern, into another tunnel. In the next cavern, lacy cream-and-red-barred fans hung from the ceiling. Will had not seen those formations before. He had never been through this chamber. Whatever had hold of his line was pulling him deeper into the labyrinth of caves.

He could see the guideline, the nylon rope glowing white ahead in the beam of his helmet lamp. It stretched across the unfamiliar cavern to a dark opening in the far side. As Will drew nearer, something moved within the darkness. Then his lamplight flashed into the tunnel, illuminating sinuous orange flesh. A tentacle at least ten metres long, and more behind, writhing in the shadows.

Will tore frantically at the front of his suit. He had attached the guide-line mounting as securely as possible, with industrial adhesive. He had known his life might depend on not losing it. Now, his only chance of survival lay in getting rid of it. He pounded it with metal-gloved fists, but it didn't budge.

Will hit his propulsion jets, twisting around to face away from the tunnel and pushing the knob to maximum. The jets couldn't out-pull the giant mutant waiting in the dark. He slowed, but the squid inexorably reeled him in. He wondered whether it would weaken before he ran out of propellant. If only he had a knife— he could cut the line. But he had not brought any extraneous attachments, except for the safety line and jet harness. The harness—suddenly, Will remembered his rock sample. The edges had been sharp enough to tear at the harness straps.

Clumsy with haste, Will pulled at the straps. He fumbled the rock free, then felt it fall from his grasp, before he could close his fingers on it. He lunged towards it, his movements nightmarishly slowed by the suit and the water around him. With his change in attitude, the jets pushed him downward, faster than the rock could fall. He reached out, and it floated into his outstretched hand. But his move down had cost him; the creature reeled him in faster, temporarily unhindered by his jets.

He sawed at the line, imagining writhing tentacles reaching to embrace him. Will never felt the line part; he only knew he had succeeded when his jets sent him shooting through the cavern, narrowly missing the fringe of rock formations overhead. He kept going, waiting for those tentacles to grab him and pull his suit apart at the joints to get at the soft, defenceless creature within, like a normal squid eating a crab. He didn't stop until he ran smack into a wall of white stone.

Will spun slowly around, shining his light. He had swum into a small chamber, a dead end. As he turned, he noticed something strange about the walls. Aside from the opening by which he had entered, they were all perfectly flat, meeting at regular angles. Ridges of shadow made patterns on the walls, as they had on the pillars. He stared at the back wall, concentrating on the pattern. Laid out flat, it looked strangely regular, exhibiting an odd sort of symmetry. As he stared at the walls, the patterns replicated outward, forming a lattice around him. Quasicrystalline symmetry. The whole damn chamber was a three-dimensional representation of a quasicrystal. Of course! The pillars had been arranged the same way, only down among them, he couldn't see it. He turned slowly, positioning himself at the centre of the lattice, the point at which the pattern originated. From there, Will gazed into infinity. He felt he had only to slide a little further into the pattern, find the exact fit, and he would be able to see the future, or the past, his mind expanding until it could contain the universe.

A shrill beeping jarred Will out of his trance. It took his sluggish mind several beep-filled minutes to recognise the suit's air level warning. He had only an hour's air left.

He made himself jet along slowly, the need to go carefully, watching for any hint of a familiar tunnel warring with the knowledge that he had only an hour to find his way out. He took shallow breaths. Assuming he had jetted a fairly straight course fleeing from the giant squid, he used his wrist compass to move back in the opposite direction, praying he would find a cavern he recognised before he reached the one where the squid lurked.

When he swam into the chamber with the bore down into the pillar room, his sense of relief was as great as if he had already reached the surface. From here, he need only head southwest to find his way out. He oriented himself with the compass, and found himself faced with a choice of two tunnels.

Will floated, caught in an agony of indecision which held him as tight as any tentacles could. The wrong choice would cost him his life. He remembered all the horror stories about divers who never returned; cautionary tales his instructor had used to drive home safety lectures. He might just end up as the most gruesome example yet.

Something moved inside the right-hand tunnel. Will started, bowels clenching. A small squid, no more than twenty centimetres long, tumbled out into the chamber. Will started laughing, the sound echoing crazily inside his helmet. He knew he should try to stop, but he didn't care. The squid had shown him the way out. Still giggling, he jetted into the tunnel.

☆

Somehow, in all his panic to escape, Will had managed to hang on to the lump of rock from the broken pillar. He showed it to Pete when he made his report on the size of the rift in the lakebed. "There's something very strange going on with the geology in those caves. Formations that just can't be natural."

Pete turned to Short. "He was down there the full four hours?"

"He was practically blue when I pulled him out," Short said.

"Is that so? And do you have any idea how deep you went?"

"I couldn't find a depth gauge," Will admitted. He hadn't been able to find a waterproof camera either, a lack he now regretted even more.

"And there's another thing, a chamber, with carvings on the walls ..." Will let the sentence trail off as he saw the expression on Short's face.

"Raptures of the deep, Will. You came up laughing like a maniac and babbling about giant mutant squid."

"The important thing is, you're fairly sure the lake won't drain much further?" Pete tried to change the subject, but Will ignored him.

"You don't get raptures in an atmosphere suit. I know what I saw."

"You saw a giant squid? How large?" Pete asked.

"I'm not sure. Big enough to think I was lunch. Twenty metres?"

"And you think it built pillars and carved things on them?"

"No." Will made an effort to keep his voice calm and even. "I don't know what made the pillars. But you know as well as I do that the squid have been mutating in that lake. Who knows what's going on down there in the depths? After all, I'm the first person who's ever been down to see."

Pete sighed. "All right. Even if there is a giant squid, it's not doing anyone any harm down there, is it? Now, I want you to let the doc have a look at you. Take the afternoon off, have a rest."

Will did go see the doctor, but not until he had taken the rock over to Maura's lab. "Have a look at this. Any idea what might have made those ridges?"

Maura ran a finger over the surface, then held the rock up to the light. "I've never seen anything like it. Where did you get this?"

"From a cave under the lake." Will didn't tell her any more; he didn't want to prejudice her judgement. More than that, he didn't want Maura to accuse him of seeing things the way Pete had.

☆

When he walked into the mess hall at dinnertime, everyone there turned to look at him.

"Are you all right?" Maura motioned him over. "I hear you had a pretty close encounter down there." Her words expressed concern, but Will heard laughter in her voice.

Pete sat across from her, smirking. "You mean he didn't tell you about Cephalogon, monster of the deep? Will, sit down and tell Maura all about how it nearly ate you for lunch."

Will made a detour past the serving hatch, where Vern handed him a plate heaped with the usual rice substitute. Tonight, to Will's relief, no tentacles stuck out. A scatter of protein flakes decorated the top of the rice instead. Will sat and picked up his chopsticks. Then, the rice moved. The surface of the lump cracked.

"Look out," Pete said. "Ricequake."

Maura snorted.

A tentacle shot out of the top of the lump. Will slid his chair back so fast he nearly fell over again.

Pete burst out laughing. Will looked around. Everyone in the mess hall was laughing at him, even Maura. The squid made a break for the edge of the plate.

"Watch out." Pete pointed at the squid. "Cephalagon's sent its minions after you."

Will tried to poke the squid back with his chopsticks. It wrapped its tentacles around them and hung on. He lifted it up from the plate and carried it dangling over to the serving hatch.

"Vern? You've got an escapee." He lifted the chopsticks and waved the squid at the cook.

☆

After dinner, Maura invited Will over to her lab.

"Watch out for Cephalogon," Pete called out as they left.

Maura grinned. "Might as well get used to it."

"I know. I'll never hear the end of it."

"Seriously though, how big was this thing?"

"The tentacle that grabbed me must have been at least ten metres long. Maybe longer; I never saw what it was attached to."

"Then it might not actually have been a squid?"

"It had tentacles. What else would it have been?"

Maura opened the door to her lab. She looked up at him, her grey eyes wide. Under the bright strip-lighting, she looked both serious and apprehensive. "A Martian," she whispered.

"Not Cepahalogon again." Will turned away. He would have gone, but Maura grabbed his arm and dragged him inside.

"Call it whatever you like." She picked up his rock sample and brandished it at him. "Something made these markings. They don't appear to be biological in origin, and they're perfectly regular in height. I think they were made deliberately. By something intelligent. And I think the patterns have some meaning, I just can't figure out what." She looked at him defiantly.

"I think so, too. I found something else down there." Will told her about the crystal room.

"So you do believe there is intelligent life on Mars."

"Was. I believe there was. Whatever made those carvings is long gone. Maura, those caves are old. Ancient. And now we've created an enormous mutant that's made its home in them. Who knows what damage it may do?"

☆

Will sat in the mess hall slurping algal porridge and wishing for eggs when Short drove up outside, shouting at the top of his voice. Gladly abandoning his breakfast, Will went out to see what the yelling was about.

"Some kind of monster attacked the base. We felt the ground shaking last night, and this morning, we found all of our hangars wrecked. Completely flattened to the ground."

"Probably an aftershock," Will said, though he hadn't felt anything in their compound.

"Aftershocks don't leave footprints."

"We'd better bring Maura this time."

Short drove them out past the lake, skirting the old shoreline.

"Stop." Maura pointed out the window. "I want a look at those."

Red dust rose around them as Short braked. As it settled, rows of three-pronged depressions in the ground faded into view, already dust-blurred at the edges. Will got out and followed Maura as she walked along beside the prints.

"These things must be a metre across." Maura looked off into the distance, shading her eyes with one hand.

Will noticed which direction Maura faced. "They come from the lake." His stomach felt suddenly hollow. "That squid must be bigger than I thought."

Maura turned to give him a look. "Squid can't function on land. They've nothing to hold their bodies up with—no skeleton or exoskeleton for support. And they'd suffocate."

"Maybe it's mutated enough to be able to? I must have seen something, the footprints prove that."

"Cephalogon." Maura grinned at him. "I told you. It's a Martian."

"Cephalogon? Martians?" Short looked from Maura to Will. "You two are off your rockers. Come on, you're supposed to be taking a look at the hangars."

Maura paid no attention to Short. She stared out at the footprints, counting under her breath.

"What is it?" Will asked.

"The footprints. I can't make out the gait."

"How do you mean?"

"Well, look at our steps." Maura pointed back towards the buggy where Short now waited. Rows of shallow depressions in the dust marked their progress out, overlaid by Short's returning steps. "You can see there are three of us, right? Three rows of pairs of steps."

"With you so far."

"And if you saw the tracks of a horse, you'd see sets of four, all in a repeated pattern, and you could tell if it had been walking or galloping by the pattern."

"All right. So what's the problem with these?"

"Well, you can see they come out and go back. That's clear from the way the claws point. But no matter how many times I count, I keep getting twenty-five legs."

"But no animal has an odd number of legs. That's impossible."

"No animal on Earth."

☆

"It's not quake damage." Will stood at the top of a small rise that was as close to the wrecked hangars as Short would let him get. He looked out over a scene of complete devastation. Every building had been systematically flattened. And all around them, imprinted on corrugated metal roofing sheets and crushed aircraft, circling and crossing the ground, Will saw three-toed footprints.

"Don't you see what this means?" Maura grabbed Will's arm, practically bouncing up and down with excitement. "It proves Cephalogon is intelligent. He knows what caused the Marsquake. He's attempting to stop them causing another."

"There's still no proof our tests caused the last one," Short said.

"That still doesn't prove it's an ancient Martian," Will said.

"It is. It has to be. Nothing could mutate that much, that fast."

"So how did it survive all this time? You think it's been waiting down there since Mars cooled off?"

"Must have been."

"I don't care how long it's been down there," Short interrupted. "That thing killed two of our men last night. Not to mention destroying every single one of our planes. What we need now is a plan for getting rid of it."

Maura stared at him. "That's what you brought us out here for? To help you figure out how to kill it? Don't you understand? This is a chance to study something truly unique. A totally new species. Not just life, but intelligent life."

"Dangerous life. For all you know, it intends to flatten your compound tonight."

Maura turned to Will.

"It's not a Martian." How could it be? Whatever built the pillar room and the infinity chamber had possessed enormous intelligence and a highly developed sense of aesthetics. They had been beings of great spiritual wisdom. Not squid-creatures. "It's some kind of heavily mutated squid. Probably caused by the weapons you've been testing." Will turned to Short. "So it's only right that you should be the ones to deal with it."

"At least, let's try to capture him alive." Maura sounded so desperate that Will felt a sudden pang of guilt. This was a big opportunity for her, after all. And as long as it got the thing out of his caves ...

"It's an extremely valuable specimen," Maura said to Short.

☆

Something moved, out in the centre of the lake. The dim moonlight of Phobos gleamed on a dark, rounded surface. Ripples spread as the ominous dome moved towards the shore. As it drew closer, it rose up out of the water.

"He has an exoskeleton," Maura whispered in Will's ear.

It tickled. Will held a finger to his lips, hushing her. Beside them, Short's troops silently checked their weapons. Will scanned the shore, trying to make out the hastily dug pits there which concealed the net crews. The net itself lay along the ground, looking like part of the layer of dried algae and dead squid which covered the lakebed. Flakes of algae swirled overhead on the frigid night breeze.

Short had insisted on placing riflemen close to the old shoreline, in case the nets failed to hold the creature. Will supposed the row of vehicles behind him, armoured and mounted with cannon, were there in case the riflemen failed. Unlike Maura, he felt relieved to have them. But then, Cephalogon hadn't tried to eat Maura for lunch. Will heard a splash, and turned his attention back to the lake.

The dome rose further, exposing a fringe of long, pale tentacles around its lower edge. Cephalogon had no discernable division between head and body, just the tentacle-fringed dome above, supported on a multitude of jointed legs below. By the time the creature stepped out onto dry land, it loomed thirty metres tall, at least.

Searchlights hummed into life, sweeping the monster with their beams. In the light, its carapace was smoky, translucent. Will could see the throb of organs underneath. He swallowed against a sudden surge of nausea, reliving the terror he had felt in the caves. He made himself concentrate on the creature, fighting off the memory. It was on their territory now, vulnerable.

Cephalogon stepped forward, not seeming weak on land at all. It moved steadily ahead on a forest of legs that shone with a chitinous orange covering. Behind it, the net men rose from concealment, hoisting rocket launchers to their shoulders. Hastily assembled that afternoon, the net had been Maura's idea. Will could already tell it wasn't big enough.

Rockets shot hissing into the night, carrying the leading edge of the net up and over the domed carapace. The creature stopped in its tracks. Men rushed forward to encircle it, jumping up and grabbing hold of the edges of the net to tie it down. For a moment, Will thought it had worked.

Then Cephalogon took another step forward. Anchoring ropes pulled free faster than the troops could stake them into the ground. Men still hung from the edges of the net as the creature took another step.

The net began to slip, still held by ropes behind. In front, men holding on to the net dangled ten metres from the ground. Some let go, falling and rolling away. One man stayed where he had fallen, clutching his ankle. A three-toed foot came down on him. There was a squelching sound, and a short, agonised scream.

The scream galvanised the riflemen into action. All around Will, the night erupted in a cacophany of rifle fire. Men yelled as they dropped from the net, some bleeding from bullet wounds.

"Come on!" Maura shouted in his ear. She pulled at his arm, trying to drag him away from the protection of the rifles.

Will pulled back. "You can't save it now," he shouted.

"Run!" she screamed at him. "Do you want to be trampled?"

Will felt the ground tremble, as the creature gathered speed. He remembered the crushed buildings and planes. He ran as fast as he could, with Maura right beside him. Behind them, the shooting intensified. He swerved around the nearest buggy, then crouched behind it to look back. Cephalogon had reached the riflemen, and was trampling them with all—if Maura was right—twenty-five feet.

"Pull back! Clear the field!" someone shouted over a loudspeaker.

The buggy rocked as the cannon on top of it fired with a resounding boom. Too late, Will put his hands over his ears. He peered over the buggy's hood, and saw more missiles streaking towards the creature as the other cannon fired. He watched as the missiles impacted the curving side of the dome. His hands dropped again, the noise forgotten, as he saw the missiles bounce off the shining surface without leaving so much as a scratch.

A few of them exploded on impact, but when the smoke and debris cleared, the creature's shell gleamed whole and unbroken in the searchlights. Most simply ricocheted off, to land among those riflemen not yet trampled.

Will didn't need to see any more. He turned to Maura. She nodded, and they both ran for it. Light came up behind them, throwing their shadows long and thin over the old lakebed. At first, Will thought for some reason the searchlights were following them. Then a buggy pulled up beside them in a cloud of stirred-up algae particles. Short was driving.

They followed Cephalogon out into the desert. It quickly outdistanced them, but they followed its trail, catching the occasional glimpse of it in the distance as they reached the top of a ridge. It led them through part of the Conglomerated Armouries testing range, unimproved land that still bore the marks of old meteor hits, the craters softened into dips and ridges by a heavy layer of dust. Their progress slowed, as Short steered carefully around new pits left by recent testing.

"What about those experimental bombs of yours?" Will asked. "Would they work on it?"

"They might, if we had a plane left to drop one with."

"Ah."

"There is something else we can try. It's only a prototype, but as far as I can see, we've got no other option." Short sounded eager.

"Except leaving it alone," Maura said.

"That thing killed at least twenty men tonight. Who knows how many it will kill tomorrow?"

"It only killed your men because they shot at it."

Will could feel her shaking with fury. Reluctantly, he thought about how he had felt in the cavern when the creature tried to pull him in. Trapped, ready to do anything to try to get away. Perhaps their attack had felt exactly the same way to Cephalogon. It had only begun trampling the men in its own defence, desperate to escape. "She's right. Before they fired, it wasn't coming anywhere near them."

"I thought you were on my side," Short said. "It tried to eat you, didn't it? Isn't that proof of hostile intent?"

"I don't know if it was trying to eat me or not." Though Will hated to admit it, he *had* panicked back there in the caverns. He might have misinterpreted the situation. "I just assumed it was. It could have been attempting to communicate."

"What about our hangars? It crushed every single one of our planes. That was no 'attempt to communicate'."

"Maybe it was," Maura said. "Maybe it didn't like you bombing its planet."

Short opened his mouth to reply as the buggy crested another ridge. His mouth stayed open. There, at the bottom of a kilometres-wide crater, stood the creature. Short killed the headlights instantly, letting the buggy roll back down the ridge.

Will held his breath, watching for the reflected moonlight which would show them the creature's dome rising above the crater edge ahead.

"I don't think he saw us," Maura whispered.

Beside him, Will heard Short muttering into the buggy's radio. "Out." Short turned to them. "We've already tried to capture it once. You saw how well that worked. Now, we do things my way."

Will and Maura got out of the buggy and crept up to lie just under the top of the ridge, peering over at the creature. Cephalogon wandered back and forth over the crater floor, the movements of its legs so slight it seemed almost to float like the huge bubble it resembled.

"What's it doing?" Will whispered.

"I don't know. Dancing?"

Maura shivered. The Martian nights were cold, but Will knew it was more than that. He put his arm around her shoulders.

Maura shrugged it off. "We have to try to warn him."

"How? Go down there and wave our arms at it? Shoo it away? Even if you're right, even if it is intelligent, how would it understand?"

"I don't know. But we have to try."

"What if you're wrong?" Will persisted. "What if it really did try to eat me? What if it thinks we're more soldiers? You can't go down there, Maura. It's suicide."

For a moment, Will feared Maura would get up and run down into the crater anyway, but she merely lay where she was, watching the creature drift to and fro across the crater floor. After a while, he heard a vehicle drive up.

Will turned and saw a buggy mounted with a bizarre object he could only assume was a weapon. It consisted of three spheres that gleamed with a glassy sheen in the moonlight, linked in a straight line by metal tubing. At one end, perforated metal flanges spread out to form a half-metre-wide dish, like a flower at the end of a glass-and-metal stalk.

"You two. Put these on." Short crawled up and handed them dark goggles, donning a pair himself. "You're about to see something top secret."

With the goggles on, Cephalogon became merely a shadow among shadows on the crater floor. Then a line of light, searingly bright even through the goggles, came into being above them. The beam transfixed the creature's dome, lighting it from within.

"Is that radioactive?" Will glanced at the strange gun. The glass orbs glowed now, though not as brightly as the beam coming from the metal dish. The weapon hummed at a frequency so high Will could only just hear it.

"Classified." Short grinned at him, teeth shining in the light from the beam. "Works a treat, doesn't it?"

The monster's shell now glowed like a giant lantern. Will could see organs throbbing underneath, coloured in lurid purple. Bubbles formed, rising to the top of the dome as the creature cooked from the inside. Its guts turned from purple through orange and yellow to incandescent white as Will stared.

"Get down." Short pushed Will and Maura face down on the ground.

Will heard a tremendous boom. Then, all noise ceased. He knelt up, deafened. At first, he couldn't see anything. Then he remembered the goggles. He took them off and looked again. A rosette of legs, most still upright, marked where Cephalogon had stood. Blobs of slime and fragments of smoking carapace littered the ground around them.

Across the crater, the horizon was beginning to lighten. Will took Maura's hand, and they watched the sky flush red as the sun rose. Will looked down into the crater again, and felt his knees go loose. He sat down hard, still staring.

"Not dancing," Will whispered, as though the Martian might still hear him. "Excavating."

Familiar curving patterns swirled out beneath him. The same patterns he had seen in the caves, reproduced here on a gigantic scale. Stumps of pillars and the remains of walls filled the crater floor, casting bloody shadows in the Martian dawn.

SCHRÖEDINGER'S FRUITBAT

ROBBIE MATTHEWS

G iant Fruitbat!"
Not again. It's a well known fact that it takes an observer to collapse the wave state between Giant Monster and seaweed. That, and lots of psychedelic drugs.

"Toshi! Stop seeing giant flying mammals at once! You know it only encourages them."

"But Boss!" he screamed. "It's coming right for us!"

"You can stop quoting South Park as well. Has it destroyed Tokyo yet?"

"No."

"Then we have plenty of time. Prepare the poison gas capsule and the photon!"

Toshi looked at me oddly. I decided to explain.

"Surely you've heard of Schröedinger's Cat? Indeterminacy Theory? Thought Experiments? Prussic acid? Really pissed off cats?"

He continued to look at me.

"But Boss," he said, "what about the giant fruitbat devastating Tokyo?"

I sighed. One day I must really find an assistant with an IQ point or two.

"You fail to understand. All these creatures are the direct result of the human collective unconscious reacting with radiation from the Van Allan Belt.

"Therefore, they are all subject to the Uncertainty Principle."

Toshi reached for the emergency Valium and the backup straightjacket.

"No, Toshi, I mean it. We can once and for all defeat the Giant Monsters that continue to raze Tokyo on such a depressingly regular basis."

"Who cares?" said Toshi. "We live in Canberra."

A man with a very short attention span.

"What happened to *it's coming right for us*?"

"I panicked."

"Fair enough," I said, and put away my equipment. "So ... what's happening on *Neighbours* this week?"

FLESH AND BONE

ROBERT HOOD

The world has already changed, whatever else we find, thought Zara Watabi as she lay on her bed, alone, on the night the Bone Computer began its work.

There had been little to recommend the actual beginning—a simple command fed into what looked like an ordinary, if rather clunky, computer. But afterwards they'd partied, all of them, even Director Dalgrave. It was, after all, the most significant scientific event in DRC's illustrious history. At such a moment, everyone felt inclined to bend the rules, even Zara; when she noticed Anton Dalgrave giving her one of his sly, aching looks, she'd almost offered to accompany him home. Almost. She had long held the opinion that the wisest course was to keep a proper distance between her personal life and the Director's, despite his ill-hidden desires and her own frankly ambiguous feelings on the subject. She didn't want to jeopardise their work—and nor did Anton, apparently, going on his continuing failure to push their relationship beyond its professional limits. This time, once again, commonsense had proven stronger than the alcohol she'd consumed.

So it wasn't desire nor regret that kept her from sleep. It was thought of the Bone Computer that preyed on her mind. Despite every effort to acquit herself of responsibility for the project, she sensed that something was wrong and that it was up to her to correct it.

☆

In the darkest part of the night, as though in confirmation of her fears, the world trembled. An ornament on her dressing table, balanced close to its edge, slid off and toppled toward the floor. Too late, Zara reached for it and felt it brush past her bitten-back fingernails. It shattered violently.

She swore, combing her fingers through the burnt-umber tangle her hair had become.

But she didn't crawl from her bed to investigate—the whole thing seemed too much like a dream. When nothing else happened, she fell asleep—she must have, because another tremor woke her and she found that the world had become lighter. Pre-dawn was a faint discoloration on the ceiling. She swung off the bed this time. A low-level, irregular vibration trembled in the floor beneath her bare feet. Stumbling on broken porcelain, she made her way to the window, which looked out across DRC City's urban neatness toward a rugged escarpment in the east. The suburb itself was still; a few lights came on, no doubt in response to the vibrations. Darkness seemed to have sunk low over the houses, forced down by the approach of dawn. She stared toward the Skull.

The structure was an absurdity that had never been properly rationalised, no more than the creature it had once belonged to. Both remained an anomaly. Decades ago, the Monster had caused untold damage to the world and its economies, rampaging across the industrialised continents and killing millions. To have used the skeletal remains of such a monster as the structural framework of the DRC's main building seemed an act of symbolic exploitation so incredible that, at times, Zara could scarcely believe it had happened. Yet a few minutes spent with Anton Dalgrave was enough to remind her that such hubris was possible. The Director's every word, every gesture, expressed his uncompromising determination.

Sometimes, however, despite his self-importance, he could be both emotionally inept and indecisive—almost comfortably human. Yesterday morning, for example, Zara had come across him at the Skull's entrance, staring toward the mountainous horizon. "Anything wrong, Mr Director?" she'd asked.

She imagined his nostrils twitch as they caught the scent of her presence. But he didn't turn. Her "provocative, warm beauty", as he had once described it, was a permanent fixture in his imagination. His stance now confirmed his awareness of her.

"Occasionally I wonder what horrors lie ahead," he'd remarked pompously.

Her gentle laughter made him turn to face her. She'd been dressed in a conservative light-green shirt and dowdy black trousers, she recalled, yet for a moment sight of her sparked fire in his eyes. Then he'd raised one bushy eyebrow, a silent rebuke, to hide his admiration.

"Sorry," she'd responded, answering his criticism of her mockery rather than acknowledging his desire, "but at times you can be so melodramatic."

"The world requires it of me." He'd smiled distantly, reverting to his normal air of cold leadership. "Sometimes I feel responsible for too much."

☆

There was one thing for which he was unquestionably responsible: DRC.

Over three decades ago, against incredible opposition, media mogul Anton Dalgrave—then a young, self-assured businessman from a rich family—had bought the Monster's bones along with the land they lay on. Destroyed by its own nuclear fire, the Monster had left these remains as a memorial to the fact that the world was not governed by the rules of Man alone (as the Gigantheists would have it)—but Dalgrave had been determined to turn that aphorism on its head. The Bones' radiation nullified, he incorporated the gigantic skeleton into a vast research establishment designed to study the creature and the many diverse issues arising from its existence. Thus the Dalgrave Research Centre was born.

The DRC—most of which lay beneath the surface of the Earth, with egress only through the Skull—had been functioning ever since. The full extent of its achievements had never been revealed, though it produced a continual trickle of innovative research papers and a plethora of practical applications that served to make Dalgrave ever richer. For herself, Zara had been content to give her life to the project—nearly 15 years of it so far. Over that time, success in understanding the Monster had been slow but comfortably satisfying.

Or at least it had been until Dr Kumala came with his theories and his startling proposition. The prominent palaeontologist had gained access to Dalgrave thanks to the Director's long-running fascination for the researcher's Lost Monster mythologies; but it was the lure of possibility that had most recommended him. If what he claimed proved true, it held vast implication for the future of DRC and the world.

If. Something in Zara whispered doubts and reservations.

She had no evidence to support such negative intuitions, of course. On the contrary, Kumala's achievement had all the beneficent dazzle of a Great Insight. As often as the molecular structure of the Monster's bones had been subjected to study and analysis, no one had made the unlikely leap from dead monster to quantum computing that Dr Kumala had. The palaeontologist, with little or no knowledge of information technology, had bridged the logic chasm with stunning results.

Development of the Bone Computer hadn't been straight-forward, however. After all, this was a problem physicists had been failing to solve since the mid-20th century. There'd been technical problems to overcome first—problems dealing with fragmentation of the bone itself, problems refining communication within its sub-atomic structure, problems of data access and recovery. But six months after Kumala's initial revelation, scientists had been ready to power up the first fully functional quantum computer and to set it the task of analysing and re-configuring an unimaginably huge volume of data, in the first instance seeking for evidence of Kumala's Lost Monsters. Researchers had estimated that a conventional computer would have taken well over five years to analyse the totality of existence as presently understood, if it could manage it at all. The Bone Computer, working its spooky magic, would perform the same procedure in a week. A Great Leap Forward indeed—but it made Zara nervous.

☆

Movement in the pre-dawn gloom sent a tingle down her spine. She focused through her own reflection, staring toward the Skull. Her eyes widened. The structure appeared to be shifting!

But that was impossible. Zara unlatched the window and slid it open. The air that flowed in around her was unnaturally warm for this time of year. But, yes, it looked for all the world as though the DRC building was moving. The rounded roof of the Skull appeared to be higher than normal, and the rest of its skeleton fuller and more solid. As she watched, it jerked sideways, shaking off the walls that had been added to it over the years as though they were dust.

Then dizziness overcame her, her mind hazing into a momentary disorientation. She staggered, clutching at the windowsill. Blinked to clear the mist from her eyes. When she re-focused on the DRC complex, she saw that the Skull was unmoved. The Monster's skeleton, too, lay still, prone behind the Skull and patchily enclosed by man-made walls and annexes—as it had lain for decades now.

Unnerved, she slammed the window closed.

☆

Another hour passed. Endless pounding in Zara's temples had contributed to her insomnia, or so she thought as she sat biting at her nails even more determinedly than ever. Had she been asleep the whole time? Perhaps, but when the world shook, twice as violently as before, it felt as though she'd been jolted awake, fully conscious now with sudden and painful urgency.

She forced herself to stand. Halfway to her feet, reality trembled again and she lost her balance. This time she hit the floor hard. Automatic lighting snapped on.

What was happening? An earthquake? Impossible. This was a stable part of the planet—it had never experienced a tremor this savage, not in recorded history. Another shockwave hit, so intense the air seemed to shimmer.

Unsteadily, she headed for the window. The sky was heavy with cloud, the horizon barely visible in the gloom. When wind slashed against the walls, Zara thought she could hear screaming in it.

Then her lights flickered out.

Sight of something moving in the dark haze beyond the window was accompanied by a fleeting sense of déjà vu. Whatever the something was, it was big. More than big—gigantic! Like a vast shadow it rose out of the dawn, growing larger with every step.

She breathed in sharply as another, heavier shockwave caused the corners of her room to split apart. The view from her window disappeared, replaced by a mottled, dark-green mass. Liquid splattered onto the glass. Zara leaned closer. Blood.

She pulled away as a ragged shape plummeted toward her, tossed sideways and from above as though by some monstrous predator. The window shattered and a torn, desiccated scrap of human prey, riding a wave of foul breath, crashed against her in a shower of glass splinters. Zara went down, even as she tried to scramble to safety.

Then her walls caved in, and the world followed in a fury of wind and sound, driven by a gigantic clawed foot and the stench of ancient violence.

☆

Zara woke in dim sunlight. The morning was calm and she lay in the quiet, for a moment empty of thought. As memory returned, she thought: Kumala was right about this, too. There is more than one of them.

"The Lost Monsters?" he had queried at his first meeting with Dalgrave. As DRC's leading gigantophysicist, Zara was present, though at that time she hadn't known why. Appropriately enough, the meeting had taken place in Dalgrave's office within the Monster's cranial cavity. "The term is not mine," Kumala continued disdainfully. "A journalist from Fortean Times *coined it. His lurid article gave the theory much limited, and unwanted, publicity about four years ago. I've published only a little since, having been involved in lengthy expeditions to various prehistorically significant regions—"*

Dalgrave waved the explanation aside.

"Okay, then you know my theory that this Monster ..." Kumala pointed upward at the curved bone of the ceiling. "... That it wasn't unique, despite the common view."

"The common view being that the Monster was a one-off mutation inspired by some rather foolish nuclear activities in the mid-20th century?"

Kumala nodded. "It was a time of massive fear and paranoia— some say the Monster manifested the apocalyptic anxieties of the period. And there exists considerable evidence of its power. Newsreel footage. The famous documentary made by a Japanese film crew, chronicling its attack on Tokyo. Scarring across the surface of the planet that still hasn't healed ..." Again he gestured at the surrounding Bone. "This skeleton itself is indicative enough."

"Surely there'd be evidence of others," Zara commented, "if they'd ever existed. Written accounts, at least—and their bones."

"I came to believe that such evidence could be found, somewhere. For years I've dedicated myself to doing so."

"Any success?" Dalgrave asked with a hint of irony.

The man's eyes seemed to glaze over briefly. "Success? That remains to be seen. However, last July, in a remote location in Africa, we found something more tangible than belief ..."

Another tremor broke Zara's reverie. Its abruptness made her cry out, afraid the primeval creature had returned. But no, there was no sign of a monster.

The walls of her house were still standing; as far as she could tell, they had been completely unaffected by either earthquake or monster. No torn, drained corpse. No busted masonry.

She peered through the unbroken window. An unusual amount of activity twittered across neighbouring blocks, especially for this time of the morning—but all of it seemed relatively innocuous.

A dream?

Zara might have thought so if not for the scared faces she saw peering out from windows up and down the street. *Something* had happened.

She reached for the comm-link pad and keyed in Dalgrave's private code. Access was denied for over an hour.

☆

"The experience was more-or-less universal," Kumala said—to himself as much as to the rest of them. He was deceptively young in appearance, but with a weathered look that spoke of fieldwork. His skin was a coppery colour, a trait determined as much by genetic pre-disposition as by exposure to the sun. His "ancestral home" (as he put it) was the island Mafu, situated 20 kilometres east of the Vava'u archipelago, a once-fertile rock that had been rendered uninhabitable by the Monster back in 1955. Everyone bar his then-pregnant grandmother had died in that attack. "Such a dark familial heritage has given me purpose," he'd declared at Zara's first introduction to him, his fists clenched.

Now his hands moved about restlessly, as though lost without that grim emotion to guide them. "It was a shared hallucination," he added, referring to last night's monster.

"Okay," Dalgrave pressed, his tone demanding, "but what the hell does it mean?"

"Mean? When the computer's finished its run, we'll know. We can only guess at this stage—"

"Guess then."

"Very well." The palaeontologist went into lecture mode. "I believe that thing was a fragmentary but actualised transpositional image of the first Monster to occur in history ... the primeval Monster—at the dawn of Man. The coincidence is too great for this incident to have occurred just as the Bone Computer began its analysis. The two events must be connected." His hands gripped each other tightly.

"A dinosaur?"

"No, no. It was much bigger than any dinosaur ever known, its physiology totally divergent."

"I can see similarities."

He grunted in annoyance at Dalgrave's contradictory manner. "I'm convinced it's of a different phylum at least—but more probably it's non-linear ... a one-off."

"Absurd. How could that be?"

"I don't know. It doesn't matter." He breathed out noisily and continued. "Look, quantum weirdness has been a topic of some debate for decades. Speculation is frequently fantastic and highly dubious—yet how can we know for sure what the consequences of dabbling at the high end of theory might be? Would you agree,

Dr Watabi?"

Zara recalled times when she'd had premonitions of the rise of a Monster, later dismissed as the after-effects of dream and largely forgotten. Was the Monster a potentiality in humanity or in the world that the Bone Computer could draw on? A reflection of some alternative history? "Most of the speculation has been dubious at best," Zara responded simply.

Not getting the answer he'd wanted, Kumala ignored her. "What if the Bone Computer's activities are causing perceptual ripples at a sub-material level, re-creating the past it is trying to analyse? I believe that what it showed us was the Original Monster, not simply the descendent of some prehistoric species—and it will point the way toward physical evidence for the creature's existence. I will be fully vindicated."

Dalgrave frowned thoughtfully. "I assume then we'll be subjected to more of this mind-shit before the damn computer's finished?"

"Oh yes," exclaimed Kumala, his enthusiasm reaching toward a state of ecstasy. "Yes indeed. In our dreams there are Monsters untapped. More will arise, I believe ... many more."

☆

Zara was still trying to fathom Kumala's motives. His own account of them left her dissatisfied.

Over two years before, deep beneath a dried-out landscape that had been mountainous terrain until prehistoric seismic activity turned it topsy-turvy, the palaeontologist and his team had stumbled upon a Neolithic archive. According to Kumala, the primitive paintings that adorned the seemingly endless underground walls told a tale of calamity and fear.

"Look!" Kumala had demanded during their first meeting, powering up an air-screen he'd projected over the Director's desk. An image appeared on it—a faded, barely distinguishable sketch, executed in red paint on stone.

"A giant monster?" Zara suggested.

Kumala pointed to a small figure running at the foot of the monster. "We get some idea of the scale involved from this, which appears to be a human."

"It's just a painting, Kumala," Dalgrave huffed. "And a somewhat ambiguous one at that. Isn't it reasonable to assume that ancient Man possessed imagination?"

Kumala gestured for patience. He ran through a collection of images, detailing his belief that they represented the destruction caused by a giant monster. "How it was finally killed, I don't know, but this—" He displayed what looked like a celebratory scene. "This depicts its fate."

"You mean they ate it?" Zara could make out what might have been huge bones being picked clean by the tiny stick figures.

Kumala nodded. "And I further believe that consumption of the monster's flesh gave a powerful shove to human development, precipitating a major increase in intelligence."

Dalgrave laughed. "I assume you have some basis for a claim as outlandish as that one?"

Kumala waved the question aside. "A case can be made. I believe this theory explains the nature of the Monster: opposing possibilities, both utter destruction and significant advancement. It's up to us which potential becomes reality. The Monster is merely a catalyst." He paused, studying their expressions. "However, that's not important right now. This is!"

The screen filled with symbols and lines.

"Dozens of walls in the cavern complex were filled with these hieroglyphics," Kumala said. "Remarkable. Nothing elsewhere can compare—"

"And these say what?" Dalgrave interrupted.

Kumala was near bursting with excitement. His hands swirled about like wind-blades in a storm. "Translation was demanding and we expended most of our allocated computer time in the process. But we eventually determined that these scrawls were an attempt to give the monster a name, based on an intricate mathematical system that the primitives derived from proportional measurements of the creature's body factored into some sort of mystical schematic of its activities when alive. Do you see? It's remarkable. They were trying to define the monster according to the science of their time—and re-structuring that science as they did so!"

To her own amazement, Zara could already appreciate some of the sophisticated computational qualities of the symbols.

"And how does this help us?" Dalgrave asked.

Kumala leapt around the desk and leaned toward the Director. "I believe that we can use the parameters outlined by this ancient symbology as a basis for analysing existing data—with a view to ... well, finding evidence of giant monster activity throughout history."

"I see."

"The implications are almost inconceivable!" Kumala edged even closer. "We could ... we could learn where the Monsters come from, perhaps control them. It offers unequaled potential—"

Dalgrave gestured for silence and amazingly Kumala obliged. "I can appreciate your excitement, Doctor." Dalgrave paced away from the over-eager palaeontologist. "But as I see it there are some significant hurdles. For a start, this whole edifice rests on a few rather dubious assumptions. That there was another Monster, for example. What do you think, Zara? Dr Watabi?"

Zara had heard the Director's question but she continued to stare at the wall of symbols Kumala had projected onto his virtual screen. "There might be something in it," she said at last. "I can see conceptual relationships in those symbols that are surprising to say the least, given where they come from—"

"But you think he might be right?"

She turned to Kumala. "I assume your aim would be to trawl through all available archives in the DRC's network, sorting and re-ordering data using some kind of decoded version of the paradigm. Shaping it as you go, in fact."

"That, for a start. But not just secondary archives. I want to reference everything."

"Everything?"

"Encode the world itself as primary data! Quantify reality!"

"You'd need enormous computational power to make any sort of headway in a reasonable timeframe with that aim in mind. The DRC's on-site database is huge enough, but we have direct and indirect connection to literally millions of digital libraries worldwide. Encoding the natural world itself is a huge leap beyond that!"

"Which leads me to an important question," Kumala replied.

"Yes?"

He glanced slyly at Dalgrave. "How's the development of your quantum computer progressing?"

☆

The next vision hit at midday. Frustrated that her own research had become a side issue in the face of the Bone Computer's potential benefits, Zara had left the lab early and was driving to the supermarket to pick up a supply of chocolate and vodka. The DRC employed over ten thousand people and Dalgrave had arranged for a mini-mall to be built for their convenience—malls were a central factor in creating a sense of goodwill and contentment, he'd said. DRC City must have one.

An earsplitting thrash-metal/latino-cross pop song was blaring from her on-board netlink and filling her vehicle with noise—but Zara heard the roar anyway. It was so loud it made the windscreen vibrate.

She glanced out the side window, looking for the source of the sound. On the pavement, people were scanning the distance nervously.

An old-fashioned car braked in front of her—Zara saw the warning-lights out of the corner of her eye. She'd already slowed and her reflexes were good—but she'd turned off the proximity detectors when she switched to manual and, regardless of its high-tech nature, her vehicle slipped forward too far. The impact was little more than a nudge, however, jolting her and pushing the car she'd hit forward a few centimetres. The driver—an older man—didn't even look at her. He was staring off to the right.

Zara followed his gaze—and saw what had him so mesmerised.

This new monster was even larger than the last one—a dark, billowing mass against the cloudy lightness of the sky. Was it reptilian? It gave the impression of cold flesh and scaliness but the way its skin gathered into huge folds made it seem as though it wore a cowl and flowing robes, like a giant priest. Darkness churned around it despite the daylight. In fact it seemed to attract every scrap of shadow it passed, infusing it into its flesh, keeping it close. Two huge blazing eyes stared from the folds of skin surrounding its head, coldly challenging the world that scurried around its hoofed feet.

Zara tasted blood from her bitten lip.

People were panicking now, leaping from stalled vehicles, running; some remained in their cars and accelerated into stalled lines of traffic in an unthinking desire to simply *move*. The Monster was still some way off, but the effect of its impossible size was to make its presence immediate and fearsome. It appeared to tower above the tallest building in DRC City's central business district. As Zara watched, a long, ropy tail with a bony end swept upward like a censer, then slammed down on a row of warehouses. Smoke, dust and rubble shot into the air, swirling into mini-tornadoes in the Monster's wake.

Zara's body went numb. She wanted to do something, but the sight wouldn't allow her to think. She stared through the window as the thing ploughed across rows of houses, demolishing them with ease. It met with no resistance. Why should it? No one had expected this, no one had been prepared. And besides, surely it was another vision, one of the Bone Computer's random pieces of multiverse flotsam. Once the moment had passed the world would revert to the way it was before the thing's arrival.

Yet the Monster didn't look like an hallucination. Zara could feel the rumble in the ground, could see very detail of the destruction, could hear the cries. Suddenly the Priest Monster leaned down, opened a cavernous mouth in its upper body and breathed out a cloud of vapour. As the fumes settled on them, its victims collapsed, their flesh blackening, then becoming pustulant. Reflexively Zara checked that her vehicle's windows were sealed and flipped the air filter on, even though the cloud hadn't reached her.

Her front-panel comm-light flashed on and off. "What?" she snapped.

"Zara, can you see this?" It was Dalgrave.

"If you mean the Monster, yes, I can. Far better than I like!"

"So far it's wrecked half the warehouse district. I hope to hell it's an illusion."

"I was just thinking the same thing. I'm out in the street, near the Mall. It's killing people with its breath."

"What, a firestorm?"

"Not like the Monster from the 1950s. This isn't nuclear. More like ... I don't know ... a plague. Hallucination or not, I think this is dangerous, Anton. We should stop the program—"

At that moment, her vehicle was struck by a soundwave and sloughed sideways. A woman, hands flapping madly, the skin of her face inflamed, crashed across Zara's windscreen and bounced away. Zara's link-up shrieked and went dead. She glanced toward the sky.

Seething blackness towered above her. A hoof the size of a house smashed into the ground a block away, sending a shockwave through the town. Buildings collapsed, slabs of broken concrete, vehicles, people heaved into the air. A wall of dirt and smoke rose from the chaos, roiling down the street and engulfing her. Zara was plunged into a thick grey twilight.

The Monster's voice thundered above it.

☆

Even mentioning DRC's interest in developing a quantum computer had been a daring one, and Kumala had known it. The DRC's obsession with the holy grail of information technology was supposed to be a secret. How someone like Kumala had come to learn of its existence suggested serious security implications to be dealt with further down the line.

"Quantum computers are a myth," Dalgrave growled.

Kumala nodded knowingly. "But I understand the DRC has come close."

Further deception seemed pointless. Zara shrugged. "No significant inroads have been made into the decoherence problem, Dr Kumala." Dalgrave frowned at her. She'd scowled back at him before adding, "Either here or elsewhere. Five, six qubit capacity is still the limit. Sad, but true."

"Six qubit processing? That's impressive, isn't it?"

"Impressive, but not good enough. Barely worth the effort."

Kumala nodded again, displaying a growing sense of arrogance. "What if I said I could provide you with a substance both stable and malleable enough to be used for quantum computation? A substance that might become the basis of an infinitely robust system allowing easy control of superimposed states and the provision of a simple logic gate that isn't susceptible to breakdown? An ideal quantum 'chip', in fact?"

Dalgrave had laughed. "Give me that and you could write your own ticket."

Kumala pointed to a series of prehistoric glyphs displayed on the screen. "That's it," he said.

"That's what?"

Zara felt the first stirring of an intuition she could scarcely believe. "The Monster's bones," she whispered through teeth grinding at her thumbnail.

Kumala grinned at her, spreading his arms as though offering the universe to a surprisingly clever acolyte. "Bone chips. And you have plenty of them to experiment with."

☆

"I managed to access some current data without interrupting the program," Kumala insisted. "The Computer identified this latest Monster as having plundered vast areas of Europe in the late 5th century through to about 1000 AD. It explains so much."

"The Dark Ages," Zara commented grimly. Once again she hadn't been awake to see the Monster's passing. She didn't remember when her consciousness slipped into oblivion, but at some point it must have. She recalled the cloud thinning, however, drifting away on a gentle wind that had sprung up from nowhere. She'd found herself looking out on a scene of chaos and confusion. A few vehicles had been burning, several bodies had littered the street, but nearby buildings were still standing and there'd been little sign that a Monster had rampaged through the area moments before. Minor damage only.

"It looked like a monk or a priest," she added.

Kumala snorted. "You're being a bit romantic about it, don't you think?"

"Seems appropriate though. The rise of knowledge driven back by the spread of the Church's monolithic influence—"

"Please, doctor, your historical ignorance is showing." Kumala shook his head. "The Church as a whole fostered the growth of knowledge, but political instability, superstition and the plague—"

Dalgrave slammed his hand down on his desktop. "No history lessons!" he growled. "I want to know about that thing *now*. Two warehouses burned to the ground, doctor. People died—"

"Damage was caused by panic and accident, not by the Monster. Chance factors only. The Monster was transitory!"

"But the likelihood of actual injury is escalating with each manifestation," Zara pointed out.

"And what is that conclusion based on? There have only been two instances. Hardly a valid sample."

"So should we wait for a few more Monsters to turn up? See how many people die each time? Get the Bone Computer to assess risk factors?"

Kumala ignored her sarcasm. "This is too important to let knee-jerk reactions dictate how we respond. We need this information."

Dalgrave gestured for both Kumala and Zara to be calm. "I don't know about *need*, but there is rather a lot of money and reputation tied up in this, Zara. More than you know."

What Zara did know was how the discussion would proceed from there; ethical considerations had a traditionally low priority in the commercial sphere. "People are scared, Director."

"So we'll placate them. Some generous compensation—and a bit of propaganda to prepare them for what's to come. How long has the program got to run? Three, four days? We'll discourage unnecessary movement, bring in a partial curfew. At least it's localised." He looked straight at Kumala. "Can we predict—roughly—when the visions are likely to happen?"

Kumala frowned. "Perhaps."

"Try."

Zara protested, but Dalgrave's look silenced her. "It's safe enough as long as people don't panic," he said. She went off to initiate development of a program of appeasement and containment. Then she headed for her own lab deep beneath the surface, determined to undertake investigations of her own. Memory of Kumala's smugness and mocking smile spurred her on.

What did he really want?

☆

The next Monster appeared at about two the following morning. Zara hadn't been to bed yet; she was still slogging away on her computer, looking for ... she didn't know what. Information. Inspiration. Idly she'd typed in <MAFU> and was reading a history of the island when, once again, the world shook violently. She glanced at the ceiling and muttered, "Here we go." She was some distance underground, so didn't expect any direct confrontations with the Monster this time around—no matter what form it should take.

Not surprisingly it was huge like the others, but surprisingly it didn't look organic at all. It manifested as a vast machine, multiple piston-legs pounding the earth as it progressed with slow, determined inexorability. Steam, thick smoke, bursts of flame churned around it. For about 30 minutes Zara watched it via the network channels as it blackened a wide path through DRC City. At one point the distant news cameras got close enough to reveal the texture of the Monster's surface. Oddly, up that close, it seemed to have a sort of hard, steel-grey skin.

Then transmission ceased. The connection went dead. When it came back on, moments later, the creature was gone, as was the news media's recorded evidence of its presence.

Much of the Monster's destruction remained, however. Flames continued to scorch the horizon for several hours.

☆

"Let me guess," Zara said to Kumala, once again in conference within the Skull. "The spectre of Industrial Revolution?"

He nodded. "This monster killed millions and caused untold damage just as the Industrial Revolution was reaching its peak, attracted by the factories and the refineries. I've found abundant material on it."

Somewhere at the back of her mind Zara recalled a time not so long ago when none of this information was available to them— when there existed no mention of the Monsters in history or cultural tradition. The 1950s Monster had been unique then. But that was absurd. Had her memories been affected? She thought back, delving deeply into her own past, and there it was: she recalled reading a chapter on the Mecha-monster twenty years ago during a university course in global technological history. Of course the evidence had to have been there all along. Yet the recollection sat uncomfortably in her mind.

"What stopped it?" Dalgrave asked.

"According to several prominent historians, a rag-tag coalition of technologists developed a chemically unstable but potent gas that became highly corrosive when mixed with certain industrial by-products. They arranged for the substance, in controlled quantities, to be ingested by the Monster, and caused it to break apart from within."

"Remarkable."

"Do you see?" said Kumala. "Like the Priest, the Mecha-monster was a terrible threat, but once again the end result was progress. It encouraged growth. Just as early Man ate the Original Monster and doing so caused an unexpected increase in mental ability, and developing a biological approach to disposing of the Priest Monster ushered in an age of enlightenment, so the Mecha revitalised industrial technology. There is evidence that many subsequent developments were founded on surviving scraps of the monster's carcass, feeding many fields, including, I'm sorry to say, munitions production. So, it's a two-edged sword that inevitably led to the Atomic Monster we are more familiar with."

"The way things are going," Zara commented dryly, "the Atomic Monster will be walking down DRC Main Street to say Hi! any moment now." She looked straight at Dalgrave, her sharp features grim. "And that worries me a lot. Have you seen the damage reports? The Mecha-vision was, in its effect, much more physically real than the others. We lost an entire district. Over 1000 people were killed. And about 100 of them stayed dead."

Dalgrave frowned, but said nothing.

"Regrettable, but again, merely incidental." Kumala's face had lost the softness it had once displayed. Zara wondered at how chameleon-like he was, how unstable. She suddenly felt that any insight into his character she'd once had was completely false.

"Regrettable?" she echoed. "We're talking real, irretrievable death here, Doctor Kumala. But the essential issue is: what happens next? It seems to me that each manifestation is more permanently destructive—the closer to us in time, the greater the objective effect. The next one—our friend the Atomic Monster, I'd guess—is way too historically close for complacency."

Kumala's eyes were cold and evasive. "Nonsense."

"Is it?" Zara's assumed her own gaze had become equally cold, though more direct. "Sometimes, Doctor, I find myself wondering what exactly your motives are in this."

Kumala didn't move, his rounded face unreadable. Dalgrave, however, glared at Zara. "I think you'll have to explain yourself, Dr Watabi," he said.

Zara turned to him, made even colder by her friend's—no, her superior's—tone.

"I've been researching background to the current events, Director—rather widely, I admit, not knowing what I was looking for. At one point, I did a search on 'Mafu' with no aim other than wanting to understand the Monster's history. Well, it seems we were wrong, even Dr Kumala. The Monster didn't destroy Mafu, not directly anyway. According to certain de-classified government reports I managed to dig up, the island was destroyed by friendly fire."

"What?" The look on Dalgrave's face was a curious mixture of puzzlement and irritation.

Zara glanced at Kumala. *His* face was stonily indifferent.

"Friendly fire. The US airforce tried to nuke the Monster—and missed. They annihilated Mafu instead. The story that the Monster was responsible was seeded into the press and popular histories—fairly normal ass-covering tactics. But the reality is there in official documents and the writings of certain fringe commentators."

The Director turned sharply. "Did you know about this, Kumala?"

Kumala stared at him, making no sound, barely breathing.

"Of course, he did," said Zara, "and that's what started me thinking late last night. I realised that Dr Kumala has been so determined about this project it's blinded us—what do we know of it really? We were wooed with the promise of a quantum-processing chip and didn't look very hard at anything else. Few of us read the technical specs, and those who did were easily bamboozled by its overlay of socio-scientific jargon. It seems probable that Dr Kumala knows more about it—about the possible outcome of this experiment—than he's been letting on. True, doctor? You even did final adjustments on the program—and there's no record of what exactly those adjustments were intended to achieve."

Kumala smiled nastily from one side of his mouth. The asymmetry of it was unsettling.

"You don't know anything," he growled. "This is professional jealousy, nothing more or less."

Having started, Zara found that ideas came thick and fast. She directed her on-the-run deductions at Dalgrave, needing him to understand fully so he'd let her act against his best commercial interests. "What if Dr Kumala harbors resentment toward the nation responsible for destroying his forebears, his native island?"

"But, Zara, really! To what end would he start an experiment that can only result in the glorification of the DRC?" Dalgrave shrugged. "The Bone Computer is working. It's an incredible success."

"But what's it doing, Director? So far we've experienced the visionary manifestation of historical monsters—monsters that rampage through the city, then disappear, as though settling back into their proper times. If the Atomic Monster should appear—as we all assume it will—then its career will probably be similar. But what then? What comes after that?"

Dalgrave frowned.

Zara stepped closer to him, knowing his attitude to such proximity: her closeness would likely affect his judgement in her favour. "Anton, I think Kumala has planned this, and the end of it is the creation of a history of monstrous visitations defining moments of crisis—a history that didn't exist before the Bone Computer went on line—and the institution of a new universal regime. It's changing history, defining it in terms of a succession of monstrous beings!"

"That's absurd."

"Is it? The physics involved here is quite twisted, believe me. Alternative time-lines have been a much-discussed tenet of quantum thought for decades, along with a huge indigestible mass of pseudo-scientific metaphysics. But what *is* the Bone Computer doing, Anton? Do you really know? I don't—and I'm the most highly qualified physicist in this place. I can only go on what I see—and what I see is the manifestation of Monsters that should have been consigned to the past, if they existed at all."

"But why do it, even if we concede that it's possible?"

Zara gestured at Kumala. "Ask him! Ask why—as I discovered last night in my net-searches—he's a member of the Gigantheistic movement."

"The Monster-as-God faction?" Dalgrave glowered at Kumala. "Is this true?"

He shrugged. "Why would I deny it? There is such a thing as religious freedom."

"The Gigantheists are crackpots, man."

"If that's what they are," Kumala said, "why should you care about them?" He snorted. "The fact is, Mr Director, I *am* an affiliate of the Gigantheist Church—and I joined because of my people's history, because I believe it is not the Monster we should be afraid of. Indeed, I and my fellow Gigantheists believe that the Atomic Monster was not enough. We wanted something more, something much greater."

"More?" Dalgrave stood and prowled toward him. "You've been using me ... exploiting the DRC to further some stupid religious conviction?"

Kumala formed a barrier with his hands. "Don't you touch me!" he warned. "I'm the only one who understands that computer. Hurt me and you'll regret it, I promise you."

"Oh?" Dalgrave glared. "So what's the damn thing supposed to produce?"

Kumala looked ostentatiously at his watch. "By my calculations," he said, smirking, "you'll find out soon enough."

His words filtered into Zara's mind slowly, but as their meaning hit, the thunder began. Soundwave impact threw them from their feet, overturning chairs and tables, as though somehow an electrical discharge had taken place within the room itself. Zara's skin felt hot.

"What was that?" yelled Dalgrave.

Zara wanted to answer but the ringing in her ears inhibited her ability to talk. Kumala, more prepared perhaps, growled, "Merely a beginning!"

Zara made it to her feet and, despite the effects of further percussive shockwaves, concentrated on getting to a bank of monitors that lined one wall. Dalgrave's office had no windows, the Skull's walls having defied early low-level attempts to slice an opening in them.

"The control's are here!" Dalgrave collapsed onto his desk as the earth wrenched upward, then settled again. He reached toward a panel.

Images transmitted from the western-facing cameras were enough to take her breath away. Huge, vicious and exuding an aura that made the air visibly shake as it moved, the Atomic Monster strode across bushland, houses, streets, the fleeing inhabitants of DRC City, breathing destruction as it went. Fire rose behind it. Its tail was like a gigantic scythe, demolishing whole districts with one sweep. A fierce yet impersonal anger glowed in its eyes, plucking at Zara even from this distance. So this was what it had looked like in action, all those years ago! Incredible! Zara was forced to glance away.

What she saw when she did so was Kumala, opening the main door and lunging out into the corridor.

"Kumala!" she cried.

Dalgrave turned, howling an inarticulate curse. But the door slammed shut before either of them could act. Zara heard the high-pitched whine of the emergency seal being activated.

"He's locked us in!" she said, bashing against the thick steel. Nothing happened when she pressed the internal release.

"How did he know the code, damn it?"

"He's prepared himself for this, Anton."

"So what's he think he's doing?"

"Making sure we don't interfere!" Zara gestured back at the images on Dalgrave's monitors. "That thing is going to incinerate the whole town. And then—"

Again the thunder hit, louder now, closer. The room trembled and shook—shifted, in fact, as though waking up after a long sleep.

"Then?" yelled Dalgrave. "What's going to happen, Zara?"

"After the Atomic Monster?" She stumbled over to him and leaned toward his ear, desperate to be heard above the hurricane battering at the walls. "Like the others, the Atomic Monster doesn't belong here ... I think it'll raze the city, as it did before, elsewhere. Then it'll phase-shift back to its own time. But something else will follow, something new."

"A new sort of Monster?"

"A Monster for these times. Unlike the others it will belong here ... now." She paused, tasting her fear. "For real!" Possibilities tumbled through her mind—grim, awful possibilities. "Whatever form it takes it's going to be bigger and meaner and harder to kill ... damn it all, Anton, back in the 1950s the Atomic Monster was practically invulnerable. It consumed itself—*we* were helpless.

If the Monsters are somehow a crystallisation of the dangers inherent in contemporary experience, then maybe ours will be some kind of cross-over between the real and the virtual. Given that the last one provided us the means for creating a revolutionary and powerful computer."

"A Monster that straddles quantum realities—manipulates them perhaps?"

"A logical enough jump from the idea that the Monsters encapsulate crucial moments in history. It's precisely the dilemma we face. And to be honest, I think the Bone Computer has already opened the gate to a multilayered reality in which events that never happened and objects that never existed except as a sort of suspended potential can be inserted into the past ... A monster that gains its conceptual nature from a scenario like that could totally destroy humanity, wiping us from history."

"And replacing us with what?"

"With whatever reality it wants!" She grabbed his arm and pulled him closer, partly to ensure that he heard her over the thunderous noise of the approaching Monster, but mostly for the re-assurance of contact with him. "We've got to turn the Bone Computer off, Anton."

He nodded. It was obvious. At that instant Zara glanced over his shoulder toward the bank of monitors. The Atomic Monster, glowing with a deadly heat, was so close Zara could no longer see all of it. Its gigantic foot crashed to earth just out of view, the screens showing an expanse of mottled grey skin. The air quivered with an urgency that made Zara's flesh crawl. One of the more remote cameras automatically refocussed so she could see more of the creature. Its image leaned toward the Skull. Zara stared into its fierce eyes and a widening maw that opened to release a nuclear flood—

She threw the Director and herself to the floor. Zara felt the radioactive inferno engulf them, wave upon wave of atomic fire washing over the Skull, clawing at its molecules, trying to rip the densely powerful bone apart. The room shook and lurched from side to side, tossing Zara around as though she were nothing. Through the flames she saw the Monster rear up again, about to send another burst of radiation their way. How much of its nuclear heat could even its own bones take?

But as it did so it began to break up, its outline wavering, dimming. It was as Zara had predicted—what she was seeing was the creature's departure, dragged back through time presumably, to where it belonged. The Monster roared as though in anger and a final burst of flame shot out of it, rolling toward the Skull in a last ditch attempt to annihilate this symbol of its own mortality. External cameras finally succumbed and the images on the screens above her pixelated into darkness. The room vibrated, rocked, groaned in agony. The air flared in an incandescent rage.

☆

But it wasn't the end. Not yet. Zara opened her eyes and found that neither the room nor themselves had been vaporised. Presumably the Atomic Monster had gone and all was back to normal. Yet she knew that normality was problematic at best. She could hear the sound of fire and destruction—DRC City burning around them. The air reeked of change, a smell she would not have been able to describe even if she'd tried.

Then she realised that what she sensed was coming from the Skull itself. It was glowing, the energies within it intensifying as she watched. Power seemed to leak from within its molecular structure and form a translucent matting over its entire surface, as though ... oh God! Zara thought, it's growing new flesh!

As the idea struck her, the Skull shifted beneath her feet again. But this time the movement had come from the substance of the Skull itself, not from movement of the ground on which it lay.

"Anton," she screamed, grabbing the Director, "we have to do something!"

He shook her off. Determination had re-entered his eyes.

"Internal override can only to be achieved centrally."

"There must be a way out. We have to get to the Bone Computer before this thing—" She gestured widely at whatever was taking shape around them. "Before this new Monster becomes real."

The Skeleton moved, stretching its long-dormant fibres.

Breathing erratically, Dalgrave made it to his desk, where he paused to recoup his strength. "I have some access to the full DRC network here," he said.

He punched a code into the keypad at one side of his desk. A large panel rose from the smooth surface, covered with dimly glowing touch-points. He poked at them, then recited his entry code in a formal manner: "I am Anton Dalgrave, DRC's living monster."

Zara raised her eyebrows mockingly. Dalgrave ignored her, his attention on a three-dimensional hologram of a computer network that formed over his desktop. The room shuddered.

"I doubt we'll be able to gain physical access to the labs," he said, "but if you can connect into the Bone grid from here, we might stand a chance of affecting the Computer's program." His hard grey eyes stared at her from across the room. "So hurry!" he said.

☆

That Dalgrave might have such a powerful linking facility in his office was an arrogance that hadn't occurred to Kumala—he hadn't known the Director well enough. So he hadn't constructed appropriate barriers, even had he had the knowledge to do so. He was a palaeontologist, after all, not a professional geek—even less so than Zara. Yet despite this, Zara found herself struggling to break in.

"It's too unfamiliar, Anton," Zara shouted above the wrenching sounds the Skull was making. The room seemed to be crowding in on them as it incorporated furniture and fittings into its new brain—sooner or later, Zara recognised, it would incorporate them, too. "The coding is too complex for me to fully understand. I have no idea what these data matrices mean."

"Can you edge me through the lab's backdoor at least?"

"Maybe." She swept her fingers over the hologram, enforcing connections between gateways and probing virtual facilities. "Ah," she yelled suddenly, "I *can* do this."

The emergency door to Dalgrave's office ground open about half way, then seized.

"Well, nearly."

"Enough," Dalgrave said. He forced her out of the seat. "I think I've got the hang of what you're doing. You leave. Now. Get out while you can."

Zara glared at him. "You can't stay here."

"I've got to gain control of the program," he said with forceful determination. "If it can be done at all, it can be done from here. In fact..." He glanced around. "If this place is destined to be the brain of the Monster, then I'm in the perfect place to infiltrate and influence its actions."

"You'll be killed!"

"Perhaps. Either way, this is my responsibility, Zara. All of it. It was never anybody else's."

"But—"

"There's no time!" The look he gave her said it all, and she knew with utter certainty that this was an argument she couldn't win.

"I'll try to get to the main computer room," she said.

"It's inaccessible. And if it isn't at the moment, I'll make sure the path is blocked when you try." He stared into her eyes. "You don't doubt I'd do it, do you?"

"No."

"I want you out of here, Zara, through the closest exit. Out and far away from whatever this place is becoming. I want you safe. Someone worthy has to survive this."

"Anton, this is—"

"The way it will be."

Zara leaned down and kissed his forehead. For a moment she thought he was going to say something to express the emotion that was driving this particular act of determined sacrifice. But he pulled away from it and instead growled: "Get out! I know what I'm doing! I'll see you later."

She doubted that was true.

The floor lurched. Most of the room was squirming with tendrils of nearly solid energy—dodging them would be tricky. The central area around Dalgrave's desk was still clear, however, though Zara knew that that wouldn't last. Dalgrave's attention was focused on the network hologram as he punched at its visual codings. Zara gave a second or two to checking that what he was doing made sense, then, reassured, turned and headed for the door. As she pushed through the gap, she glanced at Dalgrave, hoping he'd look toward her so she could catch his eye one last time, perhaps express some hope that she'd see him again—that he'd stop the Monster from forming and escape from this place.

But his attention was fully on the grid.

She pulled away and ran toward the entrance to what had once been the DRC and was now a churning, burgeoning mass of virtual Monster flesh.

☆

Getting out was easier than she'd thought. Monstrous growths of thickening energy-matter seemed to draw away from her, as though the substance of it had been instructed to avoid touching her.

Was that something Anton had achieved? Even if she never found out for sure, she'd choose to believe so.

The outside world was a vision of hell. The fiery trail of the Atomic Monster was burning in the surrounding acres, leaving parkland, forest and suburbs blackened and scorched. Everything was in ruins. Ignoring it all, Zara simply ran, stumbling over smouldering debris, avoiding the huge footprints crushed into the ground, recoiling from barely recognisable human remains. Her mind was numb, her lungs filled with a pain caused by breathing in the seared air. Every part of her body ached.

Then the world shuddered violently. Zara stumbled, nearly tripping. Recovering her balance, dizzy with shame and horror, she glanced back. The Skull—fleshed out in a translucent covering of solid light—rose high above her, featureless, eyeless, yet somehow human. The rest of its skeleton, too, had been transformed and, like some mythical sea beast emerging from the depths of the ocean, it rose from the ground—the whole extent of the DRC complex having been incorporated into its new body. Earth and stone fell away from it as it rose ... up and up ... endlessly, huge wings opening from its back, spread wide across the country. It cast no shadow, but around it, everything it touched shook, burst apart, re-formed anew. Even the air was changed—it remained air but seemed different now. As it drifted toward her, Zara took it into herself and it filled her with a strange numbness.

Fully revealed, the Monster landed back on the earth. Its feet touched down in DRC City, causing the buildings to atomise in a vast cloud of gaseous turbulence. Through the haze it turned from side to side. Though it had no eyes, Zara knew it was searching ... and suddenly, with no physical sign to tell her, she was positive it had found what it was looking for.

Her.

☆

Though absorbed into the Monster's substance—swirling through its interdimensional multiverse reality—Dalgrave still retained some scrap of consciousness that was his own. Seeing Zara filled him with relief. As she gazed fearfully up at him, recognising nothing of Anton Dalgrave at all, he took all the emotions that had been seething nebulously within him and released them into the space-time continuum, carrying all his passion and hope. Then he pulled back—and the Monster followed. Its gaze swept over the City streets ... and came to rest on one particular figure. This one was standing on top of a building exulting in the destruction, shouting words Dalgrave didn't care to hear, worshipping the dangerous thing that Dalgrave had become.

If he could have, Dalgrave would have smiled. He was not the god Kumala had worked to create—he was something much more vengeful. Reaching out, he let the flesh of the Monster trail across time and space, sweeping the man into the waves of power that surrounded him. In that instant Mafu Kumala ceased to be. Whatever the future would be like, Dalgrave was content—for Zara Watabi would be in it and she would thrive. But Kumala, Creator of Monsters, would not.

Then he let himself rise skyward again. With infinite grace he grabbed hold of existence and began a final rampage, not of destruction this time but of creation.

Sub~Continent

Robin Pen

Prologue

This is all true.

While at a small regional convention in late 2003 I attended a screening of forthcoming movie trailers. It featured the usual kind of Hollywood stuff, but as I'm a monster movie enthusiast, there was one movie promoted that greatly intrigued me. The problem is, I've never heard that the film was released nor have I seen anything of it since; I've read nothing in any magazine nor found any reference to it on the internet. Intriguing, isn't it? To admit to this is extraordinary, I know, but it is as if the film never existed. Yet I did see the trailer; and the complexity of the scenes in it tells me that the film was made.

With no evidence other than those few fellow witnesses, hidden in the dark of that screening room, in the early hours, three days into an exceptionally drunken con, there is little else I can do except give you a detailed description of the trailer as best as I can recall. The rest is up to you.

The Trailer

Fade-in to Universal™ logo with music of low ominous strings and faint harp tinkles.

Cut to helicopter shot of a large science vessel in deep blue ocean.

Narrator, voice over: Deep in the Indian Ocean, man is about to discover a past once thought to exist only in legend.

Cut to a net being raised out of the water. A large lump of pitted lava-like rock hits the ship deck. Close up of a hammer hitting the rock and the rock breaking open to reveal a hint of gold. Over-the-shoulder shot of nondescript science-type lady who looks back towards the camera.

Nondescript science-type lady: Doctor, take a look at this.
Bob Balaban enters shot in close-up from below to look at off-screen object.

Bob Balaban: My god.

Wide shot of Brendan Frazer on a higher deck, unshaven and with long hair.

Brendan Frazer: What have you got there?

Close-up of part of a gold statue poking out of the dark rock. A symbolic statue of a strange creature, fishy yet reptilian and with a hint of squid.

Medium shot of Frazer and Balaban looking at object out-of-focus in foreground.

Balaban: What does this mean?

Frazer: A legend comes true, my friend.

Cut to a press conference with Frazer and Balaban at a table, the golden statue all shiny next to them. Lots of media rumbling and cameras flashing.

Close-up of Frazer leaning to microphone.

Frazer: We have found the lost continent of Lemuria.

Voices rumble louder, cameras flash faster.

Marching drums style, getting things done music starts with shots of a fleet of ships chugging along. Helicopter shot fly-over of the armada of vessels of varying types. Cut to mini-sub being lifted and swung over the side.

Close-up of Frazer in the sub with a headset on.

Frazer: Okay people, let's make history.

Cut to black and silence for a nano-second before the sub's lights go on and ominous music returns. Close up of Hank Azaria as sub driver. His eyes go wide as he sees something. Sudden image of mega-ugly fish with knife-like teeth.

Hank Azaria: Whoa, that's one ugly fish.

Close-up of Brendan Frazer looking into a monitor with super serious expression and stare of intense concentration.

Close-up of Hank Azaria also looking into the monitor.

Hank Azaria: My god.

Frazer moves to porthole, and we get a moment of his excited expression reflected in the dark glass.

Black is quickly replaced by sub lights silhouetting a large encrusted statue in shape not unlike the original gold statue.

Cut to close-up of Frazer back on deck, all very excited.

Frazer: I'm telling you, there's a whole city down there.

Female voice, out of shot: A city of gold.

Wider shot of Frazer and Balaban. They lean back to reveal Jennifer Connelly, pony-tail and round-rim glasses.

Close-up of Frazer: So who invited you?

Medium shot of Connelly, pans up to Terry O'Quinn climbing down a ladder, wearing blue blazer and a pencil moustache.

O'Quinn: I did.

Close-up of Frazer looking unhappy.

Close-up of Connolly eyeing off Brendan Frazer, who's off-screen.

Voice of Quinn: This is Doctor Reynolds of The Institute of Ocean Archaeology. She knows everything there is to be known about the lost continent of Lemuria.

Medium shot of Frazer and Balaban. Frazer looks angry. Balaban leans over to Frazer and mutters under his beard.

Balaban: Not everything.

Close-up of angry Frazer: This is my expedition and I choose—

Medium shot of O'Quinn as he walks up to an uncomfortable Connelly.

O'Quinn: No, Doctor. I paid for this jaunt of yours. It's my investment.

Close-up of ship captain Delroy Lindo holding a radio mic.

Delroy Lindo: Lower the cargo.

Close-up of a crate being lowered to deck with a *thunk*. Close-up as a crowbar cracks open the lid to reveal automatic rifles.

O'Quinn, voice over: And I intend to protect my investment.

Medium shot of Connelly and Frazer.

Connelly: I hope we can work together, Doctor.

Frazer: Well, I hope you brought good hiking boots.

Close-up of fake radar image of a cross-section of city with a cave under it.

Frazer, voice over: ... because it's hollow under the city and dry.

Shot of underground lagoon and the mini-sub surfacing.

Wide shot of Frazer, Connelly, Balaban, Azaria and non-descript others in caving outfits surrounded by rock. Very wide shot of team in a huge digital matte of a cavernous terrain with huge ancient city ruins all around. Tracking shot towards a huge shiny statue, torch lights wavering across it. The statue looks like the two previous ones shown. It's a fearsome creature, like a reptilian ape but scaly and with a fish-like tail. The claws and teeth are prominent.

Balaban, voice over: My god. What is that?

Medium shot of actors looking at statue, torches pointed.

Connelly: It's Emirah, the god that was said to protect Lemuria from enemies who threatened to plunder it.

Close-up of nondescript character pointing a video camera at the statue.

Close-up of O'Quinn back on the ship looking at a monitor. Close-up monitor image of statue's shiny surface.

Close-up of O'Quinn.

O'Quinn: My god, that's solid gold.

Close-up of Balaban close to the ground looking at something. He calls to Frazer.

Close-up of Balaban's hand picking up and showing a very large tip of a razor-sharp, curved claw.

Balaban, voice over: Look at this fossil.

Close-up of Frazer looking serious.

Frazer: That's no fossil.

Camera tracks towards actors as they turn to camera in response to a bizarre loud howl.

Close-up of frightened Azaria.

Azaria: I don't like the sound of that.

Close-up of very serious Brendan Frazer.

Frazer: Let's get out of here.

Music turns to action as we see the actors running down a slope toward the sub in the lagoon.

Close-up of Frazer about to close the hatch when he looks up to camera.

We get a point-of-view shot of something running down the slope, moving towards Frazer and the sub. We hear heavy breathing and a *thump thump*.

Medium close-up of Frazer looking wide-eyed.

Frazer, shouting: Dive! Now!

Close-up of sub hatch slamming shut.

Cut to characters cramped in the sub. Azaria is wrestling with controls.

Azaria: Hold on.

External shot of sub in unrealistic light in deep water. It's another creature P.O.V. shot as it slams into the sub.

Inside the sub, everything shakes, sparks fly.

Close-up of Connelly and Frazer, obviously getting close. Connelly is now without glasses.

Music stops.

Wide shot of sub bursting to surface. It's raining. The skies are dark. There is thunder. A storm is brewing.

Medium shot of Frazer storming onto the bridge. Other ships can be seen out of the bridge windows. Frazer shouts to Lindo.

Frazer: Get the hell out of here. Right now!

Medium shot of perplexed O'Quinn.

O'Quinn: Now just hold on there.

Close-up of Frazer: You said it. Hold on! Tight!

Underwater, P.O.V. shot of bottom of a ship. Low bubbling underwater sounds. We are moving quickly towards the ship.

Wide shot of deck of a transport ship, obviously different to main ship.

We see a sailor in rain gear battening down hatches on deck when a huge claw, the massive dark talons glistening, grabs onto the rail. Then another claw.

CGI shot of whole ship being quickly pulled under. Then it bursts out of the water again with the creature on it. But shot is too quick to get a good look at the beast.

Close-up of Lindo with binoculars. Awestruck, he lowers binoculars.

Lindo: My god. What terrible thing have we unleashed?

Wide shot of bottom part of creature, scaly belly and four claws ripping up the bridge of the transport ship in the wind and rain.

Close-up of Frazer: Get us out of here, captain. Now!

Wide-shot of far away transport ship as seen through the bridge windows. The monster, obscured by the storm, is turning about on the distant ship but finally directs itself towards camera. It goes to crouch and, pushing the ship back under the ocean as it does, leaps high.

Close-up of Lindo staring in amazement.

Wide-shot of the figure of the creature as it falls towards the camera very fast. It blankets the shot and we hear a loud crunch.

Big beat music begins as we get a rapid montage of action shots:

Frazer leaps off a ledge.

O'Quinn points a hand-gun.

Frazer lights a flare.

Azaria screams.

Connelly jumps as a huge claw comes through a metal wall.

An explosion among the ancient Lemurian ruins.

A shot from under the water of Frazer falling towards camera, breaking the surface.

Connelly climbing out of a muddy claw print.

Delroy Lindo, covered in blood, swinging an axe.

Close-up of Bob Balaban with a hint of jaws reflected in his glasses.

Frazer and Azaria running down an ancient stone stairwell.

Extreme close-up of Frazer obviously in a perilous situation, staring intently.

The music stops with a clang.

Cut to black.

Original ominous music returns.

Medium shot of Frazer standing among ruins.

Narrator, voice over: Brendan Frazer.

Close-up of Connelly shakily holding a rifle toward camera.

Narrator, voice over: Jennifer Connelly.

Fade to black and fade in title, which voice-over announces:

SUB-CONTINENT

Fades away, then we see cast and crew credits with sound of sonar beeping.

Fades to black.

Cut to extreme close-up of Brendan Frazer in an earlier quiet moment from the film. He is holding up the small golden statue.

Frazer: Man has only explored five per cent of the world's oceans. Who knows what could be out there (pause) waiting for us to find it.

Quick fade to black.

Cut to Frazer and Azaria, bruised and weary, on a raft. It's raining, but flames are on the water all round them.

Azaria: We have to kill that monster.

Frazer: Out here we're the monsters. And to protect itself it will kill us.

Cut to black and momentary silence.

Cut to Connelly slowly turning around to large figure behind her. Pull focus to figure to see it as a set of sharp-toothed jaws. It howls.

Cut to black and silence.

Fade in: IT'S COMING

Fade out.

Fade in: SOON

Epilogue

Now, before you ask the obvious questions, yes, I chased up the guy responsible for showing that trailer. He was very enthusiastic in his passion to talk about his collection of rarities—except for that piece. He remained adamant he didn't know what I was talking about and refused to enter into any kind of discussion. But the last thing he said was most telling. He said to me, "I have never seen any trailer for a film about Lemuria and if you are smart you'd say you haven't see anything either." I didn't let it go, however; but every letter to the studio, to any and all of the actors I recognised in the trailer, met with no response. I had failed to read the crew credits at the end so I didn't know the names of the writers or the producer or director and thus had no further leads. I decided to give up on this quest, get on with watching the next groovy kaiju flick and forget I'd ever seen a trailer for a movie that apparently does not exist.

Then, not long ago, I found a letter in my post box—no stamp, no return address. Inside was a small newspaper clipping. It read "Research Ship Mystery. *Deep Sea Voyager*, a research vessel for the Lemurian Institute, has gone missing in calm seas 800km South-West of Mauritius. It was on a second expedition to an undisclosed location where previously the institute claimed to have found evidence of a submerged continent that was once above sea level and had harboured a civilisation of unknown history. No wreckage or bodies have been found. All that was discovered by rescue vessels was a marker buoy left from the previous expedition. The Lemurian Institute has made no statement and the disappearance of *Deep Sea Voyager* remains a mystery."

At the bottom was a handwritten message, "But they did find something. They found a parchment attached to that buoy and whatever was written on it *they* wanted it kept secret at any cost. Tread carefully or you might meet the same fate as the crew of *Deep Sea Voyager* and any others who found out too much."

This is all true, as true as I am sitting here typing these words—and you are reading them.

That is, if I haven't already met an unsavoury end and I, too, am now only the trailer to a film that never existed.

CAPSULE MONSTERS:

GIANT MONSTER FILM REVIEWS IN A FEW WORDS

ROBERT HOOD AND ROBIN PEN

Godzilla: Original Series (1954–1974)

1. Gojira (1954; dir. Ishiro Honda) aka Godzilla: King of the Monsters (US, 1956; dir. Ishiro Honda/Terry Morse)
    Nuclear icon attacks Tokyo!

2. Gojira no gyakushu [Counterattack of Godzilla] (1955; dir. Motoyoshi Oda) aka Godzilla Raids Again, Gigantis, the Fire Monster (US, 1959)
    Big G and spiky buddy wrestle on various Japanese landmarks.

3. Kingu Kongu tai Gojira [King Kong vs Godzilla] (1962; dir. Ishiro Honda) aka King Kong vs Godzilla (US, 1963; dir. Ishiro Honda and Thomas Montgomery)
    Rubbersuit monster vs mangy-furred ape and a bunch of comedians.

4. Mosura tai Gojira [Mothra vs Godzilla] (1964; dir. Ishiro Honda) aka Godzilla vs The Thing (US, 1964)
    Fifty tons of mothballs, please!

5. San daikaiju chikyu saidai no kessen [Three Giant Monsters' Decisive Battle for Earth] (1964; dir. Ishiro Honda) aka Ghidrah, The Three-Headed Monster (1965)
    Are three heads really better than one?

6. Kaiju daisenso [War of the Monsters] (1965; dir. Ishiro Honda) aka Godzilla vs Monster Zero (US, 1970), Invasion of the Astro Monster
    Planet X, flying saucers and Godzilla dancing.

7. Nankai no daiketto [South Seas Giant Battle] (1966; dir. Jun Fukuda) aka Godzilla vs The Sea Monster (US, 1968), Ebirah, Horror of the Deep
    Giant lobsters need love, too.

8. Kaiju to no kessen-Gojira no Musuko [Battle of Monster Island—Godzilla's Son] (1967; dir. Jun Fukuda) aka Son of Godzilla (US, 1969)
   Family camping trips! If it's not bugs, it's bad weather.

9. Kaiju soshingeki [Parade of Monsters] (1968) aka Destroy All Monsters (US, 1969)
   Cheaper by the dozen?

10. Oru kaiju daishingeki [All Monsters Giant Attack] (1969; dir. Ishiro Honda) aka Godzilla's Revenge (US, 1972)
    Life lessons learnt from the Big G(uru).

11. Gojira tai Hedora [Godzilla vs Hedorah] (1971; dir. Yoshimitsu Banno) aka Godzilla vs the Smog Monster (US, 1972)
    This is what happens to the fans when the shit hits back.

12. Chikyu kogeki meirei-Gojira tai Gaigan [Earth Destruction Directive: Godzilla vs Gigan] (1972; dir. Jun Fukuda) aka Godzilla on Monster Island (US, 1978), Godzilla vs Gigan
    Planet of the Apes comes to Godzillaland.

13. Gojira tai Megaro [Godzilla vs Megalon] (1973; dir. Jun Fukuda) aka Godzilla vs Megalon (US, 1976)
    Badly dressed guys and gals—and their giant cockroach.

14. Gojira tai Mekagojira [Godzilla vs Mechagodzilla] (1974; dir. Jun Fukuda) aka Godzilla vs The Cosmic Monster (US, 1978), Godzilla vs The Bionic Monster, Godzilla vs Mechagodzilla
    When one Godzilla isn't enough, build another one.

15. Mekagojira no gyakushu [Mechagodzilla's Counterattack] (1975) aka Revenge of Mechagodzilla (US), Terror of Mechagodzilla, Terror of Godzilla
    When two Godzillas aren't enough, add a dinosaur.

Godzilla: "Heisei" Series (1984–1995)

16. Gojira 1984 (1984; dir. Kohji Hashimoto) aka Godzilla 1985 (US, 1985; dir. Kohji Hashimoto and R.J. Kizer), The Return of Godzilla
    He's come back from holidays to deal with the Cold War.

17. Gojira tai Biollante [Godzilla vs. Biollante] (1989; dir. Kazuki Omori) aka Godzilla vs Biollante (US, 1993)
    Be careful how you fertilise your rose garden.

18. Gojira tai Kingu Gidora [Godzilla vs King Ghidorah] (1991; dir. Kazuki Omori)
Time-travel, WW2, cyborgs and King Ghidorah make Godzilla inevitable.

19. Gojira tai Mosura [Godzilla vs Motha] (1992; dir. Takao Okawara)
Mothra meets her dark side.

20. Gojira tai Mekagojira [Godzilla vs Mechagodzilla II] (1993; dir. Takao Okawara)
To destroy Godzilla, build a big robotic version of him. It's the only sensible thing to do.

21. Gojira tai Supesu Gojira [Godzilla vs Space Godzilla] (1994; dir. Kensho Yamashita)
Combine black holes and Godzilla cells and you know there's going to be trouble.

22. Gojira tai Desutoroya [Godzilla vs Destroyah] (1995; dir. Takao Okawara)
Godzilla suffers from heartburn.

"Alternate Reality" Series (1999–)

23. Gojira ni-sen mireniamu [Godzilla 2000 Millennium] (1999; dir. Takao Okawara) aka Godzilla 2000 (US, 1999), Godzilla vs Orga
Information-hungry alien monolith.

24. Gojira tai Megagirasu: Jii Shômetsu Sakusen [Godzilla vs. Megaguiras: G-Eradication Command (2000; dir. Masaaki Tezuka)
More blackhole troubles. What's that buzzing noise?

25. Gojira, Mosura, Kingu Gidora: Daikaiju soukougeki [Godzilla, Mothra, King Ghidorah: The Giant Monsters' General Offensive] (2001; dir. Shusuke Kaneko) aka Godzilla, Mothra and King Ghidorah: Giant Monsters All-Out Attack
Metaphysics and mysticism make Godzilla blank-eyed and cross.

26. Gojira tai Mekagojira [Godzilla Against Mechagodzilla] (2002, dir. Masaaki Tezuka)
Lovely bones: the memory lingers.

27. Gojira tai Mosura tai Mekagojira: Tôkyô S.O.S. [Godzilla, Mothra, Mechagodzilla: Tokyo SOS] (2003, dir. Masaaki Tezuka]
Lovely bones Part 2: Mothra steps in!

28. Gojira: Fainaru uozu [Godzilla: Final Wars] (2004; dir. Ryuhei Kitamura)
Destroy All Monsters in a Matrix of Independence Day pub brawls.

Gamera: 'Old'

1. Daikaiju Gamera [Giant Monster Gamera] (1965; dir. Noriaki Yuasa) aka Gammera the Invincible (US, 1966)
    The flying turtle arrives.

2. Daikaiju ketto Gamera tai Barugon [Great Monster Duel: Gamera vs Barugon] (1966; dir. Shigeo Tanaka) aka War of the Monsters (US, 1967)
    Big crocodilic thing ejects rainbows and freeze-gas.

3. Daikaiju kuchesen Gamera tai Gaosu [Giant Monster Air Battle: Gamera vs Gyaos] (1967; dir. Noriaki Yuasa) aka Return of the Giant Monsters, Gamera vs Gaos (US, 1967)
    Giant reptilian bat what's-it with sonic-ray squawk!

4. Gamera tai uchu kaiju Bairasu [Gamera vs the Outer Space Monster Virus] (1968; dir. Noriaki Yuasa) aka Destroy All Planets, Gamera vs Viras (US, 1968)
    Friend of children but not pointy-headed alien squids.

5. Gamera tai daiakuju Giron [Gamera vs the Giant Evil Beast Guiron] (1969; dir. Noriaki Yuasa) aka Attack of the Monsters, Gamera vs Guiron (1969)
    Friend of children but not cannibalistic alien babes and their pet Staysharp shishime knife.

6. Gamera tai maju Jaiga [Gamera vs the Demon Beast Jaiga] (1970; dir. Noriaki Yuasa) aka Gamera vs Monster X, Gamera vs Juiger (US, 1970)
    A Fantastic Voyage through the Friend of Children.

7. Gamera tai shinkai kaiju Jigura [Gamera vs the Deep Sea Monster Zigra] (1971; dir. Noriaki Yuasa) aka Gamera vs Zigra (1971)
    Friend of children but not space sharks or the bankruptcy court.

8. Uchu kaiju Gamera [Super Monster Gamera] (1980; dir. Noriaki Yuasa) aka Super Monster (US, 1980)
    Friend of children returns from exile to fight lots of stock footage.

Gamera: 'New'

9. Gamera daikaiju kuchu kessen [Gamera: Giant Monster Midair Showdown] (1995; dir. Shusuke Kaneko) aka Gamera: The Guardian of the Universe (US, 1995; dir. Shusuke Kaneko and Matt Greenfield)
    Friend of children becomes friend of the Earth and shows Superman a thing or two in the process.

10. Gamera 2: Region shurai [Gamera 2: Attack of Legion] (1996; dir. Shusuke Kaneko) aka Gamera 2: Advent of Legion, Gamera 2: Assault of the Legion
    Genetically engineered turtle takes on alien crabs.

11. Gamera 3: Iris kakusei (1999; dir. Shusuke Kaneko) aka Gamera 3: Revenge of Iris, Gamera 3: The Awakening of Iris
    Hero, yes. But who is the enemy?

12. Gamera: Chiisaka yusha-tachi (2006; dir. Ryuta Tazaki) aka Gamera the Brave
    Gamera is dead. Long live Gamera!

Other Daikaiju (Japanese)

Sora no daikaiju Radon [Rodan, Giant Monster of the Sky] (1956; dir. Ishiro Honda) aka Rodan (US, 1957)
Mutant pteradons meet tragic end.

Chikyu boeigun [Earth Defence Force] (1957; dir. Ishiro Honda) aka The Mysterians (US, 1959)
Earth vs the flying saucers -- and their robotic chicken.

Daikaiju Baran [Giant Monster Varan] (1958; dir. Ishiro Honda) aka Varan the Unbelievable (US, 1962)
Rocky the Flying Squirrel was never like this.

Mosura [Mothra] (1961; dir. Ishiro Honda) aka Mothra (US, 1962)
All she wants is to get her singing twin fairies back.

Kaitei gunkan [Undersea Battleship] (1963; dir. Ishiro Honda) aka Atragon (US, 1965)
Manda was feeling horny, that's all.

Uchu daikaiju Dogora [Space Giant Monster Dogora] (1964; dir. Ishiro Honda) aka Dagora, the Space Monster (US, 1965)
Humungous jellyfish adrift in the upper atmosphere.

Furankenshutain tai chitei kaiju Baragon [Frankenstein vs the Subterranean Monster Baragon] (1965; dir. Ishiro Honda) aka Frankenstein Conquers the World (US, 1966)
Frankenstein's monster gets bigger thanks to Nazis and that darn Bomb.

Kai tatsu daikessen [Decisive Battle of the Giant Magic Dragons] (1966; dir. Tetsuya Yamauchi and Kunio Kunisada) aka The Magic Serpent (US, 1968)
Dragon vs giant frog vs giant eagle vs giant spider vs magic vs Star Wars.

Dai Majin [Great Majin] (1966; dir. Kimiyoshi Yasuda) aka Majin, Majin, the Hideous Idol (US, 1968)
Huge statue gets cranky.

Furankenshutain no kaiju-Sanda tai Gaira [Frankenstein Monsters-Sanda vs Gaira] (1966; dir. Ishiro Honda) aka War of the Gargantuas (US, 1970)
Ugly ape-like siblings are always fighting: bad singer gets eaten.

Dai Majin ikaru [The Giant Majin Grows Angry] (1966; dir. Kenji Misumi) aka The Return of the Giant Majin (US, 1968)
Huge statue gets crankier.

Dai Majin gyakushu [The Great Majin's Counterattack] (1966; dir. Issei Mori) aka Majin Strikes Again
Huge statue steps on naughty samurais.

Uchu daikaiju Girara [Giant Space Monster Girara] (1967; dir. Kazui Nihonmatsu) aka The X from Outer Space (US, 1968)
Giant space chicken objects to groovy '60s fashions.

Dai kyoju Gappa [Great Giant Monster Gappa] (1967; dir. Haruyasu Nogushi) aka Monster from a Prehistoric Planet, Gappa, the Triphibian Monster (US, 1968)
Gargantuan reptile family go sight-seeing across Japan.

Kingukongu no gyakushu [King Kong's Counterattack] (1967; dir. Ishiro Honda) aka King Kong Escapes (1968)
Spy-thriller with big ape, big mecha-ape and big melodrama.

Ido zero daiakusen [Laitude Zero: Great Military Battle] (1969; dir. Ishiro Honda) aka Latitude Zero (US, 1970)
Was there a giant monster in this? Oh yeah, Cesar Romero.

Kessen! Nankai no daikaiju Gezora, Ganime, Kameba [Decisive Battle! Giant Monsters of the South Seas: Gezora, Ganime, and Kameba] (1970; dir. Ishiro Honda) aka Yog—Monster from Space (US, 1971)
Giant cuttlefish, crab and turtle holidaying in a tropical paradise.

Yamato Takeru (1994; dir. Takao Okawara) aka Orochi, The Eight Headed Serpent (US, 1999)
Very big medieval serpent with lots of heads.

Mosura (1996; dir. Okihiro Yoneda) aka Rebirth of Mothra (US, 1999)
Ecology-conscious Moth vs development-spawned Ghidorah.

Mosura 2 (1997; dir. Kunio Miyoshi) aka Rebirth of Mothra 2 (US, 1997)
The Moth is all at sea. So transforms into Aqua-Moth!

Mosura 3: King Ghidora Attacks (1998; dir. Okihiro Yoneda)
King Ghidorah is back and this time he's brought the Baygon!

Wakusei daikaiju Negadon (2005; dir. Jun Awazu) aka Negadon: the Monster from Mars
Giant all-CGI martian mechanism comes to town.

Ultraman

Urutoraman (1966–) aka Ultraman (various TV series)
Multi-generational space giants fight neverending invasion of weird things, all gigantic, over 40-odd years.

Ultraman (2004; dir. Kazuya Konaka) aka Ultraman: The Next
Humanoid space giant reborn to face ill-tempered nemesis.

Non-Japanese Giant Monsters

King Kong (US, 1933; dir. Merian C. Cooper and Ernest B. Schoedsack)
Big scary monkey with soul and charisma.

Son of Kong (US, 1933; dir. Ernest B. Schoedsack)
Little less soul and charisma, but cuter.

The Beast From 20,000 Fathoms (US, 1953; dir. Eugene Lourie)
Giant radioactive sea lizard. The first to come ashore.

Them! (US, 1954; dir. Gordon Douglas)
Big ants mean business.

The Monster From the Ocean Floor (US, 1954; dir. Wyatt Ordung)
Darn big one-eyed amoeba.

It Came From Beneath the Sea (US, 1955; dir. Robert Gordon)
Awesome octopus short two of its terrifying tentacles for budgetary reasons.

Tarantula (US, 1955; dir. Jack Arnold)
Big hairy spider takes to the road.

X-The Unknown (UK, 1956; dir. Leslie Norman)
Sentient radioactive mud.

The Amazing Colossal Man (US, 1957; dir. Bert I. Gordon)
More terrible than amazing, but still colossal.

Attack of the Crab Monsters (US, 1957; dir. Roger Corman)
Big crabs with excellent speaking voices.

The Beginning of the End (US, 1957; dir. Bert I. Gordon)
Magnified grasshoppers with no speaking voices.

The Black Scorpian (US, 1957; dir. Edward Ludwig)
More than one, but big and black and they drool, too.

The Deadly Mantis (US, 1957; dir. Nathan Duran)
Bomber-sized mantis with nice detailing.

The Giant Behemoth (US, 1957; dir. Eugene Lourie) aka
Behemoth, the Sea Monster
Radioactive sea lizard visits the old country.

The Giant Claw (US, 1957; dir. Fred F. Sears)
Bug-eyed buzzard on strings.

Kronos (US, 1957; dir. Kurt Neumann)
Energy-hungry Rubik's Cube on the march.

The Monolith Monsters (US, 1957; dir. John Sherwood)
Towering shards of non-sentient malevolence.

Monster from Green Hell (US, 1957; dir. Kenneth Crane)
Ruddy big, lumbering wasps can still ruin a picnic.

The Monster That Challenged the World (US, 1957; dir. Arnold
Laven)
Killer sea snails of mechanical grace.

Twenty Million Years to Earth (US, 1957; dir. Nathan Juran)
Reptilian ape beast from Venus.

Attack of the 50-Foot Woman (US, 1958; dir. Nathan Juran)
50-Foot woman with sharp lacquered nails.

The Blob (US, 1958; dir. Irvin S. Yeaworth Jr)
A giant killer mound of strawberry jam.

The Crawling Eye (UK, 1958; dir. Quentin Lawrence) aka The
Trollenberg Terror
Family of blood-shot eyeballs with wavering tentacles.

Earth vs the Spider (US, 1958; dir. Bert I. Gordon)
Spider might be big but Earth is to scale.

War of the Colossal Beast (US, 1958; dir. Bert I. Gordon)
It's that colossal man again but with a nasty rash.

The Giant Gila Monster (US, 1959; dir. Ray Kellogg)
He makes the toy cars and trains look really small.

Konga (GB, 1960; dir. John Lemont)
Big lady monkey. Not happy.

Gorgo (GB, 1961; dir. Eugene Lourie)
Big scary reptillic monster and his mum in London.

Reptilicus (Denmark, 1962; dir. Poul Bang and Sidney Pink)
Spitting skink with bad dentures.

The Creeping Terror (US, 1964; dir. Arthur Nelson)
Cheap rug swallows B-actors.

Les Escargots (Fr, 1965; dir. René Laloux)
Big land snails attack French restaurants.

Taekoesu Yonggary (South Korea, 1967; dir. Ki-duk Kim) aka
Yongary, Monster from the Deep
Horny-nosed lizard with Soeul battles toy tanks.

The Mighty Gorga (US, 1969; dir. David L. Hewitt)
Big hairy ape needs a tailor.

Beware! The Blob (US, 1972: Larry Hagman) aka Son of Blob
Yes, a blob but less blob more gloop.

The Giant Spider Invasion (US, 1975; dir. Bill Rebane)
Truth in advertising: Giant spiders invade!

King Kong (US, 1976; dir. John Guillermin)
Guy in monkey suit, but it's a nice suit.

Queen Kong (UK/Italy, 1976; dir. Frank Agrama)
Giant lady monkey in unrequited love.

Hsing Hsing wang [King Hsing hsing] (HK, 1977; dir. Ho Meng-
Hwa) aka The Mighty Peking Man aka Goliathon
Giant Yeti takes scantily clad jungle blond out on the town.

Q—the Winged Serpent (US, 1982; dir. Larry Cohen)
Quetzalcoatl takes a bite out of the Big Apple.

Pulgasari (North Korea, 1985; dir. Chong Gon Jo and Sang-ok Shin)
Metal bull monster fighting for communism.

King Kong Lives! (US, 1986; dir. John Guillermin and Charles McCracken)
Two Kongs in love, war ensues.

The Blob (US, 1988; dir. Chuck Russell)
Yes, still a blob, but real blobby.

DeepStar Six (US, 1989; dir. Sean S. Cunningham)
Sea crustacean of hydraulic proportions.

Tremors (US, 1990; dir. Ron Underwood)
Graboids are like giant ant lions. Neat.

The Relic (US, 1997; dir. Peter Hyams)
Lion, lizard, mutant; just tall enough for the ride.

Deep Rising (US, 1998; dir. Stephen Sommers)
Real nasty, spiky tentacled squid thingy.

Gargantua (US, 1998; dir. Bradford May)
Giant lizard, great with kids.

Godzilla (US, 1998; dir. Roland Emmerich)
Who would have thought a guy in a rubber suit would look better?

Yonggary 2001 (South Korea, 1999; dir. Hyung-rae Shim) aka Reptilian (US, 2001)
Giant lizard monster but he's handsome.

Reign of Fire (UK, 2002; dir. Rob Bowman)
Hey, why wasn't Dragonslayer (US, 1981; dir. Matthew Robbins) included?

Garuda (Thai, 2004; dir. Monthon Arayangkoon)
Vengeful bird god barely makes it into the giant monster books.

King Kong (NZ/US, 2005; dir. Peter Jackson)
Big scary ape still has charm and charisma.

D-War (South Korea, 2006; dir. Hyung-rae Shim)
Big mythical serpents trash LA.

Gwoemul (South Korea, 2006; dir. Joon-ho Bong) aka The Host
Trust me, mutant tadpoles can be scary.

CONTRIBUTORS

Lee Battersby is the multiple award-winning author of over 50 stories, with publications in Australia, the US, and Europe. His first collection, entitled *Through Soft Air*, was released by Prime Books in 2006. He lives in Perth, Western Australia with his wife, writer Lyn Battersby, three kids, and as many finches as survive his attempts to look after them. He is far too fascinated by Daleks and serial killers for his own good. You can find his website at <www.battersby.com.au> and his weblog, The Battersblog, at <http://battersblog.blogspot.com>.

Richard A. Becker is a working writer and a native of Los Angeles, with degrees in film production and literature. He's also a filmmaker, promotes a burlesque show, and enjoys participating in many other arts. Some of his fondest memories are of giant monster movies, and that's why he's written this depressing story about them. Go figure.

Leigh Blackmore, writer, editor, manuscript assessor and occultist, lives in Wollongong, Australia with his two partners, several cats, and way too many books. Leigh's fiction has appeared in the first two *Agog* anthologies ("Uncharted" was a Ditmar nominee for Best Novella in 2003) and also in *Avatar, Bold Action, Micro, Phantastique, Pulse of Darkness, Tertangala* and online at <www.ligotti.net> and <www.writingshow.com>. Leigh is currently doing a Double Degree in Creative Writing and Journalism at the University of Wollongong. His website, The Blackmausoleum, is at <http://members.optusnet.com.au/lvxnox/>.

Born and raised in West Texas, which is renowned for its *kaiju*-like tornadoes, **Michael Bogue** now lives and breathes and has his being in the state of Arkansas, USA. Sporting three college degrees (none of which make him much money, alas), Mike currently works at Arkansas Tech University; there he supervises a freshman-mentoring program called Bridge to Excellence. Mike enjoys writing, singing, reading and occasionally playing (some would say defaming) the sport of tennis. In addition, Mike is a life-long fan of kaiju movies of all stripes.

Steven Cavanagh was first published in *Andromeda Spaceways Inflight Magazine*. His fiction has won competitions from the NSW

Writers Centre and the Australian Horror Writers Association, and popped up in *AntipodeanSF*, *Infinitas* and *Shadowed Realms*. Anthology appearances include the year's best *Australian Dark Fantasy and Horror 2007*, *Book of Shadows Volume 1*, *Shadow Box*, *Black Box* (Brimstone Press) and *Outcast: An Anthology of Strangers and Exiles* (CSFG Publishing). He currently exists in Sydney with a long-suffering wife and three short-suffering children. Steven's full bibliography is online and can be reached from his writing blog, <http://stevecav.blogspot.com>.

Terry Dartnall has published speculative fiction in *Oceans of the Mind*, *Ideomancer*, *Planet*, *AlienSkin*, *Aphelion*, *Mytholog* and elsewhere. His anthology of short stories, *The Ladder at the Bottom of the World*, was published as an eBook by Trantor Publications in 2006. Before retiring in March 2007 he taught Artificial Intelligence and Philosophy at Griffith University, Nathan, Brisbane, Australia.

Nick Fox and John Heeder co-authored the supernatural adventure novel, *Judgment Day* (as J.J. Ace), which received strong reviews, such as "There is non-stop action, great character development and an exciting storyline in this unique speculative fiction work. J.J. Ace has written a work that will be put on the readers' keeper shelf." (The Readers Guild) Separately, Nick and John's work has appeared in various anthologies, e-zines, and magazines. They're currently working together on several projects, including a comicbook series based on the characters in "Action Joe™ to the Rescue." Readers can contact them at <nick-fox@excite.com>.

Tony Frazier worked as a waiter, a newspaper movie critic, and a military intelligence noncom before settling down to his current job of watching television for money. He lives in Tulsa, Oklahoma with his wife and daughter. Two other Digger tales have been published on-line by *Baen's Universe* magazine.

Robert Hood is an author of horror-fantasy, SF and dark crime. His stories are numerous, and his books include *Day-dreaming on Company Time*, *Immaterial: Ghost Stories*, the upcoming *Creeping in Reptile Flesh*, the *Shades* series of YA supernatural thrillers and *Backstreets*. He has won awards for stories, edited books and film commentary. Editing anthologies of giant monster stories with Robin Pen seems to have become an obsession. His website is at <www.roberthood.net>.

Tessa Kum is but a tiny grasshopper. She has published a handful of stories, which have appeared in various Canberra Speculative Fiction Guild (CSFG) and UC publications. "One Night on Tidal Rig #13" was savaged at the 2005 Clarion South workshop, and survived. She lives in Melbourne, does shiftwork, and melts when exposed to direct sunlight.

Robbie Matthews has been active in the local publishing scene since about 1999, not coincidentally after the World Science Fiction Convention was held in Melbourne. He was a founding member of the Canberra Speculative Fiction Guild (CSFG), and currently Editor-in-Chief of the *Andromeda Spaceways Inflight Magazine*. He's into roleplaying, computers, cycling, guitar playing, amateur theater, unexpectedly falling off roofs and random attacks of editing. A collection of his "Johnny Werewolf" short stories is due to be published in April 2008 by ASN.

Robin Pen is the founding editor of the prestigious Australian science fiction and fantasy literary magazine *Eidolon*. He is the author of *The Secret Life of Rubber-suit Monsters*, a book of humorous criticism directed at fantastic cinema. He has won four Australian science fiction Ditmar awards for his writings, and co-edited the previous two *Daikaiju!* volumes with Robert Hood.

Steven Savile has written for Games Workshop (the *Vampire Wars* trilogy), *Star Wars*, *Dr Who* and most recently *Torchwood*. He has written another Greyfriar's Gentleman's Club adventure, *The Hollow Earth*, which is published by Bloodletting Press in the US. Steve readily admits that when growing up Godzilla scared the living crap out of him. He has never gotten over it.

Alys Sterling shares a small flat in London with the Cult of Khoshek, who refuse to leave due to a prophecy that the Great One will manifest any day now, via her television set. They're quiet, except for the chanting, and they do their own cooking. As the TV is now permanently tuned to grey static, roiling with brain-twisting spirals, she has turned to writing in the attempt not to look.

Nick Stathopoulos grew up in the outer Sydney suburb of Blacktown, Australia, in a halcyon time when Channel Seven ran black-and-white monster movies every Saturday afternoon. When he wasn't glued in front of the TV drawing, he performed evil experiments on his sister's dolls, converting them to Frankenstein monsters or simian inhabitants from the Planet of the Apes. In the backyard, he constructed elaborate Martian cities, which were always obliterated by explosions. His appearance in this collection as a writer is testament as to why he's won so many awards for artwork. He still draws in front of the TV.

Kiel Stuart is a member of SFWA, HWA and the Authors Guild. Her poetry and fiction have appeared in *Long Island Quarterly*, *The Potomac Review*, *Beyond the Last Star* and elsewhere. An avid pen collector, she also produces audio material for radio stations and the web, and is struggling to learn Japanese. In 2007, one of her stories ('How The Swan Queen Celebrated Mother's Day', *Zahir* magazine) was nominated for a Pushcart Prize.

Mikal Trimm's stories and poems can be found cluttering far too many venues in Australia, England, and the US. Recent or forthcoming appearances include works in *Strange Horizons*, *Postscripts*, *Weird Tales*, *Black Gate*, and others, and several anthologies as well. His first novel will be published as soon as he writes and sells it ...

Printed in the United States
101190LV00002B/303/A

9 780809 572335